THE SHE-KING: BOOK ONE

THE

SEKHMET BED

LIBBIE HAWKER

Running Rabbit Press
Seattle, WA

CONTENTS

THE SHE-KING: BOOK ONE

THE
SEKHMET BED

So said Amun-Re, Lord of Waset, presider over the Holy House:

He made his form like the majesty of her husband, the King Thutmose. He found her as she slept in the beauty of her palace. She awakened at the fragrance of the god, which she smelled in the presence of his majesty. He went to her immediately. He imposed his desire upon her; he caused that she should see him in the form of a god.

When he came before her, she rejoiced at the sight of his beauty. His love passed into her limbs, which the fragrance of the god flooded; his fragrance was of the land of Punt.

-Inscription from Djeser-Djeseru,
mortuary temple of Hatshepsut,
Fifth King of the Eighteenth Dynasty.

PART ONE

GOD-CHOSEN

1506 B.C.E.

CHAPTER ONE

AHMOSE WOKE TO A TERRIBLE, high-pitched wailing. She fought against sleep, kicked and scratched at it until it released her. She lay in her bed for a long time, eyes staring wide but seeing nothing in the dark, transfixed by the distant rise and fall of the cries. In the moments just after waking she could not place the sound. A cat? Some strange bird? Her mind cleared, and with a chill she recognized the sound of weeping women.

She found her way through the chamber in the dark, still naked, her feet cold against the mosaic floor. Before she reached the door, she *knew*. The presence of the gods was heavy about her, thick as honey in the air, pressing, warning. For Ahmose, the gods were always explicit.

She pulled the door open with numb hands. The hall of the House of Women was alive with moving shadows. In the darkness, the painted forms on the mural walls stretched and distorted, reaching arms toward Ahmose where she stood, shivering. The close air was dense with the odors of perfume and flowers, too sweet to be appealing. From far up the corridor the wailing drew closer. Women's shapes formed out of the darkness, leaning on each other, hands clawing at faces, gowns ripped in mourning where any were dressed at all. Ahmose watched them come. Then she watched them pass her door, heedless of her presence. Renenet, Hentaneb, Khamaat, Baketamun – all the faces of the harem she knew and loved, reddened with sorrow, mouths distorted with crying. They moved past her as a single body with many weeping eyes, many clawing hands, one being with many grief-stricken kas.

Behind them, Mutnofret walked.

The First King's Daughter was dressed and wigged, though evidently she had had no time to paint her face. Her gown was not torn. Her body was straight, shoulders square, face a controlled mask that nevertheless could not hide her eagerness. Not from Ahmose. She looked half a Great Royal Wife already, there in the darkness of the House of Women.

Mutnofret stopped at Ahmose's door. "Our father is dead."

Ahmose nodded, mute. She knew.

Mutnofret's eyes were like fires in the night. "Get dressed. We must go to our mother."

"No." Ahmose didn't know why she said it, only that she must. As she stood staring at her elder sister's calm, expectant face, a tight, cold snake coiled up in her belly. It wasn't fear. Not exactly.

"What do you mean, *no?*"

"I must...I should go to the Holy House. And pray." A good excuse for her refusal, and once she'd said it, it became true.

Mutnofret grunted, impatient. "Always praying. Go, then. But don't go naked as you are. And be back by dawn; it's only a few hours away. Our mother will be expecting us." *Will be expecting me*, Mutnofret's eyes said.

Ahmose shrugged into her red tunic-dress, a thin, faded old thing from her childhood. Hardly appropriate for the Pharaoh's daughter, but she wanted comfort now, not beauty. She would walk to the great temple complex at Ipet-Isut. No time to arrange for a chariot and escort. An hour there, an hour back – she would have just enough time to offer at the shrine of Waser. And the walk would help her sort through the clutter in her head. She pulled a wig on – not her best, but who would see her in the hours before dawn? – and slipped through her door as silent as river mist.

The Pharaoh's harem was a lush and sweet place, sprawling gardens thick with herbs and flowers and shade trees, row on row of pillared porches, cool rooms full of music and laughter. Ahmose loved to while away her days there, talking with her friends, trying on their prettiest gowns, playing senet beneath the olive trees. But tonight the House of Women crouched, mourning, beneath a weighty canopy of stars. All its beauties were dimmed and dulled by night and sorrow.

Eager to leave the weeping behind, Ahmose tied her long shawl tightly about her shoulders and all but ran through the courtyard and out onto the road. "I am only going to take the air," she said to the guards at the gate, and when they saw the the worry on her young face they let her pass without complaint.

Though the hot season of Shemu had long since set in, the night was unusually cold. Once well away from the harem, the night's peace comforted her a little, and the chill piqued her senses. It was not the Pharaoh's death that worried at her heart. It was the sharp, desperate certainty that this night, this moment, this scroll in the gods' hands was about *her*, tipped on her. She was the fulcrum of the coming day's balance. This moment was crafted just for Ahmose, and she wanted nothing of it. Outside the tall sandstone walls of the harem, with no sounds but the singing of night insects and the deep, dark, distant voice of the Iteru, she could order at least that much of her thoughts.

Tell me, she begged the gods as she walked, *what is to come. As I am your true servant, show me mercy, and tell me.* But the gods remained silent.

Behind her on the road, she heard the hoof-beats and breath of trotting horses. *What a stupid idea,* walking *to the Holy House! Alone, in the night!* Ahmose looked around wildly for a place to hide. The hard-packed dirt road stretched north to the temples and south to Waset, a long, wide, uncaring line. The shoulders of the road were bare, save for the season's usual tangle of dry, knee-high weeds. She did not have so much as a dagger in her belt – nothing. She glanced back the way she had come. The House of Women was there, lamps lit, glowing golden in the chill night, bright as a scarab. But it was too far to run; and anyway, the chariot was between Ahmose and the safety of the House. She might cross the road, dash out into the stubble of the harvested wheat field, and make it to the river – but no. It was many spans from road to river bank, and once she reached it, there would be nothing but mud, reeds, and a few skinny palms holding to the bank. Nowhere to hide. The guards on the gate would never hear her shout from this distance.

She stood still, fists clenched, and prayed as she watched the chariot come on: "Khonsu, who protects night travelers, see me! Cast evil from my path!"

The chariot was close enough now that she could see moonlight sparking in the horses' eyes. "Slow, slow," the driver said, and drew his reins. The horses stopped, blowing, beside Ahmose.

"Well," said the driver, leaning a forearm on the rail of his chariot. "The king's daughter."

Ahmose blushed.

"Not dressed like a king's daughter tonight."

"What business is it of yours how I choose to dress?" She stared at the impudent man, hoping her look was regal and intimidating, painfully aware that she was thirteen years old and barely a woman, for all her royal blood.

The driver smirked at her like a boy, though he was at least twice her age. The corners of his eyes creased, and his kohl was smeared where he'd carelessly rubbed at his face. Nose and chin were both sharply pointed; his cheeks were lean and flat. His face was all long angles. He brought the image of Anupu instantly to Ahmose's mind. Anupu, jackal-god of the underworld, who could condemn or reward. Would this man be her friend or her enemy? She did not know, and not knowing intrigued her.

"I am more concerned with the safety of Amunhotep's daughter than with her clothing, to be sure," the man said. "What are you doing out here, alone in the darkness?"

"*You* are not to question the *Pharaoh's* daughter – or to use the king's name so lightly."

The driver laughed. Not just a chuckle; he laughed hard, a string of loud, high barks like the call of a lapwing. His amusement revealed a prominent jut of upper teeth. Ahmose frowned at him. Was he mad, to laugh at a daughter of the king? Then a prickle of fear ran up her spine. If he was mad, she was alone with him, and no one to see or hear what he might do to her. She took a step back.

"Oh, I am sorry, King's Daughter," he said at once. "I've frightened you. Fear is the last thing you need tonight, poor girl."

What did he know of tonight's sad news? The harem had only just found out. The Pharaoh's women and children should have been the first to know of his departure for the Field of Reeds, save for his stewards and closest advisors. And *girl*? She wore a wig, even if it was a rather shabby one, not a child's braid. It should be obvious to even the simplest rekhet, the most ignorant peasant, that she was a woman now.

"I am not afraid of you or anyone else," she said. "You have an appalling lack of respect, that's all."

"Where are you headed?"

"Nowhere. I am taking the air."

The driver snorted. "King's daughters do not wander about aimlessly on the road. You have palace courtyards for *taking the air*, yes? Would you like a ride to wherever you're going, Great Lady?"

"I would have to be simple to get into a chariot with a strange man who laughs at the Pharaoh's own blood. And who can't even keep his kohl around his eyes."

Incredibly, he laughed again. He stretched a hand down from the back of his chariot as if to help her up. She looked at it, then at his face, and did not move.

"I am General Thutmose," he said, "your father's best soldier and his closest friend. I have reason to be out taking the air tonight, too. The same reason as you, Great Lady. The Pharaoh is dead. I have heard."

"Already?"

He nodded, his face solemn but his eyes still bright. "It wasn't a joke, that I am your father's closest friend. *Was* his closest friend. I am...grieved." Thutmose looked away, out through the cold night toward the river. "And confused," he said, quietly, to Ahmose or to the night; she was not sure.

"Then you lost a friend, and I am sorry for you." Ahmose had never experienced the death of a loved one. Even her father's death did not truly grieve her. She knew Amunhotep only as a king, the figure on the throne, the hands that held the crook and flail. She wondered – what would it be like to lose her closest friend, the pretty Northern girl Aiya with her unshaven, golden hair? Or Mutnofret, who was haughty, but always kind to Ahmose? She should be happy for the dead, she knew. They were the privileged ones who lived in glory forever with the gods, who hunted eternally in the Field of Reeds in boats made of sun-fire. But to never again see the ones she loved with her eyes.... Sympathy for Thutmose welled up inside her. A familiar voice spoke in her heart. *Trust this man. Trust him.* There could be no mistake: it was Mut speaking, the mother of the gods. Her voice was soothing and direct, a calming contrast to the uncertainty she felt just moments before, begging the gods for clarity.

Ahmose had never defied Mut before. She would not begin now. She stepped to the edge of the chariot's platform and reached up a hand.

Thutmose smiled at her – a gentle, pleasant smile – and took her hand in his own. She felt its calluses and hard strength, allowed him to pull her up to stand beside him. Before she let his hand go she heard the gods murmur their approval, a whisper in her heart like water among reeds.

Thutmose clucked to his horses. "So where were you headed, Great Lady?"

"To Ipet-Isut." She hesitated. "I am not sure I want to go there now, though." She still felt the gods leaning their weight on her, watching her. The feeling made her skin itch. Perhaps, after all, the Holy House was the last place Ahmose should go tonight. "Do you have a destination in mind, General?"

"I was going nowhere in particular. I just do my best thinking while standing in a chariot."

"And has it helped you? Tonight?" Ahmose looked behind her as she spoke, at the House of Women receding into the night, growing smaller, darker, and colder.

Thutmose's breath made a sharp sound. She wondered if her words pained him somehow, but when she glanced at his face he was smiling, showing his big front teeth. "I'm not sure there's any help for me, tonight or any night."

"What do you mean?"

The General shook his head. "It's nothing for a pretty girl to worry over. Tell me, have you ridden in a chariot before?"

"A time or two. Never very fast, though," she admitted.

"Ha! Then we'll ride in the fields as fast as you like." He hissed, and the horses lashed their tails, jounced into a trot so abruptly that Ahmose had to clutch for the rail. The cold air stung her skin, vibrant and sharp with the dun-colored smell of barley.

She smiled. "It's good! The wind feels good."

The general laughed like a barking jackal. "Do you like adventure?" He flipped the reins. The horses trotted faster. Pale shapes formed on the road ahead of them, brightened into linen-white. Two men in the short kilts of commoners stood whispering together by the side of the road. Ahmose watched them as the chariot passed. If she'd walked to the Holy House, she would have met these men. Alone.

"You should have brought more men with you, General. What if we're robbed?"

"Bah. Robbers. This is for robbers." Quick as a cat, he pulled a dagger from his belt, flipped it without so much as glancing down. It spun blade over handle; the hilt smacked back into his thick hand. He laughed at the startled look on Ahmose's face. Then, as fast as he'd drawn his knife, his laughter died. "Are you the one who reads the women's dreams?"

She hesitated. "Yes. I am god-chosen. I'm surprised a general in my father's army would know of anything that goes on in the House of Women."

Thutmose ignored the implied question. He watched the road, his face still and serious. The light of stars and moon muted the colors of his skin. His profile leaped bright and stark against the black of the night sky. Even smudged, the kohl around his eye made it seem as dark and fierce as the eye of Horus. Suddenly, despite the awful cold, despite the urgency of the night and the unformed threat of the morning, Ahmose was caught up in wild excitement. Whatever her future held, whatever the gods would give her with the rising sun, here she was in a ragged tunic, flying through the night, free as a leaping fish. This was her first time alone with a man, and nobody knew but Ahmose. A reckless surge rose up in her middle. She felt deliciously bad, like a hero-princess from one of her nurse's stories; she felt secretive and powerful.

She laid a hand lightly atop Thutmose's. The general looked down at her, his dark eyes wide. "Faster," she said.

He hissed the horses into a canter, then a gallop. The wind tried to rip the wig from Ahmose's head. She steadied it, and steadied herself with the other hand, gripping the rail near where Thutmose held the reins.

"My name is Ahmose," she shouted into the night.

Chapter Two

THEY STOPPED ON A LITTLE hill, not nearly as high as
the great bluffs across the river on the western bank, but
elevated enough that they could look down on the valley.
Late fields of wheat shook their pale leaves in the moonlight.
To the south, weak lights burned in the miniature House
of Women, and beyond it, pale distant points of torches
flickered on the roof of the great palace above Waset. The
palace raised broad shoulders over streets and dwellings, a
stern brow frowning at the river. Its lit windows were many
eyes, unblinking, staring across miles of field and road to
see Ahmose in the chariot. Her skin prickled. In that palace,
stretching so great and tense along the flank of the land,
the Pharaoh had died. In that palace, beautiful and rich and
stifling, the gods tended her fate. They could not have her
yet, though. Not until the morning.

She looked away from Waset deliberately, turning her
cheek against the gods' eyes. She would enjoy tonight while
it was here. The day would come soon enough. But for now,
Ahmose was free, and the sky was mirror-bright with stars.
This moment was all that mattered. Tonight was all she cared
for.

Smiling, she jumped down from the chariot's platform,
kicked her feet in the spicy-sweet summer grasses. The dark
shapes of a few olive trees huddled not far away, leaning
together to whisper their secrets. "It's beautiful here." The
exhilaration of the ride was still in her, and as long as she did

21

not look at the palace, her anxiety was gone.

Thutmose hobbled the horses, his face serious. "A good ride, but perhaps I should pray after all. I have a weight on my heart tonight. Will you excuse me, Great Lady?"

"Of course." Ahmose watched him move along the crest of the hill to stand looking down at sleeping Waset. He faced the setting moon, a gold half-disc sinking among a scatter of stars, and raised his palms in prayer. She kept her eyes on the general's silhouette for a long time, allowing her own tangled thoughts to lie untouched.

She sat, watched the river in the moonlight, lay on the ground staring upward so her eyes were full of stars. The earth was cool and hard against her back. Click-beetles popped in the grass. The horses stamped; she felt their weight and life shiver through the ground beneath her. Ahmose closed her eyes, breathed in the scent of horse and hill and night air, and thought of nothing, nothing, nothing at all but Thutmose praying to the moon. If she held onto this moment with all her strength, perhaps the gods' strange morning would never come.

"Dawn," the general said.

She opened her heavy eyes, blinked up at him.

He stood above her, grinning. "You fell asleep."

"How long?"

"Oh, an hour maybe. I thought it best to let you lie."

Ahmose sat up. Her wig had slipped off. She shook it, flicked at its braids, plucked stray leaves away. When it was in its proper place again, she stood stiffly. Thutmose remained apart, gazing down again at Waset. Ahmose leaned against the chariot and eased a pebble from her sandal, watching him. He was strong as a bull, though short for a man. He stood with his legs apart, a stance of natural confidence. The cleft of his bare back held a deep shadow like a furrow in a field. Beyond him, the western sky lightened; the stars shut their eyes one by one. And still Waset's palace waited for her, huge and immovable, paler in the morning light but not subdued. Ahmose blinked at the eastern horizon; a pink swell was building there. Soon the sun would be up. She had to get back to the House of Women, to Mutnofret.

"General."

He did not move. Perhaps he had not heard. She slipped to his side, touched his wrist.

Thutmose looked down at her. His eyes moved over every part of her features, as if he searched for something in the shape and color of her face. "Ahmose," he said, barely more than a whisper, as if her name were the answer to a question.

Her face heated. She stepped back. The general tossed his head, a small shake. His smile returned. "Shall we get back to Waset, then?"

"I...I promised my sister I'd be home by dawn."

"You'll be a bit late, I'm afraid. I hope you won't be in trouble."

"No one need know except Mutnofret, and I can probably keep her quiet." Probably not. Mutnofret was difficult to control at the best of times, but perhaps with her ascension to the throne so near her mood would be light.

Ahmose climbed back into the chariot. "Do you think your prayers tonight will be successful?" she asked when the general joined her, tucking the horses' hobbles into his belt.

"Successful?" His brows drew together. "It depends on how you define the word."

They drove back to the House of Women at a brisk trot. Thutmose kept his eyes on the road, and Ahmose, feeling once more the weight of the morning, did not try to engage him in conversation. When the chariot swung into the harem courtyard, she took his hand.

"Thank you for being so kind to me. I hope I will see you again soon."

Thutmose gave a single, shoulder-shaking, mirthless laugh. "Ahmose, Great Lady, you will see me again sooner than you'd like. You and I will be seeing much of one other."

"What do you mean?"

But a voice was calling from the walls of the House, shrill against the peaceful morning sky. "Ahmose! You're late! Get in here and get dressed!"

"Mutnofret," Ahmose said. "My sister. She's only two years older than I, but she's just like a Great Royal Wife already."

Thutmose pressed his lips together, hiding his big teeth. "Better not keep that one waiting any longer. She sounds ferocious."

Ahmose jumped down into the dust of the courtyard. She turned to offer the general her thanks once more, but he hissed to the horses, and, snorting, they burst into a run. He was gone, flashing down to the road in a rattle of wheels. Ahmose stared after him for one, two heartbeats, then hurried inside to dress. She and Mutnofret would be expected at court today – today of all days. The king was dead.

In the throne room a great crowd of nobles and priests justled, all talking at once, some of them shouting and shoving. Ahmose and Mutnofret stood together in the doorway, clutching one another. The room was a mess of color: red and blue linen, bright gold glinting from every neck and arm, beads in every wig, the whole crowd moving and pushing against itself. The smell of so many men, even washed and perfumed with myrrh, overwhelmed Ahmose. She was accustomed to order and restraint at court, not this ceaseless commotion of a drunken festival. Even the huge painted pillars along the walls seemed to lean away from the crowd in offense. Stewards moved through the crush of men, restoring order, hauling away those who refused to be restored.

"What do we do, Mutnofret?"

The First King Daughter's eyes narrowed. Then she grabbed

Ahmose by the elbow, dragged her roughly into the room. "Make way for the king's daughters," Mutnofret shouted. No one made way, or even paid them mind. Mutnofret growled in rage.

"There you are!" An unfamiliar steward pushed between two fat men in long, pleated kilts. He bowed to Ahmose and Mutnofret, palms out. "I beg a thousand pardons, Great Ladies. I was told to look for you and escort you to your chairs, but the Great Royal Wife has just announced..."

Mutnofret cut him short. "Then take us to our places."

"Yes, Great Lady. As you wish."

The steward held a short, thick staff carved like a papyrus frond. He used it to tap-tap on shoulders, to wedge between bodies, slowly opening a path across the long hall to the dais where the thrones sat. Ahmose and Mutnofret followed him closely; in their wake the crowd closed again, all talking and stinking and shoving together.

"Steward, if you please, what is going on here? Why is the crowd so unruly?"

The young man, soft-faced with kind eyes, paused to answer Ahmose. "You arrived at the worst possible moment, Great Lady. Your mother just announced that none of the Pharaoh's sons are of the royal blood. There is no heir to the throne. The people are angry; some are frightened." He turned again to his business of clearing their way. Ahmose peered at the faces of the men they passed. She noted a glimmer in each dark eye, but was uncertain whether it was fear, anger, or cool deliberation she saw.

Nearer to the throne the crowd became denser and more frantic. Here the shouting was angrier, and directed not from one man to another, but toward the Horus Throne on its dais. Their steward had to raise his voice, too, commanding the crowd to make way, and the taps of his papyrus stick sometimes turned to blows. Then, so suddenly Ahmose staggered, they broke through the crowd to stand in the empty space at the foot of the dais.

Great Royal Wife Meritamun sat upon the Horus Throne,

the gilded chair, carved and inlaid with a hundred lapis scarabs. *The rightful place of the Pharaoh.* Ahmose's skin prickled to see a woman sitting in the place of the king. It was a kind of wickedness, but one that filled her with nervous excitement. An enormous wig framed her mother's severe face, sweeping from crown to shoulders like a pair of great black wings. Meritamun's eyes were swollen, red, but her gaze was steady and unflinching. Ahmose knew little of the Great Royal Wife. She saw Meritamun as infrequently as she had seen her father, at court or festival, where everything was proper and stately. She had never known Meritamun's eyes to be anything but steady, assessing. The evidence of tears, dry though they may be, surprised Ahmose, and did nothing to still the fear in her heart.

Nefertari, Ahmose's grandmother, stood beside the king's throne, one hand on her daughter's shoulder. She was the God's Wife of Amun, the highest priest in the empire, and possessed of nearly as much power as the Pharaoh himself. The old woman seemed carved of ebony: hard, dark, and permanent. Nefertari stared at Ahmose with a directness that chilled her ka. Then the gnarled sticks of her hand tightened on the shoulder of the Great Royal Wife, and decisively, confidently, as if the queen and the God's Wife shared a single heart, Meritamun rose, plucked the Pharaoh's crook and flail from their stand beside the throne, and crossed them over her chest.

The crowd hushed in one abrupt instant. In the silence, Ahmose's pounding heart filled her ears like a shout. The holy scepters of the crook and flail were for the king alone to wield. She held her breath, unable to tear her eyes from the shocking impiety, though sense told her she should look away from her mother's shame. Then the roar of voices crashed back to life, so loud that Ahmose fought the urge to press her hands over her ears.

Old Nefertari's eyes smiled if her mouth did not. Lightly, she nodded toward the two smaller seats behind and to the left of the Horus Throne, granting permission or issuing a command. Ahmose climbed the steps on shaking legs and lowered herself numbly into her chair.

Meritamun raised the flail above her head. Its heavy beaded lashes swung beside her face. Silence returned to the hall reluctantly.

"As I am the body of the goddess, hear me. I have told you the Pharaoh named no heir before his death. And the gods did not see fit to grant Amunhotep a son of my royal body."

As the clamor rose again, this time with a note of panic, a cold wind blew through Ahmose's ka. No heir. Egypt faced a severe danger. She knew her history well: it was times like these, when the Horus Throne was weak, that Egypt's enemies attacked. The scale tipped over Ahmose; it bore its terrible weight upon her. The moment the gods had promised – had threatened – had at last arrived.

Someone in the crowd called, "But still, the Pharaoh *has* sons!"

"Indeed. A few infant boys born to lesser women of the harem. None old enough to rule. None of the blood of Horus. And I tell you true, my own ka cries out to be free. I, too, will soon join my husband in the afterworld. I cannot rule Egypt as the regent of a child. Not for long."

If one of their young brothers could sit the throne, Meritamun might well rule Egypt in his name until he came of age. But the Great Royal Wife on the verge of death? Why? She was not a young woman, but not so old that jackal-headed Anupu yet knew her name. It could not be. Voices murmured their fears, and Ahmose was unsure whether they came from the great hall or from her own heart. *What of the inundation? Without a Pharaoh the river will fail! The Heqa-Khasewet will take Egypt back! Without a king, we will be invaded again, subjugated!*

"I tell you that until the new Pharaoh takes this throne, I speak with the ka of Amunhotep, who was my brother and my husband. Who doubts me?" Meritamun's voice was a fired arrow. No one spoke against her. Still holding the crook and flail, she continued, "In the voice of Amunhotep

I tell you that the God's Wife, Nefertari, has chosen an heir. In her holy wisdom, in communion with the gods, she has already found the one who shall rule and protect Egypt." Ahmose gripped the armrests of her chair, rigid with anxiety. The crowd seemed to draw one pained breath, waiting. "By the will of all the gods, the heir to the throne is General Thutmose, may he live!"

The crowd surged, voice and body. The stewards shouted as loudly as the nobles and priests. Meritamun raised the crook and flail and shook them, crossed, in the air. A wary silence returned, broken here and there by mutters.

Someone fought his way through the crowd. Ahmose saw the pate of his shaven head first, then glimpsed between bodies the familiar angular profile, the big teeth.

Thutmose bowed low before the throne. "Great Lady and voice of the Pharaoh, if the gods will it, I shall take the Horus Throne, though I am only a common man."

Meritamun's eyes tensed, the only sign of her amusement. "Not so common, I think. Many times Amunhotep told me of your greatness in battle, General. Many times he awarded you the Golden Flies for your bravery on the field."

A hot spear struck Ahmose's heart. Thutmose was not surprised. He had already known. Last night he had known. This – this must be what had troubled him, what had caused him to pray on the hill above Waset while Ahmose slept in the grass. It was not just the death of the Pharaoh, his friend. It was *this*.

Thutmose nodded in humble acceptance of the praise. "This is true, and you honor me by saying it. Yet still, I am a man of low birth. How can the gods choose me for the Horus Throne?"

His words had the sound of practice. He and the Great Royal Wife had planned this speech. And Nefertari – the God's Wife was an implacable force. If she appointed a common general as Pharaoh, no man in the empire could stop her, or even speak against her. What else was she capable of? How else might she flout convention? What could Great Royal

Wife, God's Wife, and heir accomplish together? Ahmose felt the scales tip above her, wavering, pushing down until she knew she would shatter like a dropped pot. She was helpless before the court, helpless before the power of her family. Tears stung her eyes. She blinked them away.

From behind the throne, Nefertari smiled down at Thutmose. Her voice was dry with age, but strong enough to fill the hall. "You will be royal by marriage."

On her small throne beside Ahmose's, Mutnofret stiffened. Her back straightened. Her hands gripped the arms of her chair until they turned white.

"Your Great Royal Wife will be the King's Daughter, Ahmose, may she live!"

In a heartbeat, the moisture left Ahmose's mouth. All her bones turned to hot honey, weak and melted. Mutnofret lurched to her feet, staring at their mother and grandmother. Ahmose would not look at her sister's face, but she knew how Mutnofret's eyes must burn, how her jaw must clench as she struggled to gain mastery over shock.

Meritamun glared at Mutnofret, and after a long moment, the First King's Daughter sank back into her chair. Ahmose risked a sidelong glance at her sister. Mutnofret was shaking and pale; she looked away from the throne, away from Ahmose, out across the crowded expanse of the great hall. Her eyes were blank, cold, the eyes of a slain animal.

Ahmose stared helplessly at the queen, the God's Wife, Thutmose, her sister. She could think of nothing to say, and so she said nothing. She heard nothing of the remainder of the court proceedings but Mutnofret's ragged breathing. When they were at last dismissed, she needed a steward to guide her back to her litter, and a guard to help her stagger back to her room in the House of Women.

Alone at last, she stripped off her clothes and opened the sluice in her bath without summoning a servant for help. She lay back in the cold water, let it cover her face and carry away her tears.

CHAPTER THREE

A HMOSE WAITED IN THE ANTEROOM of Meritamun's apartments for a long time before the Great Royal Wife could see her. It was a beautiful place, a wide room cooled by windcatchers near the ceiling. Ahmose leaned her elbows on a table of oiled carob wood and took in the richness of her surroundings. The sheer force of opulence was a welcome distraction from the morning's madness in the throne room. Heavy, bright draperies hung from poles; they stirred softly in a breeze that smelled of flowers and spice. In one corner of the spacious room cushions were piled near several ornate stands where instruments – a tambourine and sesheshet, a long-bodied lute, a double-reed horn of slick black wood – stood waiting to be played. A great floor harp arced up above the rest, its stand carved into the form of a sphinx. Did Meritamun play these instruments herself? Or did she keep a troupe of musicians whose only duty was to amuse the Great Royal Wife?

A long couch stood in the center of the room, and beside it, a cabinet full of papyrus scrolls. Ahmose considered stealing across to the cabinet to peek at the scrolls. They might contain anything: letters from viziers and foreign kings, or romances, or poetry written by the Great Royal Wife. Or perhaps correspondence with General Thutmose about his appointment as heir, and who he was to marry. Ahmose resisted the temptation. She must make a clear, sure impression on Meritamun. Being caught sneaking through her mother's cabinet would not help her cause. Only children peeked at scrolls, and Ahmose was no child. Not anymore.

A great electrum mirror stood against the opposite wall, flanked by two slender wood carvings of the goddess Iset. Ahmose stared at herself in the shining surface, at the small, young woman sitting so still and proper on her carved chair, distant and untouchable across the reflected double span of tiled floor and couch and cushions. The quiet, good girl overwhelmed and buried among the persistent pressing hands of wealth and state.

She wanted to cry, but she had cried enough today. Her kohl would smear. The thought brought back the memory of Thutmose in the chariot, the black line around his Horus-eye blurred so carelessly, the lines that crimped his face when he laughed so loud. He had been kind and gentle to her. He had kept her safe, and she had trusted him, ridden all alone with him. And the whole time he had known what today would bring, and had said no word. She did not know whether she was angry at him, or grateful.

Her stomach hurt and rumbled. It was well past the dinner hour. Ahmose had eaten nothing all day. She rose, peeked outside Meritamun's door, spotted a serving woman, and sent her for food. Thank the gods, it was not long before a tray of bread and figs arrived with a cone of soft white cheese and a jug of beer.

The Great Royal Wife arrived as well. Ahmose was stuffing figs into her mouth when Meritamun swept through the door. "You thought to send for food. Excellent. I will join you. I haven't had more than a sip of milk all day."

Ahmose nodded, blushing and swallowing hard around the half-chewed fig.

"Quite a day." Meritamun sighed. She folded a bit of bread, pinched up some cheese and popped it into her mouth with none of her typical courtly grace. "A regular show at court. I suppose that's why you have come to me."

"Yes," Ahmose admitted. "This must be a mistake."

"It is no mistake, Ahmose." Meritamun leaned an elbow

on the table, rested her forehead against one strong, slender hand. She breathed deeply. Ahmose looked at her mother's swollen eyes and wondered whether she would weep again for the dead king. But then Meritamun straightened, resolute as ever, and said, "Nefertari was quite adamant that you should be Thutmose's Great Royal Wife."

"You've been planning this since before the Pharaoh died." It was not a question. There was simply not enough time between Amunhotep's death and that spectacle in the throne room. Not enough time for Thutmose to find out, and to accept the order of the God's Wife with as much composure as he showed before the court. No man could have remained so calm amidst so much chaos; not even a general.

Meritamun nodded. She drank beer straight from the jug, then passed it to Ahmose. "I loved your father, but he was a stubborn, stupid man. He simply *refused* to name an heir after he fell ill. Refused! He thought he would recover – a man of his age."

"He was ill? I did not know."

"Mm," Meritamun bit a fig in half. She must truly be hungry, to eat with so little poise. Ahmose was still hungry, too, for that matter, in spite of the fear clawing at her belly. The Great Royal Wife chewed, swallowed, then said, "Late in the month of Djehuty he collapsed with a pain in his chest. The physicians made him rest for weeks. When they finally let him out of his bed he could not remain active for more than a few hours. His breath was always short. Nefertari and I knew he was preparing to leave this world. We begged him to name an heir. He would not. He was certain his health would return.

"Putting one of his sons on the throne was never an option. Can you imagine, a harem girl's suckling babe with the Nemes crown on his head? No. Your grandmother and I saw how it would go – *see* how it will go. The situation with the Heqa-Khasewet is tenuous. Since your dear grandfather, may he live forever, drove them out of the kingdom they have been itching to take Egypt back. A decisive ruler is needed now: one the Heqa-Khasewet will fear; one for whom Egypt's soldiers will fight with confidence and pride. Not a baby. We were in despair, Ahmose, I tell you truly. Then Nefertari had the idea of..."

"Of a common-born soldier?"

"Of *you*. I confess I have paid less attention to you than I ought over the years, but you are god-chosen; that I know. The gods speak through you. Do you think only the House of Women knows of your gifts? You have a reputation among the court, Ahmose. Oh, yes," she said, for Ahmose's mouth had fallen open. "You've been bleeding for – how long? – five, six months? A short time only, but word has made its rounds. You have a way with dreams, or so the women say. Omens, too. How often do you read dreams at the House of Women?"

"Every fifth day."

"You should do it more. You're so accurate, they say, the nobles' wives have come to look on you as something of a good-luck charm. Having one's fortune told by the king's daughter has become quite fashionable in the court of Amunhotep."

Ahmose blushed, folded her hands in her lap. It was true that some noble women visited the House of Women every fifth day to share their dreams and hear Ahmose's interpretations. But noble women all over Waset had friends and relations in the harem. Ahmose was not *famed* for her dream-reading. Surely not. She kept her words humble. "It is the power of the gods, and none of my doing. I only speak the words they give me when I hear the women's dreams."

Meritamun tapped the table with a dark hennaed fingernail, rap-rap, a sound of great finality. "Well, there you are, then. You are a channel through which the gods speak. Everybody who has seen you believes it to be true. *You* believe it to be true. And it is true, surely. And you are the daughter of the king. With you standing behind the Horus Throne, Nefertari and I could put any man we pleased on the seat itself and no one would question the arrangement."

"But Mutnofret! She is the elder daughter. This is *improper*, to say nothing of being unfair to my sister."

"Nothing about this is proper. Nothing about this is fair." Meritamun's face was suddenly grave. She rose from her seat and walked to her dressing table. With some difficulty she pulled the giant wig from her head and rested it atop a tall, carved stand.

Ahmose stared. She had never seen the Great Royal Wife without one of her great, wide wigs. Now, knuckling her back, freed of her trappings, Meritamun lost her royal grace. She was still poised, still powerful, but the image of a strong woman was marred by the crookedness of her body. The line of Meritamun's spine from her nape to the top of her gown kinked like an olive branch. The wig hid all but the slightest slant of her shoulders, and masked completely the terrible deformity of her back.

Relieved of the weight, Meritamun sighed. She shook her head wearily. "And now you know my secret, child. My bones are bent. Every year it grows harder to breathe, harder to move about. All the physicians have told me I should have died years ago." Her voice twisted like her backbone, sharp and ugly. "It's only by the gods' grace that I've lived to see such days. I wanted to try for a son, but the physicians made me stop after you were born. They were afraid another pregnancy would kill me. I feared my daughters would have the same affliction. You have no idea how closely I watched you both as little girls, waiting to see whether your backs would twist. Thank all the gods your bodies are sound. You are all I have to give Egypt."

"I don't know what to say. I had no idea."

"No, indeed. Only your father and grandmother knew. And my body servants and the physicians, of course. They have been well paid to keep quiet. The court would not look favorably on a crippled Great Royal Wife."

"So this is why you said...in the throne room...."

Meritamun nodded, her face calm. "I can feel my body weakening. It will not be much longer for me. Soon I will go to the Field of Reeds, to meet my husband there."

Ahmose nearly groaned under a sudden weight of misery. She barely knew Meritamun, but already she could sense the difficult times ahead. She only realized now, when all hope of a guiding hand had died, that she had been hopeful of her mother's shepherding. How comforting it would be to have Meritamun's advice and support, even if they had been all but strangers until this day. The gods' will would be done, though, Ahmose knew. She of all people knew.

"But why this General Thutmose, of all men? Is there even a drop of royal blood in his veins?" She'd ridden with him just last night. She knew he was a good man, trustworthy and kind; yet Ahmose could not help but feel a flush of indignation. She was the daughter of a king, after all. She had always expected a suitable marriage to a nobleman or a high priest, or perhaps to a very powerful governor. A common general? This was nothing short of absurd.

Meritamun laughed as she ran a hand over her bald head. "Not a drop, not a speck, so far as anybody can tell. As to why, he is absolutely brilliant with strategy. Amunhotep relied on him heavily, Ahmose; he was not only the most elite of the king's soldiers, but your father's dearest friend. Thutmose is more than just a strong arm. He knew the mind of the Pharaoh in ways no prince or priest ever could. He is better prepared to take the throne than any child of Amunhotep's blood, and far better able to command the army than Mutnofret. Or you."

"So you need a sword arm to keep our enemies at bay, and you think to legitimize him by marrying him to a king's daughter. To me."

"*Think to*, nothing. It will be done. The Heqa-Khasewet wait at Egypt's northern border. The Kushites wait to the south. To which of these will you give Egypt, Ahmose?"

"Neither," she said fiercely. "And to no one else besides. I know what life was like for us under Heqa-Khasewet rule. I will never let Egypt return to such shame. But the rekhet, Mother. What will they do? What will the common people think of a common man ruling them?"

"I imagine they'll be thrilled." Meritamun chuckled, finishing off the cheese. "What a tale to tell their children. 'Be a good boy, and even you could grow up to be Pharaoh.'"

"But don't the rekhet expect a person of the royal blood to lead them? It is the Pharaoh's divinity that brings the floods. The rekhet know this."

"Ah, true. But it is not the rekhet you need worry over. The nobles and the priests are the ones who need convincing. If they don't accept Thutmose, the Kushites and the Heqa-Khasewet will only need to decide how to divide up the land between them. It is the priests above all, and the nobles as well, who hold this land together."

"How so?" Ahmose's tutors had always told her the rekhet – the commoners – made Egypt live or die.

Meritamun raised one hand, palm up and cupped as if it held water. "The priests take taxes and offerings to the gods. They store them away for times of need. They oversee the food surpluses in the name of fairness, so that those with riches cannot keep all the grain and cattle for themselves. They are the voice that speaks to the gods on behalf of the rest of us." She raised her other hand in the same gesture. "The nobles oversee the working of the land. They ensure the crops are planted and harvested. They make sure flax is spun and cloth woven. They keep trade routes open and relations with foreigners intact, so wealth flows into Egypt." The Great Royal Wife brought both hands together, pressing as if she clutched some brilliant and fragile fruit between her palms. "Without the priests, the rekhet might be forgotten by the nobles and the food stores might fail. Without the nobles, the wealth of Egypt would quickly dry up and all the people would be back to living as they did in the times before cities, when there was no Egypt as we know it today. If both do not work together as one, the rekhet become dissatisfied and rebellious. They refuse to fight in the army. They refuse to work the fields. They refuse to build. You can see where this leads."

Ahmose nodded. She was not completely convinced, though. So it *was* the rekhet who made Egypt live or die. They *were* important. But Meritamun's point was well made. "The horses pull the chariot," she said, "but a driver must guide them. The rekhet are the horses, the priests and nobles together the driver."

Meritamun smiled. "Nefertari was right about you. You will make a good Great Royal Wife."

"I understand now why you have chosen Thutmose. And I understand the importance of keeping harmony in Egypt. But I still do not see why you've set Mutnofret aside. She is just as royal as I am, and she is the First King's Daughter."

"Is that why you have come? To try to convince me to make Mutnofret Great Royal Wife? It will not happen, Ahmose. It cannot. Mutnofret is the elder; this is true. And she is beautiful, I know. But age and beauty are not enough to guide Egypt through what lies ahead. Mutnofret is as hot-headed a woman as the gods have ever made – oh, yes, I have heard all about her temper! – and a hot-headed Great Wife could damn Egypt forever. Mut knows I've tried everything I can think of to cool that girl's heart, but she has always been an ember waiting to fall on tinder. It cannot be overstated how eagerly the Heqa-Khasewet wait for Egypt to show any sign of weakness. Mutnofret ranting on the throne beside a common-born king may be just what they need to chisel a few holes into our walls.

"Thutmose will be in a difficult position, as dangerous as any of his battles. He needs every bit of legitimacy we can give him. Today I claimed the voice of Amunhotep to name him the heir. It was barely enough. Thutmose needs the voice of the gods speaking for him, or the priests and the nobles will never be satisfied."

"It's because of me, then. You are breaking Mutnofret's heart because I am god-chosen."

Meritamun pinched the bridge of her nose. "The gods know I tried my best with Mutnofret. Her nurse and I, we did everything we could think of to curb the girl. But she was born with too much fire in her. She is a wild horse that will not be caught. Setting her loose on a common-born king – even a man experienced in battle – could be disastrous. Thutmose will need unity and peace in his family, not just legitimacy.

"I am not without sympathy for Mutnofret, Ahmose. And I know how you love her; I love her, too, for all her fire. She is my own child – my first child! I regret the pain this will cause her. But I cannot go to my death leaving Egypt to face disaster. Caring for this land has always been my life's devotion. If one true thing can be painted on the walls of my tomb, it will be this: Egypt was so important to me that I sacrificed anything – everything – even the happiness of my daughter – to save it from ruin."

Because she saw the sadness in Meritamun's eyes, Ahmose said nothing. But her ka whispered restlessly. *Will I, too, be required to make such a sacrifice? What will be said at the funeral of Ahmose, the Great Royal Wife?*

"Mutnofret will not be forgotten, I promise you," Meritamun said. "She will be Thutmose's second wife, and a queen in her own right, not a concubine. She will have rooms here in the palace and will attend court if she chooses. I hope you will treat her as a near-equal, Ahmose. Your duty is to speak with the voice of the gods on Thutmose's behalf, so none will challenge his rule. But it will be for you and your sister both to love this new Pharaoh and please him. To bear his children."

The skin on Ahmose's arms raised into gooseflesh, a prickle of foreboding. "If we are to be near-equals, and both of us royal wives, who will bear Thutmose's *heir?*"

Meritamun looked steadily into her daughter's eyes. "That will be for you to decide."

CHAPTER FOUR

A HMOSE TOOK THE SPINDLES AND distaffs from Aiya's arms and helped her sit in the shade of the olive tree. The girl was Ahmose's dearest friend, a pretty, shy, golden young thing. Aiya was the daughter of a foreign king far to the north. She had been given to the Pharaoh as a peace offering three years ago, along with casks of wine, animal skins, horses, and chests of copper and gold. Aiya seldom spoke of life in the north. It must have been a terrible place, and her father a beast of a man. What kind of a king would send his daughter to a distant land?

Surely life in the Pharaoh's harem was better than life in her savage homeland. Aiya seemed happy enough. She was chatty – with Ahmose, at least – and was the best spinner in the House of Women despite her young age. It was Aiya who had taught Ahmose to spin, and they often passed their afternoons together beneath the largest olive tree in the garden, laughing and gossiping while they dropped their spindles in the shade.

The girl spoke the Egyptian tongue well. Her accent was thick, but she had picked up the language quickly. She wore Egyptian clothing, loved Egyptian music and sang with a pure, clear voice. The only concession she refused to grant Egypt was her bright yellow hair. She flatly refused to shave her head and wear a wig like a proper Egyptian woman. It sometimes made her the target of snide remarks in the women's quarters, but Ahmose loved Aiya's golden hair, and

41

often combed her fingers through it, weaving it with flowers while they passed their hours in the garden.

Aiya was also pregnant – hugely so – and proud of her unborn child. She was certain it was a boy. She would bear the son of a Pharaoh, the last of Amunhotep's children. The girl was just fourteen, only a year older than Ahmose, but already eager for motherhood.

"I heard you are soon Great Wife," Aiya said, playing with the spindle in her lap.

"You heard rightly, I am afraid. Mutnofret hasn't spoken to me in the two days since our mother made the announcement."

"Poor Mutnofret."

Ahmose propped her distaff against her hip.

"I suppose she has every right to be angry with me, although I didn't choose this for myself. I would undo it if I could."

Aiya shook her head. "She should be angry with mother. Ahmose is not for blaming."

"I know you are right, but if I were in her place I think I might feel the same way." Ahmose licked her fingers and twisted her flax fibers, pulling them smoothly away from the distaff, securing them to her spindle. Her threads were not always perfect, but they were usually even and strong. One day she would spin as well as Aiya, with threads as fine and strong as a spider's web. She'd had plenty of practice of late. Spinning relaxed her, allowed her mind some measure of peace. It seemed Ahmose had done nothing but spin since the Pharaoh died.

"When is wedding?"

"Ten days," Ahmose said, concentrating on the weight and speed of her spindle instead of on the specter of her wedding. "I hope you will sit beside me at the feast."

"If baby is not coming!"

"I cannot wait to meet your son. Have you chosen his name?"

Aiya's smile was shy. "How you say it in Egyptian?" She lapsed into her native tongue, and after all the time they had spent together, sharing secrets and stories, Ahmose understood the words well enough. *"He stands first among the great men."*

"Hatshepsu." Ahmose gave her the Egyptian word. "It is a good name, Aiya. Very strong. Perfect for the son of a Pharaoh."

Aiya beamed, her lovely, pale eyes on her spindle. At last she said, "You should visit Mutnofret, tell her your heart."

"I have been afraid to talk to her. She must be so hurt and so angry. I don't think I can bear to see her in such pain." *Or to face her rage.*

"She needs her sister."

Perhaps it was true. For all Mutnofret's fierce temper, she had always been close to Ahmose. There was no one Mutnofret loved or trusted more.

"You should be a priestess, not a harem woman. You always know exactly what to say. You are right, Aiya. Mutnofret needs me now. I will go to her this evening. Gods protect a fool, but I will give it a try."

Mutnofret received Ahmose graciously, but her eyes were puffy and red beneath fresh, neatly drawn kohl. They made their awkward greetings, both of them perched tensely on the edges of the ebony stools in Mutnofret's elegant room. A dish of fragrant figs lay untouched on the table between them. A tiny, silent fly circled the fruits.

"I had no idea this would happen," Ahmose said, dejected.

"I know."

"I went to see our mother. I asked her to take back her decision."

Mutnofret looked hopeful for a moment. Reluctantly, Ahmose shook her head. Mutnofret's mouth turned down, but her eyes remained calm. "I've been crying for two days straight. I feel like a fool, but I can't seem to stop."

Ahmose laid a hand atop her sister's. "I don't blame you, Nofret. I would cry, too. I *have* cried, in truth. This is so unfair to you. I didn't want this. *Don't* want this; you must believe me. But I don't know how to change it."

Mutnofret's chin quivered, but no tears welled in her eyes. "I don't know how to change it, either. I just wish I understood why."

"It's because of my gift. My being god-chosen. Mother thinks it will make the priests and nobles accept Thutmose more readily, if a god-chosen wife stands behind his throne." She thought better of disclosing to Mutnofret the rest of Meritamun's reasoning.

Mutnofret rolled her eyes. She pulled her hand out from under Ahmose's. The gesture stung, but Ahmose chided herself. *She is hurting. You must keep patience.*

"Thutmose," Mutnofret said. "You say his name with such familiarity. Have you met him before?" There was a considering, almost light-hearted note in her voice. Trying to take her mind off her anger, perhaps; Ahmose gladly went along. She told her sister of the forbidden night-time ride with the general.

Nofret laughed, clapping her hands at the romance and mischief of it. Her pleasure seemed genuine. "So you think he is a good man. And he has a taste for adventure, I see. At least that is something. It could have been worse, I suppose. I guess I would rather be second wife of a good, brave man than Great Royal Wife of a naked baby."

"You must meet him soon, Nofret. I know you will love him."

"Do you love him?"

It was a startling question. Ahmose had not considered it until now. "I...I think I do," she said, just to feed Mutnofret's cheery mood. "At least, I found him to be...suitable...when we rode together."

"*Suitable!* How like a Great Wife you sound." Mutnofret laughed again. There was no barb in her words, and, warming, Ahmose smiled tremulously.

"I don't know how to be a Great Royal Wife, Nofret. Not like you do. I'll need your help. I won't be able to do it without you."

This time it was Mutnofret who took her sister's hand. Their fingers intertwined. "I will be behind you, Ahmose. When do you think I can meet your Thutmose?"

"Let's send a message to him tonight. If luck is with us, we can see him tomorrow."

"He's not very handsome, is he?" Nofret whispered. "And how old is he? He looks thirty at least."

They waited beside the palace lake. A breeze stirred the surface of the water, cooling Ahmose's skin, raising the scent of lotus. Tiny waves lapped at the raised stone lip of the reservoir. Thutmose walked toward them with a stride like a bull's, purposeful and direct. A little ball of excitement rolled around in Ahmose's stomach; she shrugged at Mutnofret's words. She had not considered whether Thutmose was handsome. He was simply Thutmose, good at driving horses, strong and kind, with a jackal's laugh.

"Good morning, Great Ladies." Thutmose bowed lower than was necessary, one hand steadying his rather plain wig. He wore the simple white kilt of a soldier, falling in pleats to his knees. The only sign of his new status as Egypt's heir was a brilliant Eye-of-Horus pectoral laid over his broad brown chest, gold set with cabochons of blue, red, and green. "Shall we?" He indicated a small craft moored against the stone wall, a miniature version of the great pleasure barges that sailed the Iteru. Food and flasks of wine were laid out on a low platform at the center of the barge.

Thutmose climbed onto the lake's lip, then offered a hand to Mutnofret. She hiked up her skirt and took his hand, cheeks coloring when her skin touched his. Ahmose, watching, bit her lip.

When Mutnofret had lowered herself gracefully to a stack of cushions, Thutmose turned to help Ahmose aboard. "I swear I've met you someplace before," he said with a wink. Ahmose giggled, which brought a horsey grin onto his face. When his hand closed around hers, a shaky heat flared through her. Her palm tingled with the memory of his rough, callused fingers even after she had seated herself by Nofret's side.

Thutmose loosed the ropes holding the barge, then found the quant and poled them toward the center of the lake. "And so the great journey began," he said. "The lucky soldier stole the two beautiful daughters from their father's house and put them on his magic boat. He took them far away down the Iteru, where nobody would be able to find them...."

"You don't need to steal me," Mutnofret said. "I'll come along willingly."

"Will you, now?" Thutmose let the boat slow, then tucked the quant into the hull. The barge drifted. He made his careful way to the table, strong arms stretched low to counter the boat's rocking. "Let's have some breakfast, shall we?"

There was honey for their bread, and berries in milk, and two kinds of cheese. Ahmose could barely eat, her stomach fluttered so. She recalled how close she had stood to Thutmose in the chariot, how strong he had looked standing on the crest of the hill in the moonlight, and her skin felt much too hot in the sun. She had never been closer to a man than she had been to Thutmose, and here he was again, sharing the morning meal. She kept glancing at the shapes of the muscles in his arms and shoulders, the path of a raised vein that ran over the outside of his arm like a tiny brown river. His very maleness fascinated her.

As they talked, Thutmose would sometimes give his big, barking laugh. The first time he did it Mutnofret blinked, obviously taken aback by his uncouth manner. He was unlike the noblemen Mutnofret was used to, Ahmose knew. But as the First King's Daughter became accustomed to Thutmose's sense of humor she soon began striving to make him laugh, coaxing the humor from him with ribald stories or bawdy jokes. At first, Ahmose laughed right along with Thutmose. But as he paid more attention to Mutnofret, each of his smiles brought a twinge of jealousy. Soon Mutnofret reclined on her cushions, stretching in the sun, eyes closed, head back, soft neck bared. Her body was long and round, like curves of the river, as ripe as Iset and lovely as a song.

"Mmm, the sun feels so nice, don't you think?"

Thutmose only sipped his wine. But his eyes wandered from Mutnofret's face down the line of her throat to her breasts, to her softly rounded belly and hips, curving bright through her sun-soaked linen. Ahmose bit her lips together and looked away, sharply aware of the smallness of her own breasts, the hard angles of her young body. Beside Mutnofret, she was as plain as a pebble. She wished they were back on the shore again.

"I've brought you both some little gifts," Thutmose said. "What about it? Are you interested?"

Mutnofret sat up at once and leaned forward, closing her eyes and holding out her hands. Thutmose lifted a leather bag from beneath their small table. He pulled out of it a little bundle wrapped in blue fabric, dropped it into Nofret's palms. She opened her eyes, then opened the cloth. "Oh! What is this stone?" It was a pendant made of some shiny, bright white rock, carved in the shape of a crouching lioness.

"Not a stone," Thutmose said. "Ivory. It's so white because I only just had it carved for you yesterday. I asked your mother about you; she said you are as fierce as anything the gods ever made. I thought a lioness would be perfect. I hope you like it."

"It's beautiful," Mutnofret said, clutching the pendant to her heart. "And carved for me. Oh, the detail is so fine! I shall wear it at our wedding feast. Look, Ahmose."

She held the lioness out so Ahmose could examine it. It was indeed a marvelous carving. The snarling mouth was treacherous with sharp white teeth. Its eye was a tiny, hard, sparkling flake of obsidian. Thutmose must have paid plenty to commission such a skilled carver.

"And here is your gift, Ahmoset." She blushed. Only Nofret and her childhood nurse ever used the familiar form of her name. It made her delightfully giddy to hear Thutmose address her with such affection.

He handed her a red cloth bundle, larger and heavier than Mutnofret's. She squeezed it through the cloth without unwrapping it. It was about as long as her hand and bumpy. Another carving, then.

When she peeled back the red cloth, the face of the goddess Mut looked back at her. She gasped. The carving was exquisite. Mut's face, arms, and bared breasts were of rosy alabaster; her hair was jet; her carnelian dress was polished to a brilliant sheen. The double crown of Egypt was upon her head, ivory and red jasper, as delicate as a feather, translucent in the morning light

"To beautify your worship, my god-chosen wife." Thutmose's words were light, as if this gift were a mere bauble, as if calling her *wife* was all in a day's jesting. But Ahmose's hands clutched the statue of Mut as if they would never let go, and her heart held onto his words as if their sound was the breath of life.

Ahmose turned to show her gift to her sister. Nofret's smile was tight. It never touched her eyes.

Chapter Five

"I BELIEVE YOU WERE RIGHT about Thutmose," Mutnofret said.

She had invited Ahmose to bathe with her after supper. They lay in Mutnofret's tiled pool, relaxed and quiet. Crushed herbs floated on the water; their earthy scent rose upon the steam. Two of Nofret's women arrived, carrying a kettle of hot water between them. They upended it into the bath, and the heat crept up Ahmose's legs, made her shiver with delight.

Meeting Thutmose, flirting with him, seemed to have brought Mutnofret around. She was still hurt, of course; sometimes it showed. But Nofret seemed committed to renewing the closeness she and Ahmose had enjoyed until that mad day in the throne room.

"How was I right?" Ahmose asked lazily.

"He is *suitable*." Mutnofret rolled over in the water. When she propped herself on her elbows, her back swept down into the bath; her buttocks rose out of the water again, two perfect round islands.

Ahmose sat up and crossed her arms over her small breasts. "I'm glad you like him. I am sure he likes you as well. I think he will be a good husband, don't you?"

"Mm, much better than a baby for a husband. What strong arms he has."

Ahmose's face burned. The bath was far too warm. "I think I am ready to get out now. Will you scrape me?"

Nofret rose, elegant as an ibis taking wing. The water streamed from her body, sparkling in the light of the bath's braziers as it ran off her rounded flesh. She reached a hand down to help Ahmose to her feet. Her eyes traveled down Ahmose's body; the corner of Nofret's mouth quirked.

"What?"

"You need a plucking, little sister. Let me call one of my women. They are very good; they never miss a hair."

While they waited for the woman to come with her tweezers and ointments, Ahmose and Mutnofret scraped each other's skin with curved copper strips, flinging the water from their bodies to the ground, where it puddled about their feet. The sensation was invigorating after the languor of the hot bath.

"And how is your little Northern friend?" Mutnofret asked, sliding her scraper down Ahmose's back.

"Aiya? As well as can be, I suppose. She will have her baby soon."

Mutnofret tutted. "Poor young thing. She is so small."

The scraper hissed like a cat as it slid over Ahmose's skin. She shivered. "What do you mean?"

"Oh, the dangers of childbirth, the risk." Mutnofret's voice was light, unconcerned. "You know what they say about all that terrible business."

"Well...of course it's dangerous, sometimes. But you don't think Aiya is in more danger than most, do you?"

"But Ahmose, she is so young."

"She is not so much younger than you."

"You don't see me with a big belly. I would never risk my life that way until I was sure I was old enough to survive."

Survive? "Nonsense, Nofret! Plenty of women have babies at Aiya's age."

"Plenty of women die having babies at her age. But let us talk of more pleasant things. This is upsetting you."

Shaken, Ahmose cast about for a change of subject. "I have never been as good with clothing as you, Nofret. What should I wear to our wedding?"

"Green, definitely," she said, unhesitating. "It looks glorious against your skin. It brings out your eyes well, too. You are stunning in that color. You have a green gown, yes? I know I've seen you in one before."

The green gown was the plainest in Ahmose's clothing-chest, except for her ratty old red tunic. The green was serviceable and comfortable, but there was nothing especially fine about it. "But that dress is so ordinary."

"Silly, you don't need to look like you've rolled out of a jewel chest be beautiful. If you load yourself with fine fabrics and gold and gems you will only appear insecure. A Great Royal Wife should look confident, don't you think? Naturally strong."

Ahmose chewed her lip. Mutnofret would not steer her wrong. And Ahmose had never paid much attention to trends. Perhaps all the women dressed in a quieter, more restrained style of late. Ahmose certainly was not one to know. At court she was more likely to mind what the politicians were discussed than how the women dressed.

"All right. I shall wear the green. What about my jewelry?"

"Hardly anything. You must keep it simple. Understated is very elegant. That's what I will do."

"Oh, thank you, Nofret. You are so good to help me."

"I'll help you any way I can, dear Ahmose. We are still sisters, above all."

Ahmose squeezed Nofret's hand. "Always sisters."

Mutnofret's body servant arrived, laid out a thick linen towel on a long, high bench. The bench stood below a faience mural upon the bath's wall. Ahmose lay back and studied the picture, wincing, waiting for the ordeal of plucking to begin. She kept her eyes upon the mural: nude women swam and cavorted in a secluded river pool screened by tall, bright papyrus leaves. A man's face peeked out between the leaves, spying on the bathing girls. Mutnofret must have found the mural amusing, but to Ahmose it was distasteful. She squinted at it, groping for conversation while the woman rubbed a soothing ointment into her legs and groin.

"How long do you suppose the feast will last?"

51

"Oh, hours, I'm sure."

"I have never been to a wedding before. Well – when I was a little girl, but I don't remember much of it."

"I remember both the weddings I have seen. There is ever so much music, and dozens of courses for dinner, and gifts for the brides and groom."

"Will we dance?" Ahmose loved to dance.

"Not us. We must be dignified. But the stewards will hire the best dancers in the kingdom, and there will be plays and acrobats and poetry recitals. Most of the nobles will drink too much. Drunken nobles are always good sport." Mutnofret slipped into a fresh gown of soft white linen. She tied it, smiling slyly. "And then, after the celebration, the wedding night."

"The wedding night?"

Mutnofret laughed. "Oh, Ahmose. Sometimes I forget how young you are, you sweet child."

The plucking-lady tittered, hid a smile behind her free hand.

"What happens?" Ahmose insisted.

"That is when our husband will take us."

"*Take* us?"

Mutnofret laughed again, then drifted over to the bench. She pinched Ahmose's cheek just as if she were a helpless baby. "He will take our maidenhood. I assume you are still a maiden, yes?"

"Oh, I know all about that. Only I had never heard it called *taking* before."

Mutnofret rolled her eyes. Drily she said, "So you are not so young after all. I was afraid I would need to explain the entire process to you. I just hope he doesn't fancy taking us both at the same time."

"But how can he? He only has one to use."

Nofret and the plucking-lady laughed aloud, as if Ahmose had made a wonderful joke.

"I wonder which of us he will want first." An unsettling, dreamy look came over Mutnofret's face. "I can almost forget the shame of being a second wife, if I can look forward to that man in my bed."

Ahmose wrinkled her nose. The plucking twinged at her nerves. Maybe Nofret was not putting the disappointment behind her as well as Ahmose had hoped. To keep Nofret's mood light, she asked, "What's it like?"

Mutnofret's eyes glittered. "I'm sure *I* don't know."

The plucking-lady stopped her work and turned away, snorting back a laugh. Ahmose stared at her sister in combined horror and admiration.

"You have done it already! With whom?"

"Of course not, Ahmoset! What a wicked idea. Rutting like cattle in the fields – that is for common women. I was raised to be the Great Royal Wife. What if I had gotten a child in my belly and it wasn't the son of a Pharaoh? Our friends in the harem would all go hoarse for weeks from gossiping over such a scandal. I could never do that to them."

Ahmose felt sure she could not trust Mutnofret's denial. But she doubted she would get any more information from her sister. "Still, I wish I knew what to expect."

"Well, from what I've *heard*, it hurts terribly the first time. And you bleed like a cut calf. But after the first time, it gets more bearable. Sometimes."

"Then why does *anybody* do it?"

"Oh, to make children, I suppose. A wife's duty is to give her husband heirs, after all."

"Yes, but...but I've heard some of the women talk as if they like it."

"I'm sure every woman pretends that she likes it to her friends. It is a woman's duty. But who could really like all that pain and bleeding?"

The plucking-woman packed away her tweezers and jars. "You are finished, Great Lady."

Ahmose sat up, suddenly weak and dizzy. "Oh, Nofret. How will I get through this?"

Mutnofret sank onto the bench beside Ahmose, pulling her close in a quick, tight hug. "I will be here for you. Always sisters, remember? For now it's best to forget about it. It is days away, and we have so much to do before the wedding feast. Stand up; let me have a look at you."

Ahmose stood unsteadily. The place between her legs smarted from the plucking; she felt tender and raw, and especially vulnerable. Her hands shook, aching to cover up her trembling body. Instead she put her hands on her hips, and hoped the gesture made her look more confident, more womanly.

"Positively beautiful for one so young," Mutnofret said, although at sixteen she was barely older than Ahmose. "How proud I am of my little sister, soon to be the Great Royal Wife. Now let's get you dressed."

As Mutnofret helped her back into her gown, cooing and fussing, Ahmose had never before felt so young, so insignificant. She wanted to cry. Instead, she made herself smile.

CHAPTER SIX

ONLY THREE DAYS REMAINED BEFORE her wedding. Soon Ahmose would move to the apartments of the Great Royal Wife in Waset's great palace. It was a lovely place, even better than the harem house. She could visit her friends in the House of Women any time she pleased. Yet once she moved she would be the Great Wife. Everything would change. Could she look on the House, on the women, with the same eyes?

Restless and sad, she left her apartment and paced through the halls, staring all about as if she could ingrain every feature of the House of Women in her memory. Her feet carried her with no logical path. She visited the leisure room, strangely empty at this afternoon hour, with its thick red rugs on the floor, its soft hair-stuffed couches, its copper vessels in the corners spilling armfuls of fresh lotus and iris. The smell of the blooms lifted in the still air, combined with the ever-present traces of exotic perfumes: spathe and labdanum, earthy cyprinum. Ahmose breathed in the leisure room, tasted it, and it seemed to her that the taste of the air had the savor of laughter and music. *Will I find the same in the palace?*

A senet board was laid out on a nearby table, its red and blue stone pawns were frozen in the midst of an abandoned game. She touched one, gently. It was cool and smooth, and *here* – undeniably a part of the House of Women. She was a pawn, too. She would be moved about the game-board as a toss of the throwing-sticks dictated, but she was made of feeling flesh, not of stone. She could be taken from her home and displaced as it suited the players of the game. None would speak to defend her.

Angry, Ahmose flattened a palm against the senet board. The cool stone pawns pressed into her hand. She slid the game pieces of out alignment; they hissed and squealed against the gold and jet squares of the board's surface. But she felt guilty, looking at the mess she had made of the players' game. One by one, he put the pieces back on their squares, hoping she remembered the pattern correctly.

In the kitchens she watched servants mix bread dough and drizzle cakes with honey. They smiled at her, and bowed, and asked if they could give her anything to eat, any juice or beer to drink; but she shook her head, and sent them back to their tasks. They were so comforting in their plainness, these simple women in their simple wigs and frocks, smelling of flour and sweat and onions. Soon enough she hurried away from the kitchen, too, when her eyes began to sting.

In the courtyard she found some relief from her sorrow. The sun soothed her; the sight of furry bees touching the throats of flowers brought her a fragile kind of cheer. But soon enough she could see only the image of Thutmose driving away on that first day they'd met – the day her life became a tangled skein. She turned her face away from the courtyard and the memory of rattling wheels.

Ahmose found the common bath empty, its wide pool drained. The tiled mural of fishes shone in the bright light streaming in through the windcatchers. A few servants sat on the benches along the walls, folding towels, refilling pretty jars of ointment. Ahmose greeted them, but did not stay long. Without the company of her friends, the bath held nothing to interest her.

In the children's quarters where she grew up, Ahmose had to pinch the insides of her elbows to keep the tears from her eyes. Here was the room where she had played with Mutnofret and the other children, sharing their dolls and learning their simple songs. Here was the worn old chair carved with Hathor's face where Ahmose's nurse had often held her, whispering stories of the gods, her arms as warm and strong as a tree's branches in the sun.

In time her restless steps took her out into the open expanse of the garden. Shemu was the time for harvesting crops and repairing the irrigation canals; the sky was white with dust from labor in the fields surrounding Waset. Under the oddly pale sky the women's garden transformed into a place of alien ripeness. The boughs of fruit trees were weighed to the ground by their sweet burdens. Figs split and rotted on the ground, giving off a cloying smell that attracted insects. Their humming was like the voices of women at work. Birds shrieked in the trees. Late flowers were everywhere, splayed open and staring in stunned disbelief at the mindless fertility of the season.

The otherworld of the Shemu garden calmed Ahmose's heart. It was pleasant to walk along the gravel paths, trailing her fingers against waxy yellow blooms. In the afternoon sun, the warm, rich aroma of leaves yielding their moisture to the air filled the yard. She found a particularly wide and neat path and walked aimlessly, thinking of nothing, allowing her dark thoughts to flee. The benches beneath the boughs of a shade-tree grove were inviting, but she moved on. Vaguely, she wondered why no women sat spinning or sewing in the grove. It was such a lovely place to work.

Her stroll took her past the garden lake, where rowing skiffs bobbed, tied to the retaining wall. On the hottest days of the year, the Pharaoh's women stripped off wigs and gowns, splashed in the lake's green water – heavenly shore-birds, long of leg, pale of body, rounded breasts and thighs, their high, shouting laughter mingling like the piping of avocets on the river. The women were transformed by the water to creatures of another, more graceful world. Ahmose loved to watch them while she perched on the lake's wall, kicking her feet in the cool shallows. But today the lake was quiet, though the air was hot.

Now her thoughts gathered once more and she glanced

around sharply, taking in the emptiness of the garden. Where were all the women? The royal harem was the home of thirty women and nearly two dozen children. Even the children were absent. They should have been gathered under the shade trees with their tutors, learning their figures and sums, or playing in noisy packs up and down the paths, the little ones riding on the backs of the bigger, tossing balls back and forth as they charged headlong through the flowering rows. The garden was silent.

Here and there a servant scuttled by, head down, more intent on their errands than Ahmose had ever known them to be. There was, despite the birdsong and the placid heat, an air of – danger? Was it danger she sensed? Some worrying tension lay thick and heavy across the rows and paths.

She moved steadily toward the heart of the garden. A figure was coming toward her, rounding a bend in the path: a female servant, head completely shaven, breasts bare. She carried something red and white in her arms. Ahmose stopped and stood to one side, straining to make out the shape of the bundle as the servant rushed past. She recognized strips of linen soaked with blood. Her hand flew to her mouth in shock. Long after the servant had fled, Ahmose remained rooted to the spot, staring. *What in the blessed name of Mut can be bleeding so in the women's garden?*

"Ahmose!"

Her head snapped around. Mutnofret loomed in the center of the path, legs apart, shoulders tense. She raised one hand, a tense beckoning. Ahmose hurried toward her.

"Did you see the blood? What is happening?"

"Shh." Mutnofret took Ahmose by the elbow, steered her between rows of flowers.

Among a grove of myrrh trees a small pavilion stood, stone lotus pillars roofed with thin cedar. Walls of heavy cloth were tied down between each pillar, blocking the outside world from whatever lay within. Someone held a lamp inside, and as the lamp moved past the nearest wall Ahmose just made out the reverse image of Tawaret, the big-bellied river-horse goddess, painted on the inner side of the cloth. The lamp moved away. Tawaret's silhouette faded into linen again.

"The birthing pavilion." In a hot rush of fear, Ahmose recalled Aiya. Her knees turned to water. She shook off Mutnofret's hand, pushed forward. The voices of many women hummed like flies inside the pavilion, subdued, confused, urgent. Ahmose scrambled around a myrrh trunk, tripped over a root, and nearly collided with another servant laden with linens as she ran from the pavilion's farthest side.

"Move, move," the servant snapped, not even seeing in her haste that it was the king's daughter to whom she spoke. Ahmose did not stop to reprimand her.

She righted herself, ducked around the pavilion's corner. One panel of cloth was rolled halfway up and tied, creating a small door. Ahmose peered around the column. Inside was chaos. The terrible stench of blood and feces gusted from the room whenever a person passed the door. Several women moved back and forth with lamps and linens. She recognized women of the harem, including her stout cousin Renenet, her plump cheeks streaked with tears. Two servants knelt around a wooden stool with a large hole in the seat. They used sheets of linen to soak up a great puddle of dark wetness beneath the stool – a very large amount of blood. Her legs and belly trembled. She stood aside for another servant to pass.

Just as she made to look inside once more, a rough hand took her by the shoulder and pulled her back. Too startled to say a word, she glanced up at the face of Wahibra, the harem physician. He carried his rolled leather kit in his arms. She stood aside for him as she had for the servant, but Wahibra made no move to enter. He clapped his hands for permission.

At once an old midwife approached, carrying a tiny brazier on a padding of thick cloth. Green, acrid smoke lifted from the bowl. The old woman waved one hand toward Wahibra, wafting the harsh incense over his face and shoulders. "In the name of Tawaret," she said somberly, "be purified, and enter the place of birth."

At once the crowd of women parted. At the heart of the pavilion, pale, golden Aiya lay on a bed of cushions soaked in red. Her face was as white as milk, eyes closed. Her arm lay limp across the floor of the pavilion, damming a pool of blood that darkened the bed and floor.

The old midwife spoke. "It is too late for the girl, I fear. Her hips are not wide enough. The door is too small. The baby cannot come on his own. She has lost too much blood, despite all we could do. She will not live."

"Yes," Wahibra said. "I can see that you are right."

"We have called you here to cut the child out."

Wahibra nodded. His face was pale and sober. He gestured toward the birthing stool. A servant leapt to obey him, positioning it near Aiya's limp body. Wahibra unrolled his leather kit, stretched it across the hole in the seat. Ahmose watched, horrified, as he selected a long copper blade from among the kit's strange instruments. Her mind screamed at her to look away, to run away, but she was powerless to do anything but stand, numbly, detached, and watch Wahibra bend toward Aiya.

The knife in Wahibra's hand caught the light of a brazier, sending a red flash into Ahmose's eyes. The spell broke.

"Wait," she called out.

Wahibra looked around, his brows furrowed. The hesitation gave her just enough time. She was at Aiya's side in two heartbeats, kneeling at the girl's shoulder. She took Aiya's face in her hands.

Aiya opened her eyes. "Ahmose." Her voice was thick and low with pain, rasped from hours of crying.

"Aiya. I am so sorry. If I could change this, if I could stop it...."

"Take care of my son. Make him a good man. Tell him of Aiya, his mother who loved him best. He is best of all the great men."

"Hatshepsu," Ahmose said, grieving, regretting. "I will, Aiya, my sweet one, the best of my friends." She bent to kiss Aiya's forehead, pressed her lips to the girl's sweat-beaded brow and held them there, tasting the salt of her skin, as Wahibra raised his knife.

The pain of the blade roused the last strength in Aiya's body. She jerked, her pale limbs convulsing, her eyes opening wide in shock. "No," she cried in a feeble voice, in the tongue of her homeland. "No!" The midwives bent to hold her down. They pinioned all her limbs against the cushions, while Ahmose stroked her hair, murmuring useless apologies.

"You will be with Hathor soon, little mother," the old midwife said. Aiya's cries were an agony in Ahmose's belly, an accusation in her heart.

At last they faded. Aiya lay still. Ahmose looked up at the midwife. The old woman shook her head. Slowly, the women removed their hands from Aiya's limbs. From one corner of the pavilion, a harem woman began to sing a prayer of supplication to Anupu, the taker of the dead; and Renenet, fists pressed to her mouth, moaned.

Wahibra made a horror of Aiya's proud, round belly. Layer after layer of flesh split beneath his blade. Ahmose stared at the bands of red and yellow, exposed in the dim light of the oil lamps. Something a sick shade of blue lay within the slit in Aiya's middle. Two of the midwives grasped it and pulled it free of the surrounding flesh, tore at its outer skin. Ahmose lurched to her feet, staggered against a lotus pillar, held it hard, willing down the bubble of nausea rising in her throat. *They are like scavengers at a carcass.*

And then she understood. It was the baby's caul they ripped away. One midwife inserted a slender reed into its throat, sucking and spitting the fluid from its lungs. The child's skin was a terrible color, the blue-grey of death. Wet, red-gold hair clung to its scalp. Its little eyes were closed. The midwives rubbed and patted the child, turned it upside down by its feet and watched as cloudy water dripped from its nostrils, but still the baby did not cry, did not move. One by one they stopped their work, until finally the baby was laid at its mother's cold breast.

The song of Anupu rose again, begging mercy for this

unnamed boychild who had never lived at all.

"Hatshepsu," Ahmose whispered. "His name is Hatshepsu." No one heard her.

Wahibra rose slowly from the ground. His hands were darkened by thick gore. Aiya's blood had spread around the hem of his kilt. "I am sorry, my ladies," he said to the midwives. "Even had you called me sooner, I doubt this child could have been saved. The mother was just too small, too young. It is a great sadness that both were lost."

Too young, Ahmose thought. Panic seized her. She took two steps toward Aiya and her baby, then the ground slid sideways beneath her feet. She fell in a heap, head spinning, dimly aware that the harem women were leaping to her side, crowding around her.

"Let me take her," she heard Renenet say. "She knows me well."

Her arm was pulled upward painfully, laid around a plump shoulder, her wrist gripped in a firm hand. Renenet lifted her to her feet and pulled her from the horror of the pavilion. Ahmose's legs refused to do their work. She stumbled and swayed.

"That's right, my lady," Renenet said, dragging her along the path. The heat of the sun beat down; Ahmose retched, emptying her stomach into a nearby flower bed. Renenet clucked in sympathy.

After several minutes Ahmose could at least support her own weight, although she made no move to take her arm from her cousin's shoulders. They continued to walk silently together. Round a bend in the path they found Mutnofret. Her arms were folded, her head high, her face a blank stone, like Meritamun's on the throne, like a queen's.

As they passed, Ahmose's eyes locked with her sister's. She stopped, forcing Renenet to halt as well. For a long moment she stood staring into Mutnofret's deep black eyes. The First King's Daughter looked fearlessly at Ahmose, wordless and triumphant.

Chilled, afraid, wounded, Ahmose choked on her words and staggered away.

CHAPTER SEVEN

"S HE COULD HAVE SPARED ME," Ahmose said. "She did not have to bring me to the birthing pavilion."

"Calm, calm. If you upset yourself you'll only cry, and smear your eyes." Renenet shook out Ahmose's plain green gown. She said doubtfully, "Perhaps Mutnofret thought you would want to be with your friend when she went to the gods."

Ahmose shook her head, at once denying her cousin's words and trying to push the image of Aiya bleeding, Aiya dying, from her mind. All through the morning's marriage, making offerings at the Temple of Amun, receiving the blessings from the High Priest, she had seen only Aiya. While she stood back to watch Thutmose place the salt of marriage on Mutnofret's tongue, tasting the salt sharp and thick on her own, she had heard Aiya's dying words, and had tasted too the sweat on her friend's cold brow. As their litter carried them back to the palace through a throng of cheering rekhet, Ahmose could think only of planning Aiya's tomb. Her wedding day had been one long blur of sadness, with Mutnofret's radiant smile and coy laugh the only things of real clarity.

"She did it on purpose, Reni, to throw me. She planned to break my spirit so Thutmose would only love her today."

Reni sighed. "I know Mutnofret is jealous and angry. But you cannot let her win. Don't allow her to ruin your wedding feast for you, Ahmose."

With shaking fingers, Ahmose managed to untie the knot of the simple white linen dress she had worn to the temple. She let it fall to the floor. She felt the need to spin flax, to center herself, lose herself in the rhythm of the spindle and distaff. But there was no time. In less than an hour she was expected at the feast, where she would sit with Thutmose and Mutnofret while drunken nobles fell all over each other and bad poets caterwauled for her approval. There was nothing she felt less like doing than feasting. Aiya's tomb needed planning, and Ahmose should check with the embalmers to be sure the preparation of both bodies was proceeding well.

But duty called. It always did.

Resigned to the feast, she held out her arms so Renenet could dress her. It was kind of her cousin to see to her today, when her heart was so badly broken. It was kind of Renenet to advise her, to care. She would do her best to make Reni happy. Thutmose, too. Though her heart was with Aiya and the baby boy, she would do her duty.

Ahmose left her apartment at the House of Women reluctantly, trailing her hand along one of the beautiful painted walls all the way to the door. She glanced back only once, looking through her open chamber doorway out to the garden. After the feast, she would be shown to her new rooms in Waset's royal palace. *Who will have this room now? Will it stand empty until I have a daughter to fill it?* A daughter – no, not that. Nor a son. The thought of her home remaining quiet and unloved through all the years to come filled her with regret. Before she could cry again, she left her old apartment, closing the door behind her resolutely.

Renenet waited in the hall. "Are you sure you will not take more jewels, Ahmose?" The woman had been trying to force rings onto Ahmose's fingers and chains about her neck all afternoon. Ahmose had given in on only a few pieces:

simple turquoise studs for her ears and nose, a wide bracelet of unadorned gold, and a bloodstone ring carved with the face of Iset.

"No, Reni. I want to be understated."

"Where did you get an idea like *understated*? This is your wedding feast!"

Ahmose felt ill. Another of Mutnofret's deceptions? But what did it matter? She was resolved to be the best Great Royal Wife Egypt had ever known. She did not need trappings to make the court see her as Thutmose's divine partner. If Mutnofret had tricked her into looking shoddy, then Ahmose would turn the deception around on her sister. She could be as confident and splendid as a goddess, even in her plain green dress.

She and Reni climbed into the fine gilded litter that waited in the courtyard. Renenet drew the curtains, then turned to Ahmose with a look that said words were on their way.

"Yes?"

The plump woman shook her head. "Just...be careful. That is all."

The litter bumped and rocked, raised into the air. Men's voices called out to one another; they were underway.

Ahmose breathed deeply to loosen the stiffness of her neck and shoulders. *As confident and splendid as a goddess*, she reminded herself. "Be careful of what?"

Renenet sighed. They traveled in silence for some time. At last Reni said, "I've known you and Mutnofret all your lives, dear Ahmose. I know what your sister is like. Be careful of *her*. She is not happy with her station, no matter what she may tell you; I need not tell you that. And when Mutnofret is unhappy, the very gods are unhappy. I know she loves you, but I do not know whether her love or her anger is stronger."

When they arrived at the palace, Mutnofret's litter was already in the courtyard, curtains drawn. A servant appeared to help Ahmose to her feet. As she rose, Ahmose caught a flicker of movement from the other litter. A curtain twitched back; Mutnofret's eye peeped out. The curtains whipped shut again. A hand emerged to twiddle its fingers in Ahmose's direction. A greeting, she supposed. Ahmose shrugged. She did not return her sister's gesture.

She had arrived early, as it turned out. The magnificent expanse of the great feasting hall bustled with servants re-arranging tables, laying here and there bundles of flowers and cones of scented wax. Great bronze braziers stood alight at the foot of every pillar, sending streamers of fragrant smoke high into the air to pool like river fog against the painted ceiling.

She could not stay here, drifting about the hall while the servants prepared her feast. She was about to ask Renenet to stroll with her in the courtyard when she saw a few of her friends from the House of Women clustered in one corner. The women stood in a tight circle, evidently listening to Iryet, whose smiling mouth was half-hidden behind the conspiratorial cup of her hand. Ahmose headed toward them with Renenet in tow, drawn by their merry laughter. It would be good to laugh today.

Iryet saw her coming and broke off, bowed her head. "Great Lady, you honor us."

"Stop that, Iryet! Don't go treating me like I'm a goddess's backside."

Iryet looked genuinely confused. "But you are the Great Royal Wife now, Lady."

"My name is Ahmose. That is what you will call me. Please, all of you. I am not used to this yet."

Iryet threw an arm around Ahmose's shoulders, pulled her into the circle. Ahmose flushed with pleasure and relief. She linked arms with her friends.

"We were just talking about your husband, Ahmose. Isn't he fine! He has teeth like a hare, but that can be forgiven beside muscles such as his. Ooh, how I'd like to get my hands on him!"

Tuyu grinned. "Soldier's arms. Much better than fat noble's arms. I hope he likes to visit the House of Women once in a while. I am first in line."

"Oh, but you don't really want to do *that*, do you? I mean, I *have* to, but you can just...avoid it." Ahmose looked at each woman's face in turn. Some of them widened their eyes, startled; others were clearly amused. "But doesn't it hurt?"

Iryet shrugged. "Perhaps the first time. It is nothing to weep over."

An awkward silence descended. Ahmose's face burned hot. She had intended to look like a confident Great Royal Wife, and instead she had revealed her fears and made herself out to be a terrified child.

The women glanced about, as if daring one another to speak first. Tuyu opened her mouth, smiling, but blinked as if her thoughts had caught up with her, and shut it again. *They do not want to admit to one another that they don't like it. It is just as Mutnofret said.*

"Your gown is pretty," Tuyu said at once, apparently reaching for a change of subject. "The color agrees with your complexion."

"You could use more jewels, though," said Khamaat, slipping an ivory cuff off her wrist. She thrust it toward Ahmose. "Here, take this. It will look perfect with the gold bracelet."

"Oh, and my necklace!" Baketamun reached up to undo the clasp of an ornate scarab collar. "It is lucky!"

"But I wanted to be understated," Ahmose said, waving away their offerings. She was determined to turn Mutnofret's trick around on her. She would not go loading herself with jewels at the last minute. Let Mutnofret see the true strength of a Great Royal Wife.

"Hisst!" Iryet elbowed Baketamun. "Here he comes!"

Ahmose raised her head from the group. Thutmose strode into the feast room, followed by the same young steward who had helped Ahmose and her sister through the crowded throne room the day Thutmose was named heir. The steward was reading aloud from a scroll. Ahmose caught her husband's eye. He stopped, smiling, and bowed to her.

"Go talk to him!"

"What will I say?"

"For Mut's sake, you're married to him, you goose! Say whatever you want."

"No." She knew it was absurd that the idea of merely talking to Thutmose should make her so nervous. Hadn't she ridden with him in the hills above Waset when he had been no more than a stranger? But he was not a king then, and she had been only the king's second daughter.

"It will be your first great act as Great Lady." Iryet's arm slipped out of Ahmose's, reached across to link with Baketamun on Ahmose's other side. Pharaoh's wife or no, she was shut out of the circle. The women giggled, watching her expectantly.

"All right, then." Ahmose took a deep breath and walked to her husband on weak legs.

"There is my Great Royal Wife," he said, smiling.

"You look...well dressed."

Thutmose laughed. "You can thank Ineni here for that. He's hired a whole army of serving men to make me look more like a king and less like a soldier. It is quite a job, I am sure."

Ahmose smiled at the steward. So Ineni was his name. "A very good steward. I remember how you led my sister and me through the crowd the day Thutmose was proclaimed heir."

Ineni's hands crinkled against his scroll. He smiled shyly at Ahmose's praise.

"Not just a steward. An architect, sometimes, eh, Ineni? He designed the expansions your father made at Ipet-Isut." Thutmose reached for Ineni's shoulder, no doubt to squeeze it in a gesture of approval, but the steward flinched. Thutmose let his hand fall again, smiling. "Ineni is not very good at talking to pretty women when he doesn't have a stick to hit nobles with, but he is always very good at reading lists. Lists are his great passion. He was just going over the wedding gifts with me. Why don't you listen, Ahmoset? You can claim anything you like for your new apartments." Thutmose waved for Ineni to continue with his scroll.

"From the jewelers' guild, eighteen casks of jewelry for the wives of Thutmose." Ineni's voice shook. "From the steward of cattle, six black bulls. You can sacrifice them or breed them, whichever you like. From the merchant Hirkhepshef, a pleasure barge with rowers. From the carpenter Huy, many pieces of fine ebony furniture. From the horse-trader Pawera, six black stallions and sixteen red mares; very fine animals from what I hear."

"Excellent," Thutmose said, rubbing his hands together. "Anything you like, Ahmose? I think the pleasure barge would look nice in your room."

She laughed. "Perhaps so, but I couldn't choose from the gifts without Mutnofret."

Thutmose glanced around the hall. "Where is she?"

"I last saw her out in her litter, in the courtyard."

Thutmose dismissed Ineni. He stepped closer to Ahmose. The smell of him came to her powerfully, myrrh and horse-sweat and leather. It made her thoughts all a muddle until she exhaled. "Mutnofret told me you lost a friend three days ago, Ahmoset. I was sorry to hear it."

"Aiya," she said, caught off guard; and her eyes filled with tears.

Thutmose laid his hand on her cheek, softly. His thumb brushed a tear out of the corner of her eye, then lightly rubbed, fixing her kohl. "No tears now. She is with the gods. The baby, too." His eyes were gentle, comforting.

"I am trying to set it aside, so I can enjoy our wedding feast."

"There is no need to set your friend aside, or your grief. Honor her by remembering her. But Aiya's ka is watching you: remember that, too. Although you cannot see her, she is here with us tonight, celebrating with us. She is happy for you, don't you think? And she will be your friend always, in your heart."

Thutmose. She wanted to say his name aloud, to show her gratitude for his kindness. His soft words made her feel calmer, more centered, the way she had always felt while spinning with Aiya. "I can feel her with me," she managed at last. "Thank you." Her throat tightened. She swallowed hard, and said again, "Thank you, Thutmose."

He leaned in close, so their foreheads nearly touched. His scent overwhelmed her. "Call me Tut," he whispered, as if they conspired in some secret mischief.

"Tut," she breathed.

Mutnofret still had not showed by the time the stewards herded Ahmose and the king from the great hall. They were ushered to a waiting room, comfortably appointed and supplied with a senet board and a harpist. They played a distracted game, chatting and joking as the hour before the celebration fled. He told her stories of his battles and showed her a fearsome scar on his scalp, impulsively pulling his wig from his head. She had to help him reposition it; they both laughed as she fussed with its locks. By the time Ineni appeared to announce the hour, Ahmose was more confident with Thutmose than she had ever been.

"*Where* is Mutnofret? Is she trapped in a privy?"

Tut jackal-laughed. "She will show. She probably wants to make a grand entrance."

Ahmose's shoulders raised like a wary animal hackling. *A grand entrance?* With an effort, she soothed her own nerves. The grandest entrance Nofret could imagine would not be enough to shake Ahmose's composure. She swore that to herself, and repeated it silently several times.

"Lord Horus," Ineni called from the door.

Tut rose from his chair, adjusted the pleats of his long kilt.

He looked so handsome and powerful in the formal dress; Ahmose blinked as she watched his hands move. "Well, then, it is time to go play king."

Ahmose followed him from the waiting room and down the corridor to the great hall's entryway. The noise of many voices carried through the great double doors. She was suddenly all a-flutter over the feast, welling up inside with anticipation and pride. She clutched at her stomach with both hands, pinching herself through the smooth fabric of the green dress. She did not think she could stand being alone, even for a few minutes while Tut was formally announced.

He stopped, turned back to look at her. The Eye-of-Horus pectoral hung askew across his chest. She reached up to straighten it on its golden chain; he caught her wrists. "A kiss for luck," he said, and before she could blink, his lips touched her own. His kiss was there and gone in an instant, but her mouth tingled with its memory as he walked away. The complement of guards on the feast hall's doors bowed to him, swung the huge carved and gilded doors wide.

"The heir to the Horus Throne, Thutmose," the steward called. Hundreds of voices rose in a cheer.

Hidden by the door, out of sight of the crowd, Ahmose pressed a hand to her heart, squeezing her eyes shut, willing her breath to remain steady. *Confidence. Confidence is all I need. I will make them see me as the Great Royal Wife. None will doubt me.* When the shouts of the people died back, Ineni coughed politely. She sprang away from the wall. When she moved into the great hall, her steps were even and sure.

"The Great Royal Wife, King's Daughter, God-Chosen, Ahmose."

As one the guests rose to their feet, clapping hands, shouting approval, raising golden cups filled with sweet wine in her direction. She walked down the wide aisle between rows of tables, her eyes on the three thrones at the head of the room. Thutmose sat upon the center one, grinning down at her. His smile was all that mattered.

When she reached her throne, high-backed and adorned

with a shining sun disc, Ahmose had one brief, soaring moment to look down upon her approving subjects. *I am their Great Lady. They know it.* A proud bearing had been all she needed to win their hearts.

But hardly had Ahmose settled into her throne when the steward announced Mutnofret. Her sister swept into the hall like the Iteru's flood, undeniable, essential, rich. Far from being understated, Mutnofret glimmered like a vision. She wore unbleached linen of the loosest weave; every part of her body shone through the earthy fabric, more revealed than covered. Her breasts beamed like goddess' faces, her nipples were dark jewels, her navel a pool to quench any man's thirst. About her hips was a belt of golden links, hung with bright-beaded fringe. As she swayed toward Thutmose the fringe danced and parted, revealing the delta of her groin, a brazen invitation. Her arms, bound in countless cuffs and bracelets, sparkled like the river; gems clustered all about her, glowing, enthralling. Ahmose gasped, torn between admiration for Mutnofret's beauty and shock at the audacity of this betrayal. She had expected some small deception. She had not expected Mutnofret to look like perfection made flesh – like Iset, like the queen of the gods herself.

Ahmose only realized how loudly the crowd had cheered Mutnofret when at last they quieted. Shamefully aware of how poor and child-like she truly looked, she found herself unable to meet any eye, especially her husband's. As it happened, this posed no great trouble, for Thutmose's full attention was on his second wife. He helped Mutnofret fix her perfumed wax cone to her lovely gleaming wig, touched her soft hand, told her she was beautiful, so beautiful.

Ahmose's belly soured.

The night dragged on forever. Mutnofret was a perfect woman, graceful and winsome, beaming her approval at all the performers, brushing her arm now and then against Thutmose's, her cheek against his shoulder. Thutmose was not unmindful of Ahmose, to be sure; he offered every dish to her first, asked her opinion of each performance. But all his attentions had the flavor of duty, not the adoration she craved.

Is this to be my marriage, then? A dutiful husband who cannot take his eyes off my sister, even for a moment? Then she recalled Meritamun, sacrificing everything for Egypt, and stilled her heart. The gods had given the throne to Ahmose for reasons only they knew. She had never failed the gods before. She would not fail them now. If her divine task was to be a dutiful wife, then so she would be. The harem women may read their love stories and dream of romance, but for Ahmose her heart and body could only be given to Egypt. This had been her fate and her obligation from the day her nurse laid her in her cradle.

She would tend to her task, and Thutmose to his. If she was lucky, their mutual work would grow into – something. Friendship, she may hope. But love? She leaned her elbows on the table to look past her husband at Mutnofret; the second wife tilted her head toward the king, laughing musically at something he had said.

Mutnofret would have his love, it seemed, while Ahmose must content herself with duty.

Chapter Eight

THE FEAST DRAGGED ON MERCILESSLY. When at last it ended, thank all the gods, Ahmose escaped to her new quarters. The Great Royal Wife was granted an entire arm of the palace, a great pillared hall separated from the larger body of the complex by a courtyard, dappled now in moonlight. She nodded to the pair of guards on her chamber's entryway, allowed them to open the ornate doors for her.

Happily, a brazier had been lit earlier in the evening. The oil in the bronze dish was low, a dark and shallow pool of honey-colored light, burned nearly away while the feast went on and on. The flame sputtered. A fire box waited floor, full of twigs, striking stones, and a jug of oil. She dismissed the guards back to their post and lifted the jug herself, trickled new oil carefully into the charred bowl, watched as the flame resurrected. The growing light revealed another brazier further along the wall. She filled it, then carried a burning twig to it, lit the oil; its pool of light reached yet another brazier. When the third was burning, the red-orange glow showed her an empty cavern of a room. All of Meritamun's fine things were gone, moved to a large estate to the south, which she would now share with Nefertari. The gallery of the chamber murmured with the same deep echoes that woke in temples when the priests had left their duties and only the lone worshiper remained.

The floor was exquisitely tiled in bits of faience; an image of Mut with her perfect white wings outstretched spanned the length of the room, more than twice as long as Ahmose was tall. Several doors were set into the walls around her. She gazed at the bare walls a moment, helpless, paralyzed with exhaustion. One door must lead to her bed chamber. She chose one and headed toward it with hesitant steps. The sound of her sandals on the tiles rang too loud in her ears. When these apartments had been Meritamun's and full of rich, ornate things, Ahmose had never noticed how large and grand the room itself was. It took an eternity just to walk across Mut's figure to the line of doors.

Ahmose was lucky. The first door she tried revealed the bed chamber, nearly as large as the anteroom from which she had come. To her delighted pleasure, there was no need for a brazier here. The rear wall was cleverly made, a series of flat-faced pillars, soaring rectangular columns divided by spaces the width of two hands. The gaps reached from floor to ceiling; ample light from moon and stars poured into the room, turning the great bed – its only furnishing – to dull, beaten silver. In the center of one pillar, the largest, a doorway opened like a friend's palm onto a private garden. Ahmose sighed in deep relief at the sight of the garden. So she would have a refuge, a place of peace. The knowledge comforted her in the midst of her bewilderment.

The pillared wall meant that the chamber would stay cool during the warmest months, and during the chill of the sowing season rugs could be hung over the wall's gaps to keep out the wind. Patterns of black and silver reached toward her across the floor, shadow and pale light playing through the miraculous wall. She stumbled toward the bed, shedding sandals, jewelry, and gown. She removed her wig. The braids were soaked in the fragrant oils of the festive wax cone she had worn, melted down now to a sticky white stub. She tossed wig and wax alike carelessly on the floor. There was nowhere to set them anyhow – no stand, no table. And if the braids stuck in the wax, she could get another wig. She was the Great Royal Wife.

The bed was double the size of the one she had used in

the House of Women. It was piled with clean linen sheets, strewn with cushions of cool-sided silk. An aged ivory headrest, padded with a blue bolster, stood at the top of the bed's gentle slope. She ignored the headrest. Naked, she crawled atop the bed and huddled into the cushions, pulled a thin sheet over her exhausted body, and watched the bars of moonlight creep across the chamber floor.

She imagined she was a gazelle fawn, fragile and fearful, cowering in a thicket. The hunter would come for her soon with his bloody spear. She shivered, recalling the physician Wahibra's words. *The mother was just too small, too young.* Ahmose did not know how old or how large a woman must be to survive bearing a child, but her hands crossed defensively over her narrow hips, shielded her small, high breasts, and she knew she was too young. Like Aiya.

She lay paralyzed in the striped shadows of her bed chamber for hours before sleep took mercy on the Great Royal Wife. She fled into her dreams, bounding and kicking, gasping, a gazelle before a lion.

Late morning sun lanced into the courtyard, filtered through the climbing vines of a plant with huge, flat leaves. The vine grew over the columns on Ahmose's side of the yard and provided a pleasant, sweet-smelling shade. She had ordered her servants to set up her breakfast in the yard this morning, for troops of servants filled her chambers, moving the fine new ebony furniture she had claimed into her rooms; she could not eat there, with so much bustling and scraping.

She had slept late, waking to the morning sun full in her face, shining insistently through her columned wall. A good night's sleep had done her well – that, and the fact that Thutmose had not come to take her. She felt calm and determined now, ready to face her new life head on, like a barque under full sail.

Ahmose had asked for two chairs at her breakfast table, intending to invite Renenet to join her. But her cousin was still abed, sleeping off the previous night's wine. Instead, Ahmose imagined Aiya's ka for company, silvery as moonlight, with the perfect, soft belly of a virgin, holding her son on her knee. In her thoughts Ahmose chatted with Aiya about the wedding feast, gossiping over the singers, the dancers, the scandal of the High Priest kissing Iryet in the back corner. Ka-Aiya laughed and smiled, cradled her baby boy, told Ahmose how pleasant the life beyond was; though of course Aiya was not there yet in truth, could not be there until she had been properly entombed – and that would not happen for two months yet. Still, the fantasy was a pleasant diversion from the noise of the servants struggling with ebony couches and chests to hold Ahmose's gowns.

"Good morning, sister. Did you sleep well?" Mutnofret padded across the courtyard. Evidently her own new apartments were not far from Ahmose's. She wore a more modest gown than last night's spectacle, simple white linen with no adornments. *Understated.*

"I did, thank you," Ahmose said tersely. She bit into a melon and looked pointed away from Mutnofret.

Her sister seated herself in the other chair. Ka-Aiya vanished. "I did not sleep *this* much." She snapped her fingers to show how little. "I hope you enjoyed the wedding night as much as I did."

Ahmose flushed. So Tut had been with Mutnofret all night. Her relief at avoiding the pain was replaced in an instant by anger. As Great Royal Wife, he should have visited her bed before any other. But she could not show her feelings to Mutnofret. She crossed one knee over the other, leaned back in her chair, and flipped her sandal repeatedly against her foot – *flap-flap-flap* – a display of nonchalance.

Mutnofret tried a different approach. "What did you think of my dress last night?"

"I thought the oldest and fattest nobles would poke their eyes out on your nipples, they stared at them so."

Mutnofret burst into perfect laughter. "Oh, Ahmose. You are always so clever. I think our husband liked it, though. He wasted no time in coming to see me. I barely had time to bathe. I think I kept him happy. I might have worn him out." She dipped her finger into the jar of honey and sucked it.

Ahmose made a disgusted noise. "What if the servants see you sticking your fingers into the honey?"

"Let them see. I'm the king's wife. *Second wife*, at any rate."

Ahmose's sandal *flap-flap-flapped*. "About that dress. You told me you planned to look understated."

"Oh, I intended to at first, but I changed my mind." She gazed across the table at Ahmose for a moment, all wide eyes and innocence. Then her mouth opened in shock. "You can't think – but Ahmose, I would never *mislead* you! Oh, by Hathor, I didn't even remember I'd told you how to dress. Don't I just feel a perfect goose. I should have told you the plan had changed, shouldn't I? Anyway, it is all for the best. You did not want our husband and all the whole world besides to see that you still have a girl's body, did you?"

Flap-flap-flap.

"Well, regardless of the dresses," Mutnofret went on, helping herself to Ahmose's pitcher of juice, "you looked perfectly lovely. Really. Like a Great Lady."

Ahmose rolled her eyes. She could not have looked less like a Great Lady if she had rolled in mud and wheat chaff before the feast. *How to get rid of this buzzing fly?*

Mutnofret propped her elbows on the table. "So, did he...?"

"Did he what?"

"Did he...*visit you?*"

Ahmose considered lying, but no doubt the second wife would just ask Thutmose about the matter the very next time she saw him. "No. He did not. I fell asleep early anyhow."

"Oh, that is a shame. He really is wonderful, you know." Her eyes shifted about the courtyard. "I mean, up until the pain and the bleeding starts. Did you know he is going off on a campaign soon? Oh, of course you didn't know; you were asleep last night. He told me all about it while we bathed. He is going south, all the way to Buhen, to check on the fortress and the outposts. He said there might be a battle with the Kushites. I expect he will be gone for weeks. I am going to try to conceive a son before he leaves. Wouldn't that be a wonderful surprise for our husband when he returns home from battle? An heir already on the way."

While they bathed? Together? Ahmose lifted a honey cake to her mouth so Mutnofret could not see how she seethed.

"How soon is he leaving? He cannot go anywhere until the Opening of the Mouth." Thutmose would not truly be the Pharaoh until he had performed the ritual to raise his predecessor from death. And Amunhotep's embalming was still not complete. Ahmose guessed her dead father's body had rested no more than twelve days beneath the salt. There was nearly another month to wait until Thutmose could usher the old Pharaoh into the afterlife.

"Just after that, I expect. It should leave me barely enough time to conceive. If we lay together every night between now and then, a baby is as good as certain."

"You had best pray to Hathor for fertility. And Hathor doesn't like liars."

Mutnofret sighed. "Ahmoset, darling, I did not lie to you. It was a very simple mistake."

"Whatever it was, you made me look like a fool." She was proud that her voice did not shake. She was cool as night wind.

"Never! Thutmose adores you. I have heard how he calls you Ahmoset. Remember that day on the barge..."

"And the nobles, and the priests? Have you heard them call me Ahmoset as well? There is more to being the Great Royal Wife than being loved by the king."

"Do you think I don't know that? I, who was raised to be the Great Royal Wife?"

Ahmose stood and clapped for her servants. "Clear this away," she said, waving toward breakfast and Mutnofret without looking at either.

"Where are you going?" Mutnofret asked, standing and

stepping aside from the servants' work as if she had ordered it herself, as if Ahmose had not spoken a word.

"To pray for your fertility. Perhaps Hathor will listen to *me*."

She did not pray to Hathor, of course. Instead she found the cool, shadowed corridor that led out to the palace lake and made her way to its shore, aching for the solace of privacy. Mutnofret's deception weighed on her heart, dragged at her ka as a quarryman's sledge drags through deep, black mud. Between the Heqa-Khasewet and the Kushites, Egypt's freedom was at stake. Could Mutnofret not see? Did nothing matter to her but whether the throne she sat upon had more or less gilding than her sister's? More than anything else, could Mutnofret not see how this whole sorry arrangement pained Ahmose?

On the stone-lipped shore of the lake, Ahmose picked pebbles from the cracks in the wall and tossed them into the water, watching the ripples spread, breaking and reflecting the day's light, converging and merging and shattering like the shifting flash-and-dim dance of the river. The sweep of each ring of waves soothed her; she followed one ripple, then the next with her eyes; they sailed smooth as barques, pushing outward, growing, at last flattening into nothing but an echo of a wave. She threw two pebbles together; then one out of each hand, *plunk-plunk*, noting the different patterns they made, the way their ripples shivered together and rebounded away to chase each other across the face of the lake. Finally she gathered a whole handful of stone chips and sent them flying. They pattered into the water all haphazard, a splash like a fisherman's cast net. The water's surface scattered in disarray. As the ripples began to calm, settling into their familiar spread and rebound, the turquoise and lapis of sky's light and water's shade were replaced with an ever-shifting tumult of brown, black, linen-white. The lake grew calm. A man's shape beside her own broke and reformed, broke and reformed.

Thutmose.

She turned to face him. Her face was hot with shame. To be caught at such a child-like game...!

He did not say a word, but smiled at her, then searched through the stone chips at the base of the retaining wall. He found one he liked, tossed it a few times in his hand as if weighing its merits, then whipped it hard out over the lake. It sailed the length of six men's bodies, then *hep-hep-hep*, jumped across the water's surface. Ahmose, wide-eyed, stared at her husband.

"Not bad, eh?"

She shook her head, smiling.

"Do you know how it's done?"

"No, I've never."

"Let me show you." He found the right kind of rock and guided it into her hand, set it along her curled fingers, just so. With words and gestures, he told her how to make the rock jump. She pulled her arm back, hesitated, then threw. The rock plunked into the water with a single disappointing splash.

"It takes some practice, that's all, like anything else." Thutmose laughed lightly. He sat upon the lake's stone wall. Ahmose sat, too.

"I heard you are going to Buhen soon," she said, disguising the bitterness in her voice by scuffing up half-buried pebbles with the toe of her sandal. Puffs of yellow dust rose around her feet to glitter in the sunlight.

"I am leaving just after the Opening of the Mouth. Whenever a new Pharaoh comes to the throne, Egypt's enemies like to test her borders. I pray that word of Amunhotep's death will not reach Kush until after I arrive in Buhen. I must move quickly if I'm to prevent a major raid on the southern sepats."

Ahmose nodded, unwilling to say the words that gnawed

at her heart.

"I will leave good stewards in charge here," he went on. "You likely will not have to do anything but sit on your throne during court and try not to fall asleep while the nobles bicker. I will instruct the stewards to filter out all but the most serious petitions so you are not taxed by holding court."

"I can do it fine," Ahmose said. She cringed inside at how young she sounded, like a child protesting that she could climb any tree the bigger children could climb.

"I have no doubt of it. You are a strong girl, and very clever."

"I'm a *woman*."

Thutmose cleared his throat. "Mutnofret can help you, I suppose, if you need help with court."

"I have no need of *her* help." Ahmose filled her voice with as much scorn as she could muster.

It was perhaps too much scorn; Thutmose's eyebrows rose and he glanced at her from the tail of his eye. "Trouble?"

The sorrow inside Ahmose rose trembling to the surface. She could keep it bridled no longer. "You spent all night with her. You didn't come to me once."

"Oh," he breathed, looking down, then away; anywhere but at his Great Royal Wife. "Ahmose, you must believe me. I meant no offense. But you are still so young, and I thought...."

"I've had my blood. Many times!"

Thutmose pulled off his wig and scratched at his scalp with both hands, as if the gesture might buy him some time in answering.

"Do you have lice?" Ahmose said.

"Of course not."

"Then don't take your wig off where servants can see! What will they think of you? You're supposed to be the king."

Thutmose grinned, laughed. His wig went back onto his head. "This is why I like you so, Ahmoset. You keep me in line. What a fine Great Lady you are; the gods have truly blessed me."

"Then why didn't you come to my bed?"

Thutmose lowered his voice, as if he wished to spare her some kind of embarrassment, though not even servants were near enough hear. "Ahmoset, do you even know what men do with women in their beds?"

"Of course I do! I am the Great Royal Wife, not an ignorant child. I know what men and women do together. I know what you were doing with Mutnofret last night."

Thutmose nodded. "Forgive me. I misjudged you."

He had misjudged her because of her childlike body. And how could she expect any man to appraise her as womanly, when compared to Mutnofret's ripe femininity? *It is not his fault. He is only a man, after all,* she told herself firmly, to stop the sting of tears in her eyes.

He laid a rough hand on her knee. "Do you want me to come to your bed, Ahmose? Tonight?"

Ahmose's breath caught. She heard Mutnofret's words about pain and blood; she saw Aiya's belly cut open. She shoved these things away, hard. She was the Great Lady. It was not right that her husband should desire Mutnofret alone.

"Yes," she said, with finality.

CHAPTER NINE

T HE DAY CREPT BY. AHMOSE had excused herself from the lakeshore, begging some errand or other. When she was out of Tut's sight she ran through the corridors because her ka was too light, too fiery, to do anything else. Her body thrummed with a brew of tension: triumph, longing, fear. Her feet had wings, and she didn't care if the servants saw her running and gossiped about it later. When she approached the courtyard she shared with Mutnofret, she slowed and caught her breath in the shadow of a lotus column. Mutnofret was nowhere to be seen. Ahmose crossed the yard without haste, head up, steps steady.

Once in her apartments, though, she had no idea what to do. She pushed her new furniture here and there, rearranging it. Boxes of her belongings from the House of Women were stacked against one wall. Her servants had not yet unpacked everything. She found her collection of god statues, though, and set them on one dressing table, arranging them in a little shrine. At the center of the grouping, she placed Tut's gift, the carving of Mut.

She grew restless. She stripped and bathed, called a servant to shave the stubble off her scalp, then bathed again, just for something to do. Anxiety warred with victory inside her. She paced around her garden, kicking stones, swatting insects, plucking petals off yellow flowers until at length her new body servant, a tall, thin woman, arrived with supper and a musician.

The musician was a good idea, a soothing distraction. She complimented the servant on her forethought, then, feeling generous and expansive, gave her two jeweled wig ornaments as a reward and begged her to gossip. The woman – Twosre was her name – was not as good with rumors as the women in the harem, but she would do. Ahmose liked her earthy voice and the scent of figs that rose from Twosre's garments. They laughed over their shared supper, flax-seed cakes with cold white fish wrapped in musky lettuce leaves. Twosre thumped the table with a hard hand whenever she laughed.

"Tuyu is such a she-cat; she is after that poor steward Ineni all day and night! She fancies him, and she'll get him into her bed if it's her final act in the living world. Whenever she has a chance she tries to grab him under his kilt. He looks like he's about to die each time! I tell you, you've never seen such a thing."

"Why, though?"

"Why what? Why Ineni? I suppose he's handsome, in an innocent sort of way. And he's the Pharaoh's steward, and an architect besides. Maybe he will make a good husband some day."

"No, why does Tuyu want him in her bed?"

"For the pleasure, of course! Why does any woman want a man in her bed? To make her belly big?" Twosre, apparently realizing that producing an heir was indeed why Ahmose wanted her husband in her bed, bit her lip and glanced away.

"But it's not pleasure, really."

"Who told you that, Great Lady?"

"Mutnofret."

Twosre raised her eyebrows. "Well, I suppose your sister did not know anything of pleasure before last night. She was inexperienced before her marriage, of course. She might be forgiven for thinking it's not a pleasure, if she didn't know."

Ahmose held Twosre's eye with a direct look. "Tell me truly. Does it hurt?"

The woman shrugged. "Yes, sometimes. The first time, usually."

"And is there blood?"

"Well...yes. But...."

Ahmose nodded. "I thank you for the truth, Twosre. Mutnofret did not lie. Not this time, at any rate."

"Great Lady, you look so pale! Are you afraid?"

Ahmose stood and wandered to one of her jewelry chests, lifted a necklace, a broad net of red and blue beads, and draped it around her shoulders. She turned back to Twosre. "What do you think? Does this look good on me?"

Twosre seemed confused. Her face became even thinner as she puckered her lips. "Of course. Great Lady, if there is anything I can do for you...any question I can answer...."

"You have already answered the only questions I needed to ask." Ahmose turned back to the chest, replaced the necklace with great care. She would be brave. She would be dutiful through the pain. She would ignore the blood. She would make Thutmose love her. She would. Mutnofret could not have all of him. And anything Mutnofret did, Ahmose would make herself do, too. Even this.

"Very well, then." Twosre stood and began stacking the remains of dinner onto her wooden tray. "I will just clear this away. Shall I dismiss the musician?"

"No. Leave her here. I would like more music while I... while I prepare."

Twosre smiled. It was half pity, half affection. "Good luck tonight, Great Lady."

Ahmose wore the blue and red necklace. She adorned her arms with cuffs of gold and electrum, bracelets of ivory and faience; she found the box of oils in her bathing room and scented her scalp, her neck, her breasts, the place between her legs. She dressed herself in the finest gown she owned. It was not Mutnofret's enchanting open weave, but the finest bleached linen, white as the moon. She knotted it tightly; so tightly she could only take small steps, so tightly she could barely bend to do up the knots. But when she looked at herself in her big electrum mirror, the fine, tight linen clung to her body, rounded her hips, pushed her small breasts up and out.

Then there was nothing to do but wait.

She sat uneasily on her bed, squeezed by the gown, and concentrated on the harper's soothing music. The evening glow in her room deepened, reddened; quickly it faded altogether and her chamber was transformed into a temple of dim dusk-purple. She thanked the musician and dismissed her. The calls of roosting birds replaced the plucking of strings; when the birds had gone to sleep and the floor glowed with stripes of moonlight, the hum of night insects began.

She waited, still, silent, apprehensive. The shadows slanted by degrees. At last Twosre's muffled clap sounded outside her bed chamber door.

"Come."

The door creaked open. Twosre's thin face peeked around its edge. "The Pharaoh is here to see you, Great Lady."

"Send him in." She was proud that her voice did not shake.

Thutmose entered, but his hand remained hesitantly on the door. Ahmose rose from the bed. His eyes traveled her body. They were lit from without by the moon, lit from within by the same hunger she had seen when he had gazed at Mutnofret's body on the lake barge. Her heart quickened.

"Come in," she said.

He did.

Thutmose reached her in a few steps; it seemed to Ahmose as if he floated, flew across the distance that separated them. His hands reached for her, stopped in doubt. She swallowed and stepped to meet his hands, fit her shoulders between them so he could feel the warmth of her arms, the shape of her.

His touch was light, careful. "Are you sure, Ahmoset?"

She nodded, pulled the wig from her head without stepping out of his touch.

Thutmose's hand was at the knot of her gown. In a heartbeat it was undone; the fabric fell away with a sound like a bird's wings. Her body, freed from the gown's pressure, felt more exposed than she was prepared for. She gasped.

Thutmose seemed to take the sound for excitement. Before she knew what he was doing, his hands were everywhere, light and sure. They ran down her arms, removed her bracelets, dropped each one to the floor atop the gown. They crossed the span of her shoulder blades, traced down her spine, grazed against her buttocks. A curious heat spread through her; her skin was alive, insistent; her palms throbbed with the beat of her heart.

He scooped her up, easy as lifting a bow, and laid her on the bed. She stretched along her linen sheets, hot with excitement; she arched to look at him. His hands were at his kilt, undoing it, pulling it away. Naked, he climbed onto the bed beside her.

Something bumped against her leg. It was hard like a knife's handle, but silky-smooth. She looked down at it. Thutmose's member, his bloody spear. She had seen a few before, on her naked half-brothers and when rowing slaves urinated over the sides of barges. But never before had one seemed so threatening; never had she seen one like this, awake and expectant. She lurched upright and shrank against her bed's headboard.

"What's the matter?" Thutmose's voice was thick with impatience.

He would put a seed in her. She'd grow a baby like Aiya's; she'd die in a hot, stinking pavilion as Aiya had died, too small, too young.

"Ahmoset." He took her hand gently, guided it toward the thing. She stiffened, refusing to touch it.

Thutmose sighed. He lay back on his elbows. His spear fell, defeated.

"I'm afraid," she said. The admission made her feel unspeakably stupid. She pulled her knees to her chest, hugging them tight, and rocked from side to side.

"You needn't fear."

"It will hurt. The blood."

"Only for a moment. Only a spot of blood."

She shook her head. Not that; that would hurt, yes. Mutnofret had said so and Twosre had confirmed it. It was Aiya's hurt she feared – Aiya's sweating forehead against Ahmose's lips, Aiya's body jerking as the knife came down. Aiya's baby, blue and dead, lying on a bloody breast.

She could not do it. She would not do it.

Mutnofret had won.

Ahmose was certain Tut would be angry with her. Instead, he sat up and hugged her gently. His hands were comforting now, not hungry. She allowed him to pull her close. He rocked her, murmuring, planting kisses on her bare scalp. "It's all right. Sweet girl, sweet *woman*, it's all right."

"No, it is not. If I do not give you a son..."

"Then Mutnofret will. I need you by my side to keep the gods with me, Ahmoset, not to give me a son. You have no duty in a bed – unless you want that duty. *Until* you want that duty. A day will come when you do want it. You will see."

Ahmose said nothing. She would never desire such a death.

"Ahmoset, I promise you, I will not force you. I will not come to you again until you ask me. But you must mean it – really mean it – the next time you bring me to your bed. Promise me that."

She held her breath for a long time. Then she let it go with a sigh, and said, "What if I never bring you to my bed?"

He did not hesitate. "You will still be my Great Royal Wife. I will not set you aside. I will get my sons from Mutnofret. But it won't be that way, Ahmoset. You will send for me; I know you will someday. I will be patient until then."

Ahmose made no reply.

CHAPTER TEN

THE SEASON OF SHEMU DREW to a close. The Iteru crept higher, day by day filling the hot earth with the promise of renewal. The river's water rose from deep within the valley to darken parched earth, then soak it, then saturate it until all about were layers of thick brown mud and the shimmer of new insect life on morning air. At last the canals of Waset began to fill. Puddles stood in the new canal beds, reflecting a brilliant sky, throwing light into the eyes from below so that any worker in the fields must paint his eyes heavily with cheap kohl or squint through his day's labors. The puddles grew, stretched blue arms one toward another until Waset's canals filled with the gurgle and hush of moving water. The Black Land lay carpeted in a mantle of wildflowers; weeds burst into life, striving to attract their share of insects and shed their seeds before Egypt's farmers plucked them out of the ground. Akhet – the season of the Inundation – had begun.

Ahmose loved this time of year better than any other. She ordered that a small pavilion should be raised on the roof of her hall, and there she spent most of her time, from the earliest hours of the morning until well past sunset. Whenever court did not call, she took her meals in her breezy rooftop sanctuary or spun flax there with Twosre and Renenet, breathing in the bright green scent of wet earth and reawakened life.

Tut encouraged her to resume her dream-reading. The

pavilion provided a natural place to do so; it was neither as public as the court hall nor as private as her apartments. Twosre saw to her needs as she listened to the dreams of noble women and palace servants alike. Word spread quickly through the city, and by the time the Inundation was well underway Ahmose was being petitioned for dream-reading by Waset's rekhet. Soon she could not manage the demand on her own. Tut devoted Ineni to the service of the Great Royal Wife; under his careful management Ahmose's days were well planned.

Akhet was a good time for a funeral. The very land sang hymns of rebirth as the river raised its fertile hands above the valley. The royal family set out from the palace an hour after sunrise, carried in their litters through the streets of Waset where the air was still and thick with the smell of fish and refuse. Tut and Ahmose rode together on a great throned platform carried by sixteen men, Mutnofret on a smaller litter immediately behind. Even this early in the morning, even during the Inundation when there was no race to plant or harvest and sleep could be had more freely, the rekhet crowded the route from palace to river. They cheered and waved as Ahmose and Tut passed, holding children up for a view, jumping to see above the crowd.

Behind them, the wails of a throng of paid mourners rose into the sky. They channeled the grief of the family, lamenting and scooping dust onto their heads, tearing their garments, shaking fists at the sun. Amunhotep had been a great Pharaoh, long-reigning and strong. He had many mourners; their cries were like those of the great flocks of geese in early Shemu, each individual voice merging into one relentless cacophony. Ahmose smiled to hear it. It was right that Amunhotep should be loudly mourned.

At the head of the procession, Meritamun and Nefertari rode litters directly behind the king's coffin. They had moved out of the Waset palace just before the wedding, taking up in an estate on the bluffs to the south of the city. Ahmose had not seen either woman since her wedding feast. She wondered how her mother and grandmother felt today. Did their hearts cry out as loudly as the mourners? Nefertari, at least, must be sorrowful. She had only one living child left – Meritamun – and the twist of her daughter's spine was slowly taking her life away. Meritamun too would die before the old God's Wife.

At length they reached the water steps where the royal barge rocked gently in its moorings. Broad and deep, fitted with two masts and bristling with oars, the barge's sides were painted red and white, the colors of Egypt's two crowns. The litter lowered. Tut gave his hand to Ahmose to lead her down the steps and onto the barge.

He went back right away to lead Mutnofret aboard. Ahmose watched as Mutnofret and Tut walked hand-in-hand down the great steps to the mooring. Though she was at odds with Mutnofret, she still felt keenly her sister's disappointment at being second wife. *It must be possible, though, to find some stable ground with my sister.* Surely their rivalry for Tut's affections could not keep them apart forever.

As for Tut, he kept his word to Ahmose. He did not try to return to her bed, but he came to her during the day, and often. It was well known around the palace that Ahmose and the Pharaoh often rode together in the evenings, taking their chariot out into the fields, past ancient temples and tiny villages, sometimes so far they could see the desert lying red and hot on the eastern horizon. Most days they shared the morning meal, too, in Ahmose's garden or in Tut's lush courtyard. She had heard no rumors that the Pharaoh invited Mutnofret into his leisure. Perhaps Ahmose was to be the Pharaoh's companion, and Mutnofret was to be his brood mare. *I can live with such an arrangement*, she thought, smiling.

Ahmose found Nefertari and Meritamun beneath a shaded canopy. She sat upon a bench with them and sipped wine while the sailors cast off the lines. The barge shoved away from the city's shore. It lumbered out into the water, wavering; then the current took it and it shuddered a deep rumble against the rising Iteru. The oarsmen shouted to each other as they churned the current, steering the craft deftly, pointing its nose upstream. Fabric snapped hard in the wind; the sails raised, bellying out into the brisk southward breeze. The barge steadied, pulled, cut through the chopping waves with increasing speed. Waset receded on the eastern bank. Several spans downstream, another barge carrying the hired mourners cast off. They were on their way to the western shore.

"You are doing well as Great Royal Wife, I hear," Meritamun said.

"I am doing my best. I suppose that's all I can do."

"And how is Mutnofret taking it?"

"Better. She fights with me less, but I see her less, too. I think she just avoids me."

"I hear she is trying for a son."

The unasked question hung stagnant in the air between them. Ahmose said nothing, turning her eyes to a small troupe of dancers performing in the center of the barge.

"And you?" Meritamun apparently would not be put off.

"We have...we have tried," Ahmose said carefully. It was not a lie. She had tried.

"I am glad to hear it. Sons are important for a Great Royal Wife."

"You never had any sons, Mother."

"If I had, none of us would need face this mess now. Think on that, Ahmose."

"I am doing all I can do," she said, a bit sharply. "I am still new to womanhood. Perhaps I need time to..."

"I know you love your sister, Ahmose, but recall that we put you behind the throne for a reason. You must remain the Great Royal Wife. Give your husband no reason to set you aside. If he does, there is no telling how the people may react to him.

"You allow him to dote on Mutnofret in public. Yes, I know he is affectionate toward you around the palace. I have heard. But only servants see what goes on in the palace. What do the people see today on this barge? The Pharaoh walking hand in hand with his second wife, and now he sits on the other side of the boat with her while you have tucked yourself away with a couple of old women. What must they all think, Ahmose? And more importantly, what must Mutnofret be thinking? I will not have you risking Egypt's security by failing to..."

Nefertari laid a dry, bony hand on Meritamun's leg – just that, and the former Great Royal Wife fell silent.

"Ahmose was a good choice," the God's Wife said, her voice like worn leather. "Be still, Meritamun."

Well upstream of the water steps on the western shore, the crew furled the sails of the barge. Now they would coast, under guidance of the oars alone, to their mooring. Ahmose loved to ride the river downstream during the Inundation. Nothing was so exhilarating: the rush of wind, the dizzying expanse of the river, the white-tipped waves shouting and slapping against the boat's hull. She let Meritamun's tirade slide off her shoulders, and smiled as the oarsmen turned the barge nose-north. They flew down the river, angling always to the west. Gulls followed the boat, screaming above the music, squabbling over bits of food, dropping their treasures into the water. When the boat neared the moorings, the oarsmen backed water and the barge shuddered, jolted, boomed, slowing ponderously, until it coasted to the water steps. Men leapt ashore carrying ropes, tied the barge to stone pillars as thick as a circle of gossiping women.

Refreshed and cheered by the ride, Ahmose jumped to her feet. Nefertari grabbed her hand, motioned for her to bend her head close.

"You were a good choice, Ahmose, but still Meritamun is not wrong. You have a battle ahead of you, as surely as your husband has his own war."

Nefertari bobbed her dark old head toward Mutnofret. She lounged across the barge from Ahmose, her hand lightly resting on Tut's arm. He said something to her as the dancers finished their performance, and she laughed, her long, slanted eyes sparkling in the sun.

"The woman who bears the Pharaoh's sons has his heart," Nefertari said. "And the woman who has the Pharaoh's heart has at least as much power as the God's Wife of Amun."

They made the journey to Amunhotep's tomb on foot. The mourners made a sorrowful music down the length of a great ravine, green and flourishing with thick growth. Tut walked with Ahmose. She was glad to be in his company, wary all over again of Mutnofret's smiles. Nefertari's words worried at her ka.

Tut had never seen a royal funeral before, and Ahmose quietly rehearsed the Opening of the Mouth with him as they walked. In truth, she had never seen a royal funeral either, but as the daughter of a Pharaoh who might someday bear an heir, the ancient ceremony had been required learning. She knew that Tut must not place a single footstep wrong. Her reputation as a god-chosen woman would only gain her husband a measure of credence among the priests and nobles. Today, he had to be the very embodiment of Horus, conquering death, resurrecting the father. If he could give a convincing show as Horus, it would be ever more difficult for any man to doubt his right to the throne.

"...And then the bull is butchered," Ahmose said, "and you are given...?"

"The foreleg. I point it at his body."

"To convey its strength," she confirmed. "And after that?"

"The iron."

"Do you remember the words you must say?"

They went over the entire ceremony three times as they walked, their rehearsal well hidden by the wailing of the mourners. Behind the mourners the priests and nobles came, their fine clothing caked with dust from the dozens of feet that went before.

A few of the higher priests were already gathered outside

Amunhotep's tomb, preparing for the day's work. They raised their palms in obeisance when they saw Thutmose. He returned the greeting, a gesture of confidence, strength.

You will do well, my love. You must do well. She looked up at Tut's face, stoic and bold in the sun. A shadow passed over him from above, darkening his features, sliding up over the tall, white spire of his crown. She followed the shadow's path. A bird circled above them with pointed wings and long, straight tail. She seized Tut's hand.

"Look, Tut!"

He followed her gaze into the sky, his free hand going up to steady the crown. "A falcon."

"Horus blesses us." Ahmose smiled, opening herself to the gods' glow.

The High Priest of Amun raised his arms to the sun as the last of the procession drew up around the tomb. The mourners fell silent. "Let the setem priest be awakened!"

Thutmose stepped forward. Ahmose's eyes were on his back, broad and strong and straight beneath the wide jeweled collar covering his shoulders. He made the ritual response in a voice that rang off the red walls of the ravine. "The setem priest has risen."

The High Priest draped a leopard skin around Thutmose's shoulders. He did not move, but stared straight ahead as the priest adjusted the skin. He was as untouchable, as unmovable as a god.

The bearers of the coffin emerged from the crowd. They laid it on the ground, then with great care lifted the lid and raised Amunhotep's body. It did not look like a man at all; it was a man-shaped bundle, an unfinished statue wrapped in white linen, crowned with a smiling golden mask. They laid it upon a platform of sand. The priests crowded around, fanning incense over the body and singing.

Awake!
Be alert as a living one,
Rise fresh every morning,

97

Awake!
Healthy forever more,
A thousand thousand thousand times will you awake.
Awake!
The gods protect you.
Protection surrounds you every day.
Awake!
Your son Horus has come to raise you
You will fly forever as a falcon flies.
Awake!

Awake, Ahmose whispered in her heart. *Father I never knew, awake and live forever.* A pang of regret stabbed her heart. She had never known Amunhotep as Thutmose had. Surely any man who was so loved by her husband had been worth knowing. She imagined her father striding through the sky, laughing with pleasure as his funerary rites were carried out by the mortals below. *I hope I will please you as Great Royal Wife, Father. I hope I will be a good wife to your friend, and make you proud.*

The singing done, the body blessed, Amunhotep was returned to his simple inner coffin. To the renewed cries of the mourners, a troop of priests emerged from the darkness of the open tomb bearing an intricately decorated outer coffin, carved and adorned with lapis, carnelian, and gold. They lifted its lid and nestled Amunhotep inside; the wails of the mourners surged. The priests stood the brilliant coffin upright against the tomb's outer wall. It was splendid. The artisan had done well, capturing Amunhotep's features perfectly in gold and enamel. The way the morning sun caught the gilding made Ahmose's heart swell. *To be immortal, to live forever in happiness like a god. To be golden like Re.*

When they butchered the bull, Ahmose looked away. She pitied the poor creature, but its strength would go into her father's ka. It must be done. Eyes closed, she heard the axe fall and looked in time to see Tut receive the bull's foreleg. He stepped up without hesitating, laid the leg at Amunhotep's feet. "Strength will be yours as you live forever." He turned back and took the bull's hot heart from the priest's hands. Blood ran down his arms, trickled off his elbows to stain his white kilt. He hoisted the heart so all could see it, then offered it, too, to Amunhotep. "Strength will be yours forever."

The high priest shouted in a voice like a snapping sail, "Who is the son who loves Djeserkare, the king, Amunhotep, he who has gone to live forever with the gods?"

"I am the son who loves Djeserkare, the king, Amunhotep," Thutmose replied.

"Then take the netjerwy in your hand, and raise him back to life."

The priest held a carved tray of white stone. Ahmose craned her neck to see past Tut's shoulder as he took hold of the sacred metal rod. It was a bit longer than a man's foot, split into two hooks at one end. It was made from a fallen star, so Ahmose had heard. Miraculous, astounding, that a star could be made of metal, that mortals could forge it into this sacred rod in her husband's hand. A whisper of envy was in her ear. To touch a piece of the heavens was a wondrous thing.

"Horus comes," the priests chanted in one voice. "Horus comes to split the mouth of Waser with his little finger!"

Tut stepped to the coffin, the netjerwy held out before him like a divine offering. He hesitated, and Ahmose's heart burned cold. She was sure he had forgotten the words. Then he turned his head slightly, and she could see the barest glimpse of his face. Sorrow was written plain there. This was not just his king who Tut sent to the afterlife, but his dearest friend. She wanted to run to her husband, to offer him what comfort she could. Instead, she squeezed her hands into fists and prayed.

Tut's voice rose with a power that made her suck in her breath. "With gods' iron of Upper Egypt, with gods' iron of Lower Egypt, I, Horus, split open your mouth for you, O Waser the King. Breathe in the ankh, the breath of life. Awake, and live forever!" He touched the netjerwy to Amunhotep's golden lips.

The crowd in the valley shouted its acclaim. Ahmose stared

around her. Nobles' wives jumped and sang. The mourners clapped, danced, raised their voices in an ululating cry. Priests wept. Thutmose had come through the ceremony as boldly as any man born to rule. She longed to run to his side, so he could sweep her into his arms and spin her in a circle. But she remembered Meritamun's words on the barge. She walked to her husband slowly, all possession and calm, before Mutnofret could reach him first. She allowed herself only a small smile.

"You did very well."

"I had a good teacher."

"You are Pharaoh now in truth, Tut. Look at them. They all love you!"

"The ceremony was only my first test. My real trial will come on the battle fields."

Ahmose shivered.

"Don't worry," Tut said. "I'll keep the fighting as far from our borders as I can."

"When will you leave?"

"Tomorrow night, my love." He stopped short. There was expectation in his voice.

Ahmose wanted to ask him to come to her bed that night. She wanted to want him in that way. She remembered the way his hands had made her feel, the way he had laid her onto the bed so gently. But she remembered Aiya, too, and could not make herself speak the words. Instead, she stood on her toes to kiss his cheek. "I will pray to all the gods for your safety."

"So will I."

CHAPTER ELEVEN

THUTMOSE WAS GONE FOR BUHEN only two days when Mutnofret paid a visit to the rooftop pavilion. She arrived unannounced, brushing past Ineni, ignoring the steward's protests. She sank down on Ahmose's cushions, stirring the air around her face with a fan of green feathers. "Spinning on the rooftop just like a rekhet woman. How quaint," she said sweetly. "How does the season find you, dear sister?"

"Well enough."

"You're not planning on weaving your own cloth and sewing your own dresses, are you?"

"Of course not. Don't be silly. Spinning helps me concentrate, that's all. I do my best thinking when I am spinning." Ahmose finished her twist and laid aside spindle and distaff. She brushed her hands together to rid them of clinging flax fibers. "Shall I fetch you something cool to drink? You look very sweaty."

"That would be most kind. And have your woman bring me some salted fish to eat. I crave salt so; it is unbearable."

"Cravings? So you did conceive before our husband left."

For an answer, Mutnofret smiled. She looked truly happy; this was not just a sly cat's grin. Ahmose could not help but give a small smile in return. Mutnofret had been so miserable and angry since their marriage was announced. If a child would bring her sister real happiness, then Ahmose could not be entirely dismayed. Motherhood might mellow the second wife, the way whelping a litter often mellowed a fierce bitch. Besides, the baby might be a girl.

"I only just found out a few days ago. I wanted to wait to tell you until I could be certain. Oh! But I can see you are still not pregnant."

Ahmose followed Mutnofret's downward glance. The knot of her menstrual belt was visible under the linen of her gown, rumpling the fabric. She tugged at the garment as if to conceal her failure.

"No matter," Mutnofret went on. "You are still young. I came to ask whether you would like my help at court while our husband is away."

All of Ahmose's instincts shrieked at her to reject the offer. Mutnofret would seize the opportunity to make her look like a fool before as many people as could be managed. But she saw again Mutnofret leaping to her feet in the throne room the day Amunhotep died, shivering with shock. Could she deny her sister a share in the life she had always expected? *Yes, yes!* Her heart shouted. *Deny her; send her away!*

But the eyes inside her, the eyes of her ka, saw Mutnofret's eyes red from crying, and guilt overwhelmed her. Dimly, she heard herself say, "If you wish. I shall be glad of your company." She shook her head to still her heart's anger; disbelief and rage howled from within her own ka. She masked the gesture by brushing at the air as if warding off gnats, though none were near. *Stupid, stupid, stupid,* cried her fast-pounding heart.

Ahmose said, "Did you hear the rumor from the House of Women? Baketamun is also with child."

Mutnofret pursed her lips. Her eyes narrowed. "No, I did not hear. That is good news."

But what could Mutnofret possibly fear? Baketamun was not a wife, nor even a king's daughter. Her child would not be royal, and therefore not an heir to compete with Mutnofret's offspring. Unless, of course, Thutmose decided to be as unorthodox as his predecessor in matters of inheritance. It was a troubling thought, even for Ahmose. Would her Tut choose a friend or a soldier to succeed him on the throne, rather than a child of his own blood? He would have more right, greater precedent, than any Pharaoh who had come before. The nobles might accept such a thing once -- but twice? *No, not Tut. He would never do it,* Ahmose told herself sternly. Then, *Would he?*

"So her baby will arrive at the same time as yours," Ahmose said.

"Do you think Thutmose is the father?"

"Mutnofret!" Ahmose stared at her sister. True, the Pharaoh often allowed his most important guests access to the harem, but it was the height of incivility to imply that any harem woman carried a child that was not the king's.

"Well? Thutmose often visited the House before he was the Pharaoh. Why should he not permit his friends...?"

"Baketamun was your friend! How could you be so coarse?"

Mutnofret sighed. "Ahmose, you are so simple sometimes. The world is not the way you think it, all propriety and rules and...and maat."

"What in the name of Mut is that supposed to mean?"

"Real life is not like the stories. First King's Daughters can be set aside, and women in the king's harem can have children sired by men other than the king."

"I know, but you don't have to..."

"*You* know, *you* know." She sighed again, looking away, frowning. "I'm sorry, Ahmose, truly. I did not come here to fight. I don't want to fight with you. Sometimes I just can't help myself."

"I know, Mutnofret. This...arrangement...is difficult for you. For me, too. You were raised to be the Great Royal Wife, and I – with my gifts, I could have been a priestess. That is what I always wanted to do, you know. I wish I still could."

"I did not know. You never told me." Mutnofret took her hand. It had been so long since her sister had touched her in kindness that Ahmose's eyes filled with tears. "You would have made a good priestess."

"Wouldn't it be a lovely thing? The temples are so peaceful. Not like the court at all."

"Tell me, priestess, what should I do to be sure my child is healthy, and a boy?"

Ahmose smiled. "Go to Hathor's sanctuary at Ipet-Isut. Leave an offering of cow's milk, and pray to the goddess. Then take a bull calf's meat to Khnum's shrine. That should please him. They will both hear your prayers – Hathor to protect the child, and Khnum to shape him into a male."

"I will do that. I will tell the gods Ahmose sent me to them. Perhaps they will listen doubly hard, if they know I have your blessing."

Week followed week, the Inundation bringing higher waters and hotter days. The smell of water hung always in the air. The insects became nearly as miserable to bear as the heat. Ahmose's pavilion was curtained now in loose-woven linen, sheer enough to let some semblance of a breeze in but tight enough to keep out the worst of the biting flies. Mutnofret appeared daily at court, watching the proceedings without a word, but ready with good advice whenever Ahmose asked. She was careful to ask often, though Ahmose frequently found herself wondering whether a linen screen could be woven to keep Mutnofret away, too, like the gnats and flies. The second wife could be unpredictable at the best of times, and pregnancy and Akhet combined to make her moods and her tongue sharp.

Akhet was a troubling time for the court. With the fields flooded and Thutmose too occupied with war to build his monuments, many hands remained idle, and not only rekhet, but nobles as well. More disputes and petitions came before the throne now than at any other time of the year. Ineni and the other stewards did a fine job filtering out all but the direst conflicts, referring a great deal of them back to local juries. It was a tiring business, though, adjudicating disputes over land or cattle or trade goods. Ahmose was often so exhausted by her work in court that she had small enough energy for reading dreams. Mutnofret hardly seemed to fare better. She was sick most mornings, and had taken to sleeping on her roof – like a rekhet woman, Ahmose was amused to note – soothed by the night's cooler breezes.

Thutmose sent many letters from Buhen. They were addressed only to Ahmose. She had no idea whether he also sent word to his second wife, and Ahmose did not think it wise to ask. In any case, Nofret never mentioned any letters from their husband. Rather than risk hurting her feelings, Ahmose asked Ineni to add Mutnofret's shenu – her name surrounded by the formal royal ring – to the beginning of each letter. The steward did a fair imitation of Tut's hand. Once the notes had been doctored, Ahmose shared the letters with Mutnofret when she came to the rooftop pavilion to visit.

Buhen is beautiful,

one read.

The fortress here is strong. Many legions of men, well fed, plenty of horses, spears, and bows. No sign yet of the Kushites. I am hopeful.

Met with Kushite warlord yesterday, read another. *Black as night and mean as a river horse. Made threats, would not be consoled. Thinks to take the river, all the way up to the cataracts, for his own. We will teach him his lessons.*

One made her shiver:

Surprise attack this morning by Kushite force while we inspected crop fields. Came upon us from behind, out of a canyon. Were pinned against river. A near thing. Reinforcements came from the fortress and surrounded their rear. We crushed them under our heels. Warlord killed by my own spear. Kush will think hard before coming against Egypt again.

And there were more, and still more. The conflict seemed to be rising in intensity, building to some terrible climax. Ahmose watched for Tut's letters with a curious disturbance in her heart, a fierce pressure of mingled yearning and dread. Would a scroll arrive from a steward, informing her of the Pharaoh's death at Kushite hands? No – not Thutmose, the greatest soldier in all the land. Never.

Every letter was signed the same way:

Loving and missing you.

A day came when Ahmose had no dreams to read, no disputes to settle. She determined to make the most of this rare break from her duties. She made arrangements at once for a barque to carry her south to the estate Meritamun and Nefertari shared. Ahmose brought no one with her, save for Ineni and a single guard, and dressed simply, hoping she would not be recognized by the bustling rekhet crowds at the waterside. She was in luck. It was a market day, and most rekhet were busy in the higher streets of Waset, buying and trading foods and wares. The Great Royal Wife was still new enough to the throne that her face was not well known, and those who moved about the waterfront – fishermen unloading boats and folding nets, prostitutes hoping for the fishers' custom, merchants' slaves driving camels and donkeys to drink, naked children splashing in canal inlets – all these glanced her way and went back to their business, content that she was just another noble lady setting out on a journey.

Her barque was especially fast and fine. It leaped under the prevailing southward wind, as fleet and responsive as a colt just broken to the chariot. She reclined with Ineni in the soft shade of the curtained hut astern.

"You seem to be getting on well with your sister, Great Lady."

Ahmose nodded. "I suppose she just needed time. I can't tell you how often I've wanted to strangle her since Amunhotep died. Mutnofret can be such a snake when she is upset. But I am glad to see her coming around. She is with child, you know."

Ineni's eyes widened. "That is news to me. Does the king know?"

"I have not told him in any of my letters. I do not know whether Mutnofret writes to him. She wants to surprise him with the news when he returns from Buhen, though, so I should think he knows nothing of it."

"And – you, Great Lady?" Ineni fidgeted, obviously uncomfortable with the topic. Because she had come to regard him as a dear friend, Ahmose answered him forthrightly.

"No. The Pharaoh and I have not lain together."

Ineni blushed. He looked out the shade mesh covering the cabin walls for a long time, watching the east bank glide by. At length he said, "Is there...a problem, Great Lady? As your steward, I will call the best physicians if there is anything amiss."

"There is nothing wrong, Ineni. You have no cause to worry."

"You...you do not choose to lie with the Pharaoh?"

Ahmose shook her head lightly, smiling.

"Ah," he said, his brows falling as if in mild disappointment. "You prefer women?"

Ahmose laughed. "No, that's not what I mean. I suppose I prefer no one."

Ineni looked at her hard; then, apparently aware that he was treading close to disrespect, coughed and softened his expression with an obvious effort. "Great Lady, may I speak freely to you?"

Confused, Ahmose shrugged. "All right."

"It is critically important that you get a child. A son, if you can."

"I know," Ahmose said vaguely. She wanted to ask *why*, when Mutnofret was obviously fertile, but to do so would make her seem foolish. Still, Ineni seemed to hear the unspoken question.

"A Great Royal Wife who cannot do her duty is not secure on the throne. This is especially true when lesser wives wait to take her place. Great Royal Wives have been displaced before when they could not produce children."

"It is not a matter of *cannot*." She snapped her teeth shut, but the words were already out upon the air.

Ineni's fingers tangling in the hem of his kilt. Annoyed with his reluctance, Ahmose gestured for him to speak. He glanced at her, then away. "You ...will not?"

Ahmose sighed. "I need time – that is all. My sister needed time to adjust to her role as second wife. I need time to...to..."

Ineni nodded. "It is a dangerous thing, bearing children. Even men know this. Still, Great Lady, as your sister's belly grows larger she will creep that much closer to your throne."

"That is foolish. Giving birth, even to a son, doesn't mean she can be Great Royal Wife. I am god-chosen. Thutmose needs me to legitimize his rule in the eyes of the people."

"The people need Thutmose to keep the Kushites and the Heqa-Khasewet at bay. Once he has done this, he has no more need of you, Great Lady. When he has restored Egypt's sense of security, he will need nothing to legitimize his claim to the throne. The people's gratitude toward him will be more powerful a token than any god-chosen wife. Please forgive my speaking so harshly, but it must be said for your own good."

Ahmose sat back, stunned to silence. Impossible, that Tut could have no *need* of her once Egypt's enemies were defeated. They talked together, shared leisure together; he wrote to her, and not, so far as she knew, to Mutnofret. Tut valued her – if not as a woman in his bed, then at least as a god-chosen emblem to hold up before those who might question his right to rule. At least, he treated her as if he valued her, even if he did not desire her.

But what if his affection for her was a sham to keep Ahmose content with her temporary role? What if, indeed, he only needed her until he had put down the uprisings at Egypt's borders? Then, with his capability proven at last to the drivers of Egypt's chariot, would he be free to set her aside, to fully love his beautiful and fertile second wife?

Her mouth tasted of ash at the mere thought of her husband casting her aside, just at the possibility that he could even be *capable* of casting her aside. For Mutnofret! For the one who carried his child, his heir. And what would become of her then? She would be, no doubt, sent back to the House of Women, where she would be lucky if the king visited one day out of twenty, and she would be forced to compete with the harem for his attention.

She saw Thutmose from another angle then, not her laughing, boyish husband who skipped rocks across the lake, but a soldier – a general – more skilled than any in Egypt with strategies and schemes. She quailed.

"What am I to do, Ineni?" Her lips were numb, her ears ringing.

"You must conceive a child, Great Lady. You must do it as soon as you can. I am glad for you if your sister is treating you kindly again, but leave no room in Mutnofret's heart to hope for the throne. I have known the both of you for only a short time, but I think I know already which *she* would choose, if she were forced to choose between her sister or her birthright."

The captain called out the landing. Relieved, Ahmose staggered to her feet. The rowing-men leapt ashore, tying the barque fast to the water steps. Ineni offered his arm, and she took it gratefully.

"I did not mean to frighten you, Great Lady."

"I know, Ineni." She sucked in a deep breath. "You are right, of course. Mutnofret probably hasn't changed. She has always been too wily to give in so easily. I had allowed myself to hope she had settled. I must still be wary of her tricks."

"And a Royal Son?"

"Being god-chosen is not enough to keep my husband's heart. I can see that now. Even the best of men will be swayed by a son. A son changes everything."

"I...I am glad to hear you will try," Ineni said. His voice was dry. Its dryness reminded her of Nefertari, her leather voice, the brittle strength of her old hands. She recalled how, on the funeral barge, Nefertari had laid a hand on Meritamun's leg to quiet her. How in the throne room Nefertari's hand had tightened on Meritamun's shoulder, and Meritamun had sprang to her feet, clutching the crook and flail.

"It is not a son I need, but power," she said quietly.

Ineni did not hear her over the sailors joking and splashing. But when he asked her to repeat her words, she only shook her head and led him on toward Nefertari's estate.

CHAPTER TWELVE

NEFERTARI'S HOME, A SPACIOUS BRICK building with an enormous pillared porch, stood on a high hill overlooking a great orchard. Beyond the orchard, fields of barley, sun-gold, ran down to the Iteru. Fishing boats and traders' barges moved over the shining water, slow-motion, dancers in a dream. Ahmose and Nefertari sipped beer in the shade of the porch, watching the boats sail far below, while Meritamun wandered through her little garden, cutting herbs and flowers, laying them in the old, flat basket she carried propped against one thin hip. Away from the eyes of the court at last, the former Great Royal Wife had given up the oversized wigs that hid her deformity. Now fashionable rows of tiny braids swung around her face as she bent, slowly, carefully, like a very old woman, over her flowers.

"Her back troubles her more every day," Nefertari said, hardly louder than a whisper.

"Can the physicians do nothing?"

"Nothing. The magicians seem helpless, too. They have tried all the spells and charms, all the songs and prayers. My daughter will leave me soon, too, as did my son."

"Grandmother..." Ahmose laid her hand on Nefertari's shoulder, but she could think of nothing to offer in comfort, or in denial. In the short time since Meritamun had moved out of the palace, her back did seem more twisted, her movements weaker and more timid.

"It is a terrible thing, for a mother to outlive all her

children."

"Let us talk of something happier. Tell me a story from when you were the Great Royal Wife."

"Oh, cats' whiskers. You don't want to hear about that. You have your own stories to tell by now."

"But I do want to hear it. Tell me how you came to be God's Wife. I have never heard that story."

Nefertari allowed a tiny smile. "Oh, if you insist. Pour me another bowl of beer; my throat is dry. Good girl." She took the lacquered bowl from Ahmose's hands, and sat for a time watching the bubbles on the beer's surface. Her tired old eyes shone with a distant warmth. "When I married my brother – not your grandfather; I speak of my elder brother, Kamose – I was not much older than you. Our father had just died, and Kamose was burning with desire to drive the Heqa-Khasewet invaders from Egypt. He had always dreamed of it, always talked of it. When the throne passed to him, he said, 'I will not be a mere statue. I will not sit still while foreigners control my land.'

"But Kamose was always a hot-head, possessed of much more bravery than sense. He went north to make war on the Heqa-Khasewet settlers, to toss them out of Egypt if he could. The Heqa-Khasewet were growing restless, making demands: pushing hard, you see. So Kamose went to throw them right out of the empire. We all asked him to reconsider – the whole family, and each of his advisors, too. He had so little experience in battle, you see, and the Heqa-Khasewet had been rooted into Egyptian soil for more than two hundred years. But Kamose would not be dissuaded. When it was clear we could not keep him from the Heqa-Khasewet, I begged him to take me along. No, I insisted I should be allowed to accompany him. I thought I might protect him somehow, or perhaps I thought to curb him. We were both young and stupid, so he agreed.

"Those were the best times of my life, and the worst. The voyage north, seeing the pyramids – *ah!* Such beauty! Oh, and the cities we visited on the way, my girl – the feasts they gave us! It was an adventure to sing of. And it ended so badly.

"Poor Kamose was killed in the first battle, almost immediately. Our army broke to pieces. The Heqa-Khasewet very nearly defeated us then. I was at camp in Kamose's tent, and a wounded soldier brought me the news of his death. The Heqa-Khasewet were still slaughtering Egyptians on the battle field. I had to do something, so I made the slaves hitch a chariot and outfit me with a man's armor. I took a spear, but that was all. And I prayed that the gods would lead me to the heart of the battle."

Ahmose leaned her arms on the table, staring at her grandmother. She was distantly aware that her mouth hung open like a beached carp's, but she could not seem to close it. In her heart's eye she saw Nefertari, young and stern and strong and beautiful, shining in a man's armor, holding aloft great bronze-tipped spear like a holy scepter. Her heart drummed in her chest. *War drums.*

"I was all that kept Egypt together. I rode out of the hills and onto the battle field, waving my spear as if I knew what to do with it. Afterward all the soldiers swore I glowed like the sun. Maybe it was the gods' light upon me – who can say? I rallied them, pulled them back into the hills and into a draw where the Heqa-Khasewet could not get at us. We waited for my younger brother to come – he had been scouting, you see – and he led the troops back out into the fray.

"And that was your grandfather, the man we named you for. After that battle was settled, he sent for a High Priest from the nearest town and we were married in Kamose's tent. My dear short-tempered Kamose. He was not Pharaoh for three years. But as impulsive as he was, he never would have been as great a Pharaoh as King Ahmose."

Nefertari paused, watching the river and the deep green hills beyond.

Ahmose waited, but it seemed the old woman had lost herself in memory. She wondered: would *she* ever have such an exciting life? Could she even survive such adventure? She studied her grandmother's face, deep-creased with age but still with eyes as bright as stars. Ahmose's chin lifted with pride. What a fortunate thing, to have the blood of such a woman in her veins.

At length, Nefertari continued her tale. "After just a few weeks, your grandfather sent me back to Waset, and just in time. The nobles were beside themselves without somebody of the royal blood to tell them which end to put their wigs on. The country – or the city, at least – was on the brink of erupting into civil war. Fighting, fighting, everywhere fighting as if all the people were little children stealing figs from one another. I went nearly mad tending to all the little children of Egypt. When my husband came home, though, I had my reward."

"The title," Ahmose said.

Nefertari nodded. "He had uncovered stories of the God's Wives of the past while he traveled home, talking to some old priest or other whom he had befriended. He was high as a falcon after he'd chased the Heqa-Khasewet out, and he felt like giving gifts, I suppose. For rallying the troops and for putting Waset back to rights in the absence of the king, he made me God's Wife of Amun.

"To share power with a Pharaoh – that was a rich thing. Yet it was a gift with a blade in it, for I lost my privacy and freedom. I never did live quite the same way again. When the priests truly believe you to be the consort of the god, every move you make is seen by hundreds of eyes. I had power, but never again could I go adventuring as I had done with Kamose. I was chained to the temple like a hound to its kennel.

"Still, I suppose I would not give it up, if I had my life to live again. This house was part of my due as God's Wife, and much more: so much rich cloth I could have had a new gown for every day of my life, if I had wanted it; more gold and jewels than any woman could ever desire. And these fields and orchards are all mine, too. I am dependent on no one, even in my old age. And I have had control over the Amun priests – more or less – for nearly my whole life.

Power – respect: these are good things for a woman to have, and difficult to come by."

Good things indeed. Ahmose considered her grandmother's words in silence as Meritamun made her way into the shade, set her basket on the table. Ahmose made pleasantries with her mother, but her heart weighed Nefertari's story carefully. She examined every word of the tale in minute detail. And one idea stood out above all her other thoughts: if she were the God's Wife, her word would be like the word of a goddess.

Meritamun lowered herself onto a stool, sighing, massaging her back with careful hands. A servant stepped from the recesses of the porch and took over the duty, rubbing between Meritamun's shoulders until the former queen relaxed, head drooping.

"You look well," Ahmose said.

Meritamun huffed. "My back aches all the time, but otherwise I feel well enough. I never knew what a chore it is to govern a land until I no longer had to do it."

"And I am only beginning to find out," Ahmose said. "Ineni is a wonderful steward, and does all he can for me, but I have a job of work every day in the throne room. All the fighting! And the scheming! I don't know how you put up with it for so long."

"I did what I had to do, what Egypt needed me to do. That is the duty of a Great Royal Wife."

"That, and making sons," Ahmose said, frowning.

"And how goes that job of work?"

She sighed. "Very well, for the second wife. Mutnofret is with child."

"I am glad to hear it. One never knows when the gods will take a child away. The more sons your husband has, the more secure Egypt will be."

Ahmose scuffed her sandals against the flagstones. Out on the river, fishing boats crawled along like water beetles, and here and there a pleasure barge sailed. The smallest hints of music, whispers of pipe and drum, came to her faintly from the Iteru's restless flanks. The sounds were like words in a half-remembered dream, touching her mind and flitting away again before she could seize hold and identify their meaning.

"And how," Nefertari said, nibbling a date, "go your attempts at getting a child?"

Ahmose wanted to lie, to tell them Thutmose had come every night to her bed before he left on his campaign. But her ka was not up to the charade. "I have not tried." There. The words were out.

Nefertari sighed. "Your spiritual gifts make you valuable to Thutmose, girl. But your sister was always more cunning than you. She has the court in her blood and bones. She knows how to turn one man against another, how to turn a rumor to reality. Do not suppose that she has forgotten she was first in line for the throne."

"Ineni has already reminded me of this," Ahmose said impatiently. "I know Mutnofret is a schemer. I know to be wary."

"The nobles will assume you are barren," said Meritamun.

"Let them. You had only girls, after all, Mother; your right to the throne was never challenged."

"I never had a second wife nipping at my heels. No doubt if Amunhotep had taken another official wife, I would have been displaced for my failure. What troubles you so?"

She had begun with the truth; she may as well go on with it. Ineni stood at a deferential distance, chatting with Nefertari's own steward, but he was within earshot. Ahmose lowered her voice. "I saw a girl – a friend – killed by birthing. Wahibra cut her open while she still lived, but the baby died, too." So much time had passed since Aiya's death, yet still talking of it, remembering it, brought the sting of tears.

"But Ahmose! That will not happen to you. The women of our line birth easily."

"It was her smallness that killed her. Wahibra said so."

"And you think you are too small to bear?"

She nodded.

"Nonsense," Meritamun said. She sipped at her bowl of

beer, staring hard at Ahmose over the rim.

"It is not. Aiya was no smaller than I. You did not see her. You do not know."

"You sound like a goose."

"I am the Great Royal Wife. You should remember that."

"Oh-ho!" Nefertari chuckled. "So you have a little of Mutnofret in you, do you? That is good. You will need a touch of fire in the years to come."

"I will not have to behave like Mutnofret if I have your title, Grandmother. The title would give me some control over her – over the nobles and priests, too."

"Is that why you came today? And I thought you wanted to see my nice house."

Ahmose smiled. "Of course I wanted to see it. In truth, I only thought of asking you about the title on the walk up from the river."

"Well, you cannot have it."

The bluntness of the rejection made Ahmose gasp. "Why not? I am god-chosen, after all."

"It takes more than feeling the gods to wield this kind of power. And so much power is more curse than blessing. Everything you do, everything you say, must be guarded. It is no way to live a life. I would not pass the title on to you unless there was no other way for you to sort out your problems, Ahmose. I have lived under the eyes of the priests my whole life. It is only now, as a very old woman, that I get to enjoy a little peace. Even as Great Royal Wife, you have more freedom now than you realize. That will vanish if you become God's Wife of Amun. You must be perfect all the time to keep the priests."

To satisfy them, Ahmose shook her head lightly, laughed as if these ideas were only the fancy of a young girl, and spoke of other things. But the eyes of her heart saw a repeating vision of Nefertari standing behind the Horus Throne, her hand on Meritamun's shoulder. Ahmose could not deny the subtlety and strength of the God's Wife's power, the assurance with which she controlled the one who sat upon the throne.

It was not a son she needed – of this she was now certain. She needed the title. And without Nefertari's blessing, Ahmose would have to be as clever as a spider to make the Amun priests her own.

CHAPTER THIRTEEN

THUTMOSE HAD BEEN SIX WEEKS away when Ahmose received this letter:

> *Great battle at last. Ranks and ranks of Kushites threw themselves against the fortress. We held them off but ran out of arrows. Had to take to the field with all men using spears. Lost many horses and men. Captured three Kushite princes as hostages. Killed the rest of their army. Egypt is secure from the south.*
>
> *I am wounded. Cut to the leg. Should heal well but my return is delayed. Will set sail for Egypt in two weeks' time.*

It had taken perhaps a week and a half for the letter to reach her. Tut would be home soon.

Ahmose set the palace into a frenzy. Every corner was swept of sand, every floor scrubbed until it shone. Scaffolds were brought into the throne room and the great feast hall, and servants hoisted pots of water high up on scaffolds to scrub years' worth of soot from the ceilings and walls. Gardens were weeded and watered and replanted. The palace was invaded by an army of musicians, playing from sunrise to sunset to buoy the spirits of the workers. Well before the Pharaoh returned, the great palace of Waset looked as if it had just been willed into immaculate being by a goddess, as fresh and inviting as cool water.

Mutnofret, too, was busy preparing for the Pharaoh's return. She had new gowns sewn, purchased new wigs and jewels. Her pregnancy was progressing well. She had visited the temples of Hathor and Khnum several times to make offerings for a boy child, and prayed nightly. Ahmose prayed, too, though in secrecy. There was nothing she wished for more fervently than that her sister should bear a daughter. After all, if their own mother had only girls, it was possible that Mutnofret, too, might be so afflicted. Perhaps it was even likely. Who could say? Mutnofret haunted Ahmose's dreams, leading a pack of nobles to tear Ahmose from the throne as jackals tear at their prey. She often woke shaking.

At last the day of the king's return came. Late in the warm evening glow, while Ahmose spun her flax on the rooftop, Ineni clapped at the head of the stairs. "Great Lady, the Pharaoh! He is returned!"

Ahmose dropped her distaff and bounced to her feet quick as a hare. She was out of the pavilion and pelting down the stairs, brushing past Ineni – all wide, dark eyes and gaping mouth – without a care in the world for a Great Royal Wife's dignity. She caught herself up just before she reached the courtyard between her hall and Mutnofret's rooms. The shade of the climbing plant was deep and dark here, cool green-blue like the skin of a melon. She hid herself behind its leaves. Smoothing her gown, she drew deep breaths, eyes squeezed shut, imagining the sight of him, how he would look striding into the palace, the way he would sit on his throne, his hands laid atop the arms of the great gilded chair like the paws of a lion. She could see his face, hear his laugh. She would ride with him again in the hills beyond the city tomorrow – tonight!

Composed now, but still with a belly full of tickling moths, Ahmose ventured into the courtyard. There was no sign of Mutnofret. She wondered whether her sister had heard the news. Should Ahmose tell her? No. Let Mutnofret's servants inform the second wife. But then, Mutnofret did have every right to greet their husband; she had good news for Thutmose.

Ahmose turned toward Nofret's chambers, clapped outside the door.

Sitamun, Mutnofret's big-eyed, thin-bodied servant, opened the door.

"Is Mutnofret receiving visitors?"

"Yes, Great Lady. Please come in." The woman stood aside, bowing. Mutnofret's antechamber was not nearly so large as Ahmose's own, but richly decorated in spite of its smallness. Certainly Ahmose's servants had picked through the best of the wedding gifts for her own rooms. Still, what was left to Mutnofret lacked nothing in lush beauty. One corner of the chamber held an intimate seating area; the walls above the chairs and table were hung with fascinating paintings on red linen depicting stories of the goddesses, illustrated by a skilled hand. A tray with the leavings of a meal had yet to be cleared away. There were several bowls. Mutnofret must have entertained a group of friends only a short time ago. Ahmose waited in the center of the chamber, fists on her hips, while Sitamun gathered up the tray and straightened the furniture.

After a long time, Mutnofret drifted from her bed chamber. She wore a striking new yellow gown that clung to her, accentuating her swollen breasts, the slight rise of her belly. Her wig was heavily beaded in gold; it framed her face with an aura of light. "Sister," she said, smiling.

"I came to tell you, Mutnofret. Our husband has returned."

"Oh, that's wonderful news." Mutnofret did not sound surprised. Ahmose wondered how she had known so soon. "I suppose we ought go see him, then. But you look a proper mess — let us tidy you up before we go."

Ahmose was a mess indeed. She had been on her feet all day, walking in her garden, plucking leaves absently, tossing bread crumbs to birds, while she mulled the thoughts in her heart — thoughts of power and sons, of thrones and priests. Her gown was wrinkled, her face dry with the afternoon's dust. Mutnofret took her hand and led her into the bed chamber, sat her down at the dressing table.

"You must look the part, little sister," Mutnofret said. There was no malice in her voice. Once more she spoke as if there had never been any rift between them. *It is the child in her. It gives her assurance. She thinks I am no threat so long as I remain a virgin. But she is wrong.*

Mutnforet laid out a broad silver bowl, filled it with water from a pitcher, and unstopped a jar of soap. Ahmose washed, scooping the myrrh-scented soap into her hands, scrubbing the day's musings away.

"A royal wife is expected to be pretty and perfect all the time." Mutnofret drizzled oil into a pot, stirred in the shimmering green dust of powdered malachite. She whipped it into a paste, dipped a small brush, and gently painted Ahmose's eyelids. "Make yourself beautiful and your husband will always love you."

"You know all about being beautiful," Ahmose said. She could not keep a touch of jealousy from her voice.

Mutnofret reached for the kohl pot. She did not hesitate, but Ahmose saw a quick spark flare and die in Mutnofret's eye. Then the kohl brush came toward her, wet and sharp; Ahmose closed her eyes and allowed Mutnofret to line them with the cool, sooty kohl.

"It is a thing you can learn, too, Ahmose. You really must take more care of your appearance if you are to be the Great Royal Wife."

I am the Great Royal Wife, Ahmose thought. She said nothing.

Mutnofret applied the rouge to Ahmose's cheeks, then oiled her lips and dusted them with rouge as well. "Don't lick it all off."

"How do I look now?" Ahmose smiled timidly at her sister.

"You need another dress. Take me back to your rooms and I will help you choose one."

It was the first time Mutnofret had been inside the apartments of the Great Royal Wife since they had passed to Ahmose. The second wife looked around at the opulence, the soaring ceilings and bright-painted walls that stood at least twice as wide and high as her own rooms. Mutnofret's face remained blank but for a muscle that twitched once, twice, in her jaw.

To keep her sister's mood light, Ahmose joked and gossiped as she led Mutnofret to the wardrobe. They sorted through Ahmose's garments, Nofret casting some aside and placing others into a neat stack. Finally, she picked through the stack, considering each weave and drape in turn, and at last held up a bright blue dress of thin linen. It was nearly as thin as the one Mutnofret had worn to their wedding feast. Ahmose blushed. She only ever wore this gown about her apartments on excessively warm days. She would never consider going out into the palace dressed in it – it revealed entirely too much.

"It is awfully thin," she said in a small voice.

"Of course it is! Your body is starting to develop, Ahmose." Mutnofret sounded less than enthusiastic about the fact. "You would be wise to show it to Thutmose."

"All right."

Surely Mutnofret knew what she was doing. With Thutmose's child inside her, the second wife believed she had no more need of tricks. And this help with dressing – Ahmose truly looked beautiful now, not like a child at all. It was almost as if Nofret sought to make amends for her deception at the wedding feast. Ahmose stood still while her sister tied the dress, adjusting it two or three times until it draped just so, both revealing and concealing the features of her body. Her breasts, her hips were like brown stones under flowing water, to be glimpsed and hidden again by the wash of blue. She took a few shaky breaths while Mutnofret stepped back to look her over.

"Some jewels, I think. Where are they?"

Ahmose pointed to her jewel boxes, stacked neatly against one wall. Mutnofret's eyebrows rose; perhaps Ahmose had more than she. But all the same, Nofret kept her opinion to herself and rummaged through the boxes until she found the right pieces to complement the blue dress.

"Now you look a Great Royal Wife," she said quietly, fastening a necklace of overlapping gold leaves.

"Thank you, Nofret."

Mutnofret's answering smile was not insincere, for all its sadness.

Ahmose could not force herself to sit still in the litter. The ride from the palace to the water steps was too long, too stifling in the confines of the loose-weave curtains. She craned her neck this way and that, watching the bustle of Waset distort and blur through the linen. There was a certain energy in the streets, a shouting, a hurrying. Ahmose longed to be outside the litter, skipping through the alleys and merchants' stalls, calling out her joy with the rekhet. The king had returned. Kush was defeated. Egypt was victorious.

Mutnofret sat quietly, her hands folded in her lap, watching straight ahead as if the curtains were not there at all. Ahmose eyed her sister's face, but could think of nothing to say, and so she held her tongue. In a moment, though, Mutnofret's chin lifted slightly; her lips curved with the smallest touch of a smile. Ahmose squinted through the litter at the road in front of them. It swept downhill to the moorings. There were fish-sellers' booths here, boat-renters and children leading cattle to water. The pungent smell of the waterfront invaded the litter. Ships rocked against their restraints like horses impatient to run. One, painted white and blue with a massive upswept prow, was surely the Pharaoh's own war vessel, but through the linen Ahmose could see nothing more of it than a confusion of color and slashing shapes.

Mutnofret's smile turned into a low, melodious laugh.

"What?" Ahmose said. "What do you see?"

"Look harder, little sister."

Ahmose leaned forward, crooked a finger around the edge of the curtain. She drew it back just a bit, so a gap of unmuddled waterfront opened before her face. The great white-and-blue hulk must be Thutmose's — it was the largest ship on the river. But something strange, long and dark, was affixed to the prow. Ahmose stared. It was a tree trunk with gnarled, brittle limbs. No — in the space of another heartbeat she saw the object truly. Not a tree, but a man's body, dark and naked, desiccated, twisted. She gasped, let the curtain fall as she jolted back onto her cushion.

"Our husband is a true warrior," Mutnofret said.

"Horrible!"

"This is war, Ahmose," she said quietly. "People do horrible things when they are at war."

Ahmose did not dare look at her sister's face. She swallowed hard, and fought to still her hands in her lap while the litter crept toward the river.

Thutmose met them at the head of the water steps. Ahmose walked to him as calmly as she could, took his hand in both of hers and kissed his fingers again and again. Oh, how she had missed him, their chariot rides, their conversations over dinner. Steadfastly, she kept her eyes turned away from the prow of the ship. Her gentle, kind husband could never have hung a man's body there. She would not look at it. She would not believe it.

Mutnofret approached down the steps; her ladies trailed behind her in a fan of color, reds and sky-blues, whites and greens. Their gowns seemed chosen to set off Mutnofret's brilliant golden-yellow ever more brightly. The second wife extended her hand to Thutmose. He took it gently. She stared boldly into his eyes, laid a hand upon her stomach.

"Well." He took Mutnofret by the shoulders. "I suppose I should not be surprised."

She blushed a pretty shade and covered her mouth, laughing lightly. "I have made so many offerings, we cannot fail to have a son."

Tut shook his head, grinning, both hands stroking up and down Mutnofret's arms as if she were his cherished pet cat. "What news, what news! Nothing better to follow a war victory than a son on the way. When will he arrive?"

"Just a bit more than five moons."

"Come," Tut said. The massive royal litter had arrived. Twelve soldiers, strong and tall, lowered it to the ground at the head of the water steps. Ahmose climbed inside gratefully. Her face flushed hot at the look in Tut's eyes, the brightness of his eyes on Mutnofret's body. Tut told them amusing stories from his expedition as they rode back to the palace, and the three of them laughed as one. But Ahmose was keenly aware of how the king leaned toward Mutnofret, how his left hand busily stroked at her neck while his right lay still on Ahmose's own knee. She all but ran from the litter when they were safe within the palace's walls once more, and ground her teeth together when Tut invited her – and Mutnofret, of course – to his chamber. She ground her teeth, but she forced a smile.

Inside the Pharaoh's lush chambers, freshly scrubbed and scented with the sweet smoke of myrrh and bundles of fresh herbs, they sat together on Thutmose's long, low couch, the Pharaoh between the sisters, and shared their news. Tut told them of the battles, the journey, the treacherous travel through the white-water cataracts of Upper Egypt, the strange customs of Buhen. Mutnofret shared her pregnancy symptoms: sickness in the morning, and strange cravings. She had her eye on several young court women with big bellies who might make suitable wet nurses for the Royal Son, and these she discussed with Thutmose at great length. For Ahmose's part, she had nothing to share but a few unusual dreams she had read, and the disputes she had adjudicated in her husband's absence. Her news seemed paltry and dull in comparison to Mutnofret's child.

There was one thing she could share with Tut alone, though. When Mutnofret excused herself to the privy, she leaned in close to the king's ear. "We must go riding soon. Or take the boat out on the lake. Just you and me."

His eyes wandered down to her chest, and she shifted her shoulders, unsure whether she intended to show or hide her breasts from his view. He licked his lips.

"You have changed since I've been gone, Ahmoset." There was the shadow of a question in his words.

"Just to ride," she said quickly. "I meant, just to..."

He patted her hand. "Yes, all right. We will go riding as soon as I have the chance."

"Tonight! I have missed you so."

Tut barked his laugh, a sound that made her bite her lips to hide her foolish smile. "Eager! Well, I confess I could use a good, swift chariot ride after all the time I've spent on that blasted boat." Mutnofret returned, golden, ripe; she remained standing, smiling at Thutmose, one coy hand playing with a braided strand of her wig. "I will see you later tonight, Ahmoset, and we will take that ride."

Ahmose's face fell. Was she being dismissed? Perhaps Tut needed to rest or eat. The journey must have been very hard, in the heat of the day. "Yes, of course. Mutnofret, we should leave our husband to rest."

Mutnofret laughed, a low, hollow sound. She cut her eyes toward Ahmose, a look that said, *Foolish child!* Tut was at Mutnofret's side now, cat-petting her bare arms again, without so much as a glance for Ahmose. Nofret stared steadily at her over Tut's shoulder. There was a fire of victory in her eyes, a desperate greed, a reveling. *Your body may be changing,* those eyes said, *but I am still the one he wants.*

Ahmose backed toward the chamber doors. She did not break Mutnofret's gaze until Thutmose kissed her neck, and Nofret's eyes closed.

CHAPTER FOURTEEN

AHMOSE HAD LONG SINCE CHANGED out of the flimsy blue gown – *Useless*, she thought, kicking it across the floor – and into something more suitable for riding. Still Thutmose remained with her sister. An hour passed, then two. She crept up to her roof, dejected, and leaned on the parapet, watching the slim crescent of the moon drift against an emerging field of stars. The sky had gone violet with the approach of night.

A timid voice called from the stair head. "Great Lady?" Ineni approached her, mouse-like and halting. She waved to him in greeting. She tried to summon a smile, but could not conjure up even the ghost of one.

Her steward rested his forearms on the parapet, gazing as she did into the night sky. The last breath of day still clung to the horizon, a smudge of blue, the careless finger of Waser dragged across the space between heaven and earth.

"You are sad, Great Lady."

"Please call me Ahmose. I have had enough of *Great Lady* for now."

Ineni said nothing, as if his silence could coax out an admission of all that troubled her. The quiet lay heavily on the roof as the day died, the blue at the horizon's edge fading to dense black. At last she spoke. "You were right, that day when we visited Nefertari. Whoever bears sons will have Thutmose's heart. And even at my most beautiful, even when I look like a woman and not a girl – no, hear me," for Ineni

129

had stirred as if he would object, "even then I cannot hold his eye with Mutnofret beside me. How can he *want* to come to my bed, even if I invite him? He has *her*. And who is more beautiful than Mutnofret?"

Ineni looked away. Insects whirred in the gardens below. She remembered Aiya, the sound of the women in the birthing pavilion, the humming of the flies, the smell of the place. The knife in the physician's hand.

"In any case, I shall not bear a son. It is not for me. That is not what the gods have chosen for Ahmose." Even as she spoke these words in despair, her skin tingled with a thrill of truth. Somehow it seemed Ahmose herself had always known she would never bear sons. Now, here in the emptiness of the night, she gave voice to her secret thoughts and the gods heard her. She had spoken their will into being.

"And the throne? Ahmose?" Ineni's voice was soft.

The throne. She remembered her mother on the Horus Throne, how it had shocked Ahmose to see a woman sitting there. A woman wielding power just like a man – just like a king. And she recalled Nefertari, standing dark and quiet beside the throne. She saw it again, as clearly as if she dreamed it. Nefertari's hand on the queen's shoulder. Nefertari silencing Meritamun on the funeral barge. Power – power that she wielded like a king.

"If I do not have the throne, Thutmose will eventually have no use at all for me. Even if I cannot have his love, I can share in the ruling of Egypt. And ruling Egypt is, after all, what the gods have chosen for me. No, I must not give up the throne." With her grandmother's power she could help Tut, guide him. She could take half the work, leave him more time to be free, to ride his chariot in the hills and sail his boat, to make love to Mutnofret and raise his children. She could take half the weight of Egypt onto her back – half the weight and more. She could give him this, if she could not give him sons. "That will be enough for me. But I must have something more than a son, if he is to keep me as his Great Royal Wife." She turned to her steward, truly saw his quiet face and solemn eyes for the first time that evening. She saw the intelligence burning in those dark, wide eyes like embers of offered myrrh. "Ineni, the gods sent you to me. I have a plan. It will take time – a good amount of time – and it must remain secret always. Can I trust you? Will you help me?"

Ineni's hand jerked as though it were under some strange power of its own; it crept toward her arm. One thin, cool finger brushed so lightly against her wrist. A moth's touch; she barely felt it at all. "I am yours to command," he whispered.

Thutmose came to see her long after Ineni had departed. He came alone, without stewards or guards. She knew it was her husband before he reached the rooftop; his steps were too hesitant on the stairs to be those of a servant, too heavy to be those of a woman. She said nothing as he approached. She did not smile in welcome, though she knew she ought.

"I am sorry it's so late. I should have come sooner."

"No doubt you had better things to do than go riding in the hills with a child."

"You are no child." His mouth twisted into a sardonic smile. "You have changed."

"I have."

"I have missed our rides, Ahmose, and sailing, and sharing dinner together. I always feel closer to the gods when I am with you. You put me at ease."

These words slapped at her, stung her. They were all her heart longed to hear, yet he belonged to Mutnofret. His body craved Mutnofret. His eyes were for Mutnofret. He would sooner have Mutnofret as his first wife, as his Great Royal Wife, now that he knew the elder sister was the true woman – now that he knew Mutnofret would give him a son. His love for the second wife would grow, and soon enough, as soon as the people were satisfied that Thutmose was as strong on the throne as he was on the field of battle, the Pharaoh would set Ahmose aside.

Set aside – no matter what he had promised so long before. Never to ride with him again, never to laugh with him again; back to the harem, disgraced, to live forever in Mutnofret's long shadow. The thought tore at her stomach. She pressed one hand there, tightly to push away the pain. He seemed to take the gesture for girlish excitement. Confident, he stepped forward and cupped her chin, raised her face to look up at him. Something in her look made him stop with his mouth half-open. Whatever words he had been about to say wilted on his tongue.

"Do you remember the first time we rode together at night?" she said.

He was still holding her face, still held by the intensity of her eyes. He nodded.

"I knew then that I loved you. But as surely as I know I love you, so I also know that I will not give you any sons, Tut."

The conviction of her words made his hand drop from her chin. His brows came together in confusion. "But you will."

She shook her head. "I tell you this now so you can set me aside now, if that is what you wish."

He laughed, but it was a small laugh, a puff of air. "Set you aside? What kind of foolishness is this?"

"Mutnofret would make a better Great Royal Wife."

"No she would not, Ahmose. Mutnofret may be beautiful, but she has nothing of a Great Royal Wife in her ka. She cares about gossip and appearances and not much else. You – you ruled Egypt while I was gone."

"With the help of the stewards, yes. And with Mutnofret's help. She took it seriously, Tut; I asked for her guidance several times and she always made wise choices."

"But she did not pass final judgment, Ahmose. I have been a general long enough to know how these things go. Ruling an army is not much different from ruling a country. The final word is the general's to speak, even though he receives wise counsel from those around him. The final word in every dispute was yours. You made all the choices. Mutnofret might have ruled differently – probably would have, knowing her – and would Egypt have fared so well under her rule?"

Though she bore little love for her sister anymore, Ahmose did not think Tut's judgment was quite fair. Mutnofret was a gossip and as ill-tempered as a snake, but she was not unmindful of justice. Nofret had believed her whole life she would end up on the throne. She had been trained for the role, educated in justice and in rule. No matter what Tut supposed, the advice the second wife had given at court had been useful. She was a woman capable of judging wisely and fairly. Ahmose may be the only person in the world who could look past Mutnofret's flaws to see her potential, but to Ahmose, the truth was plain.

Still she could not bring herself to oppose Tut – not in this. There *was* something about Mutnofret that all who knew her surely could see. Meritamun had named it on the day Ahmose had gone to her to plead on Mutnofret's behalf. The second wife was full of heat, a fire that might burn out of control at any moment. The same flame did not burn within Ahmose. She was deliberate, calm. Perhaps this did make her more suited to rule, but there was yet the problem of a Great Royal Wife's chief duty.

"Still, Tut, if I will not give you any sons then I am not a fit Great Royal Wife."

Thutmose sighed. He ducked under the pavilion's loose-weave screens and sat upon a cushion.

Ahmose stared at him.

"Well?" he said. "Isn't this where you read your dreams?"

"You want me to read a dream?"

He nodded, bringing her inside with a curt wave. She sat, uncertain, on a cushion across from him. In the wan light of the slivered moon, every thread of the pavilion's screens stood out in sharp relief, so that Thutmose seemed surrounded by the filaments of a glowing spider's web, a creature from the dream-world.

"Here is the dream I have dreamed many times since I

became general, Ahmose – since I first met your father.

"I am climbing a steep hill above the valley. I am near death; there is some enemy behind me who I cannot see. He is reaching for me, though, and I know that my time in the living world is almost at an end. I reach the top of the hill to find a woman is standing there. Her back is always to me, and she is holding something in her arms.

"When she turns, a holy light surrounds her. She holds a baby – a boy. The boy wears the double crown; he looks at me and smiles; he reaches out for me. He knows me. I am his father.

"A voice says from the sky, 'The soul of Re is righteousness. Be at peace, Thutmose. Even as you die, your son, the Pharaoh, restores righteousness to the land.'

"I always see the face of the woman who holds my son. I know she is his mother. It is your face, Ahmose. It has always been your face."

The soul of Re is righteousness. The words rang in Ahmose's heart, a bell's peal at the breaking of day. *Maat-ka-re.*

"When I first saw you," Tut went on, "a child at court, I could at last put a name to the face of the woman in my dream. You were still young, but your face has always been the same. This beloved face..." he reached out to brush her cheek "...the same one I saw in my dream. At first I thought it blasphemy even to dream that dream, though what control does a man have over the things he sees in his sleep? I was only a general, born into a rekhet family, dreaming of fathering a child with the Pharaoh's daughter. But the vision would not go away. It came again and again, many nights in a row. I could never escape it.

"But that night – our ride – I knew it was a true dream. You told me your name that night as we rode through the fields, and the sound of your name was like a spear in my guts. I could see the boy in your arms, there in my chariot, and on the hill while I watched you sleep. I know you were shocked like everybody else when your mother named me the heir. But I was not. I know you were surprised when she named you Great Royal Wife in Mutnofret's place. I was not. How else could you give me a son, a boy who will be Pharaoh, unless I became the king, and you my Great Royal Wife?

"The gods have a purpose for us, Ahmoset. They brought us together, against all the conventions of mankind. They want me to get a son from you. They require it. It is my purpose in this life; it is your purpose. The child we will make together: that is what we both live for."

Ahmose leaned back on her hands, as if she might physically pull away from Thutmose's dream. The images buffeted her; she was a barque in a wind storm, tossed and endangered. Yet Ahmose felt the glowing inside, the deep river currents of the gods' voices as Tut spoke.

She looked steadily at her husband, as if she could read the future in the lines of his bluff face. "I...I don't know what the dream means. I need time to pray about it."

"I know what it means."

"I need time," she said forcefully. Inside, her heart and ka snarled at one another like dogs fighting in the market. *Mutnofret is the better wife*, her heart said. *Stand aside now while you still have some dignity left to you*. But her ka insisted, *I will do anything for Tut's love*.

Thutmose nodded. "Know this, Ahmose. I will not set you aside. I told you this before, and I say it again now. Whatever you think of Mutnofret, I know who I want for my Great Royal Wife and the mother of my heir."

She struggled to make sense of his words through the haze of her confusion. "Then...you will not make Mutnofret's child your heir?"

"None of us knows what the gods intend. Not even you, I think – not all the time. I hope the child will be healthy, but babies die. Or it could be a daughter. I can marry Mutnofret's daughter to your son one day. To our son."

This news, that Tut intended only a child of Ahmose's body to be his heir, should have filled her with happiness. Instead, her heart broke for Mutnofret. For all her deceptions, for all her mean spirit, Nofret was her sister. And she, Ahmose, had already taken Nofret's throne. Now, through none of her own choosing, she would take away her sister's right to birth Egypt's heir, too. "I cannot do this to Mutnofret, Tut. Don't ask me to do this."

He reached across the space between them. Moving in spite of her doubts, responding like an animal to its master, she reached, too, and his hands grasped hers. "It is the will of the gods, Ahmoset. We do as they direct us, don't we?"

She nodded. She wanted to shake her head, but she nodded.

"I promise you, I will only do as the gods bid. If they change their minds – if I have interpreted my dream wrong, and Mutnofret is to be the mother of my heir after all – I will do as they direct me."

"Name her child heir, Thutmose. You must."

"This is why I need you, Ahmose. I need you to tell me what the gods want. You are closer to their hearts than I. You can help me see their will."

"Name her child heir."

"Is that what the gods tell you?"

She licked her lips. She could say nothing.

"That is what I thought. We will wait for a sign from the gods, shall we? There is no rush for me to choose an heir. I am still young and strong enough that we need not fear. We will wait, you and I, until we know for sure. Until then, it does no harm for Mutnofret to believe what she will."

If Tut was right, and the gods would demand a son of Ahmose's body, then allowing Mutnofret to believe a lie would only cause her more pain in the end. But it was easier, here and now, to let the sleeping lioness rest.

"But the rest of them, Tut – the nobles, the priests, the rekhet. They do not need me by your side. Once they know you can protect Egypt on your own..."

"Then they will know I am their Pharaoh in truth. My word will be law. My Great Royal Wife will be who I say she is."

He still did not understand, for all his protestations. A

country was not an army. There was no absolute ruler. The currents of politics were more subtle, more strong and swift than those he was used to navigating. For that reason alone, he *did* still need her, for now, at any rate. She could see where the king was blind.

She nodded, squeezed his hands.

He smiled a dog's smile. "So, about making that son."

She laughed, despite the tangle of emotions, the pressure in her stomach. "I really do need to pray about your dream, Tut."

"You should pray, then," he said, and helped her to her feet. He tilted her chin up and up until her throat tightened. His breath fell on her cheek; his lips met hers. She let his tongue into her mouth, pressed her mouth hard against his. *I can feel his teeth*, she thought, giddy, afire; then the pavilion curtain swung and she was alone again, with the hum of insect voices and the distant susurrus of the river making music with her pounding heart.

CHAPTER FIFTEEN

MOTHER OF THE PHARAOH.
The voice was rich, black. Ahmose saw nothing but a river of stars.

Mother of the Pharaoh, why do you weep?

She reached out her arms the way a child reaches for its nurse. Comfort was what she wanted – reassurance, a soft embrace, a sweet cake to soothe her. Her face prickled with the salt of her tears.

Mother of the Pharaoh, rise up. Come to me.

She lay on her back, she now realized, looking at the sky; the thick band of celestial light arced above her. Her hands stretched toward it, a child's plea for help. Shaking, crying, she stood.

This was no place she knew. There was no hint of a city, no trace of men or women. Yet this was Egypt. The soil beneath her bare toes was as black as char, and it vibrated with life. Each step she took stirred up the scent of crushed herbs, wet stone, barley fields after the harvest. Somewhere before her in the black night, the river breathed, a living ka. Beyond it, giving up their heat to the darkness, the red hills of the desert crouched in torpor.

The voice drew her on.

Mother of the Pharaoh, lady of sorrow, bringer of the high waters.

Her feet sank into mud. She kept walking, pulling the hem of her dress high, then dropping it again as the mud became too deep and heavy to walk through easily. Her arms waved, her body tipped; each foot came free from the hot, black earth with a sucking sound and she plunged her feet back in again. Ankles, calves, knees, caked and wet. Dress stained. She did not care. *The voice.*

Now the mud grew thinner, cooler; now it moved so lightly against her skin. The clinging mud washed from her legs. Her dress floated on the water's surface. Still she pushed forward until the current tugged at her and she wavered against it. The water's chill surrounded her thighs, pierced the place between her legs. She gasped.

A figure stood upon the surface of the river, facing away, gazing out toward the red cliffs that marked the boundary of the Black Land. Its hips were wide and curved like the ribs of a harp. Where its feet touched water the stars' reflections split and ran, sailing downstream, a hundred thousand barges voyaging. It stood upon a river of light.

The figure turned, perfect face looking down on the creature trembling in the river. Vultures' wings cradled an infant that glowed like the sun.

Mut.

You would know your fate. You have already spoken it. Weeping child, do you never listen?

Mut's obsidian eyes closed, a slow, deliberate blink. When they opened, they were as blue as the midday sky. *You will bear no sons, Mother of the Pharaoh.*

The goddess took one perfect step toward her, another, another. The stars beneath the divine feet pooled and scurried away with the river's flow, as if Mut's brightness shamed them. With each step the goddess took he poor beast in the river sagged lower with the weight of awe, the beautiful burden of worship. Ahmose would have slipped under the water's surface and drifted away like a star, but the water held her up.

The goddess bent and placed the child of light in her arms. The creature of the river, this lowly thing, transfixed by glory, held the golden babe close to her heart. She looked into its face. In its eyes were all the floods, all the emergences, all the peace, all the war, all the people of Egypt crying out in sadness and in joy. Its right eye was righteousness, its left, salvation. Its lungs breathed the sweet breath of life. Its tiny fat hand flexed, formed a fist. The river roared, roared in Ahmose's ears, roared its tribute. The child opened its mouth, and its voice was the river's voice.

The bitter cold of her antechamber floor woke Ahmose. The chill had crawled inside her. Every muscle was cramped; her mouth was dry. She lay crumpled in a heap, face pressed against the floor, legs curled, breasts painful against the tiles. The lower portion of her ribs felt bruised; they had dug into the hard tile floor. With shaky arms she raised herself. Her legs tingled as blood flowed back into them.

She must have exhausted herself. She had prayed so fervently for a reading of Thutmose's dream that she had worn herself out and fallen forward onto the great emblem of Mut worked into the antechamber floor. Her god statues stood mute, looking down on her from the table where she had enshrined them. Nearby, her offering brazier was cold and dark. Greasy ash coated its inner surface. The faintest smell of blackened meat still hung about the room.

Ahmose had no idea how long she had lain on the floor. Her body was all knots and aches, stiff and clumsy. The tingling in her legs made her totter painfully all the way into her bed chamber, where the barred wall admitted dawn's pink light. She threw herself onto her bed without undressing, but restful sleep evaded her.

Massaging the pains out of her arms and legs, Ahmose considered Mut's message. To look upon the goddess's face had been more than she could bear. Even now, safe in her bed in the waking world, she felt as though her body might break from the impossible, sweet, terrible strain of worship. She squeezed her eyes shut. She could push away the image of the goddess, but not the image of the child.

There was no answer here – only more questions. She could not be the mother of the Pharaoh if she would bear no sons. Yet Mut could not lie. What was the riddle here? Would some ill fate befall Mutnofret, so that Ahmose must raise her sister's child as her own? That seemed most likely, most apt to fit the goddess's words. And Tut's dream – who knew? He could have been mistaken about the identity of the dream-mother. It could well be Mutnofret he saw, in spite of his insistence that it was Ahmose. Mutnofret was far more beautiful, but the sisters shared a certain harmony of features. In the dream world they might be mistaken for one another. One who was not god-chosen could not always trust his own interpretation of a dream.

Lady of sorrow, she called me. That filled her with a stab of fear. If something befell Mutnofret...she would indeed mourn, yes. Mutnofret was her sister, after all, and had once been Ahmose's friend. Even now, after all their bitter rivalries, to lose her would be the greatest sadness Ahmose could imagine.

Was this the answer, then? Would Ahmose become mother of the Pharaoh when the heir's true mother died? No; even that was not clear. Her god-dreams were always as clear as a mirror's reflection. This one was still a haze; she could discern no meaning at all.

It is not time to make my move. Not yet. But I mustn't stop preparations, either. Ineni must be allowed to continue. Until I know for certain what the goddess meant, I must keep on as I have planned. Mutnofret could be hiding any trick at all under her wig, and Ahmose must not be made to look foolish again.

Suddenly restless despite her aches, Ahmose levered herself up out of bed and shook the weakness out of her legs. It was still too early for many servants to be about. Her own women would still be abed. She wandered out of her hall, hesitating at the foot of the roof-stairs. But no – it was not her pavilion she wanted this morning. She crossed the courtyard and entered the palace proper, wending through corridors only dimly lit by morning's glow. Columns reached golden-hued into the deep blue shadows above her. Servants rustled in the dimmest corners, rousing to their early duties.

The rear door to the throne room stood barely ajar. She crept up on it, peered into the dense purple dimness of the great hall. From her vantage, to the side of the dais at the room's head, she could just make out the two gilded thrones and the dim suggestion of the crook and flail standing in their supports.

Mutnofret had seated herself on the throne of the Great Royal Wife, shrouded in shadows. Her form became truer as the darkness receded. Back straight, chin tipped high, Nofret stared out across the empty room. Her eyes blazed with a distant fire, as though her ka saw a hundred thousand subjects kneeling before her. She raised a hand, graceful and strong as a leopard, pronouncing judgment upon nothing.

Quietly, Ahmose backed away from the door. Her heart turned to a sharp blade. She could be the passive younger sister no more. Soon she must put her hand on Mutnofret's shoulder, and her grip must be unbreakable.

CHAPTER SIXTEEN

*Y*OUR MOTHER'S TIME TO DEPART *grows near. Her breathing grows ever more difficult. I fear she will not live another month.*

Ahmose read Nefertari's letter with the dull ache of regret smoldering in her heart. Meritamun had been a great ruler, if a distant mother. Her death would be a loss to Egypt. And poor Nefertari – she would outlive every one of her children, it seemed.

Ahmose rolled the papyrus carefully and laid it on the table beside her couch. A few more were stacked there: a week's worth of notes from her grandmother. She had been corresponding with Nefertari for months now, sending the news of the palace up the river to the old woman's estate. It was not purely for the pleasure of it. Ineni would arrive soon to collect the letters.

"Mutnofret's woman is here." Twosre stood in the threshold between bedroom and antechamber, a hand on her angular hip. Her stance said, *Shall I send her away with a kick to her rump?*

Relations had not improved between Ahmose and Mutnofret. As Mutnofret's belly grew larger, so did her sense of entitlement. She was more vocal at court, often speaking up before Ahmose had a chance. Thutmose had noticed. His eyebrows would raise sometimes when Mutnofret jumped in with her judgments before the Great Royal Wife had been consulted. Mutnofret no longer maintained her proper demeanor in public dealings, but a king's daughter and the mother of the Pharaoh's unborn child could hardly be chastised in front of the court. Whether Tut ever reprimanded her privately, Ahmose did not know. She often wanted to ask, but balked at the thought of looking so weak in her husband's eyes.

Instead she avoided Mutnofret entirely. Before she left her rooms, she sent Twosre into the courtyard as a scout to report on Mutnofret's whereabouts. If the second wife was lounging there – as she often did, with one eye on Ahmose's hall – Ahmose would take another route, or retreat to her garden to wait Mutnofret out. When Ahmose took to her roof-top pavilion and Mutnofret came to call, she was politely but firmly denied access; Ineni gave her one excuse after another until at last she gave up and went away.

So it was that the sisters hardly saw one another at all outside of court. It seemed to Ahmose that Mutnofret's belly grew in leaps, noticeably larger and more accusatory at each successive court session. During the course of her pregnancy Mutnofret had become a stranger to Ahmose, an invader in the palace, but she seemed content to harry Ahmose only now and again. For the most part she left her alone, apparently happy to have confined Ahmose to solitude and to inflict occasional embarrassment at court.

Never before has the second wife sent a servant directly to Ahmose's rooms.

Ahmose stood and gestured to Twosre, a command to bring the servant. Twosre was gone only a moment, and returned trailing the woman Sitamun.

"How is the second wife?"

The skinny woman bounced on the balls of her feet. She looked like an undersized carp jigging in the net. "Oh, Great Lady! You must come at once. Lady Mutnofret's pains have begun!"

"Where is she?"

"In her rooms. I have sent for a physician already, but my lady calls for you. Please hurry!"

A clap sounded outside the entrance to her apartments.

Ahmose sent Twosre to answer it, then laid a hand on Sitamun's shoulder. "It will be well. The goddess Tawaret is with my sister." She was not entirely certain whether the words were meant to soothe Sitamun or herself.

"Your steward," Twosre announced. Ineni was close behind her. Quick as always, he had caught the room's tense atmosphere; his eyebrows arched in a silent question.

Ahmose shook her head slightly. "There is no time for us now, dear Ineni. My sister's child is on the way. These are for you." She scooped Nefertari's scrolls up and pressed them into his hands. "Come to me tonight, please. We have much to discuss. Now, Sitamun, go back to Mutnofret and tell her I am coming. I will make an offering to Tawaret first. I will be as quick as I can."

Twosre caught Ahmose's eye with a flat stare. "You look pale, Great Lady."

"I am well."

"Do you want me to accompany you, Lady?"

"No, thank you. I will manage on my own." The door shut softly behind Ineni and the anxious Sitamun. "It will be good for me, I am sure, to see another birth. One that goes well," she said firmly, as if her words could make it so.

Ahmose stood for a long time outside Mutnofret's door. Even through the thick limestone walls, the muffled sounds beyond the door had a feeling of urgency, of strain. She could make out no words, but the rustle and bump, the murmur, the tension of the half-formed sounds brought her close to panic. Mut's dream-words prodded at her heart, scrabbled for a hold upon her ka. *Lady of sorrow. Mother of the Pharaoh, you will bear no sons.* She would not let the words in. She would not! Mutnofret would be well. All would be well. Ahmose breathed deeply, rubbed her fingers back and forth over the Tawaret charm she had tucked into her blue linen belt.

Finally, before the last thread of her courage could snap, she pushed the door open.

The anteroom was empty. The door to Mutnofret's bedroom hung half open, and the forms of many women passed back and forth across the gap. Ahmose made for it with the pounding heart of a soldier going into battle.

The moment she was inside Mutnofret's bedroom, the scene of Aiya's death sprang up before her eyes. The frightened urgency of the women was the same. The dense air of dread was the same. The same holed seat sat in one corner. Was Mutnofret in some trouble, then, too? Would she also die under a hideous knife? *No. No, it will be different. All will be well.*

"Ahmose." Mutnofret's voice called from somewhere in the press of women. She went toward it.

Nofret lay on her bed, naked, wigless, eyes shut. Her stomach was enormous, a great, swollen thing painted all around with dark lines where the skin had stretched. A midwife bent over the second wife to dab a cool cloth against her cheeks, and Nofret tossed her head. She called for Ahmose again.

"I am here, sister." A hundred painful thoughts had run through Ahmose's mind before she entered these rooms. As she had prayed to Tawaret, she had wondered whether Mutnofret had only summoned her here to play another cruel game with her, to renew her fear of birth. But now – now, seeing Mutnofret in such distress, so helpless, she wanted only to ease her sister's fears. She took her hand and squeezed.

"You must try to relax, Great Lady." A woman bent over Mutnofret, patting her forehead with another damp cloth. Well into the season of Peret, the days were cool and pleasant; yet here in the confines of Mutnofret's room, with so many women crowded around the bed, the air was stifling. "Relax everything, right down to your bones."

Mutnofret's stomach tensed, heaving; she groaned deep in her throat. Her hand tightened around Ahmose's fingers.

"What is going on? Tell me what's happening," Ahmose

demanded.

"She has begun her labor, Great Lady. The baby is making his way to the door."

"I know that. What is it doing to my sister?"

"Tiring her; that is all."

"When will the baby be out?"

"I do not know, Great Lady," the midwife said. With a shiver, Ahmose recognized the same woman who had presided over Aiya's doomed delivery. "Only the gods know. Some babies come very quickly; a few hours. Others take days."

"*Days?*" Her head spun at the thought of any woman remaining in such a state for *days*.

"The second wife is young. This is her first child. I think perhaps he will not arrive until late in the night-time."

Mutnofret panted. Her arms went limp. The pain had subsided, it seemed. Ahmose began to sweat from the heat of so many bodies.

"Are so many women necessary right now, if the baby won't arrive until night?"

The midwife looked annoyed at so many questions, but Ahmose was the Great Royal Wife, and could not be brushed away. "No," she said hesitantly. "Your sister, Great Lady. She ordered that we all attend her."

"She needs fresh air." *We all do, gods know.* "Clear some space."

"She may walk, Great Lady. It would do her good. It will speed the baby's coming. We have tried to coax her out of bed, but she refused."

"Get up, Mutnofret."

Nofret groaned and shook her head side to side.

"Mutnofret, you cannot stay like this until night. Get up and walk with me in your garden. You should be in a proper birthing pavilion, not here." She tugged on Nofret's hand. Slowly, carefully, still with her eyes squeezed shut, Mutnofret sat, then stood. The midwife helped Ahmose guide her to the garden door. The fresh air roused her; her eyes opened and she took several deep, shaking breaths. "Why is she in her rooms and not in the women's garden?"

"Great Lady, she refused to go."

"But the birthing pavilion is in the women's garden."

"Of course, Great Lady, but..."

"It's improper for the second wife to give birth squatting on her bed like a rekhet. Set up a pavilion out here, in Mutnofret's own garden," Ahmose said, struggling not to shout. Why should she have to tell these women their business?

The women buzzed, then one spoke up. "Great Lady, it will take time, and we haven't the supplies."

"Do you know my steward Ineni?"

The woman nodded.

"Tell him Ahmose commands him to procure the supplies this very hour. He will make it happen. Jump! The Great Royal Wife has given you orders!"

The midwife offered to walk with them, but Ahmose waved her off. Mutnofret seemed to be regaining some strength, now that she was out in the cool garden air. Ahmose tucked herself under Nofret's arm; they took steady, even steps back and forth through the garden. It was a pretty place, peaceful and private, if rather small and confined. Mutnofret took measured breaths. Now that she had a task her mind seemed to focus and her fear dispel.

"Thank you for coming," she said weakly.

"Of course."

"I know...I know you dislike birth."

Ahmose said nothing.

"It means much to me that you are here." She stopped abruptly, groaning.

"Lean on me," Ahmose said. Mutnofret sagged into her. The full weight nearly buckled Ahmose's knees. She stood very still while the pain took its course, then subsided. Mutnofret straightened, and Ahmose bent her knees one after the other to ease her own pain.

"I do think the walking helps. At least it gives me something else to think about." Mutnofret tried a tiny laugh.

"Have you thought of a name?" Ahmose asked, a further

distraction.

"I haven't wanted to. I thought to name him before he was born might curse him."

Or her. Ahmose smiled. "With all the praying you have done, I doubt this baby could be cursed."

They walked a long time. The midwife brought chairs outside so they could rest, but always chivvied Mutnofret back to her feet after a few minutes. Ahmose began to grow tired, and the midwife's assistant took her place, propping Nofret up, supporting her through the pains.

"I am glad you came, Great Lady," the midwife said as they watched the scene in the garden. "I believe we never would have gotten her out of that bed. It is dangerous to delay labor in that manner. So many things can go wrong."

Ahmose did not want to think about that.

The afternoon stretched on. At last, poles and bolts of cloth arrived. Gratefully, Ahmose set about directing the servants in setting up a makeshift pavilion. Soon its walls were waving gently in the cool breeze.

"Now you are ready to give birth like a proper lady," Ahmose said to Mutnofret, taking over walking duties again. She expected a wan smile, but Nofret's eyes were half closed and she breathed heavily, moaning with each breath. Sweat glistened on her lip and forehead. "I can't do this," she muttered.

"What?" Ahmose leaned closer.

"I can't. I can't do it!"

"Mutnofret. Of course you can."

"Anupu take me!" Her voice rose to a wail. Ahmose shrank back, cringing from the words, from the change in her sister's behavior. A moment ago Mutnofret had been plodding about as resolute as Hathor's cow, and now she was crying out to die! *So this is how it starts. How the danger begins.* Mutnofret would die, huge, frightened, in pain, and Ahmose would live the rest of her life knowing she let her sister go to her tomb without ever truly mending the break in their love. The midwife and her women leapt into action, steering Ahmose away, surrounding Mutnofret, guiding her to the pavilion. One brought the ugly stool from inside Mutnofret's bed chamber; another struck a small brazier alight and tossed herbs into the fire. One woman piled linens inside the pavilion. They were just like the linens that had soaked up Aiya's blood.

If Nofret could not do this thing – Nofret, the brave one, the brash one – then what woman could? Dizziness took hold of Ahmose's head. She clutched at something hard and steady – the back of one of the chairs. Her legs trembled.

"Come, Great Lady, come," the midwife said to Mutnofret, easing her toward the pavilion where death waited.

Nofret screamed.

Blackness crept up before Ahmose's eyes, obscuring Mutnofret's feet, legs, the obscene swell of her belly, and finally her face, mouth stretched open in a wail of pain that Ahmose no longer heard. The world had gone silent.

"Ahmose. Great Lady." The voice was a whisper. A hand shook her shoulder. She sat up in her own bed, and cried out in pain as a white fire leapt into her head just above her left ear. The room was awash in late afternoon light. It hurt her eyes. Ineni perched on a stool beside her.

"What happened?"

"They tell me you fainted. You hit your head on a chair. No one could leave Mutnofret, so somebody called for me."

"You carried me back?"

He flushed. "With the help of a guard."

"Where is Twosre?"

"Gone to help with the birthing."

"My sister?"

"Last I heard, she is doing well. The midwives are not afraid for her."

It was good news, but she felt only dread. The look on Mutnofret's face. Her scream. She had implored Anupu to take her life away. "I can never do it, Ineni."

His look darted from her eyes to her lips to her hands, as if he might find some words to say there. He reached out to pat the back of her hand awkwardly. The gesture was so sweet, so informal, that she lost all countenance and threw her arms around his neck with a childish impulsivity. Tears stung her eyes. Ineni's arms were around her in an instant. He rocked her very gently. Finally he pulled back, a stony look on his face. He would not meet her eye.

"I saw Aiya die, and now Mutnofret in the same state, calling out for death. I cannot bear a child."

"But it will cost you the throne. Sooner or later, it will. If Mutnofret has a son – when she has a son – it will cost you everything."

"No, it will not. You have the letters? And the feathers?"

"It is a hard thing. Few hunters are taking the right kinds of birds. It will take longer than I had hoped, unless..."

"Only egrets and sea-birds. No ibis. No vultures. Those are sacred."

"Sea-birds do not come so far south. Not often."

"Can you send to the north for feathers?"

"Ah, I can try."

She nodded. It would take time to make the right preparations, but it would work. It had to work. She and Ineni had devised the cleverest plan under the sun. It would not fail. She thought of Nefertari, of Meritamun dying, and shoved away creeping guilt. She had no time for guilt. No time, if she was to save her place in this world – her place at Tut's side. *People do horrible things when they are at war.*

"Keep working at it," she said. "I know now I cannot bear a child. Whatever the Pharaoh's dream meant – whatever my dream meant – I cannot bear a child. This is my only way to hold on."

CHAPTER SEVENTEEN

WHEN TWOSRE BROUGHT THE NEWS that a Royal Son was born, Ahmose sent the servant away. Not in anger, but so that she could have privacy to reflect upon what she would say, what she would do. As she sat quietly in her garden, stretching her legs along a bench beneath a canopy of winter-dried vines, nursing her aching head with wine and honey, Twosre arrived with more news. Baketamun's child had come early that morning, just hours after the Royal Son. A girl.

She remained in her garden for some time, alone, preparing to meet her nephew. She took great care with her appearance, just as Mutnofret had taught her, applying her paints with a careful hand, choosing the most select of her gowns, the most impressive of her jewels. When she looked the part of the Great Royal Wife, she departed for Mutnofret's apartments.

Mutnofret welcomed Ahmose into her bed chamber. The second wife walked stiffly and sat on her bed with great care, wincing, but the smile hardly left her face. Ahmose was dimly glad for her sister's happiness, but inwardly, she frowned at the wrinkled red baby lying on the bed. Mutnofret scooped him up and pulled a heavy breast free of her loose white gown. The boy sucked and smacked loudly. Mutnofret grinned.

"What are we to call the new Royal Son?" Ahmose asked, watching the greedy little thing wave his weak hands.

"Wadjmose. His name is Wadjmose."

"He looks healthy and strong."

Mutnofret looked up, a reply on her lips. Then her smile widened. She was looking past Ahmose's shoulder. She laughed; not her usual throaty, low laugh, but a girlish giggle. Ahmose didn't need to look around to know that the Pharaoh had arrived to greet his son.

"Well!" Thutmose brushed by Ahmose to sit at Mutnofret's side. His weight pulled the bed down so that Mutnofret's body slanted against his. She leaned her head on his shoulder for a brief moment, and he reached around her back to pull her in tighter. Ahmose chewed her lip. "He is a fine boy," Tut said, his voice rounded and warmed by pride.

"Wadjmose," Mutnofret said.

"A perfect name." Tut reached to touch the boy. Without releasing the nipple, Wadjmose clutched a wrinkled fist around Tut's finger. "Strong grip! The gods are good; he has his father's hands. Let us hope he does not grow up to have his father's teeth!"

Ahmose stepped closer, determined not to be overlooked. "Have you chosen a wet nurse yet, Mutnofret?"

"I had a few in mind, but I don't have to make a decision for a few days. Oh, it would be divine to nurse him forever!"

"You'll ruin your breasts," Ahmose said sensibly. "What about Baketamun? She gave birth to your daughter early this morning, Thutmose."

"Did she? I am doubly blessed! Has a man ever had a finer day?"

"I cannot take Baketamun out of the House of Women to nurse my child. She won't want her breasts ruined, either. She is the daughter of a great man, after all. No, it will have to be a servant. I suppose if none of the women in the palace can do it, I can find a nurse from among the rekhet."

Ahmose was annoyed. If she could get Baketamun's daughter into the court, perhaps Wadjmose would lose his novelty, and some of his inevitable power over the nobles – and over Thutmose.

"You won't want to take the time away from caring for

him, though, to find a nurse." Tut said. "You only have a few days to nurse him, after all. Ahmoset, why don't you find the Royal Son's nurse? I know you will choose a good one."

The last thing Ahmose wanted to do was interview big-breasted rekhet to nurse her treacherous nephew, but she was so pleased to hear her name on Tut's lips that she nodded like a fool. "That's a wonderful idea."

"Oh, will you, Ahmoset?" Mutnofret beamed at her. "It would be such a help to me."

"Of...of course, Nofret. I will do it today." The sooner she had it done, the sooner she could return to life as it was before the child arrived.

"There's a good aunt," Tut laughed. "And this evening, Ahmoset, I will take you on a ride. All the way out to the desert! I want to look on the whole land. I could shout from the palace roof, I'm so thrilled. Was ever a man as blessed as me?"

"You found a good nurse for Wadjmose?" Tut reined the horses to a walk.

Far to the west, across river and valley, the horizon was blurred with dust – a wind storm out in the dunes. The sunset would be especially beautiful tonight. Ahmose was glad to be here with her husband, gliding in their chariot along the crest of the hills above the valley. The waters of Akhet had receded, leaving behind deep black silt. From their vantage in the sky, it seemed all of Egypt lay dark and fresh below them, unrolled along the banks of the river like a dropped scroll. Planting would begin soon, the farmers treading the fields with bare feet, spearing holes into the earth, dropping seeds, praying for an abundant growing season, just as it had been forever, all the way back to the beginning of the world. This season was a time for nurturing, for making things grow. Children, ah; and plans, too.

"A palace woman. She has raised two healthy boys on her milk. I think Mutnofret will like her, and she will do a fine job looking after the prince."

"I am glad to hear it. It was kind of you to take on the duty. We will welcome her as part of our household."

"You are pleased with Wadjmose; I can tell."

"What father wouldn't be?"

"Have you been to see Opet?"

"Baketamun's little girl? Ah, yes. She's a fine one, too. Such thick hair! She will make a fine wife for a fat, wealthy nobleman some day."

"Baketamun hopes she will stay in the House of Women, to carry on for Wadjmose when he is Pharaoh."

Tut drove on in silence for some time. At length he said gently, "Wadjmose will not be Pharaoh, Ahmoset. You know that."

"Why shouldn't he be? You said yourself he is a fine boy."

"You know why."

"Because of the dream, yes. I know how you feel. But I have told you so many times, Tut: when I prayed for clarity to read the dream, it was all confusion. I cannot say what the gods intend. Not from hearing your dream, anyway."

"I know what they intend, dear one. I don't need your powers to show me the meaning of my dream, though I hoped you would be convinced yourself, after you heard it."

All those months since Ahmose had seen the river of stars, the vision of Mut and the shining child, had brought her no clarity. Nothing about Tut's dream or her own had convinced her to risk bearing a child; and Mutnofret in labor had only firmed Ahmose's fears. Surely, despite what the midwives said, Mutnofret had been near to death. Why else would she have cried out for Anupu to take her? It was a grave thing, to call on the jackal-headed one, a thing not done lightly. Mutnofret must have stood at death's very door. No – childbearing was too dangerous. It was not worth any risk. Not while there was another way to hold onto the throne, and Tut.

The edge of the sun dipped into the band of dust streaking the western sky. The desert caught fire, distant hills and cliffs flaring hot, all the crevasses and contours of the earth's bones leaping forward in sharp purple contrast. "Lovely," she said, pointing, changing the subject.

Tut stopped the horses. They stood together on the chariot's platform, admired the sight of the fiery god Re sinking into his night's rest, listened to the horses blow and snort, the struck-bronze chipping of birds among the scrub. Ahmose had to shield her eyes with her hands, peeking through her fingers at the blazing sky. Her eyes watered from the brilliance of Re's final light. She blinked the wetness away.

"The gods bless us; that is sure," Tut said. She ducked under his arm, pressed close to his body. A fine thing, to be here alone with him on an evening such as this – and a thing all too rare now. With Wadjmose arrived, her time with Tut would be yet scarcer, more precious than ever before. Tonight was almost like their first ride, when they had been strangers swept together by the gods and by the desperate night.

"I have been thinking, Tut. Perhaps it is time Nefertari passed on the title of God's Wife."

"To you, I suppose?"

"Why not? I am god-chosen, and you know I am good with political matters."

Tut nodded, looking down at her with one raised eyebrow. "You are at that. But why do you need such power, Ahmoset? As God's Wife, you would stand higher than all but the High Priest of Amun – higher even than Amun's priests. What need have you to control them? They support my rule; they are my friends."

They might not support me, *though, if I do not give you a son. Not with Wadjmose under their noses.* "Oh, I don't know." She waved a hand as if she had no cares in the world. "It is just another means of ensuring their loyalty, I suppose. Only a woman can be a God's Wife, of course. It may as well be your Great Royal Wife rather than her aging grandmother."

Tut's fingers rubbed absently at his chin. "It seems a lot of responsibility and work. Do you really want all that heaped upon your shoulders?"

Ahmose shrugged. "I am sure I will never have to use the power of the title. My grandmother never did – until she chose you as heir, of course."

"Power." The word caught at Tut. He watched the sun sink, his eyes deep in thought. At length he said, "I think not, Ahmose. I do not like the idea of dividing the power of our thrones. We should be a united force leading Egypt, not two working at different ends."

"But we would be united! Tut, I would never send the priests off in a direction you did not approve. If I were God's Wife, I would always consult with you in everything I did."

"Put it out of your head for now, Ahmoset. I am not saying no. There may come a time when we need to have power over the Priests of Amun. They are strong, and I imagine they could get up to trouble, especially with me away again. But for now there is no need. Let us enjoy as simple a life as we can manage, while it remains simple."

"Away again?" Her heart sank. "You are going out on another campaign?"

He squeezed her tight to him, then clucked the horses into a brisk walk. "It's time to confront the Heqa-Khasewet. We put down the Kushites well enough, but I have been receiving reports that the north grows restless. I knew they would meddle with the Delta soon enough."

"How long will you be away?"

"Not terribly long, I hope. Only as long as must be."

"And when will you leave?"

"Not for a few more months. The army must be resupplied, and I need to recruit many more young men for this campaign."

"It sounds dangerous. I imagine the Heqa-Khasewet are spoiling for another piece of Egypt. They will be treacherous, Tut."

"When are they not? But cheer up," he said. "With a little luck and the blessings of the gods, I will be back in a few months' time and there will be a few thousand less Heqa-Khasewet to trouble us. And in the meantime, we still have at least until the end of Shemu together." He kissed her, long and deep, setting her body aflame like the sun. Then he broke away and called to the horses. Ahmose was obliged to hold tight to the chariot's rail, exhilarating in the sudden burst of speed. It was a job to keep her feet. Tut drove like a mad man along the crest of the hill, laughing into the wind, sending up a trail of dust that glowed golden in the light of the setting sun. They flew like gods.

PART TWO

GOD'S WIFE

1504 B.C.E.

CHAPTER EIGHTEEN

MERITAMUN DIED JUST AFTER THE new year. As the waters of the Iteru rose to immerse the valley, the former queen's life ebbed away. Ahmose spent two days at her bedside, awkwardly holding her cold hand until she drew her final ragged breath. She had known so little of this woman who gave all she had to Egypt. From her childhood she recalled only a sense of awe bordering on fear when she saw her mother presiding over court. From Ahmose's own reign, she knew Meritamun as a quiet soul who tended her flowers in her estate garden, watering, weeding, cutting, keeping company with old Nefertari. Meritamun had been a stranger, an unreadable scroll from one end of her life to the other. Ahmose missed her all the same.

Three different messengers had been dispatched north to Thutmose with scrolls telling of Meritamun's death. Three, in case any should be lost on the high river, or in the land of the Heqa-Khasewet. This news was too important to risk losing. It would take an entire moon's turn to get the message to Tut's hands, and another moon to receive his reply.

Ahmose felt far more alone than she had when Tut went to war with the Kushites. Her servants were pleasant company, though. Twosre had improved her senet game enough to match Ahmose on the board, and Ineni shone some light onto her days. Whenever she could escape duties and dreams, Ahmose and Ineni would pole out across the palace lake, taking their supper on the cool water and laughing over the day's politics. It was good to laugh now and then. It seemed Ahmose had small enough reason to smile of late. She was fifteen years old with the weight of the Two Lands hung about her neck.

Some days before the annual Men-Nefer festival, Ahmose and Ineni were sharing fish cakes and beer on the lake barge, swatting flies from their bare arms. Ineni told all the news from the stewards: men of influence petitioning to get their daughters into Tut's harem, even though no one yet knew when the Pharaoh would return from the North; building projects Tut had commissioned, taking shape quickly now that Akhet had arrived and men were freed from tending the fields.

"And a rumor I heard, Ahmose – is your sister with child again?"

Ahmose sighed. "Yes, it seems to be so. I heard Mutnofret is four months along. She must have conceived just before Tut left."

"You haven't heard it from your sister yourself?"

"I prefer to keep her at arm's length. Mutnofret and her son are too treacherous for me, I'm afraid."

"Perhaps it is for the best. If you remain distant, she will have a harder time thinking of you as..."

"As a child, I suppose you were going to say."

"As a weak woman. Never as a child."

"No, I suppose not. Not with these!" Ahmose patted her chest. She had finally grown breasts. Her hips were beginning to round, too. Twosre had been the first to comment, though Ineni was surely the first to notice, if his frequent blushes and always-downcast eyes were any indication. He blushed now and coughed, and reached for his beer. Mischievously, Ahmose wondered if he had ever lain with a woman. Surely not, as shy as he was. It was hard to picture Ineni in the kind of embrace she had seen between Mutnofret and Tut.

"But in any case, I think you are right about distance," Ahmose said. "If I can keep Mutnofret from my side – everywhere but at court; I cannot seem to be rid of her there

– I may look more like a Great Royal Wife and less like a pebble for her to kick."

"If only you could hold court without her. I confess I do not trust her."

"Nor do I. She is all sweetness and 'oh-dear-sister' when we are together, but I can tell what she really thinks of me." She fell silent, gazing out across the water to the gentle green slope of the gardens. She should be used to Mutnofret's two faces by now, but it hurt all the same, to know that her own sister thought so little of her. Ahmose had coaxed a few rumors out of palace servants. Behind Ahmose's back, the second wife was all mockery and derision. Even when they were apart Ahmose could not stay out of Mutnofret's bad graces.

Ineni tugged at his sandal straps, following Ahmose's gaze. They stayed silent and melancholy for some time until Ahmose broke the spell by slapping a particularly large and stubborn fly. "A victory for Egypt!" She dipped her smeared hand in the lake.

"We know how Egypt fares against the flies. How against the Heqa-Khasewet?"

Ahmose shrugged. "I know next to nothing at this point. It takes so long for letters to arrive. Last I heard the army was in Tyre, heading north along the coast. Tut expected to meet with the Heqa-Khasewet armies soon. He said there are rebel encampments all over Canaan. I fear for him."

"He is the best warrior Egypt has seen in generations, Ahmose. If any man can come through safely...."

"I know, I know. But he is my husband. I fear for him all the same."

Ineni reached across their low barge table and patted her hand. "I know he will come back to you. I am sure he is eager to see you again. And anyway, with a god-chosen wife he is bound to have luck on the battle field."

"What is the mood among the Priests of Amun, with Thutmose away?"

"Worried. They say Ipet-Isut is in need of repairs, and

that other temples to the north had to give up most of their treasure to feed the army as it passed through."

"Bah. Tut brought plenty of food. He stripped the city's grain stores nearly empty, not just in Waset, but at Nekhen and Perhathor. And he brought ample goods to trade as well."

"Undoubtedly. But what of the people left here in Waset? And in Nekhen, and Perhathor? This season..." His voice lowered, trailed away.

"This season?"

"The Inundation is not as high as it was last year."

Ahmose had not yet heard. Still, the flood was upon them, and the fields were covered, as far as she had seen. "So? The waters are still here. It's not as if the fields won't be fertile."

"Ah, the fields will produce, but how much? The predictions are grim. With all the stores depleted to feed the army, it could be a weak harvest. And the priests think to use talk of a lower flood to scare the land owners into paying more taxes. They think to blame the lower Inundation on Amun's displeasure, and to claim that more tribute will ensure a wetter Akhet next year. With the Pharaoh gone away, they might have quite a lot of influence. And if they wring more taxes out of the people, there could be trouble."

Ahmose clicked her tongue. "I think I would have known if Amun were displeased."

"Of course. But it is a shaky time, you see, with the priests agitating the public with tales of Amun's anger, and the grain stores lower than usual."

"That is troubling. But what can I do about it now? We cannot move on the temple yet."

"I agree. A shame, but it is as you say. We must wait until the time is exactly right. A woman of your talents, though – you belong in the temple."

I belong at my husband's side, she did not say. It was the right thing to say, she knew, but with each passing day a greater distance opened between herself and the Pharaoh. With Tut away, it was easier to reflect on the difference in how he treated Ahmose and Mutnofret. He may ride with his Great

Royal Wife, and call her his dear one, and say Mutnofret's head was too hot; but his eyes when they looked at the second wife said something else. They were never so eloquent when they were on Ahmose's face, or on her body. To Tut she was only the woman in his strange dream, holding the shining prince. Until she actually cradled that child in her arms, Tut's heart would never be hers.

And Thutmose may swear the dream-son had been promised, but Wadjmose was here now, and thriving. He grew stronger all the time. He was crawling now, and babbling. Soon he would be running about the palace, learning to speak properly, winning hearts at court. It was not Tut's love for the child she feared – it was the court's. If the nobles and priests supported Wadjmose as heir, why wouldn't they clamor to set the mother of Wadjmose on the throne of the Great Royal Wife? The baby complicated everything, and another was growing in Mutnofret's belly. Ahmose had to find *somewhere* to belong, and soon.

They tied the boat to its mooring. Ineni helped Ahmose jump from the lake's retaining wall to the lush green grass of the garden. His hand was warm and soft – a steward's hand, so unlike Tut's, with its calluses and leopard's-paw strength. They walked down the garden path, close together, in no hurry to return to their duties. It was a fine thing, to have a real friend again. Aiya was long gone, and there were so few people Ahmose could trust.

A shaded bench invited them. It was set far back from the path, cast in deep green shadow, screened on three sides by a dense stand of high, flame-red lilies. They sat for a time in the evening haze, Ahmose giggling over one of Ineni's clever jokes. Another stubborn fly had begun to hound her, drawn, she supposed, to her sweet perfume. It landed on her cheek, and she slapped it hard, wincing at the blow, laughing so much she had to blink back tears.

"It is all over you! Your face is smeared with it."

"At least I killed the blasted thing." She swiped her cheek with the back of her hand, but Ineni made a disgusted face.

169

"You just made it worse. Here, let me." He licked his thumb and rubbed at the smeared fly. His fingertips lingered along the line of her jaw for a moment. The smile faded from his lips; his dark eyes were serious, intense.

A heat rose up in Ahmose's middle. All in a moment, she wondered what Ineni's soft hands would feel like on her body, touching her the way Tut had touched her the night after the wedding feast. And in one moment more, she knew it could never be. What a wicked thing, for the Great Royal Wife to consider such wantonness! Ahmose turned her face away from him, smiling to soften the gesture – and her eyes took in, all at once, a thin form with wide, staring eyes standing among the lilies.

"Oh!" Ahmose said, reaching a hand toward the woman. But she was gone in a rustle of leaves.

"Wasn't that one of your sister's women?"

"Sitamun, Mutnofret's body servant. What was she doing here, I wonder?"

"Nothing good, I am sure."

The sound of fast water filled Ahmose's head – her own blood rushing in her ears. "She was spying on us!"

Ineni stood. "I think it is best if we avoid each other for a time."

"But we weren't doing anything wrong."

"That will not be what Mutnofret thinks. I just pray the damage is not already done."

Ineni was probably right. He was always right. But Ahmose balked at the idea. Just when she had begun to enjoy a true friendship, just when she had found someone she could trust. It was so unfair, that Mutnofret should drive a wedge between them. Mutnofret had found a way to win. Again! "No. I am not going to stop spending time with you, Ineni. I need your friendship. You are the only thing that makes me happy! Let Mutnofret think what she will."

"Ahmose, be sensible, please. This is not just about Mutnofret. She will find a way to use this against you if she can. Continuing to spend time together alone will only give her more ground to build her lies upon."

"But what of our plan?"

"We can still carry it out when the time is right. We will need to communicate by letter, that is all."

By letter. Just as with Thutmose. Must all her relationships be by letter? Would she be in isolation forever? She kicked hard at a branch lying on the grass. It sailed across the path and clattered into the bushes. "I hate Mutnofret! She ruins everything. Everything!"

Ineni's gentle hand was on her shoulder. She turned to look up at him. His eyes were sad now, not hungry. "She will not win in the end, Ahmose. I promise you."

Sitamun was gone. There was no one to see. She wrapped her arms around Ineni, holding him hard against her. "She will not win in the end." Her lips brushed his cheek, a farewell kiss between the best of friends. Then she walked away from him. She looked back only once to see him staring down at his feet, his face burning.

CHAPTER NINETEEN

T HE MEN-NEFER FESTIVAL WAS OVER. The Inundation drew to a close. Day by day the waters sank lower; more of the Black Land, freshly darkened by rich silt, emerged with each sunrise. Ahmose longed for Thutmose more with each new day, too. Minding court alone was a heavy burden. She longed for Ineni as well. She laughed and smiled little now that they must see each other only at court. Ineni was her happiness, and his absence from her daily life was distressed her. All Ahmose wanted to do now was spin flax. With her heart distant, she was detached from the day-to-day business of governing the Two Lands. She was irritable, snappish; it was impossible to focus on judging and ruling. It was yet more impossible to ignore Mutnofret's impertinence.

Late one morning, as court drew to a blessed end, Ahmose felt especially restless and eager to retreat to the coolness of her rooms. Ineni approached the throne and bowed apologetically, first to Ahmose, then to Mutnofret. "Great Ladies, there is an urgent dispute. I know you are eager to conclude the session, but the governor of Waset has sent this case to you: a quarrel between the noble men Djau and Minnakht, land owners on the southern end of the city."

Ahmose groaned inwardly. "What is the quarrel?"

"A question of territory. The two men refused to allow the tjati of Waset to settle the issue. He has been working with them for over a week, it seems; they are not giving any ground, either one. The tjati asks that the throne make a final decision."

"Send them in."

Minnakht and Djau were much like any other of Waset's land owners. They were stout men, not heavy from hard work like Thutmose, but soft of body with the round features of those who eat plenty and labor infrequently. They marched into the great hall behind Ineni, looking anywhere but at each other. After they made their proper bows to the throne, Ahmose said, "What is your complaint?"

"Djau has been trying to steal my land, Great Lady."

"I have done no such thing, Great Lady, as Thoth is my witness! Minnakht tried to put up his field-markers many spans further north than he has ever done before."

"The flood knocked them down! I was putting them back up where they fell. Djau is lying about the boundaries."

"No such thing! No such thing! Minnakht is a scoundrel; everybody knows it, Great Lady."

"You dare to call me a scoundrel! You poisoned three of my cattle last year!"

"They died because you are too stupid to keep them out of the barley. They bloated! I will not be blamed for your lack of..."

Ahmose clapped her hands sharply for silence. The men, fuming, shut their mouths. "If I understand correctly, the field-markers that define the borders between your two estates fell during the flood." Djau nodded. "And you took your dispute to the tjati." Minnakht coughed, looked away. "The tjati was unable to find a suitable solution to your problem. Is this because the tjati is poor at his work, or because you two quarrel like little children?"

Neither man answered.

Ahmose drew in a breath to go on, but before she could, Mutnofret spoke up. "Either the two of you will settle this matter between you, or tomorrow I will send the Steward of Cattle to collect half of each of your herds."

The land owners gaped, but neither spoke. Ahmose's face burned.

Mutnofret went on, "And if your land-markers are not up within three days in a position that suits you both, the throne will take six spans of land between both your estates. That ought to keep you from fighting with one another in the future."

Ahmose blinked. Absurd. A punishment that did not fit the crime; indeed, there was no crime here, no reason to threaten fees and seizures. These two men needed an authority to settle their squabble; that was all. But the words were spoken – words that were Ahmose's to speak by rights, not her second wife's.

Even so, Ahmose could not contradict Mutnofret. To do so would make the throne look as contentious as these two men. She swallowed her anger, and held up a hand in dismissal. "The second wife has given you her ruling. You may go. Ineni, assign a steward to see that Lady Mutnofret's wishes are carried out."

Ineni blanched, holding Ahmose's eye for a heartbeat. She could read his thoughts on his face: *You cannot let her push you like this.*

No, I cannot, she said to herself. Thutmose should have put a stop to it long ago. But Thutmose was not here now. Ahmose had to look after herself, had to face down Mutnofret herself. *This madness will end today.*

The moment the great doors closed behind the land owners, Ahmose sprang from her throne and was gone from the hall. She slammed the hall's rear door behind her. Mutnofret! That detestable scorpion! She had stung Ahmose for the last time.

She broke into a run, flying through the colonnades, her eyes dazzled by the whip of light and shadow as she sprinted past pillars and arches. She threw open the door to Mutnofret's apartments. Sitamun, spinning in the corner below Mutnofret's goddess tapestries, jumped to her feet with a yelp of alarm. Ahmose snapped her fingers and pointed at Sitamun's heart as if her finger might fire burning arrows. "Sit down. Your mistress is coming soon, no doubt. If you know what's good for you, you will keep your mouth shut."

She stalked into Mutnofret's bedroom and shut the door.

Ahmose leaned against the wall beside the door and tried to slow her breathing. Her heart pounded so hard she could feel the furious pulse behind her eyes. Mutnofret sitting on her throne as if she owned all of Egypt. Mutnofret issuing her ridiculous judgments before Ahmose could even open her mouth. Mutnofret making love to Tut in this very bed. Mutnofret!

Feet scuffled in the anteroom. The outer door shut softly, then silence filled the second wife's apartments. Sitamun must have fled. Wise of her – Mutnofret would surely be cross once she realized her servant had allowed Ahmose into the bed chamber. Ahmose closed her eyes and steadied her heart. *Strength. Ferocity. Confidence.* She would snip the sting right off Mutnofret's tail.

The outer door opened. Footsteps: a confident, even stride coming across the anteroom. *Mutnofret!*

The bedroom door opened, blocking Ahmose from her sister's view. Mutnofret strolled into the room like a cat, all upright posture and crackling air of haughtiness.

"I suppose you think you are terribly clever."

Mutnofret jumped, whirled around. When her eyes found Ahmose standing with crossed arms beside the door, she frowned.

"What are you doing in my bedchamber? Get out."

"I am the Great Royal Wife, and I go where I please."

"Not into my private rooms, you don't. Get out before I summon the palace guards to haul you out."

She ignored the threat. If Mutnofret called the guards, Ahmose would only send them away again. They could not touch her – ot on the word of a second wife. "Threatening to take land from nobles? That's the way you think to solve a dispute?"

"It got them to settle, did it not?"

"And it will turn them against the throne. A fine job you've done."

"At least I moved decisively. At least I did not sit on my

backside and shiver like you always do."

"It is not your place to speak before me at court. I am the Great Royal Wife; I have authority over you."

Mutnofret's black eyes were piercing. "It is my place, not yours. You are a usurper. The throne is mine by birth, mine by right. You are naught but a thief, Ahmose."

The unfairness struck Ahmose like a blow. She had never wanted to be a king's wife at all, let alone the Great Royal Wife. If she had her way she would spend her days spinning and serving the gods, not settling land disputes between fat, petulant nobles. She only did what the gods required, what she was made to do. She was Great Royal Wife because she had no choice.

Ah, but Tut – she wanted him as she did not want the throne. She wanted his company, his respect, his love. She would do anything to keep Tut for herself, even rule a nation. She hardened herself. For Tut, she turned her heart to bronze. "If you ever speak to me in that manner again, I will have you caned. Do you understand me?"

Mutnofret's face registered shock, then instant derision. "Caned! You! You who can't make a single clear judgment on your golden throne! You will have me caned! Tell me, little Ahmoset, how would you have settled the dispute? Sent for a map, and wasted time with surveyors and builders putting up a wall between those men's farms?" That was precisely what Ahmose would have done. She must have blushed, for Mutnofret's mouth curled with contempt. "A waste of time and funds. Those two fools will settle the problem by themselves now, and the Pharaoh's treasure need not be tapped. If you thought like a Great Royal Wife you would have seen that."

"Now their hearts are turned against you, and against the king. If you thought like a person instead of like a crocodile, you would have seen that."

"Thutmose doesn't want their hearts. He wants their taxes."

"Tut wants their loyalty. That is what he needs. Have you already forgotten that our husband is not of royal blood? If he does not have the nobles and priests united behind him, the throne will not remain his for long. And that means it will not be yours for long, either."

"Tut. How *cute*."

Ahmose was brought up short. She made her hands into fists and pressed her nails deep into her palms to keep a triumphant smile from her face. So Mutnofret had never called him Tut. He had never given his second wife this secret name to use. The knowledge that she shared something with her husband that even Mutnofret could never touch filled her with a wash of power. She felt like Sekhmet the goddess-lioness, crouching to spring, to take down her prey. She stepped close to Mutnofret, so close that her sister drew back and crossed her hands over the bulge of her belly. "I will cane you myself, Mutnofret. Believe it. I have a duty to Egypt. My work is to rule while Thutmose is gone. If you continue to interfere, by all the gods I swear I will stripe you like a runaway slave. Stay out of my way and let me do my work."

She turned to leave. She wanted to walk away, to push Mutnofret's rage and bitterness behind her forever and never look upon it again. But the desperation in Mutnofret's voice stopped her before she could pass through the bed-chamber door. "And what is my work, now that you have taken all I lived for?"

Ahmose looked back at her sister. Mutnofret's arms and legs trembled faintly – whether from the excitement of the confrontation or from fear of Ahmose's threats, she could not tell. But still, her sister stood straight and proud, a Great Lady by birth, and to her very center.

"Give the Pharaoh an heir," Ahmose said. "That is the only work you need concern yourself with."

"A brood mare," Mutnofret said. Her lips pressed together, twisted. Tears spilled down her cheeks. Ahmose remembered the sight of Mutnofret alone on the throne of the Great Royal Wife, hand raised to an empty, dark hall. "I was raised to be the king's chief wife, and you have reduced me to a brood mare."

Ahmose left her standing there with Tut's baby in her belly.

"Does *Tut* know you're in bed with your steward, Ahmose?" Mutnofret's screech carried through her anteroom. Ahmose kept walking, never once looking round. "Have a care your precious nobles and priests do not discover it. I wonder where their hearts would lie then?"

Ahmose made herself walk slowly across the courtyard. Obviously Sitamun had told what she had seen in the garden before the Men-Nefer festival. And what else had that vile gossip seen? How often had she been sent to spy upon Ahmose? Ineni had been her only comfort, her only joy in the dark days since Tut sailed north. Any gesture, any word between them could be interpreted as romantic. A dagger of guilt twisted in her belly.

Ahmose remembered how she and Mutnofret had vowed to be sisters first, sisters forever, and remembering made her chest tighten. How quickly they had forgotten their promise; how quickly hate had taken hold of their hearts. There was a rent between them now that a thousand-thousand stitches could never mend. And would it open further? Would the gods drive this wedge between Ahmose and Tut, too? Unthinkable – impossible – unbearable. She would give it all up – her privacy, the palace itself – to ensure Tut was still hers. She would move against Mutnofret's schemes. Decisively; today.

Back in her apartments, she sent Twosre to find Ineni. She dragged a flat box out of one of the great standing chests that held her gowns. Inside was a swath of linen dyed the perfect crimson of beaded blood. She tied it tightly, and though her hands shook, they did not fail.

The garment was stifling, and so snug it was difficult to walk. But it accentuated every curve of her young body; it turned her into the very image of ripening. The red cloth was knotted beneath her breasts, exposing them, and she painted her nipples with oil and coated them with gold dust so that they shone like sun-discs. Her finest wig went onto her head, and her brilliant alabaster vulture crown settled atop it, with the goddess's finely carved white wings, worked in stone so smooth they glowed like a full moon rising, falling to either side of her face. She did not need her mirror to know she looked like a vision. She felt it. She felt Mut singing deep within her heart.

Ineni was not long in coming. Twosre helped him bear in a long box, longer than a man's height and more than wide enough for a stout man to lie inside. When Ineni straightened from his burden and looked at Ahmose, his eyes lit with a hungry fire. She looked like womanhood itself, she knew – like a goddess made flesh. *Perfect.*

"What is all this?" Twosre frowned.

"I am striking a blow against evil today," Ahmose said. She came toward Ineni and the box, her hips swaying like a bed of reeds in the confines of the red dress. Ineni swallowed hard.

"Great Lady, where are you going?" Twosre's voice was pitched high with worry.

"To Ipet-Isut, to pay a little visit to the High Priest of Amun. Ineni, do you have the letter?"

He pulled a scroll of papyrus from his belt. "It is ready. A litter is coming. The bearers will meet us in the courtyard."

"Make sure Mutnofret is distracted so she does not see me leave. I won't have her pulling some trick to ruin my plan."

There was a note of fear in Twosre's voice. "I don't understand." Ahmose turned to her, reached out in reassurance.

"Don't be afraid. The gods are with me – they always have been. They have a job for me to do, today and always. Egypt is mine, whatever Mutnofret thinks. The gods gave the land to me, and I will be its steward."

Ineni lifted away the lid. He held them up, one in each hand: two perfect wings, white as stars on water. There were dozens of feathers on each, long, strong, lightweight. She stretched out her arms.

He showed her how they worked, how her upper and lower arms fitted into the braided-linen loops. His fingers were deft and soft against her skin. She could not bend her elbows with the wings on, of course, but that hardly mattered. When she turned about and held the wings wide for Twosre to see, her servant gasped. The white feathers swept out, impossibly light, impossibly beautiful. She was winged in her ka, winged in truth. She felt she could spring up like a bird and fly over the Black Land.

Twosre half-sank into a bow, as if she stood before the goddess in truth. "You are Mut," she said.

"And today, I go to wed Amun."

CHAPTER TWENTY

IT WAS EASIER TO RIDE in the litter with the wings off. They were laid carefully beside her on the cushions, a barrier between herself and Ineni.

"Mutnofret thinks we are lovers." The sun, sliding down the sky, illuminated the litter's blue curtains and cast Ineni's face in cool planes. The steward said nothing. "Ineni, as dear as you are to me, we can never be lovers."

"I know."

"But you would have it be so, if you could."

"You would not?" He sounded defeated.

Ahmose swallowed hard. She made herself say, "In truth, I have never considered it. Not because you aren't a wonderful man. You are. But I love my husband."

He nodded. "And you are the Great Royal Wife."

"Soon to be God's Wife, too, if all goes well. Oh, what if it doesn't?"

"It will. It is a wicked thing we do, though, Ahmose."

"Is it really? With Thutmose gone, there is no one to check Mutnofret. She will drive me from the throne."

"I know all that. It's this." He tapped the scroll against his knee. "It is a lie. The gods do not favor liars."

This was the first misgiving Ineni had expressed. It took Ahmose aback. It was a lie, and a cruel one. Gods willing, Nefertari would never find out about the letter. Ineni – clever, bright Ineni – had done a masterful forgery of the old woman's shaky hand. He had studied all the notes she'd sent to Ahmose and practiced for weeks. No one would question the letter, which signed away the title, though not the wealth. Ahmose would leave her grandmother the wealth.

It was wicked, truly, to take what was not hers. But the gods intended the throne for Ahmose. They gave the throne to Ahmose. If this was the only way to keep Mutnofret at bay so Ahmose could do the gods' work, then she would be forgiven. Ineni, too; Ahmose felt sure of that. But oh, if only luck would be with her. If only Nefertari would go to the next life without ever knowing. She sent up a prayer to Iset to make it so.

Ineni reached across the wings and took Ahmose's hand. She allowed the touch. The gods alone knew when they might be together again. It would be a lonely life in the temple, with only Twosre for company. "I will miss you, Ineni."

He made no reply. They rode to Ipet-Isut in silence.

Ahmose stayed curtained in her litter as the sentries questioned her soldiers. Her heart was like a trapped bird, all flutter and beat. She could not look at Ineni, nor at the wings; she closed her eyes lightly and prayed through the avenues of the temple complex. At last she felt the sensation of lowering, at last the bump of the platform against the ground.

Ineni motioned for her to wait. He got out himself, spoke a few quiet words to someone outside. Then louder: "Inside, I say, and prepare the sanctuaries. I bring Ahmose, the god-chosen. Do as I say, or the Pharaoh will hear your name!" His face peeked back inside, hands clutching the curtain tight about him so no one in the courtyard could see into the litter. "It is time."

With difficulty, she pushed herself to her knees and shuffled about until her feet were outside the litter. Then it was a matter of levering her body, constrained by the snug gown, upright. She braced her hands against the canopy's supports and shoved hard. She teetered on her feet, nearly overbalancing; Ineni's thin arm was around her waist in a flash, righting her. She smiled at him, laughed nervously.

"This dress."

"It's enough to make anyone fall over."

"Get the wings for me, will you?" Whoever had been in the forecourt of the Temple of Amun was gone now. Ineni had sent them packing quick enough. Even the litter-bearers had their backs turned. Ipet-Isut was still and private in the cool blue of early evening.

He slid the fine white wings onto her arms. Ahmose held them out; the faintest breeze moved from the west, tugging at her feathers, pulling her arms insistently. Now she would fly. Above Mutnofret, above the court – she would set herself loose upon this breeze and sweep her will across the land. She was a sacred woman, beloved of the gods, and what she did was right; she could do no wrong. She moved toward the temple door with her bright goddess wings outstretched.

The temple's huge anteroom was empty, though faintly, she could hear the voices of men – servants or priests. The voices were urgent and forced. Whatever Ineni said to clear the forecourt, it had worked well. She faltered in the emptiness of the anteroom. Ineni ducked under her right wing and strode out into the room.

"Hear me, High Priest of Amun! The consort of your god comes! The God's Wife approaches!" Ineni's voice rang like sword on shield. Before the echo of his words faded, the High Priest swept into the room, draped in his leopard skin, a press of lesser men and women at his back. When he saw her standing there, winged, gilded, crowned, he fell to his knees, sank forward until he lay flat upon the floor. The priests behind him did the same. A murmur went up, a sound tight with wonder.

She needed do nothing but stand before them, poised and manifestly female, manifestly divine. She caught sight of herself in a great plated mirror on the temple wall: the setting sun streamed in from the doorway behind, casting her form in a halo of light, dust dancing in the air around her wings, each mote a faceted jewel. She glowed – she shone – she was as vivid as the goddess from her dream, walking on a river of light.

"Mut," the High Priest whispered, choked and awed. He stared up at her from the floor, tears standing in his eyes.

In the end, they had hardly needed the forged letter. Ahmose's appearance, white-winged, backlit by Re's holy light, young and vital, had convinced the High Priest. When she fell limp and babbling into Ineni's arms, the words she spoke brought the regiment of lesser temple servants to her as well.

My consort comes! My partner on the earth, come to heal the river! Maat, maat, maat!

It had not been a part of their plan. When she came to, Ineni was staring into her eyes, shocked and trembling.

"I am all right, Ineni." He pulled her upright again, steadied her, took the wings from her. Oh, what a bitter thing, to lose them!

"What was that?" he murmured. "What were you talking about?"

"She is the mouthpiece of the gods." The High Priest bowed to her, holding forth his palms in supplication. "Those were Amun's own words you heard. Not since her grandmother has Egypt seen such a favored woman. The gods are all around her; I can feel them."

Ineni paled. He looked from Ahmose to the High Priest, uncertain.

Ahmose nodded weakly. "I have never had it come upon me so strongly before. It was Amun. I can still feel his presence. But I am well right now."

The High Priest sent for cold wine and bread. "So you come to bring maat, then? It is well that you do. For days now when I have prayed I have seen nothing but chaos in the smoke of my offerings. The gods demand a restoration of the righteous order. The scales are close to tipping. I fear for the army in the north."

Tut. No. "This is why the gods have brought me here. I am the one to restore righteousness. The Pharaoh will strike the bodies of the Heqa-Khasewet, and I will strike their kas."

When she said it, it felt so right that it had to be true. She still shook with the power of Amun's touch. "I will spend my nights in the Temple of Mut, and I will lead all the priesthood in prayer. I need only a modest room. I must be near the gods, if I am to do their work."

"Of course, Great Lady." The High Priest bowed.

"I cannot give up my service to the throne, though. In the daytime, I will be at the palace supervising the court. The gods want a strong, young, righteous ruler on the throne, with the Pharaoh away at war."

She turned to Ineni. Sweet, clever Ineni, her dearest friend. She had just committed herself to daily and nightly work. Holy work, to be sure, but it would leave her little time for anything but court and prayer. Would she and Ineni see each other again? Of all the things she was giving up for Egypt's sake, she would miss him the most. "Bring Twosre to me, and a trunk of my clothing. She will know what to pack. I shall begin leading prayers this very night, and I won't be back at the palace until morning."

Ineni's shoulders slumped. "As you will, Great Lady."

CHAPTER TWENTY-ONE

AHMOSE RETURNED TO THE PALACE early in the morning, weak from lack of sleep. Alive with her newfound might, Ahmose had spent the entire night dancing and singing, and smoking semsemet at the shrines, crying aloud from the force of the divine fire that burned inside her. She had whirled and clapped with the sesheshet – the gods' sacred iron rattles – until her arms and legs were as weak as grass. She had prayed on her knees, bending her back, howling to the gods, and the priestesses howled with her. Such a music they had made! The gods' eyes were surely upon the Pharaoh now, far to the north, and Ahmose was feverish with power.

She arrived in the throne room before anyone else. Dressed in the white smock of a priestess with a simple wig and the golden cobra circlet – the simplest crown of the Great Royal Wife – she was as understated as she had been at her wedding feast, but now at last she was radiant with confidence. No second wife's treasure could outshine her.

She ascended the steps to her throne and sat as gracefully as if all the eyes of Egypt were upon her. The great hall stretched out before her, its pillars alive with the stories of kings of the past. The windcatchers along the eastern wall admitted shafts of golden-pink light. These, too, were like pillars, brilliant bright pillars sparkling with the early motes of morning. Soon enough, this hall would fill with her subjects, the people of her land, looking to Ahmose for

189

guidance, looking to the God's Wife for judgment. Now, though, she let the silence reach into her bones, fill her up with peace and pleasure. She felt like the king's chief wife at last, a true Great Lady, strong and beautiful on her throne. Nothing could shake her.

First one, then three, then a dozen stewards and servants moved into the hall. They were like a trickle of water from a jar, hesitant and thin, speaking low so as not to disturb Ahmose's peace. She watched them go about their business, set up their tables and benches to mind the petitioners, sweep the floors free of sand and pebbles. One servant approached her and asked if there was anything she might wish from the kitchens. Ahmose waved the man away. She was full of the gods' power. She needed no other sustenance.

Ahmose could hear the voice of the gathered people like a wind in an orchard. The second wife came in through the rear door behind the dais. Ahmose heard Mutnofret's, too, rising above the rustle of the petitioners and stewards. Ahmose did not deign to look around. Mutnofret was ordering refreshment from the serving man, and calling for her body servant to fetch a lighter wig. Mutnofret was of no consequence. Ahmose had pulled the power and the peace of the morning deep into her bones.

Mutnofret climbed the dais, her round belly swaying, leaning on the arm of one of her women. She settled onto her throne, sighed, and turned to Ahmose.

"What is that you are wearing? You look like an apprentice from the temples."

"Good morning, sister."

"You cannot attend court looking like that. Go back to your rooms and change. And be quick! There is already a crowd gathered."

"I will not change my dress. I am the God's Wife of Amun. If these people wish to see me, let them see me as a priestess."

"God's Wife? You? Did Nefertari hand you the title?"

Ahmose said nothing.

"Well," Mutnofret went on, "you look like a fool, and your

eyes are all red. By Hathor, Ahmose! You should at least try to look like the Great Royal Wife."

Ahmose turned her face, sharply, and stared into Mutnofret's eyes. The second wife pursed her lips, but she fell silent.

Beer and bread arrived, and Mutnofret turned her attention to breaking her fast. Ahmose surveyed the hall. It was nearly ready now, the stewards just beginning to fall into position. The pillars of light had crept only a hand's breadth across the floor.

Mutnofret finished her food, waved the platter away, and nodded to the chief steward.

Ahmose's mouth quirked. Amusing, that the second wife should think it was for her to begin court. Ahmose rose smoothly from her seat and took the flail from its support beside Tut's empty throne. She held it across her breasts. Mutnofret glared at her. "Steward," Ahmose said, "you may open the court to my people."

She remained standing as the crowd entered the hall, filing into their orderly lines where the stewards directed them. She looked commanding with the flail, she knew – commanding and powerful. "The throne of the Pharaoh welcomes you. Let the spirit of righteousness guide us in this day's doings. Maat."

The chief steward raised his voice. "You will be directed to the stewards first. If your petition requires adjudication, you will then be directed to either the Great Royal Wife or the Lady Mutnofret."

Now was the time. Ahmose took a step forward. "I regret to inform the court that the Lady Mutnofret will not be attending us today. Her condition troubles her." Ahmose turned to Mutnofret and smiled sweetly. "I have excused her from her duties. Perhaps when her child is born she will feel well enough to join us again."

Before the court as she was, Mutnofret could do nothing without looking like a contentious child. Any action she might take other than to retreat to her chamber would be unseemly. Mutnofret stood, holding Ahmose's eye steadily for a long, tense moment. Then she waved a servant to her side and waddled down the steps. At the base of the dais she turned to look up at Ahmose.

"You are too kind to excuse me from the burden of duty, sister. Won't you please come visit me this afternoon, so that I might thank you properly?"

Ahmose twitched the flail at her sister, a dismissal. She would not go to Mutnofret's rooms, this afternoon or any other. The God's Wife of Amun was stronger than the second wife. The God's Wife had the power to sidestep Mutnofret's traps. The God's Wife would let Mutnofret remain in her apartments and claw the walls in her useless rage.

The God's Wife had taken the throne.

CHAPTER TWENTY-TWO

A NOTHER BOY." TWOSRE STOOD, ARMS folded, eyes severe, in Ahmose's modest chamber. "She calls him Amunmose."

Ahmose bit her fist to smother a yawn. She had spent a long night dancing and chanting with the Mut priestesses. Her muscles were tight and sore. Their official mission had been to strike fear into the hearts of the Heqa-Khasewet warriors, but when an apprentice brought word that Mutnofret had gone into labor early that evening, Ahmose had slipped in a few private pleas to make the child a girl. "How is my sister recovering?"

"Quite well, Holy Lady."

Sometimes even women who had borne before still died of complications. It would be convenient for Mutnofret to slip off to the afterlife and free the Horus Throne of her oppressive presence. No such luck, though; she would carry on as capably as the brood mare she was, it seemed. Ahmose cleared her throat. "Did she ask for me again at the birthing?"

Twosre made a funny little grimace, eyebrows up, mouth down. No need to answer; the woman's face said it clearly enough. No, of course not. After her dismissal from court, the last thread between Ahmose and Mutnofret was cut forever. They were sisters no more.

"And the new baby – is he well?"

"Quite strong and healthy. He cries like a bull calf."

"I am sure the Pharaoh will be glad to hear it."

"Holy Lady..." Twosre hesitated. Ahmose nodded for her to go on, trying to erase the anger from her face. It was not Twosre who enraged her. "It is not my place to ask, Holy Lady, but all the palace servants want to know. Have you had any success with the Pharaoh? With the heirship for Wadjmose?"

Ahmose's frown deepened. "No. I get few letters from the Pharaoh these days, and they are all full of battle stories. They made Tyre a base for many weeks, and cleared the surrounding land of Heqa-Khasewet. Most of the vermin have fled north. The Pharaoh pursued them. They have had several battles along the way, he said, with heavy losses at a few. The Heqa-Khasewet ambushed them from the highlands near Kadesh. They nearly lost that one, but Tut...Thutmose turned it around on them.

"His last letter spoke of pushing even further north. He thinks to rout them from Ugarit, and to set up an outpost there. He believes he can bring the local people to him, and expand the borders of the empire. I have seen maps. Ugarit is so far to the north. I do not see how he can hold it, but he has a way with soldiers, I know. If anyone can do it, the Pharaoh can.

"That is all he tells me, though. I don't know whether the heirship is even on his mind. I do not wish to press the issue too hard, you see."

"Of course, Lady."

Ahmose was about to say more, but hands clapped lightly outside the chamber door.

"Come," Ahmose said.

An old priest bowed in the doorway. "Holy Lady, your chariot is ready. I am to drive you to the palace."

"Court calls," Ahmose said, taking Twosre by the hand. "Come; ride back with me. We have little time for gossip anymore. You can tell me all the latest stories on the way to the palace."

Twosre came along happily enough, chattering about the harem women and the servants. Ahmose listened with half her heart. The other half recalled the look on Mutnofret's face when Ahmose had sent from the throne room, and she still did not know whether she was pleased or ashamed.

Ahmose had borrowed a plain frock from an apprentice girl: unbleached linen, coarse and scratchy, loose-fitting, and a plain wig, too. She lined her eyes thinly with kohl but left the rest of her face untouched. The simplest of leather sandals were tied onto her feet. Looking for all the world like a rekhet woman paying a visit to the Holy House, she walked out from her chamber, through Amun's courtyard, out along the pillared avenue as the sun set. No one glanced at her twice as she left the complex, pacing out onto the wide road, eyes down, her sandals slapping in the dust. Waset shimmered on the horizon, seeming to float above the earth where the heat rippled the sky into the land. The growing season was nearly at its end. The desperate, thin harvest would begin soon. The air was Shemu-hot, even as evening drew on.

She walked for a long time, her eyes on Waset. To the left and right of the roadway fields of flax stretched away, bright and alive, waiting for the reaping. She stopped over a culvert to watch men at work on a canal, setting new bricks into place, shoveling debris from the bed. Was the tension in their faces from their work, or from worry? Their fields were marked with cairns, but the crop did not stretch all the way to the rock piles. Growth ended a good three spans short; the intervening space between crop and boundaries was lifeless and sere. She shuddered and walked on.

Chariots passed her, coming and going. None was the one she wanted, though. She reached the crossroads and sat upon the cairn that marked it, waiting, watching the people going about their lives. It was strange to be out among them, unrecognized. At court they were formal. In the temple they were reverent. Here, where no royalty and no gods could see, they joked and quarreled, they held hands, they picked their noses and spat on the ground. Children being herded by tired mothers screamed and caught beetles in the roadside weeds. Men driving fine ladies in chariots shouted at the rekhet to clear the way. Goatherds drove their flocks by, whistling. A string of cattle plodded past, led by a tall boy, his little brother perched on the withers of the lead beast.

She waited a long time. The sun dipped low, darkening its face as it neared the far red bluffs to the west. She was about to turn back for the temple when she saw Ineni's chariot, pulled by a pair of spotted horses. Her heart leapt to see him, lean and upright, coming toward her at a dust-kicking trot, his dear face serious and drawn. She waved to him.

"Well," he said, drawing rein. He gave her his hand, pulled her into the chariot. The touch of his skin against hers skipped her heart. "I never would have recognized you."

"Oh, Ineni! Has it really been so long?" She hugged him, kissed his cheek. "I have missed you! You got my letter; I am so glad."

"All right, all right. I have missed you, too, Great Lady, but we may be recognized, even out here. Let's go." He turned the horses past the cairn. They left the hard-packed surface of the main road, and here the horses' hooves made a soft, scraping sound on the loose soil of a farm path. The road lifted toward the low crest that marched past Ipet-Isut to Waset, the same place she had often gone to ride with Tut. There were no guards now, though, as when she rode with her husband. No one was on this road but Ahmose and her steward.

"What's this all about, then?" Ineni said when they were sure no one was nearby to hear.

"I just had to see you. I needed a friend. The harvest looks so poor, and Mutnofret has just had another son – you have heard, I am sure."

"Yes, I have."

"I just needed to be with you again, Ineni. I always felt so happy and free with you. I am so troubled now, all the time. It is too great a strain to work at court all day, and to lead the prayers each night. I knew it would be difficult being God's Wife, but I did not understand how hard it would truly be."

Ineni said nothing. The horses' hooves crunched up the path. Ahmose wavered, steadying herself with a hard grip on the chariot's rail, waiting. At last he said, "I have missed you, too." There was a curious tension in his voice.

The sun was nearly below the horizon now. It sent out a last flame, a bright defiance of the oncoming night. Ahmose tucked herself beneath Ineni's arm, pressed her body against his, rested her head on his chest. She heard him swallow hard. She was frightening him, perhaps. He had always been so shy. But she did not care. She had been too long without company, and she needed to feel his closeness.

Ineni reined in on a hilltop. They climbed down from the chariot. He hobbled the horses, adjusted their harnesses, looked anywhere but at Ahmose.

"Come here," she said, filled suddenly with a shaking, hot confidence. There was a large flat stone sunk into the ground, a natural bench. She sat there, and like a fish drawn to bait, Ineni came to her. He sank down beside her, tense, ready to dart away like a wary carp. She wrapped her arms around his neck to hold him in place, and kissed his cheek. He turned his face to hers before she could pull away, and his lips hesitated a breath away from her own.

The moment hung heavy between them, the heart-shaking, prickling moment. Then Ahmose leaned forward, so slightly. Their lips touched. Their mouths opened together. His tongue grazed the roof of her mouth, pulled her toward him, circled inside. She gasped through her nose and Ineni's smell overwhelmed her: sweet herbs, papyrus scrolls, dust from the road, the faintest taste of myrrh. It was a wicked thing. Her heart should be Tut's. But Tut was not here, and he had never looked at her the way Ineni did. And no one could see them but the spotted horses.

Decided now, determined, he loosened the knot of her

dress. It fell to her waist. Her shoulders and breasts were bare. He dipped his head to kiss each breast; she was wordless and breathless; she wanted him. She did not know how, or why. She could not have named exactly what it was she wanted so badly then, but she wanted it with a ferocity that dizzied her thoughts. His hand was on her knee, on her thigh, moving upward to where the fire burned. His fingers brushed her gently there, and she moved her legs apart, eyes squeezed shut with the sweetness of anticipation.

Something rough and warm pressed against her back. He had laid her down on the rock, his mouth busy at her neck, his hand clever and soft beneath her rumpled dress. There was a sound, and she was surprised to realize that it came from her own throat – a sigh, a moan, a surrender. She was floating away on a warm river; she had cast off all her lines, and she was floating, rushing with this strange, sweet current. He was steering her along like a captain steers a new-made barque, and now the current was faster, driving harder, spinning. She urged him on with little gasps, wordless cries. She clutched at his shoulders, and at last she sank under the waves, where there was no air, no light, just the crash of water all around her, and then drifting, drifting, drifting.

The rock had cooled. The sky was dark. The spotted horses stamped and switched their tails. She sat up, shivering.

Ineni's eyes were wide and startled. "I...I didn't plan to..."

"It's all right." She tugged at the rough dress, and he helped her re-tie it at her shoulder. It *was* all right. More than all right. Ineni...her sweet Ineni! Was this what she had wanted from him all along, all their times walking in the garden, rowing on the lake...was this what it all led to?

"I shouldn't have. I got carried away. Great Lady, forgive me."

"Don't call me that." She stood. Her legs were so weak; it was a wonder they held her, shaking as they did. There were lights in Waset below, torches being carried through the streets, braziers burning near windows. For the quickest heartbeat she wanted to admonish him, but she could not.

This was bad, this was wrong, she knew. She was Tut's, and she did love Tut, truly. But he was so far away, and Ineni had kissed her, and put his hand under her dress, and Tut had never looked on her with Ineni's eyes. "When can I see you again?"

He would not speak for a long time. Then, at last, "Whenever you want to, I suppose. But I will not...I will not step out of place again."

But she wanted him to. She understood it now, why women and men did what they did together. She and Ineni could not lie together, of course. He might get a child on her, and that was as out of the question for him as it was for her husband. But this – this they could do. They could be lovers, if it was in secret.

At least until Tut returned. Just until then.

CHAPTER TWENTY-THREE

THE FESTIVAL OF KHONSU WOULD be thinly celebrated this year. With the stores near empty and the harvest disappointing, not even the palace could afford a grand feast. Still, Ahmose planned a stylish celebration with dancers and poets enough to make up for the bland food.

After spending all her nights at the temple for three months and more, she found it somewhat disorienting to be back at the palace again by night. The courtyards in the moonlight, the fountains in the purple dusk, the richly dressed servants hurrying through the yards with reed torches: all these struck her – half awed, half appalled – as any traveler to a foreign land is stricken. The palace was a softened, mysterious place by night, dark shapes against a dark sky. There was a dizzying half-familiarity in the pillars and halls. She passed through her courtyard and paused at the stairs to the roof of her hall. They shone pale and clean in the evening glow, swept free of spider webs, waiting for her feet. With all the time she had spent on the throne and in the temple, Ahmose had not been up to her rooftop sanctuary since before she had worn her wings. Did her pavilion still stand, or had the servants dismantled it? There was no time to find out; she must prepare for the feast.

Twosre waited in Ahmose's apartments. All the braziers were lit, the magnificent painted walls dancing with copper light.

"Come, Lady," Twosre said, all bustle and efficiency. "We

don't have much time."

Twosre had laid out the finest of Ahmose's things, her best gowns and largest jewels. Ahmose held out her arms to be dressed, then lowered them again.

Twosre frowned at her, shaking out the folds of a shining blue gown. "Is something amiss, Lady?"

"I think I ought to dress simply tonight. Let the people see me as a priestess."

Twosre found a clean shift in one of Ahmose's trunks and held it up, shaking her head. "Not nearly as beautiful as your blue gown, Lady."

"I will wear it all the same. Help me put it on." The shift was pure white, softly pleated. Ahmose chose a plain belt of gold links, and considered one wig after another in her mirror. Finally she waved them all away, and set the small God's Wife circlet upon her bare head. Silk ribbons of many colors fell from the crown to frame her face.

"You can't go wigless!"

"Why not? I am the God's Wife. Who's to stop me?"

"Everyone will think you look peculiar."

"I am the bride of the god," Ahmose said, patting her servant's cheek. "Let them think what they will. The priests do as I say, and the second wife is under my control. Should I care what a lot of drunk nobles think?"

"As you will, Holy Lady." Twosre sounded doubtful, but she pulled the stopper from a jar of perfume and trickled some of the heavy oil onto Ahmose's scalp, massaged it into her skin with deft fingers. Ahmose smiled at herself in the mirror, tossed her ribbons from one shoulder to the other, watched with approval the way the white shift shaped itself to her body. The perfume filled the chamber with the rich, warm scent of galbanum. She swept from her hall brimming with confidence, a flower opening to the moon.

Even in the outer reaches of the palace the noise of the feast reached her. Cymbals crashed, flutes keened, the higher notes coming more clearly, more sharply across the intervening night. Pillars reared up above her, hot night air giving way as she strode through this land, a conquering warrior, the righteous bringer of maat.

Servants in their short wigs and plain linens grew more plentiful as she approached the great hall. They bore trays of drink and food, towels clean and soiled, cones of perfumed wax for the guests' wigs. As she passed, some of them stopped to whisper. Was this how Mutnofret felt at the wedding feast, turning every head as she passed? The guards at the great hall's doors bowed to her, murmuring her name and titles. When she nodded, they shoved open the doors.

The long room was filled with the upper class of Waset. A throng of servants waited along the walls, balancing trays of beer and watered wine, simple loaves of bread and dense cakes and withered fruits. A poor enough feast, yet there was no lack of celebrants. The crowd's mood seemed festive enough in spite of the small harvest. Ahmose was glad to see it.

She entered the room and walked solemnly to the Horus Throne. As she crossed the long hall, voices rippled behind her like a boat's wake. Her ribbons floated in the breeze of her steps, trailing her rich dark perfume.

When she was seated, Mutnofret entered, beautiful as always, and fashionably dressed. The second wife's eyes avoided Ahmose's until she was halfway across the hall. When she did look up at the Horus Throne, Mutnofret's eyebrows jumped. It must be startling, Ahmose supposed, to see such an exotic and striking figure as herself on the throne, in the white shift of a holy priestess, with her scalp shining and bare. She nodded to her sister, calm and sure.

Mutnofret took her throne gracefully, avoiding Ahmose's eye. The second wife's demeanor was happy, though, not petulant. The light mood of the crowd seemed to buoy her. Perhaps the sisters would pass a pleasant night between them. Ahmose hoped it would be so. She would not hesitate to send Mutnofret away again, if need called for it.

Ahmose listened to recited poetry, sipped wine, watched troupes of dancers and acrobats perform late into the night.

At last, feeling sleepy, she excused herself to walk in the garden. The night was pleasantly warm, and she wandered down to the lake's edge, recalling how she had watched Tut skip stones across the water. That had been so long ago. She cupped handfuls of water, splashed them over her shoulders until her white shift was soaked. A breeze lifted, cooling her skin.

"I hoped I would see you here tonight."

"Ineni." Ahmose turned from the lake's wall. He wore the formally long kilt that was stylish among noble men, folded with sharp vertical pleats. His bare chest and shoulders were pale in the moonlight.

"You are beautiful, Ahmose. You should have feasts more often, so I can look at you more."

"Be careful," she whispered. "What if someone hears us?" The garden was not empty. Men and women wandered here and there, moving from flower bed to shadow to pool of moonlight; laughter rose into the night. From a nearby hedge, densely planted, came a sigh and a moan. Ahmose's skin tingled.

"Why don't you come for a walk with me?" Ineni said.

"Are you drunk? Don't be stupid!"

"Maybe a little drunk. From looking at you."

"Oh, Ineni. You've had too much wine. No, don't come closer..." for he had taken a step toward her, smiling foolishly.

"All right, then," he said, backing off, grinning at her. "I'll just go over there, into that stand of myrrh trees, all alone."

He laughed, walked away, casting bleary looks back over his shoulder at Ahmose. She sat on the lip of the lake and watched him go, her pulse alive in her stomach and cheeks. The leaves and branches of the grove closed around Ineni, blotting out the bright white blur of his kilt and the brown of his back. For a long time she sat unmoving, the water drying on her shoulders and shift. Far up the path, the forms of a man and woman bent around each other, tangled in an embrace. Ahmose watched the man's hands travel down his lover's back, describe the arc of her hips with a graceful sweep.

From beyond the hedge, a woman's voice cried wordlessly, breathless and urgent.

Ahmose counted a hundred heartbeats, looked cautiously around the garden, and walked calmly toward the myrrh grove. *This is stupid, stupid*, she told herself. Their chariot rides were bad enough, and far too frequent. But at least in the chariot they were alone, out in the hills beyond the fields, and Ahmose was disguised. Stupid, stupid, but the night was in her blood now, and wasn't she the God's Wife? Was this palace not her own, after all? Stupid, dangerous, but when she pushed through the branches of the grove Ineni was waiting for her. His skin was warm. It smelled sweetly, greenly of the trees.

When Ahmose returned to the feast, flushed and shaking with excitement and guilt, she entered the hall to find Sitamun bending over Mutnofret's shoulder, whispering. The second wife found Ahmose's eyes, studied them while her servant spoke into her ear. And slowly, mockingly, Mutnofret smiled.

CHAPTER TWENTY-FOUR

THE DAY AFTER THE FESTIVAL of Khonsu was muggy and uncomfortable with flies. It seemed impossible that the flood could be so low on such a day as this, with the air so wet and dense that every breath tasted of reeds and mud. Ahmose waited on her cairn for the spotted horses and scratched her itching skin through the coarse linen dress. The sky was strangely subdued, hazy, as though a great length of gauzy fabric stretched from horizon to horizon.

Hardly another soul could be seen on the road. Between the light traffic and the dampness of the air, there were no distant banners of dust to give travelers away. She saw Ineni first as a dark speck fading out of Waset, detaching itself from the wall of the city, growing, forming itself into tiny horses and shrunken chariot as he drove toward the crossroads. She was on her feet and smiling before she could make out his face.

Ineni pulled the horses to a stop. She ran to the chariot, took his hand with a welling excitement under her heart.

"Kiss me!"

He frowned, and hesitated. "Ahmose, you know I adore you, but last night was..."

"I am the God's Wife! Do as I say and kiss me." She pulled him to her, pressed her mouth to his, guided his hand to her breast. It was as if her body exerted some strange control over him. His objection melted away. He pinched her nipple through the rough fabric, and it scratched at her, hurting deliciously. She shivered.

"Let's get off the road," he said thickly, and broke away from her to stir the horses into action.

They climbed the dirt path again to their rock on the hill. This was where they came most often to be alone together; the rock was as familiar to her now as her own bed.

She unknotted her dress while Ineni hobbled the horses. The cloth fell away, so she stood in nothing but her sandals and wig. When he straightened from his work, his eyes lingered on her body for a long, breathless time. Then he came to her and lifted her up; her sandaled feet tapped on the rock when he set her there so that she stood over him. He pressed his face against her belly, his fingernails pricking at her spine until she arched her hips backward. Then he hunched, and his breath was against the place between her legs, and she gasped when she felt the fire of his kiss there. She held tight to his shoulders so her shivering legs would not drop her to the stone.

Something just as hot and wet as Ineni's mouth fell upon her shoulder, then her arm, then her back. She opened her eyes. Ineni's back was speckled with shimmering light. A horse whinnied. The ground began to hiss, and in an instant Ahmose's body was soaking and chilled.

Ineni looked around, eyes wide, mouth gaping. He ran a few steps toward the horses, which tossed their heads and lashed their tails, then back to Ahmose, who hopped about on the rock and grabbed for her tangled gown.

"Get the horses," she cried over the sound of water pounding earth. She managed to pull the wet dress around herself, worked it into a sloppy knot. Water pelted her from above and below, splashing up off the hard stony ground to cover her hem with mud. She ran to help Ineni manage the beasts.

"Unhook them from the chariot," he called.

She had never hitched a horse before, but she seized one leather line running from harness to chariot and followed it with her hand. It was obvious enough where it hooked to the vehicle's shaft; it took her only a moment to pull the strap free.

"Now the other!"

She dodged around the back of the vehicle. It lurched toward her as the horse backed, screaming, and she nearly slipped in the mud, but righted herself with a hand on the muddy wheel. The other horse was free in an instant. Ineni pulled the horses, still linked together by their harnesses, away from the cart, allowing them to kick and dance in a circle around him. He held tight to the long reins. His mouth moved; he must be soothing them, but all she could hear was the roar of the rain.

At last the horses seemed resigned. They stood still, ears pinned, backs hunched against the stinging rain. Ahmose came toward them cautiously, her hands out as if to placate the beasts.

"I've never seen rain before," she said, teeth chattering.

"Nor I. I have read about it plenty. We are lucky to be on the highlands. A sudden fall like this can make floods all through the valley – kill livestock, people, too, if they're caught in a wash."

Kill livestock. With food so scarce, Egypt could ill afford to lose a single goat or calf. She swallowed hard. "What do you think it means?"

Ineni's eyes were shadowed under the dense gray sky. She could read none of his feelings in his face, but his silence spoke well enough. She looked away, ashamed. This was Amun's wrath, surely. Amun had seen their wickedness, had disapproved of their defiling the sacred Feast of Khonsu. He had opened up the skies in punishment. Now Egypt would lose precious cattle, and it was Ahmose's fault. *Forgive me,* her ka cried out. *Forgive me, Lord Amun! I will never...*even in her own thoughts the words were bitter. She forced them out, resolute, chastened. "We cannot do this again, Ineni. The gods – they will not have it. If I am to be God's Wife, I must keep myself only for Amun. Amun – and my earthly husband."

He nodded, patting a horse's soaking muzzle, avoiding her eyes. "I know."

"I would have it otherwise, if I could."

"And I."

"But it cannot be. We know that now."

One hand came free of the reins and touched her lightly at the nape of her neck, trailed down the wet cloth clinging to her back, all the way to the back of one thigh. She wanted to sob, to rail against the gods. Instead, she stood still and took the stinging lashes of Amun's rebuke. Each of the thousand-thousand drops that stung her skin shamed her. Never again.

Ineni drove her all the way back to Ipet-Isut. The rain ceased as suddenly as it had come on, and a cold wind blew the gray sky away to the south. A band of colors arced across the river between Waset and the Holy House. The foreign beauty of the arc of colors pierced her ka. *Every sensation is weightier with my heart broken.* Ahmose kept her hands on the chariot's rail all the way home.

She did not care if the temple guards saw her climb down from the steward's chariot, soaked through with a face like stone. She marched past them in her cheap wig and smeared makeup, down Ipet-Isut's avenue, which was stunned and deserted in the wake of the downpour. She kicked her chamber door closed and stripped off the gown for the second time. It hit the floor with a wet smack. She untied her sandals and threw them across the room, heaved her wig at the wall, climbed miserably into her bed before she saw the scroll lying on her bedside table. It stared at her, taunting and ominous. With trembling fingers she picked it up and untied the red cord that bound it.

You have taken my title and flaunted your treachery

before the court. You have betrayed your family. All my children are dead, and I have no more happiness in this world. I am an old woman, with no strength left in my bones to punish you in this life as you deserve; and if the priests believe you are the God's Wife, there is nothing I can do, save this. You take my last shred of joy for yourself, and so I curse you with all the unhappiness of an old woman's heart.

Ahmose sucked in a ragged breath. Nefertari. Had Mutnofret told her? Or had word simply reached the estate in the southern hills at last? It hardly mattered now. That arrow was loosed, and nothing Ahmose could do would call it back into her quiver.

Cursed with unhappiness. *Lady of sorrow.* She gave voice to her sadness at last, pulling her blanket over her head and wailing, wailing. How could it go so wrong just as it went so right? Was this Amun, or some darker god who cut at her heart? Was there any difference now? She howled beneath her blanket until her eyes were swollen and hot. When Twosre came in to sit silently at her side, patting, stroking, she stopped her keening but not her tears.

CHAPTER TWENTY-FIVE

AGAIN THE ITERU ROSE, SPANS shorter than the year before. The harvest was small, the stores near empty, the cattle thin and dull-coated. Men muttered. Women's eyes were dark. The Black Land reeled on the verge of a plunge into famine.

Nothing that could be salted and eaten was thrown back into the river. Suspicious stews were prepared in Ipet-Isut with stringy white meat or tough chunks of fish, bony fins still attached, the broth thin and greasy. There was little bread and less milk, and all the fruits were withered or over-ripe. Ahmose ate it all, and gratefully. Her belly was never empty, and she thanked the gods for that blessing. She doubted the rekhet were so lucky. No reports of death by starvation had yet reached her, but that did not mean people were not dying. She saved bits of the best fish and meat and porridge from every meal she ate, burning these offerings at every sanctuary in the Holy House by turns. She pleaded with the gods to spare her people, to intervene. But the gods were silent, and Ahmose was guilty and afraid.

There was no feast for the Royal Son Wadjmose's weaning. The boy marked two years of age quietly, without public acclaim. It was not fitting for the Pharaoh's son, but feasts were an ostentation the throne could ill afford. Even at the palace meals were smaller, simpler, and less savory. Mutnofret complained daily, but there was nothing to be done. All of Egypt must wait out the lean times and save feasting for future days. Even the Pharaoh's house was required to humble itself.

"It is not fitting that Wadjmose's weaning should go uncelebrated, though," Ahmose said to Twosre one dull, dry morning. They were picking scraggly herbs in Ahmose's palace garden in the hour before court came to session. "He is the First Royal Son. And I am sure when Tut returns, Wadjmose will be the heir. There should be some sort of acknowledgment – just not a feast."

Twosre shrugged. "But what to do? Any kind of celebration at the palace is always feasted. It would not make the nobles think highly of the Royal Son if frog stew and watered-down milk were offered them."

"Why don't we have a ceremony at Ipet-Isut? There will be no expectation of a feast at the temple, I should think. A feast would be unseemly. But it would mark the occasion, at least."

"A fine idea. You and the High Priest can hold it in the forecourt of the Amun temple. Quite a large crowd can fit there, I know. No one will grumble over a missed feast if they get the honor of attending a ceremony at the Temple of Amun."

"Exactly. And I imagine it will make Mutnofret very happy, too."

It was more than a year since Ahmose had given up Ineni's companionship, and since then she had devoted herself wholly to her duties. She still kept Mutnofret from the throne hall, telling the court the second wife was busy with the Royal Sons' tutors, or entertaining foreign dignitaries. It would impress no one to know the truth: that Mutnofret was banned from court by the God's Wife, and stewed helplessly each day in her apartments.

When Thutmose returned from his campaign, he would be cross to see such discord in the royal family. Ahmose knew she needed to reach out to Mutnofret now, to make an offering of goodwill to her distant, cold sister. She held no false hope that they would be close again. Those days were gone forever, washed downstream like a fragile leaf midriver. But some semblance of unity would please their husband when he came home. Perhaps she could at least make Mutnofret smile. A smile was worth riches, in these lean and frightening times.

"It is good to see most of Waset's greatest houses still know how to show proper respect." Twosre gave a wry smile.

Ahmose and her woman stood well concealed behind the line of myrrh trees that grew between the pylons outside the Temple of Amun. They peeked through the branches at the crowd, which swelled by the minute. There were representatives from every important family in Waset, as far as Ahmose could tell, and many faces she did not recognize – visitors from Iunet and Abedjwet, Edfu and Swenet, come to pay their respects to the king's eldest son, and to be seen doing it. Even during lean times, even with Thutmose off at war, there was strong support for the throne. Ahmose remarked on it, wondering that so many would make the journey during times like these.

"The Pharaoh has done well by the people, Lady, and that's the plain truth." Twosre tugged at her elbow, pulling her back toward the Temple of Mut. Ahmose took one last, long look at the crowd milling in the twilight, then turned to follow Twosre. *Tut has done well, but what have I done? Will he still need me beside him when he returns?*

Back in Ahmose's small temple chamber, tonight's clothing and jewels were already laid out. Faithful Twosre had been to the Waset palace early in the day, fetching this dress and that shawl, this wig and that collar from the Great Wife's chambers. Ahmose had grown so used to the simple garments of a priestess, even wearing her simple white shift and ribbon crown to court, that she hardly knew anymore how to dress herself for affairs of state. Twosre was a treasure beyond price.

Ahmose was unhappy to see, though, that Twosre has chosen the red dress – the Mut dress, the one she had worn when she took the temple. It was a hard thing to look upon. The dress carried too many painful memories – how she had plotted with her sweet Ineni, how he had swallowed hard when he saw her in it. How they conspired to take Nefertari's title – for the sake of Tut's throne, of course! – and how her grandmother had spurned her and cursed her. Nefertari's curse had been a true one. Ahmose could not recall a single moment of true happiness since the day Amun poured down his punishment upon her, that far-off day in the hills when Ineni had lifted her up to stand on the rock, when he had…

"Why that dress? Are you sure it's appropriate?"

"Never a better one. You look just like a goddess in it. And here, I've brought your nicest wig from the palace. Gold beads – very pretty! Now undress. We need to get you ready for the ceremony."

Just like a goddess. Ahmose sighed and undid her knots. It took some fidgeting and tugging to get the red gown on. Ahmose was sixteen now, and her body had filled.

"I don't remember being able to walk so well in this dress," Ahmose said, taking five or six steps across her chamber, then back again, testing the gown's give.

"I had it altered a bit to fit your new body. You are not the skinny little thing you once were."

"Thank the gods for that."

"Sit. I need to paint your face. I think your husband will be pleased when he comes home and sees how you have matured."

Ahmose's stomach pinched tight at the thought. Would she go to him at the palace, or would he come here to her temple chamber at night after her prayers were done? Making love on a ride, under the open sky, as she had with Ineni was out of the question. Even dressed as a commoner, Tut would be recognized. Two rekhet fooling about nude in the hills would not be worth noticing by passing hunters or soldiers, but the Pharaoh and the God's Wife.... Ahmose blushed at the thought. No, it would not be maat. And anyway, to be secret lovers under the open sky – that was for her and Ineni. And it was gone forever. *I will sort it out after Tut comes home*, she told herself, and resolved to stay focused on Wadjmose's ceremony.

Twosre had chosen golden torques for her arms and bright hoops for her ears. Tiny golden bells hung on chains around her ankles, so that every step chimed. There was a glittering ring for each finger. But for her brow, just the slim circlet of the cobra crown. Twosre held up a hand mirror and tilted it slowly so that Ahmose could see each part of herself by turns. She looked powerful and righteous, exactly as the God's Wife ought – and nothing like she felt.

They took a private route to the forecourt where Wadjmose's guests waited. Ahmose led Twosre through a maze of narrow lanes that snaked among the priests' living quarters and a few ancient sanctuaries. They passed beneath great painted pillars that gave way to pylons, then to walls, blacker than the sky in the warm night. The roof of the Temple of Amun choked out the starlight. With the ceremony about to begin, the interior of the temple lay quiet. To their right, a powdery orange glow scattered across the floor, deepened, strengthened. Ahmose blinked at the gathering light.

A temple servant hurried toward them holding a torch of rushes high. It gave off a strong smell: sap, earth, the smoke of offerings. "Holy Lady," the young man said. "Allow me to lead you to the forecourt."

She nodded at him, quiet and poised. There was a job ahead of her, a duty of state. She was the Great Royal Wife again, not only the God's Wife. Her ka was a cool vibration within her, a steady and confident beating like the sound of a dancer's drummer heard at a great distance. She gathered herself in. She was ready.

Menketra, the High Priest, was waiting for her just inside the front entrance to the temple. She nodded a greeting. There was a strange spark in his eye when the temple-boy's torch caught it; the High Priest's lips trembled and paled when he looked upon Ahmose. It made her wary, though not afraid – not exactly. She was like the bird that sees the approaching cat and tenses, holding itself ready for flight should the cat chance to spring.

A ripple of murmurs went through the crowd outside. Mutnofret must have arrived; only Mutnofret's frank beauty could stir a crowd in that way. Ahmose nodded at Menketra. Together they stepped around the pylon and into the forecourt. Priests raised ankhs on poles, directing the crowd back. A large half-moon cleared before Ahmose and the High Priest. The gathered nobles subsided into reverent quiet.

"Make way for the Lady Mutnofret," a steward called. The crowd parted at the apex of the moon's curve to let the second wife through. She was dressed beautifully, as always: jeweled, scented, robed in blue. A wide collar of gold and turquoise caught up the light of the stars and sent a faint aura shimmering around her face. Mutnofret was a stunning woman, if ever the gods had made one.

She carried Wadjmose on one hip. The boy looked pale with fright, but he did not cry. His solemn black eyes stared at Ahmose, unblinking. His head was shaven for the first time, the sidelock of youth tied above one ear; it was tufted, sticking out at a comical angle like a duck's tail. He studied Ahmose as Mutnofret carried him closer, then, as if deciding she was safe, smiled at her, showing dimples in his cheeks. His face was so like his mother's, with long eyes and a fine nose, that Ahmose's breath caught in her chest. A dim part of her ka yearned for her sister's love.

When Ahmose glanced at her sister, Mutnofret, too, smiled. It was tight, tremulous, and had something of an apology in it. They were standing face to face now. Mutnofret whispered, "Thank you." It meant much to her, Ahmose knew, that Wadjmose was not forgotten during Egypt's tenuous time, that Ahmose was on Mutnofret's side in the matter of heirship, if in nothing else.

Menketra raised his arms. The priests lowered their poles.

The only sound in the forecourt was the buzzing of night insects. At last the High Priest spoke in a voice that filled Ipet-Isut like struck bronze.

"Men and women of Egypt. We bring you here tonight to witness the weaning of Wadjmose, son of Aakheper-ka-ra, the Good Lord Thutmose, our king. The First Royal Son has reached his second year, by the grace of the gods, and grows stronger by the day."

Mutnofret set the boy on his feet. He clung at first to his mother's leg, staring out at the crowd, but when Mutnofret patted the back of his head in comfort he stepped away from her, facing the many eyes of the nobles like a tiny warrior, his bold little fists twisting in the hem of his kilt. Ahmose bit her cheek to ward off a laugh of delight. He was a strong boy indeed, with all of his father's bravery. He would make a fine king.

"Bring forth the bread," Ahmose said. A priestess carried a gilt tray out of the darkness of the temple. Ahmose took the loaf, broke off a small piece, and dipped it in a cup of thin, honeyed milk. She bent to Wadjmose and held it to his lips. He took it, chewed, swallowed, his somber eyes never leaving her own.

The crowd sighed with approval.

Menketra blessed Wadjmose with ankh, oil, and salt. Then he faced the crowd again. His voice had changed subtly. "And now I tell you true, O my brothers and sisters of Egypt. I have been sent a vision by the gods." The strange spark that had been in his eyes was in his throat now. There was a dark, compelling zeal in Menketra's words. "It has been given to me to know, and to tell you: the Pharaoh's son is more than any mortal prince."

Ahmose paled. What was he doing? They had discussed the ceremony in great detail. This was not what they had planned. She breathed deeply, pushing down her fear.

Menketra's hypnotic voice poured out over the listeners. "The child is the offspring not only of the king and Great Royal Wife, but of Amun and the God's Wife. This is a holy child, a Royal Son that will please the gods with his every word and deed. He will restore prosperity to Egypt. He will be the embodiment of maat, righteousness made flesh!"

No! Ahmose looked at Mutnofret, afraid her face would betray her confusion and shock to the crowd, afraid it would not show enough of her horror, her disbelief, to her sister. Mutnofret stared back at her, and her eyes were lances, her beautiful face tense and sharp with hatred.

Ahmose shook her head slightly. Her lips parted. She breathed, "No!" *No, Mutnofret,* she said with her eyes, she screamed with her heart. *I did not do this. I did not know. I did not know! You must believe me!*

Mutnofret snatched her son up and held him close. Menketra talked on; the crowd murmured; Ahmose understood none of it. All she could see, all she could feel was the force of rage in Mutnofret's heart. Both women stood still, quaking, rooted uncertainly like trees on an eroded bank. Mutnofret was poised to flee, Ahmose to fall to her knees and beg her sister's forgiveness. Neither could so much as twitch, though, with the eyes of the great houses upon them. They could speak only with their own eyes, and while Ahmose's said, *Forgive me, sister, I did not know,* Mutnofret's shouted, *I hate you, I hate you, I hate you.*

When the High Priest at last brought the ceremony to a close, Mutnofret carried her son from the temple without a word. The crowd parted for her, then closed around her. She was gone. Ahmose stared at Menketra. His eyes were dewy with reverence.

"What was that?" she hissed.

"Holy Lady." There was real worship in his voice, as on that day when she had appeared before him dressed as Mut.

"Come into the temple with me," she said, her voice shaking. He followed her like a dog.

Ahmose pulled the High Priest into the nearest empty room, a tiny alcove stocked with torches and sacks of myrrh resin. Her stomach roiled. The side of Menketra's face was lit by the faintest sliver of moonlight through the open chamber door. "The child of the God's Wife?"

"Remarkable, Holy Lady. I was granted the most incredible vision this very morning, with the rising sun. Your son, with rivers of wealth pouring from his hands. Years upon years of perfect floods. Food enough for every child in Egypt. Monuments – oh! Your son will build a great and holy temple, Great Lady! The sight of it – like nothing I have ever seen!"

"Wadjmose is not my son, Menketra."

"What?"

"He is not my son. He is my nephew. He is *Mutnofret's* son. The second wife's."

"No, Holy Lady. I cannot be mistaken. The heir to the throne..."

"Is not Wadjmose. Not yet, anyway."

The High Priest shook his head. "I do not understand. I thought he was yours, and you gave him to a nurse, as usual."

"Did that woman standing beside me look like a nurse? You have seen Mutnofret a hundred times! You know who she is. You know she is no nurse!"

"Yes, of course, but I assumed his aunt had brought him to the temple for the ceremony, and you..."

"Menketra, *I have no child.*"

He raised his hands in a gesture of total confusion. "But the gods were explicit, Holy Lady. I know my vision was not wrong."

She sighed. "There is nothing to be done about it now. We cannot make an announcement that the High Priest got his vision all wrong. We would look like fools – the entire priesthood!"

Menketra looked crestfallen. Ahmose nearly felt sorry for him. Nearly. "Holy Lady, I regret..."

"You have not yet begun to regret. We will need to appease Mutnofret now; she is humiliated. It won't be easy to make her feel she's been properly soothed, the gods help us."

"I shall write her a letter of apology first thing in the morning. I'll send her something from my estates."

"That would be a good start. But I warn you, she is not easy to calm once her anger has been roused. It would be wise of you to stay clear of her for a long time."

He nodded. "Yes, Holy Lady. But...but Holy Lady, my vision cannot have been wrong. It was too clear, too powerful. If not this child, then it will be another. It will be *yours*."

She was too sickened to argue. There was almost an apology in Mutnofret's face tonight, almost forgiveness. Ahmose had come so close to reaching her sister, and Menketra's vision ruined everything – forever, perhaps. To quiet him, she said, "All right, Menketra. I believe you. Now I must get some sleep, and you as well. You have quite the letter to write in the morning."

CHAPTER TWENTY-SIX

M UTNOFRET WASTED NO TIME. AHMOSE had just dressed for court and called for a chariot to take her from the temple to the palace. The morning bells in Ipet-Isut had hardly quieted when she heard the shouting outside her chamber door. She opened it to find Twosre attempting to fend off the second wife, attempting to block the way to Ahmose's door without actually laying her hands upon the Lady Mutnofret's person. But it was no good. It never was any good; not with Mutnofret.

The moment Mutnofret saw her, she shivered like a coiled snake and shoved past Twosre, slapping the door with her palm, throwing it wider as she crowded into Ahmose's tiny temple room. Her face was the blade of an axe. Her eyes were wide; they strained with a terrible ferocity, flashed a swift, cold fury.

Ahmose spoke immediately, seeking to still her sister's rage. "Mutnofret, you have every right to be angry. I am angry, too. It was Menketra's doing...the High Priest's. He was mistaken about his vision, that is all. He is apologetic. He..."

"The High Priest's doing! Shaming me in front of representatives of every great house? How convenient for you, that the High Priest you control should bumble before so many important people."

"No, Mutnofret! I knew nothing of this. If I had known he was going to say those things, I'd have..."

"Shut your lying mouth! I've heard enough from it!"

"Mutnofret, I am the Great Royal Wife, and the God's Wife."

Her lip curled. "Are you? You stole a title from our grandmother, and that makes you the God's Wife?"

"That's not the way it happened," Ahmose said, lowering her eyes.

Mutnofret's words trampled over her. "You stole what was Nefertari's, and you stole what was mine. You have finally pushed me over the edge of the cliff, *little sister*."

"I never stole a thing from you! This wasn't my choice! I never wanted to be Great Royal Wife, Mutnofret, believe me."

"Why should anyone believe a thieving liar like you?"

Ahmose clenched her teeth together hard. "You don't understand. I did it to appease the gods. It's to protect Tut while he's off making war...to protect Egypt."

"Protect the Pharaoh! What protection does he need from you? What have you ever given him, you timid, cowardly child? Pleasure? *Sons?* I've given him *two!* I took our mother's rebuke with grace. I've served as *second wife*, when I should be chief among women. I did my duty to Egypt. I gave more than my body, Ahmose, *more than my body*. I gave my pride! I gave my shame! I gave everything I am and everything I ever was. I gave up everything I hoped to be! I've given my husband two sons, and you conspire to take one away, like you took away our grandmother's title. You've taken *everything else* from me, and now you think take my son as well!"

Ahmose could only stare at her, struck dumb. There was no getting through to her. Mutnofret had built this like a secret palace inside her heart. The walls were already up; Ahmose could never tear them down, no matter what she said. Yet she had to say something. "I have never wanted to take your son, Mutnofret. He is yours. I have been writing to Tut, trying to get him to name Wadjmose heir."

"Oh, yes, no doubt you have. If the whole world believes Wadjmose is your son and you can get him named heir, then I've done all the hard work for you. Well, I won't stand for it, Ahmose. You shot your final arrow last night. You will pay for this. When the Pharaoh returns, he will know you for what you truly are, and so will all the people. I'll see to it myself."

"Get out. You won't listen to reason, so get out."

"Get out, says the liar. Get out, as if you still hold some power over Egypt. You think you have the power to command a royal wife."

"The second wife, yes. Get out."

Mutnofret screamed like a hunting hawk. She reached out a swift hand, never taking her eyes from Ahmose. She seized something from Ahmose's bedside table in a shaking, hard fist. Ahmose watched a blur of carnelian and jasper raise into the air, leave Mutnofret's hand, careen off the far wall with a sound like dropped pottery. Ahmose shrieked, and grabbed up the pieces of her Mut statue – Tut's gift, broken.

She stared at Mutnofret, astounded by the impiety and violence of this thing she did. Tears came to her eyes.

"Tears! You'll cry a hundred tears for every one you've made me shed, Ahmose. I swear this by all the gods. You'll *weep*." She spat the last word into Ahmose's face, and was gone.

Ahmose stood still for a long time, breathing steadily to cool her face, to still the frantic pounding of her heart. The pieces of her Mut statue were heavy in her hands. The tears broke and ran, as shame-hot as the sun.

CHAPTER TWENTY-SEVEN

SHEMU WAS ONE LONG BLACK blur of sorrow. Ahmose withdrew into her bed chamber whenever time permitted, spinning flax alone in the close air. She refused to read dreams. Dreams did not matter. Not anymore. All that mattered was her nightly ritual at the temple, dancing and chanting until she fell, spent and weeping, for the sake of keeping the gods' eyes on Egypt. Until Thutmose was home safe, that was all that mattered. There was no brightness in her days anymore, and nothing but sadness lived in her heart.

Finally, her ka was so blackened that even the news of the king's victory hardly moved her. She held the scroll Twosre brought her and sobbed over it, eyes blinded by tears, nose running. She could form no thought but *He is coming home.* If her tears had borne silt, her cheeks would have been deep black and ready for the planting.

Ahmose curled up on her bed in the summer heat, sticky with sweat and hollow with sadness. What would Tut think of the mess she had made when he returned? Their family was broken, and Ahmose was to blame. She lay for hours, drifting in and out of troubled sleep, fretting over the Pharaoh's homecoming. At last, unable to stay any longer in the close air of her chamber, she rose. There was still water in her jug. It had long since gone tepid in the heat of the day, but it cleaned her well enough. She poured it into a basin and washed the feel of hot sleep from her body. She scrubbed the crust of dried tears from her face; the skin around her eyes was tender and swollen. She pulled a fresh white frock out of a chest and belted it around her, then went out into her garden wigless and crownless.

She had not shaved her head in weeks. She had sunk so far into a depression that tending to her appearance was like carrying a boulder up a hill. The only service she'd requested was plucking. Each stab of pain as her hairs were pulled from her legs, her armpits, her groin, was a penance. She could not even say anymore what sin needed punishing. I seemed her sins were innumerable and garish, and each bled into the next, paint pots spilled on a cold floor.

A merciful breeze had come up while she slept. It stirred the mat of tight-curled hair on her head. It carried the smells of the river, papyrus plants and fish and hippopotamus dung. She closed her eyes and breathed it in deeply, so deeply that her lungs ached. She pushed it all out again quickly, sucked in another taste of air. Again and again she did this, until she was dizzy enough that she had to lean hard against the garden wall until her head cleared. When she could walk once more, she wandered aimlessly through the paths of her garden, tearing leaves from the plants and letting them fall from her hands, tangling and untangling her thoughts. Soon another pair of feet walked beside her own, pacing out this restless route. Twosre. They said nothing as they walked; Ahmose had no words.

Dusk slipped into darkness. Night birds called intermittently beyond the palace walls. Servants came to tend to Ahmose's apartments, murmuring and laughing. When they finished, torches and braziers snuffed out. The great palace of Waset darkened. At last Twosre said in her fig-and-earth voice, "What troubles you, Holy Lady?"

"You should not call me that, Twosre. I don't deserve it."

Twosre stopped walking, gazed at Ahmose steadily.

Ahmose stopped her pacing. She said, "My family – we are broken. Destroyed. my sister hates me, my grandmother has cursed me, and I have offended the gods. Oh, how I have sinned. The river – the famine – it's my doing. I am sure of it. All my doing."

"Not even the God's Wife is perfect."

"I'm not..."

Twosre raised a hand. The gesture silenced Ahmose. "How you came by the title makes no difference. Do you serve weak gods? Would they have allowed this thing if it was not their will?"

Ahmose shook her head dully. There were wads of linen stuffed inside her heart; thoughts refused to form.

Twosre seemed to take the gesture for acquiescence. "I have heard the Pharaoh returns to Waset."

"I read his letter. He should be near the Delta by now, I would guess. Two weeks, perhaps a few days more."

"You do not seem happy about this."

"It's not that I am unhappy. I've missed him so much. But I feel I've made such a mess of things here. Mutnofret, and Nefertari...."

"Sometimes the gods give us a terrible road to walk, Holy Lady. It is sacrifice after sacrifice at every step. Some pay a higher price than others."

"Ah, that we do."

"Be joyful," Twosre said. Her voice was a balm. "Your husband returns. Egypt is safe. And in Ipet-Isut, the priests dance and sing more than they ever did before. You have done much good, whatever your sins may be. *Whatever* your sins may be."

Ahmose remembered the rain on the bluffs, Ineni with the spotted horses whirling around him, the drops falling on his back. She remembered Nefertari's curse curling in her hands. She remembered Mutnofret's apologetic smile in the forecourt of the Temple. *Nofret, my sister, my only sister.* And she remembered the men in the fields, their thin, dusty crops, the barren earth. She hoped with all her heart that Twosre spoke the truth. If her life ended tonight and she met Anupu in the echoing black of the underworld, her heart would bend the scales until they broke.

CHAPTER TWENTY-EIGHT

THERE WAS NO BODY HANGING from the bow of the ship this time. Thutmose's fleet sailed into Waset at midday. Ahmose and Mutnofret stood at the head of the water steps, a nurse holding baby Amunmose on her hip while Wadjmose tugged at his sidelock with one hand and held Mutnofret's skirt with the other. A dozen guards surrounded the royal family, keeping the pressing crowd well back. There were cheers, shouts, victory songs among the rekhet and nobles who thronged through the city streets and crowded the shore. Pleasure barges sailed out onto the bright green river; wealthy men and women took their mid-day meals on the cool water, watching the return of Egypt's victorious army. The varied music coming from so many boats was a confused, vibrant jumble.

Ahmose said nothing to her sister, did not even glance her way. Mutnofret was stiff and quiet, waving Wadjmose back to the nurse's side whenever the boy tugged too hard at her dress. The tension between the two wives was thick enough that it ought to have been visible: layer upon layer of woven reeds, perhaps, or a head-high wall of mud bricks.

From the time it appeared on the northern horizon, it took nearly an hour for the flagship to moor. Ahmose could see Tut's smile well before the ship reached the shore. She smiled back, unable to constrain her joy with the proper dignity and quietude of her position. She wanted to wave to him, to jump up and down and shout like the rekhet.

231

Instead, she clenched her fists and never took her eyes away from his face.

Before the sailors had even tied the ship into place, Tut leapt from its side, splashed in the shallow water covering the lowest steps, and was striding up toward her, two steps at a time like a boy returning from a hunting trip. Ahmose could hold herself back no longer. She scurried down the last few stairs separating them and threw herself on the king, arms tight around his neck. He smelled of pitch and sweat. His skin was hot from the sun. His arms wrapped around her waist, strong, sure, as real as stone. He said something into her ear, but the crowd was roaring so, she couldn't make it out. She shook her head, grinning, and he led her by the hand to the stair head where Mutnofret and the children waited.

Ahmose broke away with difficulty, stood back as the Pharaoh held his second wife close for a long time. When she pulled back from their embrace, tears slicked her cheeks. Her eyes were closed; she bit her painted lips together. The king said something to her as well, but if Mutnofret heard she gave no sign.

Then the nurse brought the children forward, two bright, healthy boys, sturdy and dark-eyed. The Pharaoh looked them over for a long time, his eyes wide with wonder. Then he picked Wadjmose up and tossed him into the air, again and again. The Royal Son's face flashed panic, then anger; then, as Tut continued to throw him high, the boy smiled wide. Amunmose was too young for rough play; Tut held him gently and kissed his fat cheek. It was good to see them with their father. It was good to see that Tut loved them well, even after so long away. Ahmose should have no trouble convincing him to do what was right.

Two litters had come for them, and more guards as well, to push the crowd back and away. Eagerly, Ahmose climbed onto the two-chaired platform. It was good to have her husband beside her again.

The road up to the palace was lined with onlookers. They

roared, and threw wildflowers in the litter's path. The crowd was still too loud for talking, but Ahmose took Tut's hand and held it with both of her own, relieved to have him beside her again, apologetic for all her many wrongs. She hoped her touch said enough, for now.

As on the night of the Festival of Khonsu, Twosre had lit all the lights in the hall of the Great Royal Wife. The tall, slender woman bowed in the anteroom when Ahmose entered. "Is there anything you require, Lady?"

"Some wine, I think, and a bath. I will need you to shave my head as well." She wanted to have it done before heading to the quay, but after hours of offering and singing in thanks, there had hardly been enough time to dress appropriately and ride from Ipet-Isut. She set her wig on a stand in her bedroom and tugged irritably at the long stubble on her head. It itched in the heat. Most unpleasant – hard to believe she had allowed her appearance to slide so far. Well, that was at an end now. The Pharaoh was home, home, home! She would rejoice, and send up more prayers of gratitude, and tonight, she would bring Tut to her bed to give him her love, as she had done with Ineni.

She took her time bathing, then oiled her skin with the sweetest-spiciest scent Twosre could find. Her own hands running over the smoothness of her body excited her; she found it difficult to sit still while Twosre scraped away the hair on her scalp. When she looked proper once more, she dressed in the sheer blue gown and painted her face. She was just sliding a silver torque onto her arm when a sharp clap sounded outside her door. No woman's hands ever sounded so strong, so ready. She waved Twosre to the door, then hissed after her, "Leave us once you've let him in!"

Tut was across the antechamber and through her bedroom door in a few eager strides. She took a step back, all unaware, surprised by his powerful, unfamiliar presence. It had been so long since she had been alone with him, she had forgotten how he could dominate a room just by entering it. Words were lost to her. She stared at him, unblinking.

"You have changed. Again. You're a lovely woman now, Ahmoset. It's what I said on the water steps."

"I beg your pardon?"

"When you could not hear me. I said, 'You look like a goddess.'"

Her face flushed. She said modestly, "I suppose I did look more like a child when you saw me last."

His eyes fell from her face to her breasts, rounding out proud and firm beneath the bright gauze of her dress.

"I am eager to hear about your battles. In your last letter you said..." she struggled to recall exactly what he had said. Her thoughts were all white and dense, a river fog. "You said...a fortress at Ugarit."

"That and more. I have made good with the people of Ugarit. A few have sent daughters for the harem. We will trade with Ugarit now, and through their land we have access to goods from..." He still gazed at her breasts. "You've changed."

"You said as much already."

His eyes met hers again. Then he was across the room, and she was in his arms so fast her breath caught. He kissed her; his mouth tasted of barley. She pushed her tongue into his mouth and flicked it past his teeth, as Ineni had done to her. Tut groaned. His hands were rough, urgent on her back and hips. She pushed away from him and went to her bed, started to undo the knots of her dress.

"Wait," he said.

Her hands fell, uncertain, at her sides.

"I did not intend to come here and do this. I thought you would still be too shy."

"What did you intend, then? I thought after so long away you would want to do this."

"I do. I do. But we need to sort out a few messes first, Ahmoset." His voice was gentle, but the words pricked her with fear. *What does he know?*

"This business of spending all your nights at the temple – it is not maat."

"But I can't stay here with Mutnofret, Tut. I am here for court every day. Isn't that enough? Mutnofret is wicked; she threatened me recently."

"Threatened you? With what?"

"She threatened to...to hurt me." It was true, in a sense. She crossed her arms over her half-bared breasts, as if to hold back the rest of the story – the rest of what Mutnofret knew.

"The floods, Ahmose. Something in my kingdom is not maat, and your spending so much time at the temple is the only thing that has changed."

"*Mutnofret* is not maat. The gods never wanted her to be your wife; they gave it to me. She is a danger in the palace, Tut."

"I am not so sure about that."

"Has Mutnofret been telling you not to listen to me? She would. She's been awful, *awful* since you've been gone. You were with her the whole past hour, weren't you?"

"What of it?"

"And I your Great Royal Wife!"

"Don't you start with this, too." He threw up his hands. "I cannot see why any man would have more than one wife. At least the harem women stay out from under my wig."

"She's mad, Tut! She's mad with jealousy. She wants to destroy me. She hates that I'm the Great Royal Wife; she will do anything to bring me down." Like a struck spark, a solution flashed in her head. She said it before she could think. "Divorce her! Set her aside!"

"What?"

"She is dangerous, Tut, I tell you! She'll tear us apart if she can."

"Stop it. You sound like a petulant child."

Ahmose pulled back, stung as if he had slapped her.

"All those nights in the temple have not been good for

you, I think." His chest stirred beneath his golden pectoral, the jeweled Eyes of Horus staring at her in rebuke. He was breathing heavily, and his gaze was hard and cold. At last he said, "This business with the Temple has allowed you to separate yourself from your sister too far. We are a family, Ahmose. The royal family. We must be together, as one being, as one body."

"I can never be as one with her." Tears came to her eyes, so easily. *Like a child*. She swiped at them, angry and ashamed.

"You will be. Your husband requires it. Your king requires it. You will move back here to your apartments, day *and* night, and you will be a dutiful wife."

"I am the God's Wife."

Tut was silent. He turned away from her. Her lips trembled; she looked at his back, at the space between them, and felt defeated.

"I will not accuse you of lying," he said. "I will not accuse you of stealing. I won't believe such terrible things about my wife – my god-chosen wife. I don't know the truth of what has happened, but I know what I will and will not believe."

Ahmose could say nothing. She hugged herself tighter.

"Move back to the palace," he said. "Mutnofret will attend court again, and you will sit beside her and be at peace with her. I will not have my wife making such a fool of herself."

Ahmose choked on a lump in her throat, half sob, half scream of rage. It fought to come out, but when it escaped her lips all it made was a weak coughing sound.

Tut turned and looked at her. "You have made poor choices, Ahmose. You're young. I know what it's like to be young and to have power. I was not much older than you when I led my first troop into battle. I know – I know the trouble we can get ourselves into when we are young."

The forgiveness in his voice was too much to bear. She needed no forgiveness; she was the God's Wife. She deserved no forgiveness; she was wicked.

"You need guidance. You need a husband to help you see which choices you should make."

"So I must leave my praying, and spend all my nights here alone in my bed while you lie with Mutnofret. And what will the people think of me? What reason will we give them for my abandoning my duties at the temple?"

"I am sure that clever steward of yours can think of a reason. Why don't you ask Ineni?" Tut bit the name off sharp. Ahmose glanced at his face, then away again. A slick, treacherous silence fell between them. When Tut spoke again his voice was light, as if what he said was of no consequence. "Incidentally, Ineni has asked to be released from service. He is off to become an architect. I expect we won't be seeing him around Waset anymore. A shame. He is a bright lad."

Ahmose stilled her face, stilled her heart. What he said was of no consequence. "I wish him well," she said, as if it did not matter at all. Then she saw Mutnofret's sly smile again, her crackling eyes at the Festival of Khonsu, Sitamun whispering in her ear. She could not do it. She could not give up what little power she had over Mutnofret. Her life would be a constant misery. "You must leave Mutnofret, Tut. Send her away. Please."

"I will not hear that kind of talk, Ahmose." His voice was powerful, commanding. It was the voice of a general, the voice of a king. Ahmose shrank. "Mutnofret is the mother of my sons and my wife. It is your duty to find a way to live with her peacefully."

"An heir," Ahmose said, her voice nearly a wail. "Name Wadjmose heir, Tut! It will appease Mutnofret. It will make her easier to live with."

"No."

"Why do you do this? Can't you see how this tears our family apart? Amunmose, then, if Wadjmose displeases you."

"Neither of my sons will ever displease me."

"Forgive me. But why?"

She knew why. The dream – his accursed dream. He looked at her steadily, stern, expectant. Her arms were still wrapped around her body; she dug her nails into her back to keep from looking away from her husband's fierce eyes.

"I am going now. I expect you to be in the palace tomorrow

237

night. You may make your excuses to the temple this evening. You were my wife before you were the God's Wife, and my wife will live with me as a woman, not in the temple as a goddess."

CHAPTER TWENTY-NINE

AHMOSE SELDOM LEFT HER ROOF-TOP pavilion anymore. She had left Ipet-Isut defeated, and she came home defeated. She was a useless chief wife, an absent God's Wife, no sister at all. Thutmose all but ignored her; she attended court each day as he required, and he would nod a greeting to her, eyes tight, mouth severe, and speak to her only when courtesy prompted him. She was an ornament again, just as in her childhood, set upon her throne for the subjects of the Pharaoh to admire.

Twosre, at least, seemed relieved to be back in the palace day and night. She bustled about cheerily, cleaning, organizing trunks of clothing, polishing gems and rings. Ahmose would often lie on her bed, watching Twosre at her busy-work, feeling a blunt gladness for her servant's pleasure. Twosre found fulfillment in her work. Twosre knew her duties. Twosre had a purpose here in Waset's shining halls. Ahmose had no purpose, no work, no fulfillment. She seldom did more than rest now. It took so much from her to dress herself and bear her husband's scorn on her gilded throne, every day, every day. It took so much from her to present herself to the court beside Mutnofret's radiance, Mutnofret's confidence. Every day. Her bed was a blessing, her garden a haven. Her hands were idle, her mind fading like a waning moon.

Twosre still brought gossip, and Ahmose allowed it, listened to the woman's reports with little interest. Had there been a time when tales of Mutnofret's doings raised her hackles?

It was hard to believe it was ever so. The second wife was favored, by Thutmose and by the gods. It had always been this way. Why had Ahmose ever been concerned? The sun set in the west, the Iteru flowed north, and Mutnofret was favored. Mutnofret would always win.

Sometimes in the garden's shade she would close her eyes and reach out for the gods. It was harder to do here than in the temple, where the incense and the offerings drew the gods near. She was out of practice now, and her curious, languid distress made it all the harder. Still, sometimes she could touch them. The gods were in a stupor, too, it seemed. They had no words for her, no images – just a misty sort of sorrow, an untenable pity. She seldom tried to reach for them at all anymore.

The New Year came again. *Seventeen*, Ahmose thought with a dull kind of wonder as early morning light crept in through her beautiful pillared wall. *I am seventeen now.* She should have had sons by this age, like Mutnofret. Like Aiya. She should have surrendered to the physician's knife long ago, and spared herself this wreckage of a life.

But Twosre was coming in through the door, clapping briskly. "Up, up! Out of bed! It's the Birthday of Waser! Festival!"

There had been a time when the five days of the New Year made Ahmose squeal with anticipation. A long time ago, when she was happy, she had loved the feasts, the parades, and the holy ceremonies most of all.

"Up!" Twosre seized her hand and pulled. Ahmose came after it, obedient, a tired old hound. "Oh, Lady, when will you come out of this daze?" Twosre stripped her and made her get into the bath. The water was cool, but Ahmose hardly shivered. "It does you no good. It does the people no good, to see you sitting on your throne unsmiling."

"I am nothing anymore."

"Nonsense! Goose gabble! Nothing. You are the Great Lady."

The lady of betrayal. The lady of sadness. Ahmose sank into her bath up to her chin, cherishing the thrill of self-pity in her stomach. She said nothing.

Twosre made her sit up again. "You are to ride in the parade."

"Again?" She had done it last year. It had been more exciting then, to be carried on a beautiful painted platform through the city and down to Ipet-Isut. As God's Wife she had led the services, told the festival story to a crowd of a thousand or more. *A man was drawing water from a well long ago, in the place that would become Waset, our city, brothers and sisters! A voice came from all around him: go back to your people, to your herds and children, and tell them that the Great Lord has come! Waser! He who raises the river, he who will grant new life after death. Rejoice, children of the earth, for death is no more and life is eternal!* She had always loved the story of the man at the well. The Sky-Mother's Message, it was called. As a child she had dreamed of being the one to stand in the temple forecourt and lead the ceremony. This year, it seemed an impossible task.

"I don't have the energy to lead the ceremony. I am so tired."

Twosre's hands paused on Ahmose's shoulders. "Well, as to that, it seems Nefertari will be leading the ceremony this year."

Nefertari. *But the God's Wife tells the story and opens the festival.* Ahmose stared at her bath's tiled wall. The lilies set there in fragments of faience confused themselves into a meaningless jumble of color. There was one thought clear in Ahmose's heart. *Thutmose gave the title back to Nefertari.* Only the Pharaoh had the power to do such a thing. Twosre resumed her work, and words came to Ahmose with the rhythm of her servant's scrubbing. She opened her mouth, and they fell out all on their own. "Tut hates me."

"Never say that. Your husband does *not* hate you. He is the Pharaoh, Great Lady. You seem to forget that sometimes, if you will forgive my saying so."

"I have never forgotten it." Her voice quavered, though no tears came to her eyes. Perhaps she had cried that river dry. "We used to be close, Twosre. He used to spend his time with me. We used to ride together. We used to talk."

"That was before."

Before the war. Before the Royal Sons. Before Ineni. How was she to face her subjects today? How could she face her grandmother at the temple? How could she ride in her gilded litter behind her husband's and know that he would feel no urge to glance back at her and smile?

"Out now, and I will shave you."

Obedient, mindless, Ahmose took the offered hand and came from the bath. It was best to do as she was told now. Better to be like a puppet, made to dance and sing by another's hand, than to be like a chief wife.

She was dressed, perfumed, beautiful and empty-headed, never minding Twosre's scowls. Her servant wanted her to set this shadowy illness of the heart behind her, she knew, and dimly, distantly, the part of her that wanted to please tried to do just that. She fought to summon up a smile and painted it on her lips. Then the absurdity of smiling when her heart was in a tomb redoubled the formless pain. She had to blink hard to keep sudden tears from ruining her kohl.

Twosre made her sit down to breakfast and told her to eat. Ahmose did as she was told. She tasted nothing of her thin porridge and hard bread.

A clap sounded outside her anteroom door. Twosre and Ahmose both looked up from the meal. Who could be calling on the Great Royal Wife at this hour, when preparations for the festival were underway all over the palace?

Twosre puttered over to the door and opened it a crack. A thin, high voice leapt into the room.

"I must see the Great Royal Wife!"

"She's busy. She's eating."

"Please, Mistress Twosre. It is so very important. You must let me in."

"Let her in." The command in Ahmose's own voice startled her. Twosre looked round, eyes wide, then stepped back, swinging the door open.

It was Sitamun, Mutnofret's skinny servant. Her big eyes

watered. She ran across the room and fell to her knees beside Ahmose's chair. "Do not go to the festival, Great Lady. You must stay away."

"What?" The words pierced Ahmose's haze. "What's going on? Speak up!"

"Lady Mutnofret. She plans something – something to humiliate you."

"Do you think I am so foolish as to trust your words? You have spied on me and betrayed me to my vile sister."

Sitamun's face crumpled. "Great Lady, please, I beg your forgiveness. I did only what I was made to do. I have never wished you ill. Mutnofret...Mutnofret requires me to...to tell her things. Mut frowns on me for betraying the God's Wife; I am afraid of the goddess's wrath. But I am Mutnofret's servant; what can I do?"

"If you truly fear Mut's wrath, you can atone for your spying by telling *me* things. What is Mutnofret planning?"

"I wish I knew. All I can tell you for certain is that she told me you are to get your *payment* today at the festival."

Ahmose's face flushed hot. She tasted her breakfast on her tongue suddenly, the sweetness of honeyed porridge so cloying she wanted to retch. "Isn't it enough?" Her voice was high and loud, desperate, angry, violent.

Twosre was at her side, one hand steady on her shoulder. "Calm, calm. It will do you no good to rage." *Not in front of Mutnofret's creature*, Twosre's hand said.

"Calm is not for Mutnofret," Ahmose replied, though her words were more controlled.

"Great Lady, she plans something to mortify you." Sitamun held her palms out now, as if appealing to a goddess. "She is relishing it. I can see it in her face. She has been as smug as a crocodile all morning. Stay away, I beg you. Claim illness. I do not want to be a part of this anymore. I do not want to see you harmed. You are favored by the gods – everybody knows it – and Mut will curse me for the part I've played in harming you. Oh, Mut, forgive this miserable servant!"

Moments before, Ahmose had been reveling in the

surrender of control. It was pleasant enough to be under Twosre's command; Twosre would never do her any harm. But to give command to Mutnofret? As well throw herself into a crocodile pool as allow herself to be the plaything of the second wife.

Her sister's challenge fanned the last ember back to light. The temple was not her home anymore, Ineni was gone, Tut wanted nothing of her. There was not a thing left for her at all, but this: to put Mutnofret in her place at last. In this one battle she would claim her victory.

"Whatever happens to me today, Sitamun, the gods have heard your heart. You will be forgiven. Do you want me to find a new assignment for you in the palace? Or perhaps in the temple?"

Sitamun's eyes widened. Her hands shook. "Can you, Great Lady? Oh, please."

Ahmose waved at the woman, a quick, ready dismissal. "It will be done. Go now, and clean your face up. Don't let Mutnofret know where you have been."

Sitamun stood in paled, shaking silence for a long moment, then bowed, and crept away.

"I am ready to go to the temple, Twosre. It is time."

"You don't believe that creature, do you? No doubt that is exactly what Mutnofret told her to say, to lure you out! Sitamun feels guilty...*bah!*"

"It does not matter whether she told the truth, or whether Mutnofret intends to draw me out today. I am going to the festival to face my sister, no matter what her *payment* may be."

Chapter Thirty

THEY WERE HALFWAY TO IPET-ISUT when it happened. Ahmose's palanquin, a lone golden chair on a slender, red and blue platform, was borne by eight strong men through the streets of Waset. There was no humiliation, no outcry, not an eye batted at her that seemed suspicious. Mutnofret rode behind her on her own litter, quiet, unconcerned. Thutmose, the embodiment of Waser on this day, rode alone at the front of the procession, splendid and serious with the tall double crown on his head and a bull's tail tied about his waist. He had greeted Ahmose distantly, but not unkindly. She did not care. She was prepared for her husband's distance.

She was tense, braced, all through the city streets. She waited like a horse waits for the whip, but no blow came. Mutnofret was placid; Tut was his accustomed far-off self. The people cheered dutifully, looking somewhat more ragged and strained than they had a year ago. There were fewer flower petals scattered in their path, perhaps, but the people were in a mood for a festival and they had turned out to see the royal family's procession to the Temple of Amun.

Guards walked in two rows beside each rank of litter-bearers. Last year the people had cheered Ahmose's name with real fervor. The guards had been necessary then, to keep the crowd back, to keep the path down Waset's broadest street and out toward the Holy House cleared of the people who would crowd around to touch Ahmose for luck. Now, cattle and children were thin and Egypt had little to show for its depleted grain stores but a fortress in Ugarit that had as yet failed to show its worth. The trade would come in, Ahmose was certain, and make Egypt secure again, even in the midst of this cursed drought. But the certainty of the Great Royal Wife meant nothing to the rekhet. Who among them, after all, could know her thoughts? So their cheers lacked zeal and had the sound of obligation – better cheers than silence.

Waset receded behind them. The crowds along the long road to Ipet-Isut were different here, out among the fields, in the open spaces beneath an impossibly blue sky: herders and planters of grain, trainers of dogs and horses – the people of the earth, mud between their toes, unshaven heads, like the man who had heard the voice of the goddess at the well so many thousands of years ago. They wore shabbier clothing than the city-rekhet, perhaps, but the people here cheered with a real excitement. They did not chance to see royalty often, living as they did beyond the city walls. This was true festivity for them, even if their cattle were thin. The real happiness in their voices lifted Ahmose up out of her tension, out of her clenched anticipation. She smiled a genuine smile, waved here and there.

Then she heard it.

"There rides the unfaithful lady!"

Her head snapped sharply to the left. She scanned the faces on that side, but her litter glided past. She must have heard wrong; no rekhet would dare to call out such an accusation to the Great Royal Wife.

"Whore!"

The word was clear this time, shouted, meant to be heard. It had come from the right.

"Stop," she said to her bearers. They did not hear her. "*Stop!*"

The litter lurched to a halt. She sat forward and turned to the crowd. No face looked guilty there, but plenty looked confused. The rekhet stared about them, muttering, heads turning this way and that as if they, too, sought the speaker. So she had not imagined it.

"Flood-killer!"

Ahmose snapped fingers at her guards. They needed no other command; six of them were in the crowd on the instant, jostling, shoving. Women screamed. Children cried. The rear rank of the crowd, butting up against a field of scraggly fig trees, surged, bulged, and scattered. The guards' white kilts flashed here and there among the figs as they gave chase. The hissing of the orchard leaves was drowned out in an instant by the crowd's roar. She caught a word here and there: *Unfair! Let him go!* ...*she did do it!* ...*wickedness! The gods are punishing Egypt!* And again and again she heard it. First as a question, first as disbelief. Then with conviction. *Unfaithful lady!*

"Go on," she said to her bearers. They did not move for a long moment. She turned around in her chair and looked back at her sister. Mutnofret was looking about her with a hand raised to her mouth, eyes popping, the very picture of shocked disbelief. She caught Ahmose's eye and shook her head, as if to say, *I knew nothing of this.* Ahmose sat forward again and said fiercely, "*Go on!*"

She thanked all the gods that Tut's litter had not stalled when hers did. His bearers, oblivious, had carried him on toward the temple, and the crowds ahead cheered him. She had stopped for only a handful of heartbeats – a minute, barely – and it took almost no time for her own chair to catch up to her husband's. He made no move to stop and never looked back. If the gods were good, he had not even marked the disturbance in the crowd. So far ahead, how could he distinguish treacherous words from the cheers of the rekhet?

She gripped the arms of her chair hard and bit her cheeks to keep her face calm. Mutnofret's look of innocence – as if Ahmose could be so easily fooled! Whore! Flood-killer! None of them understood, none of them cared to know! They listened only to Mutnofret, beautiful Mutnofret, perfect, unfailing, dutiful Mutnofret. Evil, hissing scorpion Mutnofret.

She only needed confirmation of Mutnofret's guilt, and

after perhaps half a mile, it came to her. The six guards were back in formation, panting and sweating.

Ahmose looked down at the nearest as they plodded toward Ipet-Isut. "Well?"

"We caught him. He tripped over a downed tree and dropped this." He pulled a ring from his belt pouch. The band was small – a woman's ring, set with faceted milky quartz. She recognized it at once. A mere trinket to the second wife, but a treasure beyond riches to a farmer with mud between his toes. *A cheap price to pay for revenge.*

"And the man?"

The guard glanced at his comrades. "Dead."

A shame. She would have liked to have a confession from him. A confession was more, much more, than a ring. But the ring would be enough. She held it in her fist, squeezed it hard until its edges dug into her flesh. She did not let go all the way to Ipet-Isut. As her litter was lowered and Tut helped her to her trembling feet, she held tight to the ring. As she stood beside the smiling Mutnofret, as she watched her wrinkled, stooped grandmother deliver the ceremony and open the festival, she held it. She held it all the way back to Waset, while the crowds cheered around her and the people shared cakes in the streets. She held it hard, and it bit at her, left red indentations and a bruise in her palm. It striped her, shamed her, brought her back to life.

CHAPTER THIRTY-ONE

THERE WAS TIME BEFORE THE feast began. Ahmose changed into the pure, unadorned white of a priestess. She set the cobra crown on her forehead. She left all jewelry behind, save the quartz ring. She carried in the other hand now, the left hand, for the right was too bruised and cut by the ring to hold it tightly.

She walked to Mutnofret's apartments amidst green, river-deep calm. There was no clapping for entrance. There was no storming inside and waiting like a snake in the grass, as she had done the day she put on her wings. She was far inside the center of her own self, assured, knowing, prepared.

Mutnofret was not in her anteroom. She was not in her bedchamber. Ahmose passed through these like an implacable wind and stepped out into the bright sunlight of her sister's garden.

A nurse, watching over the Royal Sons as they played in the flower beds, was the first to see her. The nurse's body tensed; her face went dark with fear and sympathy.

"Nurse," Ahmose said, her voice like a drum, "take the boys out of here."

Mutnofret, sitting on a bench with Sitamun, her back to the palace, turned slowly around. Her eyes met Ahmose's. She smiled.

"I gave you an order, woman," Ahmose said.

The nurse stooped, propped Amunmose on her hip. Wadjmose's fat arms reached up to her; she scooped him up, too, and hurried out of the garden, looking down.

"You do not give orders to my women in my presence," Mutnofret said languidly, pleased with herself.

"Sitamun, leave us," Ahmose said.

Sitamun looked from Ahmose to her mistress, sitting like a skinny toad on the bench.

"Stay where you are," said Mutnofret. She did not look at the thin woman. Her eyes never left Ahmose's.

Deliberately, Ahmose turned her face away from Mutnofret's and stared at the quaking servant. The woman gulped and rose to her feet. "Please," Sitamun said.

Ahmose pointed out of the garden.

Mutnofret's tone of sleepy amusement was unchanged. "You have no right to dismiss my servants, little sister."

"Sitamun," Ahmose said. The thin woman ducked a bow to Mutnofret, but she ran from the garden.

With her women gone, Mutnofret's anger rose to the surface at last. "It's funny, Ahmose, how far you'll go, how much you like to prod at the limits of what a woman can do. If you can call a traitor funny." She stood and came toward Ahmose, tense, ready to strike. It was no matter. Ahmose had her weapon. She flung it at Mutnofret's feet.

The ring bounced on the pebbled garden path, rolled, tipped, stopped a hand's span from Mutnofret's toes. The second wife looked down at it with a blank face.

"You call me a traitor," Ahmose said. "You buy dissension from your husband's subjects and you call me a traitor."

Mutnofret bent and picked up the ring. She slipped it onto a finger. "I told you you would pay," she said quietly. "For everything you've taken away from me. My position. My son. My life."

"You never would listen to me. You have only ever heard the words you wanted to hear. You have made yourself bitter because being bitter pleases you."

"Pleases me? You think it pleases me to have my throne taken away by my sister?"

"I won't explain myself to you anymore, Mutnofret,"

Ahmose said. "You've stepped too far out of line. Our husband should have put you in your place long ago."

Mutnofret barked a laugh. "Yes, he should have! Should have made me Great Royal Wife when I gave him Wadjmose! Should have put Wadjmose in his place, too. But where is the announcement that Egypt has an heir? Where is my son's place? Tell me that, *Holy Lady*. Tell me how you have managed to steal my son's birthright as well as my own."

"I never stole your son, Mutnofret, and I will never take his birthright. Do not push me. Wadjmose is my blood, too."

"Your blood! You dare to say such a thing to me?" Mutnofret was on her now, her snarling face hanging before Ahmose's own, near enough that Ahmose could feel the heat of her breath. "You are no blood of mine, you beast! I have no sister! No, not even by marriage! When Thutmose hears how the crowds jeered you as a whore, he must put you aside. You're finished, Ahmose! It won't even be the harem for you; you'll have to go all the way to Ugarit to escape what you have done."

Ahmose wanted to step back from the force of Mutnofret's rage, it was so hot, so palpable. But to step back was to admit defeat. So instead she put her hands out and shoved Mutnofret's shoulders, hard – hard enough to make the other woman lurch backward. Mutnofret's face registered shock; she looked like a hare in the moment the eagle's talons close. Then a ragged scream ripped from her throat, and she flew back at Ahmose.

Ahmose never saw her sister's hand coming. A white cymbal crashed in her ear and across her eyes with the speed of an asp's strike. She staggered sideways into a flower bed, clutching at her face by some instinct, though her cheekbone had not yet begun to hurt. Then a slow throbbing began, a lancing pain, a wincing heat, crept across hre face.

Mutnofret's teeth were clenched as tightly as the fist she held.

Ahmose straightened. She made herself drop her hand to her side. "You struck the Great Royal Wife."

"I struck *no one!*"

"Get down on the ground."

"Before you? Never!"

Something in the garden brushed Ahmose's fingertips. It was a sapling, young and pliant, just a long reed of a tree with here and there a twig branching away from the finger-thin trunk.

"Get down on the ground. The Pharaoh's wife commands you."

"*I* am the Pharaoh's wife. *I* have been true to him. What have you ever done for him? What have you given him? Shame and hurt! Dishonesty! Disloyalty! Why is it you have given him no sons, Ahmose? Did you discover with your foul steward that you're barren?"

Ahmose took hold of the sapling and tore at it, viciously, powerfully. The cuts and bruises on her right palm were nothing to her now. The hot pain in her left cheek was nothing. The sapling came out of the ground with a sound like a shocked gasp. Mutnofret stared at her, wide-eyed; Ahmose took hold of her sister's shoulder and shoved her down, hard. The force of her own strength surprised and pleased her.

Mutnofret cried out as her knees buckled and hit the pebbled walk. She caught herself by falling forward onto her hands, would have levered herself up again, but Ahmose kicked savagely at one wrist. Mutnofret collapsed into a heap with a shriek like a netted bird.

There was a sound like arrows, a slicing of the air, a whip of wind, again, again. A smack of flesh. A scream, and another, and another. Ahmose felt her shoulder rise and fall, her arm ply like a sapling. It was she who made the wind whistle, she realized. It was she who brought these cries from the second wife, who sprawled, writhing, on the ground. The sapling was lashing against the backs of Mutnofret's thighs, *crack crack crack*. And the sapling was in Ahmose's hand. She paid Mutnofret a stroke for every pain she herself had felt by her sister's doing. For the wedding feast! For the mockery!

For the spying! For the quartz ring! For Ineni, for Ineni, for Ineni!

And now there was another voice screaming, a wordless keen of suffering. Ahmose's throat was being torn raw, red-raw – it must be her voice, her sorrow and shame and rage in her ears, mixing with Mutnofret's frantic sobs. More voices, spinning in her head – words, but she could not understand them. All she understood was the lashing, and the scream in her ears and throat.

A strong hand gripped her wrist. She tried to force her arm down, just one more strike! Just one more payment of this long-overdue debt! The muscles in her chest and armpit strained against the hand that held her until she cried out in pain, and she subsided, sobbing. And arm around her waist – a man's arm pulling her gently back, step by step, away from the torn, shivering heap that was Mutnofret.

She thought it was Thutmose who held her. She would have buried her face against his shoulder and cried, but the voice pierced her heart at last. *Great Lady, you must stop. Leave off, I beg you!* A man's voice, surely, but not Tut's. A palace guard, then. Just a guard.

Mutnofret pushed herself up on unsteady arms. The wailing nurse came to her side, black tears streaking kohl down her face. She supported her mistress, one hand around her shoulders. Mutnofret had bitten her lip; her mouth and teeth were bloody. The front of her dress was soaked with urine. Her wig was gone, her scalp scratched and red.

Through the mess of her face, Mutnofret laughed. "What have you ever given him? I carry another son, Ahmose – another son for the Pharaoh. What have you ever given him?"

Ahmose tore herself from the guard's grasp, threw down the sapling, and ran.

CHAPTER THIRTY-TWO

IN THE COURTYARD, A FINE chariot stood waiting. Soldiers held the bridles of two black mares. Who waited to ride? Tut? *I always do my best thinking in a chariot*, he said to her from a great distance. She remembered him leaving her in a rattle of wheels, and Mutnofret calling to her from the harem rooftop.

Ahmose was disheveled, she knew. When she wiped her cheek with the back of a hand, kohl smudged dark as a falcon's eye. She took off her sash and used it to clean her face as best she could. Then she approached the chariot.

"Is this for my husband?" Her voice was cooler than it should have been. Her ka trembled, sour and sharp.

The nearest man stared at her, curiosity lighting his eyes. "Er – yes, Great Lady. He wants to ride before the feast."

"I am taking this chariot," Ahmose heard herself say through a roaring in her ears.

"Great Lady, forgive me, but you cannot. Please!" The man left his horse and lurched for her as she stepped up onto the platform. The reins were wound around the rail. She tugged them free. She had never driven a chariot before, but how difficult could it be? She had watched Tut drive a hundred times.

"Get away from me," Ahmose shouted, as the soldier raised one foot to the platform. He hesitated. "I will have you killed if you touch me!"

"Great Lady, I beg your forgiveness, but this is dangerous.

You cannot drive a chariot on your own! Let me drive you, please, Great Lady! I will take you anywhere you wish to go, only please, do not do this yourself."

Nefertari had done it. She had led the Egyptians to battle against the Heqa-Khasewet. She had been armored in sunlight, with a spear in her hand.

The other soldier was pleading with her now, too. "It is much too dangerous, Great Lady. Please, don't risk yourself!"

"Leave me," she screamed. The black mares threw their heads, their mouths gaping. They screamed with her.

She knew how it was done, driving horses. She shook the reins, snapped them against the horses' backs, and hissed as Tut had done on their rides together, back when he had still loved her. The men shouted as Ahmose and the chariot sprang away from them. She wasn't prepared for the sudden movement. She lost the reins, lurched against the side rail, righted herself in time to grab the leather straps before they slid over the bow of the chariot and beneath the horses' pounding hooves. Her hands were cold and stiff with fear. But she was pulling away from the palace, out into the open ocher heat of the day.

She chanced a look back at the courtyard. The men were in a frenzy, brown mice scampering and shrinking as she sped north. It would not be long until they were after her in chariots of their own. She did not know where she was headed, only that she wanted to run, as fast and as far as she could from the palace, from all the terrible things she had done, from Mutnofret's bloody face. She urged the horses faster, faster. Their black bodies stretched and contracted, fluid, lithe as eels. The wheels on the road sounded like sesheshet in the temple. And all at once, she knew where she was going – where she must go.

Horus, her ka cried as she sped north past the House of Women, where Tut had first touched her hand. *Waser*, her spirit wailed as the failing crops fell into a long, colorless streak to either side of her. *Mut*, she sobbed, as she passed the cairn at the crossroads, and the path that lifted to the flat rock on the hill. *Forgive me, I beg you. Forgive me.*

At Ipet-Isut, she slowed the horses – the gods alone knew how – and threw herself from the chariot when an apprentice priest caught the mares' reins. She stumbled, fell flat in the dust, and staggered to her feet again, knees and hands scraped and stinging. "Great Lady," the boy said, an edge of panic in his voice. She ignored him, and ran toward the Temple of Amun.

The temple crouched like a lion, golden in the sun. It watched her approach. *I'm sorry,* she whispered. *Forgive me. I'm sorry.* The temple made no reply, only watched her come.

Priests clustered outside the entrance, shielding their eyes, watching the southern horizon. "Chariots," someone said. "Coming from Waset. Great Lady, what has happened? Is there trouble at the palace?"

Ahmose shoved through the crowd. When she passed beneath the temple's roof she turned back to the men. "Do not let them in here. No one is to touch me. No one is to come into the temple while I am here." Her eyes must be terrible to see, she knew – the grief, the anger in her eyes, as bright and hot and vast as the desert. The priests cowered at the force of her command. She saw the desolation of her face reflected in their eyes. Ahmose turned from the priests. She ran.

Into the temple, into the cold, dark heart of the temple. She fled past statues and painted walls, the frozen images of Amun's judgment. As she passed, the god's eyes followed her. She shoved hard at the great sanctuary door, and it gave just enough for her to push past it. Inside, the sanctuary was cold and blacker than the river bottom. Ahmose threw herself into the darkness, tripped over her own sandals, and hit the ground hard enough to steal the breath from her lungs. She pressed her face into the tomb-cold floor, fighting to draw air. *Lord Amun! Give me the breath of life! Forgive me, and let me live!* Her body cried out in pain, her heart faltered, and just when she thought she would choke like a fish on the sand Amun heard her, and pitied her. Her lungs expanded in a warm, greedy rush. She lay on the ground, writhing, gulping air until her heart slowed. When her shaking subsided, she raised herself to hands and knees and crept toward the back of the room.

Somewhere, she knew, clothed in darkness, the god waited. He was in this very room, brooding, savoring the blackness. Waiting to judge her. But it was his judgment she needed; only Amun could set her right again.

It seemed she crawled for hours, for days on weak, water-boned hands and knees. The darkness touched her, felt her body as she moved through it with a thousand unseen hands. When at last her fingers brushed the feet of the god, she shivered with relief. She was not alone in this black room. Amun *was* here.

Her eyes were closed, though there was nothing to see. She worshiped him with her hands, the feet, the strong legs, the seated lap. She pulled herself into the great statue's embrace, weeping with shame and regret, buried her face against his chest, rocked herself in his arms, kissed his cold, unmoving mouth.

Forgive me, my god. Forgive me, and set me to rights.

CHAPTER THIRTY-THREE

THIS WAS A FINER PLACE than any Ahmose had ever known. She knew it even with her eyes closed. The bed was dream-deep and soft. The air smelled of comfort and ease: wheat cakes baking, warm honey, breath of myrrh, wind on the river. Ahmose sighed, safe, content. She was happy to lie here without looking around. She knew she was in a place of safety and pleasure, and knowing this was enough.

There was a trouble in her heart. A small, tickling thing, a fly walking on exposed skin. Curious, indolent, she reached toward the trouble to toy with it, to tease out some meaning from its faint, quiet flutter. Losing her husband, that distant stirring seemed to say. Mistakes. Shame. Fear. A sapling in her hand. Most of all, though, Thutmose slipping away from her.

It made no matter. This trouble was a small, far-away thing, and she was lying, eyes closed, in a very fine bed, with a very fine breeze soothing her. Breath of myrrh. Wind on the river.

When did you arrive? There was a voice somewhere out there, far from her soft bed. It was a man's voice, deep and rich, low. It brought to mind a fast chariot under a sky flying with stars, and a knife spinning end over end. *How long has she been like this?*

What the voice said made no difference. It was not here, anyhow – not really. It touched her mind with a feather's touch; it was the pay-no-heed glance of an idle, passing thought.

The bed was here. The bed was real. The odors of water and bread were real.

She opened her eyes, though she did not feel wakeful. She did not feel tired, either; there was no point in keeping them shut.

The room – if it was a room; she saw no walls – was a dark, penetrating red. This was not Mut's red, the bright crimson of carnelian stone. It was a low, sweet, mysterious color, the red of wine, the red of the moon's blood. There was no light here, yet she saw. Her arms and legs lay easy on the wine-dark bed linens, soft angles, bent flax stems waiting to be spun. The bed's footboard, red like the rest, reared up to dominate her sight. It was carved as if by the hand of Ptah with the perfect image of nine striding boys, their arms interlinked. Ahmose stared at the boys, wondering. She raised herself up onto her elbows. The carved boys smiled as if they knew she looked upon them, and they were glad her eyes saw them at last.

She has slept for hours, Mighty Horus. Forgive me. I brought her back from Ipet-Isut as soon as I could. That voice – she knew it, too. A woman's voice, an earthy comfort like goat's milk, like fresh figs. But the woman wasn't here, either. No one was really here but Ahmose and the nine striding boys.

There is nothing to forgive. I am the one who should be asking forgiveness. Gods forgive me, they hand me a throne and an empire, and I cannot even keep two women from tearing each other apart.

"Ahmose. God-chosen. Come to me, my daughter."

This voice, now – this was real – high, female, a mild night-music. Drumming among the reeds. Dancing in the fields. She swung her legs over the bed's side and stood on moon-blood nothingness. It held her. She walked.

"Come to me. I will give you a gift tonight. I will put a gift inside you."

Ahmose went toward the voice. The voice came toward her. They met in the dark never-there. The goddess stood before her: Heket, the lady of frogs, clad in green, holding her fine towering staff, smiling. Heket took her hand. The goddess's skin was smooth and cool, damp like leaves in the morning.

"A gift for you, a gift for Egypt, a gift inside you," Heket sang, *a-thrum-thrum-thrum*, "a gift for the river."

They walked through veils of red. Breath of myrrh.

Can they ever forgive me? Faint, far, buzzing man's voice, of no consequence. It did not matter at all, at all.

Lord Horus. Do you mean the gods? Or your wives?

The man did not answer.

Heket led her forward, and forward, and forward still. She did not look back, but she knew the very fine bed was no more. Another veil parted. A glowing back to her, the creak of a wheel, the musky scent of a drover's herd. The broad back turned. He looked up at her with golden eyes shining beneath an arm's-breadth span of twisted horn.

She bowed to the ram-god, the shaper of spirits, hand to heart. "Khnum."

"Show the god-chosen what you spin on your wheel, on your wheel," Heket sang.

Khnum stood aside. The wheel at his feet spun once, twice, thrice, slowed.

She was praying at the Temple of Amun, Lord Horus. She prayed for nearly twelve hours without taking food or water. The priests finally let me in to see her. They would admit no one else. I begged her to come home, but she would not speak to me. I do not think she saw me or heard me at all, Lord. She was desperate, I think. She exhausted herself. The physicians say she will recover, that she needs only to rest, but I fear for her. I have never seen her like this. I never saw her pray that way before.

What did she pray for, Twosre? That distant voice sounded tired, hunted.

An amendment to her wrongs, my king. She prayed for salvation.

The wheel stilled. Ahmose blinked at what it held: a golden boy-child, shimmering, perfect in form, freshly shaped by Khnum's hands. The ram-god nodded: his work was good. A bright, strong boy, a prince's ka.

"So you see him, Egypt's gift," Heket said, and took her

hand again. In an instant Khnum and the boy's ka were gone. In their place there appeared another bed, greater than the one she had left. Its legs were a lioness's paws with claws unsheathed. The footboard bore the head of Sekhmet, she of the stern eye and the bloody hand. This bed was a place of power. Heket waved and its bare slats were covered with cushions and linens, all as silver-bright as beaten moonlight. The frog-goddess gestured to the bed, and Ahmose, obedient, fearless, eager, climbed onto it and lay waiting.

She has forgiveness from me, by all the gods, the man's voice said, far from this red and silver place. *I have wronged her. She was barely more than a child when she came to me. I should have protected her better. Let me go to her. If she is not awake, so be it. I just want to sit with her. I just want to see that she is all right, the poor thing.*

Veils upon veils parted. A tall, blue shadow rippled within the red. Its misty parts came together. The shape of a man – no, not a man, for this being was too perfect, too fine and strong, to be a man. Two great golden plumes rose from his crown. His face was maat.

"My lord Amun," Ahmose breathed.

He raised a hand to her face. The ankh was there, between his fingers. The breath of life. It – he – was too perfect to look on. She closed her eyes, and inhaled.

Breath of myrrh. Wind from the river.

A spark came to life inside her.

The room was black striped with silver, not red. And there was a floor. There, walls, painted and solid. Plain – oh, how plain, after the beauty of the veils! Hinges muttered. She turned her eyes toward the noise. A black form appeared, backlit by brazier light. The light was coming from her anteroom and this poor place was her bed chamber in Waset. Yes, of course – Waset. She lay on a bed that was not the Sekhmet bed of her dreams, but an earthly bed, the Great Royal Wife's bed, so plain after the glory of Heket's gift.

She could bear to look on the man who came through the door, and so it was not her consort, not Amun the god. She raised herself up on one tired elbow to look at him over the curving bluff of her hip.

Thutmose stared down at her. A shaft of light from her pillared wall fell over half his face, split it with precise symmetry so his right eye was lost in blackness, his left, bloodshot and surrounded by smudged kohl, lit with the moon's divine brilliance. His look was kind, and forgiving, and asking of forgiveness.

Ahmose reached out a hand. He took it. Wordless, she pulled him down onto the bed.

CHAPTER THIRTY-FOUR

IT WAS NOT EASY TO resume life in the palace. Ahmose had grown so accustomed to Tut's absence that having him here again was a melancholy sort of delight. Ahmose heard nothing of Ineni; perhaps it was better that way. She wondered often what had become of him, where he was, what his clever mind was up to. She never mentioned his name, not even to Twosre, though she often dreamed up ways to send him a message or a reward. Surely he had earned something – gold, an estate. Ahmose owed him a treasure. His gentle ways had erased Ahmose's fear of the bed. She had lain with Tut many times since the night Twosre brought her back from Ipet-Isut so exhausted she could not stand. She had lain with him and found joy in it, and pleasure, too. She had lain with him and conceived a Royal Son, though she had needed only one time – the first time – for that. She was certain the child who stirred in her belly had sparked to life on that still, silver-black evening when she had dwelt in the presence of the gods. And she was certain it was not Thutmose's child. Or, not *only* his.

With their husband returned, Ahmose and Mutnofret had built a shaky truce between them. For weeks after the beating, the second wife avoided Ahmose carefully, not even speaking of the Great Royal Wife as far as Ahmose could tell – not a word, not a whisper. Mutnofret was behaving herself. Whether being caught out in treachery did the trick, or whether it was the physical punishment, Ahmose could not guess, and did not want to know. The memory of the harm she had caused her sister, the blood on Mutnofret's face, her brittle laughter, was an arrow through Ahmose's heart. For many days, she wondered whether Mutnofret's ka had been broken, whether she had beaten it out with her sapling. Then Ahmose saw the second wife in their shared courtyard, and though Mutnofret would not look Ahmose in the eye, she still held her head high and proud, a Great Royal Wife to her center. So she was not broken – only chastened. Ahmose slept easier at night, knowing Mutnofret's ka was safe.

The babies in the two wives' bellies grew in tandem. Ahmose heard no more whispers about infidelity, but still it comforted her to know that any who looked at the pair of them on their thrones saw two women with the Pharaoh's children, growing larger together, growing riper together. It gave her a sense of security on her throne, and a oneness with her sister she had never felt before.

But there were changes Ahmose could not bring herself to accept entirely. Thutmose was dutiful and kind, but his failure to protect his wives from each other weighed on him, and he was not the same man who had left to fight the Heqa-Khasewet. He was more pensive now, spending long hours alone in his chamber or riding through the hills without Ahmose, with only his guards for company. He visited the harem more often than either wife's bed, where he must surely find a sense of peace he could never again feel in Ahmose's or Mutnofret's arms. Ahmose did not grudge him this. She loved her friends in the harem, and was glad that they should have some of the Pharaoh's attention. She knew they would be kind to her distant husband, would do their best to lift the shadow from his heart. Tut needed his comfort, too, in the wake of the trauma that had almost torn his family apart.

Ahmose's former life – her childhood, the days of leisure with Thutmose, her time as God's Wife – all these were gone. They could never come again. She would have wept daily for the loss, but she had the Royal Son. She loved him with a love so fierce it frightened her. How was it possible to love a thing so? How was it possible to *be* a thing so? For Ahmose was her son, and the prince was Ahmose. They were body and ka; one could never have existed without the other. The Ahmose who had lived before the boy was conceived had not really lived at all. There was no life before him. There was no love before him, not even the love she felt for her husband. It was like ashes on the wind, compared to the way her heart swelled whenever she felt the child move inside her.

When he kicked or turned, she would lay her hand against him and wonder what he would be. Would he be fierce or thoughtful, playful or serious? Would he be as strong as a bull, like his father? How could she love him so, when she had never seen him? And when she did see him at last, how could she bare the doubling, the tripling of this tearing, singing adoration?

And she would see him, she knew. She would see his face. Death in childbed held no more fear; it had vanished in the red room. It had burned away on the Sekhmet bed. It was not that she was certain of surviving. She was still small; she would always be a small woman. No, life after birth was not a surety for Ahmose. But to see her son, at least once – to see him take his breath and scream his challenge to the waiting world – this she knew she would be granted. The Royal Son was her gift from the gods. She would be allowed to look on their gift at least once. She would be allowed to feel that great cloudburst of love at least once. She knew it in her ka. She knew it with the kind of certainty only the god-chosen possess.

And if the gods had forgiven her for her sins, she would be allowed to see her boy grow into a man.

"What will you name him?" Tut asked one cool evening as they drifted on the lake barge, picking at their awkward, uncomfortable supper, trying to rekindle a flame between them.

Ahmose cast her mind back like a net, back into the time

before she had lived. The net brought back all things good and sweet. Spinning, the feel of the fibers twisting in her fingers, the spindle dropping and rising, the distaff against her shoulder. Aiya, golden, freckled, smiling tremulously with one hand on her big belly. Yes, it was a good name.

"Hatshepsu," she said, and cradled the Royal Son in her hands as he turned like a falcon on the wind.

Ramose was born just as the harvest began, when the sun was hot and the sky was thin. Mutnofret labored from one sunrise to the next, and when her third son was laid at her breast, she sent for Ahmose.

The second wife looked weak, limp, wrung out like an overused towel. She lay on the slope of her bed with her knees bent; Wahibra the physician was crouched between her thighs, plying something there that Ahmose could not see. She drew closer. Mutnofret's eyes were closed. Her breath was steady. Wahibra's hand came up, trailing a coarse thread. Something in his fingers shone – a copper needle. Ahmose gasped.

At the sound, Mutnofret opened her eyes and smiled wanly. "Ahmose. My sister."

"Are you all right?"

Mutnofret glanced down at Wahibra, who never looked up from his work. "I tore badly, but he says I will be well. The bleeding has slowed."

"It must be painful."

"The sewing? I cannot feel it. I will feel it tomorrow, no doubt." Her eyes were sleepy, and not just from the birth. The acrid smoke of the pain-dulling herb semsemet hung in the air.

"Thank you for coming. I wasn't sure I would..."

"I would have been here no matter what, if you had been in danger. Whatever our past wrongs against each other, I would have been here."

"Thank you."

"Your third son. He is a lovely one. He has so much hair."

Ramose nursed, one wrinkled fist near his mouth. Mutnofret smiled at him. "He is bigger than the others, too, when they were newborn. No wonder I tore. He will have to be my last, I think."

"Three sons make a good life's work."

"I am eager to see your own son. What are you going to call him?"

"Hatshepsu."

"*The greatest of the great men.* A good name for a Royal Son. He will be the heir, then." Through the fog of the semsemet smoke, Mutnofret's voice was defeated.

There was no sense trying to spare her feelings. Ahmose would be square and level with her sister from now on. She would be square and level with everyone. Mutnofret saw how it had all turned out, anyway. She was resigned. It was better this way. Ahmose said, "Yes."

"I wish him well." Mutnofret's lips thinned in a little smile. "Send for me after his birth, won't you?"

"I will, Mutnofret."

The second wife settled her head against the padded head-rest and sighed. Wahibra straightened, dabbed at the place between Mutnofret's legs with a clean towel, and pushed himself off the bed. A midwife came forward from where she crouched on a stool against the wall, struck up an earnest exchange of whispers with the physician. There was nothing more here for Ahmose to say or do. She gazed down at Mutnofret's slack belly and blood-spotted thighs for a long moment.

Not so long ago, the thought of lying in Mutnofret's place, torn and vulnerable, would have terrified her. Now, she was almost eager for it. Not for the pain, and not for the labor. But to hold her son to her breast, as Mutnofret held Ramose – that would be a sweet thing.

She walked back to her apartments singing.

Chapter Thirty-Five

AHMOSE WAS SPINNING IN HER garden when the pains began. It was morning, a clear day with a sky echoing with the cries of shorebirds. She'd had false pains for days. The first time a pain had taken her, sneaking up quietly, pulling at her belly, she had been so startled she dropped her bowl of beer. Twosre called for the midwives, and they examined her for hours. But there was no labor. "False pains," they called it, and warned her it might happen again. That was nearly a week ago. The false pains had come and gone every few hours, gentle pains, just enough to make her wonder whether her child was on his way. But always they subsided again, and Ahmose became increasingly frustrated.

It was several weeks after Ramose's birth. She had been marking the days since she'd seen the new prince laid on her sister's chest. Soon, soon – *sweet Hathor, let it be soon!* – her son would arrive, Egypt's blessing. The false pains taunted her, dangling a treasure before her and snatching it away again. They were beginning to make her very cross. Being hugely pregnant was uncomfortable enough without the gods toying with her. Ahmose's feet had been achy for weeks. Her ankles were swollen all the time, no matter how Twosre wrapped them and rubbed them with soothing balms. The baby stuck out before her everywhere she went, preceding her every move, as bold and confident as a king's son should be. The weight of her belly astonished her. Since the last new moon, even lying in bed made her feel like a brick thrown into

271

water. She spent one sleepless night trying to make herself comfortable, then pushed her headrest away, woke Twosre, and made her bring cushions instead. With silk pillows cradling her head, she lay on her side like a rekhet woman and slept with her knees tucked up against her belly. It was improper, but comfortable. That was all that mattered.

Now, as she idly dropped her spindle in the pleasant shade, her belly tensed. She frowned and kept spinning. Another false pain, she was sure. The spindle was a blur at the end of its pale thread. She caught it deftly. She was about to drop it once more, but the pain intensified. It was sharper and more insistent. She took a deep breath, let it out slowly. The spindle waited patiently in her hand. She breathed in and out. The pain was still not gone. It was longer than the others had been, she was sure.

At last it receded. She sighed with relief. *Just another false pain*, she told herself, unwilling to allow a thrill of excitement. She resumed her spinning.

Minutes later, though, the pain was back. This time she set her spindle aside and closed her eyes, taking measured, steady breaths. When the pain receded, she did not retrieve her spinning. She remained still and gathered, waiting, willing herself to stay calm, to keep her hopes at bay.

And again it came. This time it was more forceful than ever before. She opened her eyes and looked down at her belly. It tensed perceptibly, tightening and pulling. She sucked in a deep breath, and was startled when it came back out as a groan. She shut her eyes again and bent the groan to an unsteady hum. She sang a few lines of one of Hathor's hymns until the pain left her.

Then she pushed herself up from her bench, leaving spindle, distaff, and tangled thread where they lay. She shouted for Twosre.

Ahmose had carefully avoided venturing into the corner of her garden where the birthing pavilion stood. It had been set up more than a week ago in preparation for the Royal Son's arrival, and she did not want to annoy the gods by mooning around its perimeter. Now, with Twosre beside her and the midwives behind, she shuffled around a bend in the path and there, beneath a brilliant sycamore, was her pavilion. Its poles were painted red, and a white canopy covered the cleared ground where Ahmose would bear her child. There was a mattress covered with cushions, and a holed birthing stool, and braziers for sacred, purifying smoke – and for light, should her labor last until dark. The painted fabric walls were rolled up and tied so the air could flow freely. A statue of the goddess Tawaret stood beside the bed, her tongue hanging like her breasts. Ahmose smiled to see the water-horse-mother. She would have a friend here. But still, as she passed beneath the canopy, she tingled with fear. The last time she had been inside a birth pavilion, she had watched Aiya die.

No, her ka said firmly. *It will not happen to me.*

Won't it? whispered her heart. *Aiya was young, too.*

I am eighteen years old. I have been a woman for many years. Tawaret is near, and I bear a gift for Egypt. Even if I die, my son will live. How can he be a gift for Egypt, if he is to die?

She smiled at her women; she smiled at the midwives. The smile only slipped a little when the pains came on her, pulling, pulling, making her grunt with the effort.

They made her lie down, fanned her with plumes. They wafted incense across her body. They chanted prayers to Bes, the fearsome dwarf god, protector of newborns, beseeching him to drive away the evil spirits that waited to torment the child as he came from the womb. Ahmose felt the tension in her body rise and recede, rise and recede, like years, like eons of the river's floods. It was hard work, this lying still and breathing. It became harder when they made her walk. Dimly, she remembered supporting Mutnofret as she paced about her garden. Had her sister ever been so exhausted? Ahmose had never done anything in the world but walk, and groan through the inundations of pain that squeezed her back and her sides.

She talked to Twosre to pass the time, only pausing in her words at the peak of her contractions. They spoke of the child, and of Tut, and of the goings-on at the temple and in the House of Women. Idle talk, optimistic talk; talk to distract her. But when the waters broke and rushed down her legs, she could talk no more. Her whole being was given over to walking, walking, walking, and stopping to lean on any convenient shoulder when her body shook with the pains.

They made her drink often, and helped her squat over a jar to relieve herself. They pushed honeyed beer on her – to keep her strength up, the midwives said – until she never wanted a drop of honey on her tongue again.

She was sipping obediently at a bowl of the cloying drink when a powerful contraction came on her. At once she knew that it was different from the rest. It squeezed her with a ferocity that made her stop and stare about. The faces of the women were unfamiliar blurs, stretches of pink and brown under shapeless black wigs. The garden's bright light and shade blazed into a mosaic of overwhelming green. Her legs shook violently. She had to sit down. She had to walk – she had to run! All in a heartbeat, she was certain death had come for her at last. Her body would fail. She could go on no longer. She was finished, finished. She dropped the bowl of beer into the grass.

"Twosre!" she cried. "Aiya! I can't go on!"

Twosre was at her side now, the familiar features of her face coalescing out of the confusion of the garden. She patted Ahmose's cheek with a hand that was at once gentle and insistent. "Patience, patience, Lady."

"No! I cannot go on!" She did not know where to go, what to do. The confusion was more agonizing than the terrible squeezing pain that pushed in all around her. She stumbled forward, then back, darting looks around the garden as if she were a hunted beast searching for cover.

"The baby comes now," one of the midwives said, her garlic-sharp breath in Ahmose's face. "Come, come, to the pavilion."

"No!" Ahmose reeled away from the midwife, clutching her belly. She looked at the placid birthing hut, its canopy flapping in the benign afternoon breeze. It was a horrifying thing, this place of death and stink. "I cannot," she wailed, and her feet carried her into the pavilion. There was not even another woman guiding her. Her body went, obedient, subservient, though her heart cried out to run.

They sat her on the stool with the hole in its center. Fingers pushed inside her. "To feel the baby's head," a voice buzzed. It could have been Twosre's, or the midwife's, or the baby's, or Ahmose's own. She knew nothing but urgency and fear. A pain ripped at her and she screamed, though her heart said from a cool distance, *It doesn't hurt. Not really. Curious, that it shouldn't hurt.* She screamed anyway, until her voice was raw.

"He is coming soon, Great Lady." The buzzing voices chided her off the stool and onto the bed, and they told her to lie still, to relax, to loosen up, to go limp. She tried to do as she was told. One voice told her to go so still she would sink down into the mattress like going under water. She held her breath and waited for the river to close over her head. It never did. She breathed again, and the pain was easier. Now and then she called out for Mutnofret. The only clear thought in her head was that Mutnofret wanted to know when the Royal Son was born. She would honor her sister's wish. She called for Nofret again and again.

There was no counting how many times the buzzing women harried her up from the mattress and back onto the accursed stool, and each time they reached beneath her and prodded inside her. Somewhere in the odd, fuzzy space between mattress and stool, her belly had begun to push downward, a deep, confident, powerful thrust that made her bellow like a cow in a field. It was not exactly pain that made her empty her lungs with this inhuman sound; it was the shock of having an animal inside her. There was a beast within her now, a force unknowable that strove down, down, wresting control from Ahmose as easily as a child snatches a blade of grass from the earth. It was terrifying, and it awed her. She was sitting on the stool when the word came into her heart: *push.*

She pushed. And the beast subsided. She was working with it now, guiding it, being guided by it. She pushed. She pushed.

"I see his head!"

"Keep pushing," a midwife said, though Ahmose did not need telling. She pushed once more, and the beast went to sleep. She panted, reached out her hands for water, drank deeply when the cool, sweating bowl was held to her lips.

"You are doing well," said a new voice. Not a buzz – a musical, low voice. Mutnofret.

Ahmose looked for her. She stood beyond the knot of midwives that crowded around the birthing stool. Mutnofret tapped one midwife on the shoulder; the woman stood aside for the second wife.

"Sister!" Tears distorted Ahmose's voice.

Mutnofret put her arms around Ahmose's shoulders, pulled her tight against her chest, though Ahmose was soaked with sweat.

"I am afraid," Ahmose said, sounding tiny; and her heart, awed and confused, whispered *No I'm not.*

"I'm sorry." There was real regret in Mutnofret's eyes when she pulled away to look at Ahmose. "I'm sorry you're afraid. I'm sorry. There is nothing to fear. Tawaret is beside you. Bes is here. You are doing well."

Ahmose wanted to respond, but the beast had awakened. Unwilling to anger it, she pushed submissively. Fire-hot pain consumed her, so intense and sudden she could not tell what part of her body cried out. "It hurts," she screamed, and for once, her heart agreed.

"Lean forward," Mutnofret whispered, and Ahmose doubled up at the waist, her roiling belly pressing against her knees.

There were women on either side of her, crouching around the stool, their hands busy beneath. Ahmose screamed again.

"The head is free," Twosre said. Her hands were clutched together under her chin.

"A lot of black hair, like his mother," came one midwife's report.

Ahmose panted.

"This is the worst part, the shoulders," Mutnofret said. She kissed Ahmose on the forehead, one quick peck. "It will hurt. Be brave. You are almost done."

The pain was so pure, so white, that Ahmose *saw* it. Then there was a rush, a wet sound, the delighted cries of the women gathered around her.

And a tiny, rasping sob. And a crackling, triumphant little scream.

"Oh!" The women all said it, as if they shared one mouth between them.

"Stand up," somebody told her. Mutnofret and Twosre helped her to her feet. There was a slick blue cord coming out of her body; one of the midwives seized it and passed it through a slot in the birthing stool so Ahmose could walk. "You need to lie down now, to rest."

A woman carried the baby close beside Ahmose as she hobbled to the mattress. The cord bloomed out of his red belly, pulsed faintly where it lay over the midwife's arm. Ever so carefully, they eased her down onto the mattress, always keeping the crying bundle close to her body.

"Let me hold him," Ahmose insisted.

"Not yet, Great Lady. We must wait for the cord to die."

She lay back and sighed, feeling the awful ache in her back, her abdomen, between her legs. But the ache did not trouble her. She could hear the bellowing of her child, to know that he was live and fit. They brought her food and drink while the midwives, clustered around the child so tightly she could not see him, wiped and clucked and cooed. Mutnofret bathed her brow, murmured praise in her ear. She had done well, she had done well. The worst of her work was through now.

At last they cut the cord. Mutnofret stood to watch, peering over the backs of the midwives. Ahmose watched her sister's face nervously. The timid, sad smile the second wife wore wilted when she looked down at the baby. There was hesitation in her eyes, and, when she glanced up at Ahmose, a sudden flicker of calculation.

"What's wrong? What's wrong with my baby? Mutnofret? What's wrong?"

Mutnofret opened her mouth, then shut it. She looked back down at the crying child.

"Give me my baby," Ahmose said sharply.

The midwife edged forward on her knees, cradling the child tightly in her arms. She tucked the baby against Ahmose's chest. Ahmose clutched him close, staring down into his miraculous face. It was wrinkled, creased, bright red. The toothless mouth opened and shut in time with the hoarse cries. Ahmose smiled, adoring the tight-shut eyes, the thatch of wet black hair, the funny curved ears. His fists pounded the air, the nails bright white and sharp. His chest rose and fell with each howl, red, soft, and perfect. He kicked one foot free of her arm and worked it in the air, then let it fall again. Perfect tiny toes. Perfect fat knees. She shifted him against her chest to bundle the perfect leg up again.

And she saw.

Between the baby's legs, a perfect little cleft.

"The king has a daughter," Mutnofret breathed.

PART THREE

MOTHER
OF THE GOD

1500 B.C.E.

CHAPTER THIRTY-SIX

IT WAS LATE IN THE evening before the Pharaoh could come to see his new baby. Ahmose rested in her bed, and stroked her baby's soft warm skin, breathed in the smell of the child. Her body ached, but it was nothing beside the bright, honey-sweet ache in her heart. Egypt's treasure, lying beside her, beautiful and perfect, perfect, perfect.

When Tut's obligations at court were through, Twosre showed him in. He came to her bed and stretched out beside Ahmose, kissing her forehead, her cheeks, her lips. Then he scooped the baby up and laid the perfect pink body atop his chest. His hands, so large and strong, the hands that had brought death to Egypt's enemies and justice to the Black Land, covered the baby's form almost entirely, gentle as a wind in reeds.

"What is her name?"

"Hatshepsu," Ahmose said, drowsy.

"Hatshepsut, do you mean?"

"That's a girl's name!"

Tut coughed, and the baby complained. Ahmose sat up and took the child to her breast. Tut sat up, too, and peered into Ahmose's face, a look of worry tightening his eyes. "Ahmoset, our child is a girl."

"Oh, on the outside, yes."

"On the inside, too, I assume."

"No. I saw his ka. This child is a boy – a Royal Son. Your heir."

"The midwives gave you too much semsemet. I will have to speak to them about it."

"They did not give me any. I didn't need it."

"You are talking foolishness, my love."

It had been so long since he had called her that. *My love.* "But this is the one – the child from your dream."

"Ahmose." He ran his hand along her shoulder, carefully. "She's a fine, healthy, beautiful girl. I am very pleased with her. One day you will have another baby. A son. He will be my heir."

Ahmose jerked away from his hands. "All those years you had the dream of me holding your heir..."

"You will have more children. A son will come along."

"No, *this child* is your heir, Tut! She is more than that. She is Amun's own daughter. No matter how perfect and strong any son might be, there could never be one better suited to the Horus Throne than Hatshepsu. *Hatshepsut,* if you insist."

Tut shook his head, the corners of his eyes crinkling with anxiety. "Ahmoset, you're talking like a madwoman. Think about what you say."

The baby released the breast, and waved a fist at her father.

Ahmose said in a low voice, "I know what I am saying. I know it's...unusual. But as I am god-chosen, I know that what I am telling you is the *truth,* Tut. Hatshepsut is Amun's daughter."

"She is my daughter."

"On the night we conceived her, Amun came to me in your body."

"What?" Tut stood, took a step back from the bed. There was real concern on his face now.

He thinks I have gone mad, she realized. How to make him see? She took in a deep breath, let it out slowly. Ahmose put an easy smile on her face. "I am not mad," she said lightly. "You always trusted your vision. Even before you were Pharaoh, you believed in the dream the gods sent you. You knew in your heart that it was the truth. You knew I would bear your heir. Am I right?"

"Of course."

"No less do I trust the vision I was given. Do you remember the time I spent all day and night in the Holy House, praying? After...after Mutnofret and I fought?"

"I am not likely to forget that night."

"Just before you came to me, Tut, I had a dream. It was more than a dream. It was a holy vision." She reached out for his hand. She wanted to touch him, to will the power of her vision through his skin and into his ka. He hesitated, but took her hand in his own at last. "Haven't you ever wondered what changed me that night, what made me want to lie with you?"

He shrugged. "I assumed you had just grown into a woman's desires."

"No. I lost all my fear of birthing because the gods granted me a glimpse of my son. I knew he would be strong, healthy, proud. I saw him formed on Khnum's wheel, a beautiful, fierce *boy*. I spoke with Heket. She promised me a son, a gift for Egypt. And Amun came to me. Amun, Tut!" Her voice shook with the memory of that tall blue shadow forming out of the red mist. "He put the spark of life inside me that night. It was your body I lay with, but it was Amun who made the Royal Son."

"Hatshepsut is a King's Daughter." Tut's brow was creased now. Was he growing angry? "You may have seen a boy's ka in your dream, but she is still a girl. And why have you never told me of this vision before?" He sounded doubtful, as if he questioned whether she'd had the vision at all.

"I am not making it up," she said, a hard edge to her voice. "She may have a girl's form, but I swear to you by all the gods, Thutmose, her ka is male."

Starlight came in through her pillared wall, lit Tut's face as it had done on the night they made Hatshepsut. He waited a long time before answering, but when he did, he dropped her hand. "I cannot speak to her ka. All I know is what I see with my eyes. And that is what the people will see, too."

"No, Tut. Listen to me." There was a rising desperation

in Ahmose's chest. The will of the gods was explicit. What Hatshepsut looked like on the outside mattered not a bit; not to the gods. It was her ka that mattered, and her ka was the ka of a king. "There will be no male children from me, my love. I think I have known this for many years. The gods intend Hatshepsut to rule Egypt when you are gone. Not as a Great Royal Wife; as the Pharaoh. For Mut's sake, Thutmose, she is half divine – the child of Amun! The gods will have their way, no matter what you may wish."

"This has never been done before," he said. His voice rose in anger. Ahmose cringed on her bed, holding Hatshepsut protectively to her chest. "It would be folly for me to make such a move. I have never forgotten who I really am, and neither have the nobles, nor the priests. I'm a rekhet-born soldier, Ahmose. Oh, I am valuable enough to Egypt so long as I keep the Kushites and the Heqa-Khasewet in line. But the most royal of all Pharaohs could only expect to push tradition so far. How far would a mere soldier like me be allowed to push before he was thrown out of Egypt altogether?"

"And have your forgotten why I am your Great Royal Wife? To legitimize your choices, Tut, no matter how strange they may seem. My spiritual gifts were given to me so that I could help you on the throne. Why have I suffered so under Mutnofret's anger, if not to aid and support you?"

Tut nodded, sympathy easing the anger on his face. "I know, Ahmoset. I know things between you and Mutnofret have not been...ideal. And I know how hard you work to please the gods, and me. You...you haven't always made the best choices in your work, but I know that your intent has always been beyond reproach. But if there are things even a Pharaoh cannot do, then surely there are things even the god-chosen cannot do. We cannot push the people too far, you and I. Everything we have they can take away, if we go too far."

"The gods would never let that happen," she said.

"The gods often let happen that which the priests most desire," Tut said with a wry twist to his mouth. "I have to be careful, Ahmose. *We* have to be careful. Our children's futures will be secure so long as we are careful."

"Hatshepsut's future is on the Horus Throne. She is *half god*, Thutmose. She is the *son of Amun*. And if I were you, I would fear what Amun thinks more than what his priests think."

"*Daughter*," he said, in a voice that was half a snarl. How quickly he could change from the gentle husband to the general. "She is a daughter, not a son. She is *my* daughter." Abruptly he turned away, shaking his head, sighing. "I need to take my leave of you. I am growing too angry. I don't want to be angry with you; not now. Not tonight."

Outside, the river of stars spilled across the sky in a thick silver band, and striped Ahmose's bed with its light. Hatshepsut, in her arms, was illuminated.

"Take one last look at Hatshepsut before you go, my husband," Ahmose said, as gently as she could. "Do not leave us in anger. Look at our child, and be happy."

He did as she asked. He turned to look at the baby, who was the gods' gift to him, as well as to Ahmose. The frustration smoothed away from his eyes. The tension in his cheeks relaxed. His big front teeth showed themselves when he smiled in spite of himself.

Ahmose turned her eyes from her husband to her child. Hatshepsut's eyes were open for the first time. She looked at her father with bold black eyes, with the impudence of a Royal Son.

"Amun's will shall be done, no matter what either of us may wish," Ahmose said, quietly, so only the stars would hear.

CHAPTER THIRTY-SEVEN

HATSHEPSUT STOOD ON HER STURDY legs at the edge of the dais, hands balled up in fists as she surveyed the crowded hall. The king's daughter held herself apart from her parents and her nurse, gazing out over her subjects without a trace of fear. Ahmose looked down at the top her of the girl's head and smiled. *Such a little lioness -- such a little lion.*

Hatshepsut was two now, and her weaning celebration had begun. Sitre-In, the sweet young nurse whom Ahmose had chosen to raise the King's Daughter, had needed the Ahmose and two other women to help restrain her charge for this morning's head-shaving. As was the custom, the girl's hair had been left to grow in a thick black cloud, forever tangling, until the day of her weaning. For their weaning ceremony, most girls would have their hair combed carefully over to one side and plaited into the traditional sidelock braid, the hairstyle they would wear until they matured, the end of the lock curled and hung with ribbons. But Hatshepsut was not like other girls. Ahmose had called for a razor.

"Shave her head like a boy's," she said, and once Hatshepsut could be restrained, Sitre-In had done as she was told. The girl had put up such an admirable fight. She'd screeched and bitten like a whole army of angry cats, and kicked as hard as her chubby legs could kick. But at last the four women managed to hold her still enough that Sitre-In could safely shave away the bird's-nest of hair. Watching it fall to the ground was bittersweet. Ahmose could not see where the past two years had flown. Was her prince already so big, so strong? The careful black braid hung over Hatshepsut's half-moon ear, standing out against the smooth, bald scalp of a boy.

"My brothers and sisters," Thutmose said, raising his golden crook and flail. The crowd quieted. "We are gathered here in celebration. We have much to thank the gods for on this day. The Iteru has risen beautifully this year, praises be to Amun! And my two youngest children, the Royal Son Ramose and King's Daughter Hatshepsut, have been blessed by the gods. They are healthy, and infants no more!"

The nobles cheered, raising their drinks in salute. The sudden noise frightened Ramose; on the other side of Tut, Mutnofret tried in vain to untangle the boy from her skirt. He cried as he clung to her. Hatshepsut peered around her father's legs at Ramose, her fat lower lip stuck out in an expression of mingled curiosity and disappointment. Ahmose bit her cheek to keep a laugh at bay.

"Bring the bread," Tut commanded.

A priestess brought the tray of bread and sweet milk. She bowed low before the royal family, and blessed the food in the names of Amun and Mut.

Ahmose bent to her girl, held Hatshepsut close in a sweet embrace. These were the last precious seconds of her baby's infancy, and Ahmose would savor them. But the girl squirmed, growling in frustration, and reluctantly, Ahmose let her go.

The priestess went first to Ramose. He came forward only after Mutnofret gave him a gentle push, and his eyes studied the bit of milk-soaked bread in the woman's fingers with mistrust.

"Eat it, stupid," Amunmose hissed from where he stood behind Mutnofret. Wadjmose elbowed him in the ribs. The two elder boys glared at each other and stuck out their tongues; Mutnofret shot them a look full of unpleasant promise, and they snapped to attention, their dark eyes wide.

"Eat the tasty bread like a good boy," Mutnofret said, an edge of worry coloring her voice. "Mmm, mmm!"

At last, Ramose allowed the priestess to place the bit of bread on his tongue. He made a face and stumbled back to his mother's skirt. Mutnofret poked her finger into his mouth to be sure he'd swallowed it.

Now the woman bent before Hatshepsut and offered the sweet bread, pinched in her thumb and forefinger. Like a hungry carp, Hatshepsut lunged forward, mouth agape, and clamped down on the priestess's hand.

"Oh!" Ahmose rushed forward to grab her daughter by the arm, while the priestess, shocked out of her dignity, jerked back her hand and yelped. The crowd cheered.

"Hatshepsut, we do not bite! Biting is very wicked!" Ahmose crouched in front of her daughter, eye to eye. She struck Hatshepsut on the back of each wrist in reprimand. The King's Daughter did not flinch. "Tell the priestess you are sorry for biting her." She turned the girl around to face the priestess, whose eyes struggled to hide a smile.

Hatshepsut said nothing, grinning at the woman, chewing the bread while milk and honey dribbled down her chin.

"I still can't believe she bit the poor woman," Ahmose said, holding Tut's arm as they strolled through the great palace garden.

Two days after the weaning celebration, and Hatshepsut already seemed to be delighting in her new status as a big girl. She ran screaming down the garden path, chasing grasshoppers, full of a wild new energy. Her fat buttocks flashed away into the gathering darkness, the pat-pat-pat of her tiny sandals coming from here, now there, now here again as she explored the flower beds at chariot's speed. The girl preferred to be naked. Neither Ahmose nor Sitre-In could keep the proper boy's kilt on Hatshepsut for more than a few minutes.

"The guests at the feast seemed to think it was a good way

to start the party," Tut said, chuckling.

Ahmose smiled. "I'm glad she's as fierce as she is strong, I admit it. Egypt will need an heir as fierce as you, if peace is to be kept once you have gone to the Field of Reeds. Many years from now, of course."

Thutmose sighed. "I do need to name an heir, don't I? Four beautiful children, and none of them heir. What must the people be thinking?"

"You know how I feel about it." They had discussed the issue many times since Hatshepsut's birth. Ahmose was reluctant to tread the same path again. It always ended in anger, with Tut storming away and Ahmose biting back tears, and nothing resolved.

He put his hands on either side of her face. "Ahmoset, let's be serious about this, just once. I don't want you to get false hopes. Hatet is my gem, but she is a *girl*. She cannot be a king."

Ahmose breathed deeply, closing her eyes so she did not have to see him, though he still held her face.

"Aren't you going to say anything, Ahmoset?"

"What is there to say that I have not said a thousand times already? I will never have a son. I know that. You are wasting your time waiting for me to bear you a son, when you have the promised heir right here, running naked through your garden." From a flower bed, Sitre-In shrieked, and Hatshepsut laughed. Ahmose broke out of Tut's grasp. "It has always been clear to *me* that Hatshepsut should be the heir. She came from my body. I saw her holy father with my ka as I see her earthly father with my eyes, standing before me now. Of all your children, the choice is *obvious*, and we should not be having this same argument again.

"Just look at her! She is a warrior already, and only two years old. You saw how brave she was at her weaning feast. Tell me, did your son face the crowd as confidently as your daughter? Would Ramose have bitten a priestess? Clearly her ka is male, and what matters but her ka?"

"An ill-mannered little girl does not have to have a male ka to be wicked," Tut said, but there was fondness in his voice. He loved Hatshepsut, Ahmose knew; perhaps more than he loved any of his other children. And who could fail to love such a wild creature? "It is true that she is a warrior," Tut went on. "But Egypt is full of strong women. No one accuses them of having the spirits of men."

"Can you deny that the gods intend great things for Hatshepsut? Can you deny that her blood is holy? In the year of her weaning, the river has risen again, after five years of failure. She *is* a gift for Egypt."

"Ah, something has pleased the gods this year, to bring back the flood. And *I* intend great things for my daughter. She will be Great Royal Wife someday. We will have a son together, and she will marry her brother."

Ahmose turned away from him. "Tut, you know my feelings. If you disregard the gods' will, you risk...who knows what? Famine? Plague? Invasion? There are worse things than these. Why do you insist on being so foolish?"

"Have a care," Thutmose said, not unkindly. "You do speak to the Pharaoh, Ahmose."

"Do I? A king rules. A king commands. A king has confidence in his own words and actions. A king does not go in fear of what his subjects might think."

"Now you are angering me."

"I did not intend to. But whenever we speak of this, we can never agree."

"If you would give some ground, it would be easier for both of us."

"You are asking me to relinquish my child's birthright, and to deny the gods' will. I can never do either. Not even for you, Tut."

Sitre-In came out of the twilight, the squirming King's Daughter caught up in her arms. The nurse's dress was ripped, and her wig hung askew. "I am sorry, Sitre-In. Truly. I know she is a handful." Ahmose reached out her arms, and gratefully, the nurse passed Hatshepsut over. Once in her mother's arms, the child quieted, and looked expectantly at the king.

"You should choose an heir soon, Tut, regardless of who you name. My father went his whole life without making his choice, and it nearly cost Egypt's security. It *did* cost the happiness of his daughters. Do not make the same mistake with your own family."

"I won't. You are right, Ahmose. I must name my heir. But once the choice is made, it is final, unless...unless the heir should die. I still hope that you might..."

"I will never have a son, Thutmose. I know it. I have my son already. Make your choice soon, and for the gods' sake, make the right choice."

Before he could argue, she turned and left the garden. Hatshepsut was very solemn in her mother's arms.

CHAPTER THIRTY-EIGHT

THE GREAT COMMUNAL GARDEN AT the House of Women made an ideal neutral ground. Ahmose would often meet Mutnofret there, and together they would walk the paths, chatting about things of little import, taking careful, uneasy stock of one another while Hatshepsut and the other Royal Sons played with the harem children among the flower beds. Sometimes the sisters joined in women's games in the shade groves, or watch the harem girls practice their dancing and singing. Always the children flickered about them like a flock of brown birds, bobbing and screeching as they played, their sidelocks flying like pennants in the wind.

Here in the garden of their youth, Ahmose could almost love Mutnofret again. She had allowed herself to hope, on the evening of Ramose's birth when her sister had spoken through a semsemet haze, that Mutnofret had accepted her place – her children's place – at last. But although Mutnofret no longer seemed likely to fight with quartz rings and rekhet, there was still a gleam in the second wife's eye whenever she looked at Hatshepsut. Ahmose did not like it. She could never speak to the second wife as she had to Tut, of Amun's son, of a King's Daughter that was really a Royal Son. Mutnofret would never understand. Tut did not understand, come to that. And so, because Ahmose could tell her sister nothing of Hatshepsut's ka, Mutnofret must still harbor a secret hope for her own children. Ahmose had only a single pawn on the senet board – female – while Mutnofret had three, and all were sons.

Ahmose kept her thoughts to herself, and watched the children play.

She had come to love her nephews well since her pregnancy. The boys looked very much alike, all of them with Mutnofret's black eyes and wide mouth, but their personalities were as dissimilar as could be.

Wadjmose, the eldest, was serious and proper, with a smile that was grudgingly given but dazzling when it appeared, like the sun through Peret's fog. He was their general, leading all the children in games of war among the flowers. He would often sit beneath a sycamore to fashion toy bows for the other harem children from branches and twists of flax thread. He was stern as he worked, with a furrow between his brows that was just like Tut's. He was eight, quick with his tutors, and excited that soon he would enter basic military training: caring for horses, throwing a spear, running, climbing, firing a real bow.

Amunmose, six years old now, was the mischief-maker of the group. When he smiled, the spaces between his teeth hinted that he would grow to have his father's big, toothy grin. Of all Thutmose's children, Amunmose was the one who most resembled the Pharaoh. He even had his father's jackal-bark laugh, and he let it fly frequently, especially after he had leapt out of the bushes, hands held up like a lion's claws, to send a band of little girls scattering in all directions, or after he'd tossed a spider into a harem lady's wig. Neither Mutnofret nor his nurse could rein him in. Both had stopped trying. Ahmose always tried to keep from laughing at the boy's pranks; she usually failed.

Ramose, at three, was still soft and timid, though Hatshepsut's influence had brought out some courage in the boy. He followed Hatet everywhere, her quiet shadow, getting up to all the same trouble and crying every time they were scolded. With luck, he would mature into a stronger boy and would, perhaps, make a fine husband for Hatshepsut. He was biddable, at least, and always ceded to Hatshepsut's whims.

Though it posed a problem: what would his title be, as the husband of the king? *A puzzle for another day.* Ahmose put it out of her head and went on with her senet game in the shade of the women's favorite grove.

"Mawat!" A plaintive voice carried across the garden.

Baketamun, bent over the board, looked up in alarm. "Opet, I'm here, under the trees."

Baketamun's girl, willowy and bronze-haired, stumbled around a bed of flowers. She carried a ripped doll in her hands, and her thin, fine face was red with tears. "She's dead!" Opet waved the doll in the air. Bits of goose down drifted out of the rent in its side to float away through the flowers.

"Oh, by the gods," Baketamun said, sighing. "What did you do to your doll? I shall have to stitch her back up again."

"She's dead! That beastly little girl who dresses like a boy killed her!"

Baketamun glanced at Ahmose. There was a cringing apology in her look. She turned back to her sobbing daughter. "Opet, you must not speak so rudely of the King's Daughter."

Ahmose sighed and stood up, brushing her dress clean. "Hatshepsut did this to your doll?"

Opet stared up at Ahmose in horror. "Great Lady, I'm sorry. I didn't mean to insult the King's Daughter." The girl bowed so low the torn doll brushed the ground.

"It's all right, Opet. You need not ask my forgiveness; Hatshepsut must ask yours. And Hathor knows she certainly can be beastly sometimes. Where is she?"

Baketamun laid a gentle hand on her daughter's back, urging the girl to speak up. Opet took a deep, shaky breath, then pointed toward the big sycamore.

"I will make it right," Ahmose said. "You wait here."

She strode off toward the sycamore, but after no more than four or five steps, she faltered. There was a sudden sickness in the air, a heaviness that chilled her. She paused to listen. The children's voices were farther away than the sycamore. Had Wadjmose led them off in some game? Her skin prickled. Something was not right here – not right with the garden, not right with the day. She looked back to the grove, but if any of the other women felt as she did, none showed it. Baketamun and her friends were bent around Opet and her doll, and Mutnofret, gathered on the other side of the grove with a crowd of harem women, led them in laughter over some bit of gossip. In the close air, the sound of merriment was as discordant as the noise a harp makes when it is dropped upon the ground. Ahmose turned back toward the great tree, wondering. She reached out to seek the gods, and found there a bleary, diffused bluster, as if they were hard at work and could not be bothered to speak.

Then, like a voice in a nightmare, her own words to Tut on the night of Hatshepsut's birth floated up in her mind. *Amun's will shall be done, whatever either of us may wish.* It had been more than a year since Ahmose had dared mention the heirship, but she knew with a deep, shocking chill the day of reckoning had come.

She ran.

The children were not under the sycamore, though dolls and Wadjmose's twig-bows were scattered on the ground as if they had been dropped in a moment of distraction. She swallowed hard and held her breath, listening. A murmur of children's voices came from beyond a stand of fig trees. She ran toward it, left the path, pushed through the branches.

On the other side of the figs, the garden swept out in a wide arc of grass. The children clustered on the far side, whispering and staring at a heap of gray-brown that lay on the lawn between them and the fig trees, between them and Ahmose. She stared at the heap, too, and took one hesitant step toward it. It was a hare, she realized. Dead. A rather large hare, with blood coming from holes in its back where some great bird had once held it. The sight filled her with dread.

Movement from the knot of children: three forms broke from the group, three little bobbing brown birds in dirty white kilts. Wadjmose, tugging at Ramose's hand, trying to hold him back. And out in front of them, cocksure, Hatshepsut.

She strode toward the dead hare with her fists doubled up at her sides. Ahmose put a hand out, trying to summon up a voice to shout at her daughter, to stop her, though Amun's will would be done. She remained mute and frozen.

"Stop, Ramose," Wadjmose yelled, but the smaller boy bit his brother's hand, suddenly possessed by his half-sister's spirit; and when he was free, he ran after Hatshepsut.

The girl glanced back to see her playmate running toward her, and all at once it was a race to see who could reach the dead hare first. Hatshepsut's knees made her kilt fly up as she pelted across the lawn.

A slithering blue shadow passed over the grass, then two, three, circling, drawing a cold ring around the running children and the still hare. Ahmose looked up to see the white bodies of vultures kiting on broad wings, silhouetted against the sun. They had come for the carcass.

In an instant, as one vulture's shadow passed over Hatshepsut's body, the girl stumbled and fell, sprawled out her full length several spans from the hare. The knot of children, watching from afar, shrieked and laughed. But Ramose did not fall. He kept running, passed his sister, shouted in triumph as he reached the hare.

Another reached the hare, too, at the same time. The white bird moved, as it landed, like a swimmer's legs in deep water. Every movement of the vulture's body was clearly defined, slowly enacted, precise and dragging. The black-edged wings shouldered up; the white-crusted talons came forward, touched the ground, hopped as wings folded back against the sleek body. Ramose jerked to a stop above the hare. The vulture's beak, curved like a blade, opened in a hiss.

The boy hesitated, staring, and the bird hesitated, too, the feathers on its back raised and bristling. Then it lunged at him. Its beak pierced his arm above the wrist. Ramose screamed.

Ahmose was at his side in a flash. The vulture loped away across the ground and lumbered into the air.

She scooped Ramose into her arms, held him tight against

her chest, while he shrilled his terror into her ear. Wadjmose was beside them now, running in front of the pack of children. "Aunt Ahmose," he wailed, "I told him not to go near it!"

"Go get your mother," Ahmose said, and Wadjmose, ever the good boy, went flying off into the garden.

Ahmose carried her nephew into the fig grove, where at least the shade might comfort him. With luck, the vulture's bite was not severe. Perhaps it did not break the skin at all. She pushed through the branches, shielding Ramose as best she could from their clawing fingers. Hatshepsut was right beside her, gazing up from the garden floor with solemn eyes. When Ahmose looked into her daughter's face, hope for Ramose trickled out of her.

Amun's will shall be done.

She set Ramose on the ground. His bitten arm had been folded against Ahmose's chest; when he was lying beneath the fig trees, she could see the severity of the wound. It bled badly; it had soaked the front of her gown.

Hatshepsut watched the scene with mild curiosity in her eyes, sucking on her lower lip.

"Take off your kilt," Ahmose told her daughter. Hatshepsut complied and handed the garment over.

Ahmose wound it tightly about the boy's arm and knotted it, praying it would hold until a physician arrived. "Shh, shh," she said, scooping Ramose into her arms again and rocking him. "It hurts, I know, but you will be all right."

"What happened?" Mutnofret was beside them now under the fig branches. Ahmose passed the boy to his mother.

"A vulture," Ahmose said. "It bit him."

"A what?"

"There was a dead hare, and vultures came." Ahmose glanced at Hatshepsut, who stood naked and rocking on her heels, hands clasped behind her back. Better not to mention that Ramose had been racing the King's Daughter. "Ramose ran toward it before anybody could stop him. A vulture landed near the hare, and the bird bit him."

Mutnofret stared at her, eyes wide, mouth dropped open

in shock.

"He needs a physician," Ahmose said. "It's bleeding badly."

Mutnofret glanced at the stain on Ahmose's dress, nodded. Awkwardly, she took Ramose in her arms and hurried down the path.

Ahmose knelt once more and grabbed her daughter, hugged her fiercely. If Hatshepsut had reached the carcass first... but no. No, of course. Ramose's fate was not Hatshepsut's. An icy hand clutched at her heart, and she let her daughter go. The King's Daughter wandered to the path, peered after Mutnofret, and said nothing.

Ahmose became aware of miserable sniffling nearby. It was Wadjmose. His head hung low, and now and then he brushed at his eyes with the backs of his hands. "Come here," she said to him, holding out her arms. He drifted to her without looking up. She pulled him close. "You are not to blame, Wadjmose."

He shook his head and sniffed.

"Tell me what happened. How did you find the hare?"

The boy, struggling to marshal his voice, said nothing for a long time. He tugged at his sidelock, kicked his toes in the dust of the fig grove. At last he said, "Amunmose saw a hawk fly by. He said it looked like it had something big, but it couldn't fly with it. We went after it – you know, the way it flew – to see if we could catch it." He paused, wiping his tears. "We saw it drop the hare. Then the hawk flew away. Some of the children wanted to go get the hare so we could say we caught it, but I didn't think it was safe. I said no." He looked at naked Hatshepsut. As if she could feel her brother-cousin's eyes on her, the girl turned back from the path and held his gaze with her own bright black eyes. "Hatshepsut ran for it, and I couldn't keep Ramose back. You know he always follows her everywhere. Then...then..."

"It's all right. This is not your fault, sweet boy. Now I need to change out of this dress, and then we can go visit Ramose. I suppose the physician is sewing up his arm right now."

"Sewing him?"

"Just like a rag doll," she said, and though she tried to make her voice cheery for the sake of the children, she thought of Opet's torn doll — *She's dead!* — and shivered.

CHAPTER THIRTY-NINE

HOW IS HE TODAY?" AHMOSE asked.

Twosre shook her head and looked away. "Not well, Great Lady. The fever has grown worse. I was at his bedside this afternoon when they changed the bandage on his arm, and the smell..."

Numb, Ahmose nodded. It was no more than she expected, yet it still tore at her to know that innocent Ramose, soft little Ramose, suffered. She allowed herself to hope, though. Perhaps he would not be taken by Anupu. Perhaps a warning to the Pharaoh was enough for the gods. Perhaps the boy's life would be spared. "How is my sister?"

"She is frightened, of course, but bearing up." Twosre paused, watching Ahmose's face for a long moment, and then said, "I do not think she blames the King's Daughter, if that's what you are asking."

It *was* what she was asking. Ahmose was comforted to know that Hatshepsut would not be blamed. This was not the girl's fault, after all. If blame lay anywhere, it was with the king. He had tempted the gods by disobeying their wishes, and now she feared Ramose would pay the price.

"Has the Pharaoh been to see Ramose?"

"Ah, Great Lady. He has hardly left the boy's side the whole two days since Ramose was bitten."

Ahmose knew she should go to the boy's bedside, but she felt too angry, too frightened, to look her husband in the eye. "Is there any hope he will recover, Twosre?"

Twosre fell quiet, looking out over Ahmose's garden. Darkness was gathering over Waset. Bats piped from the branches of the trees and insects murmured among the flowers. At length she said, "I think it is unlikely, Great Lady. I am sorry."

The words unseated Ahmose's fear. "I will go to him tonight."

It was a long and daunting walk across the courtyard, lit now by the first touches of starlight from a deep purple sky. The door to Mutnofret's chamber was open slightly to allow the breeze inside. She pushed it wide and went in.

The antechamber of the second wife's apartments had been converted into a sickroom. A small bed was set up in the center, and Ramose lay sprawled atop it, his linen-wrapped arm held stiffly out across the mattress, his small body bent and shining with sweat. He seemed to be asleep, though his head tossed restlessly. Thutmose and Mutnofret sat on stools beside the bed, their backs to the door. Two serving girls worked palm fans up and down, up and down, stirring and cooling the air over the child's body. A musician played soft temple hymns on a harp in one corner.

Ahmose came to Tut's side and rested a hand on his shoulder. He jerked, as if he had been dozing, and looked up at her. "Ahmoset."

"How is he?" she asked, although she knew the answer already.

"Not well," Mutnofret said, and her voice was thick with exhaustion. "The wound has festered, though they packed it with a poultice and chanted spells to chase the demons away."

Tut shook his head slowly, side to side like a hound searching for a scent. "I don't know what to do."

"Have you been to the temple?"

Tut made no reply for a long time. His eyes wandered over Ramose's body, the small chest, the thin legs. "No," he said at last. "I have not left this room, except to see to my own needs."

"I will go," she said. "I'll bring any offerings you wish me to take. Mutnofret?"

She meant only to ask whether Mutnofret wanted anything in particular left at a shrine, but the second wife stood, slowly and carefully, as if she were an old, old woman. "I'll come with you. I need to pray."

They waited in the palace courtyard under the night sky for a chariot to take them to the temple. There were guards nearby, standing at a respectful distance, voices low so as not to disturb Egypt's grieving ladies.

Mutnofret breathed the fresh air deeply and pulled off her wig. There was no one to see but the guards; Ahmose supposed she was beyond caring about propriety, anyhow.

Mutnofret ran a hand over days-old stubble and sighed. "I needed to get out of that room, the gods forgive me."

"I imagine you did. I think the gods will understand."

"I am a terrible mother for leaving my child. He could die at any time, but I had to do something other than sit and stare."

It chilled Ahmose, to hear how matter-of-factly Mutnofret spoke of her son's death. If Hatshepsut lay in a fever, Ahmose did not believe she could face it so calmly. But Mutnofret had hardly slept for two days, and lack of sleep could do strange things to any person's mind.

"You are not a terrible mother," she said, squeezing Mutnofret's hand. It was clammy, unresponsive. She let it drop again.

"He's going to die," Mutnofret said flatly. "What am I to do? What will I do without him?"

Ahmose wanted to say, *You do not know that. He may yet survive.* But *she* knew it. She had known it the moment the vulture landed. Anupu had marked Ramose for his own. Amun's will would be done.

"There is no mortuary temple for my sons." Mutnofret's voice was low and monotonous. "I will have to lay him in my own tomb, until one can be built."

"*If* he dies, we will build him a tomb. The gods will know where to find him."

Mutnofret nodded, dull and dark. "Yes. They will know where to find him."

"Mutnofret, I think you need sleep more than you need to go to Ipet-Isut. Look at yourself; you can hardly stand."

Hooves popped against paving stones. The chariot swung into view. Mutnofret watched it draw close, and said, "I will sit in the chariot. It will be easier than standing the whole way. But I need to go to the temple before Ramose dies." There was an urgency in her voice now.

Ahmose raised no more protests. She helped her sister into the chariot.

Mutnofret sat, her back propped against the side of the vehicle, her head leaning back and bumping whenever the wheels rolled over a rough patch of road. The driver walked the horses, and they rode to the Holy House in silence.

Ahmose held their offerings wrapped in fine red linen and watched her sister's face. Mutnofret had aged so much in the past three years; the finest net of lines spread out from the corners of the second wife's eyes, maturing her face but marring her prettiness not one bit. Mutnofret's beauty was a serene one now, where before, when they were younger and more at odds, it had been a fiery beauty. She was still like a goddess, though, with clear skin and penetrating dark eyes. No passage of years would ever make Mutnofret anything but beautiful. Ahmose wanted to touch her, to embrace her, to forgive her for all the wrongs of the past, now that Mutnofret was so delicate and fine in her sorrow. Instead, she clutched the bundle of meat and bread to her chest and turned her eyes toward Ipet-Isut.

The guards at the Holy House's gates allowed them to drive the chariot all the way to the two great temples at the heart of the complex. When they arrived at the forecourt, Ahmose helped Mutnofret down from the platform and steadied her while she trembled. Then Mutnofret took the bundle and led the way into the dark heart of Mut's temple herself.

"Wait for me, please," Mutnofret said when they reached the doorway to Hathor's sanctuary – Hathor, the protector of mothers. "I would be alone with the goddess." Mutnofret disappeared into the black bosom of the sanctuary.

Ahmose sat on the floor of the temple, her back against a wall alive with painted figures. The temple was quiet, deserted in the night. Ahmose sat very still, feeling the ache of exhaustion in her limbs and heart. She closed her eyes, breathed, quiet and still.

And in a moment or an hour – she could sense no passage of time – she saw again, on the dark side of her closed eyes, Mut walking on the river of light, carrying in her arms the boy Hatshepsut.

Why? Ahmose asked, bold and challenging. She should be afraid of questioning the goddess, especially here in Ipet-Isut, in Mut's own home. But grief had taken her beyond fear.

When Mut's mouth opened, Ahmose's own voice came out. *The will of the gods shall be done.*

Don't do this to us. We will not survive it.

And now it was Twosre's voice, figs and earth: *Do you serve weak gods?*

Ahmose sagged in the dream-river, bending this time not under a weight of worship, but of sorrow.

Mut bent forward, forward, until her shining face was a hand's breadth before Ahmose's own. She smiled lovingly. She reached a white wing forward, and it became an arm, a hand that pointed a finger, a finger that touched the surface of the Iteru. The water stilled, as smooth and clear as a mirror. Ahmose watched the water. Her own face looked back at her, and now beside her reflection was Thutmose, and Hatshepsut. Just beyond them she saw the faces of Mutnofret and the boys. And beyond them, all of Egypt, faces as innumerable and precious as stars.

It is for these, my beloved children, that I raise up the prince with nine kas.

Though her eyes were closed, Ahmose *blinked*. And saw again the red veils, the comforting bed, the nine striding boys, smiling at her, knowing her. *Nine kas.* Hatshepsut was more than even Ahmose had suspected. With nine kas, she could be anywhere, everywhere. She would have power unknowable. Ahmose's heart wavered, unable to fully understand.

Nine kas? My child?

Eight male, one female, and each one pleasing to the gods. As you are pleasing to the gods, God's Wife.

You cannot call me that, Ahmose said, never knowing where her boldness came from. *I was never the God's Wife.*

On the contrary, child. You were, and are. Did you not lay with my husband Amun to conceive our child, our bringer of the floods, our soul of maat? Our prince?

My child is a girl, Ahmose said, weeping.

Mut was amused. Her perfect face shone with her laughter. *Believe that if you must.*

I must. The Pharaoh thinks Hatshepsut is a girl. What can I do? I have tried to convince him. He will not believe.

Nor will he ever believe. And that is why we do this thing.

Ramose. The name was blood in her mouth, tears in her eyes. *Please.*

Mut's white finger stretched forward again and touched the water. Ripples spread from the place, rings spreading and multiplying, a handful of pebbles thrown into the palace lake. The ripples surged outward, shaking the water as they went. They distorted the world as they passed, broke the surface of the mirror into glimmers of light. All the people of the land were touched by the spreading ring; all the people were shaken. But the first to be shaken was Tut.

A sigh from the sanctuary opened Ahmose's eyes. Mutnofret leaned against the door frame, her eyelids fluttering. Ahmose pushed up from the ground stiffly, went to her sister and nudged beneath one arm, holding her up.

"Let's go home," Ahmose said. "You need rest."

"No. Help me to the next altar. I will need you to say the prayers now; I am tired. But I will be with you."

Ahmose hesitated, torn between appealing to the gods – *Perhaps there is still hope* – and seeing to her sister's immediate needs. Mutnofret's chest quivered. She drew a ragged breath.

Ahmose made her decision, took the bundle of offerings from her sister's hands, and helped her to the next sanctuary door.

Tut may shake, and Mutnofret may shake, and all of Egypt may shake. But Ahmose would stand at the center of the spreading rings, and for her family's sake she would not be shaken.

CHAPTER FORTY

RAMOSE WAS LAID IN A tiny golden sarcophagus in Mutnofret's tomb. The sun was high and scolding. Ahmose kept her face turned toward the ground and held tight to Hatshepsut's hand as Menketra, the High Priest, recited the ceremony to commend the boy's ka to the gods.

He had died the same night Ahmose and Mutnofret went to Ipet-Isut. While they prayed in the Holy House, Ramose's tiny flame flickered out with no one near but his father, the king. They had returned to find the Pharaoh weeping silently over his son's body. Mutnofret, her face as blank as a statue's, stared at the scene, then wandered into her bed chamber and fell onto her mattress, still dressed and wigged. Ahmose and Tut undressed her gently while she slept, her body as heavy and formless as silt. She stayed asleep for nearly three days, and when she woke she cried for a week. But now, seventy days later, she watched the ceremony with calm, wistful eyes.

The tomb lay in a lush green valley not far from Ipet-Isut. A dark rock bluff rose above the entrance, hung with a rank growth of vines, smelling of green life in the afternoon air. It was a good place to await eternity. Ramose's sweet little ka would be happy here.

While Menketra recited prayers, a shadow passed over the ground where Ahmose's eyes rested. Her scalp prickled with foreboding. She tracked the shadow with her eyes: a flying bird, the gentle sound of feathers in the wind. She looked up to the bluff above the tomb's mouth in time to see a vulture alight, just as it had done before the dead hare in the women's garden, with a careless shrug of its wings. It looked down on the mourners, its white crest raised, strange obsidian eyes glittering in its naked face. It spread its wings wide and held them, basking in Re's light, triumphant. Ahmose held her breath. *Nekhbet, the vulture goddess, come to see that we finish the job she started.*

Ahmose glanced at Mutnofret. The second wife saw the vulture, too. She looked at it unafraid, a simple question hanging round the black lines of her eyes. Then she looked away again, as if she knew she would receive no answer from this god or any other.

Hatshepsut, dressed properly today in a girl's long belted tunic, tugged at Ahmose's hand. She pointed up at the vulture and seemed about to speak, but Ahmose held a finger to her lips. The girl frowned – frowned at her mother, frowned at Ramose's funeral. She frowned at white Nekhbet, too, as if to say, *You took my friend away.* Ahmose could feel a storm of words building in the King's Daughter. She looked around for Sitre-In; the nurse swept in and quietly took Hatshepsut away, off to the edge of the crowd, and distracted her by picking flowers to weave into her sidelock.

"As the Royal Son Ramose journeys into the afterlife, we know that he will be guided by Hathor. He will be with the rising sun each morning, so that we will never forget him." Menketra finished the rites, and blessed the sarcophagus with salt and oil and ankh. Then it was time to carry Ramose down into the tomb. Tut and the other bearers came forward, lifted the pitiful small golden sarcophagus between them, and stepped over the tomb's threshold. The darkness swallowed them. The vulture took flight.

Mutnofret sighed, a desolate sound, a wind in the desert. Wadjmose and Amunmose held onto her two hands, both boys fighting back tears. Ahmose knelt and held out her arms to her nephews. They both leaned into her; she shielded their faces from the gathered nobles while they sniffled and sobbed.

"Where is he?" Amunmose asked.

"He is with Waser," she told him. "It is a wonderful place, always green, because Waser makes all the green things grow. It is never too hot there, and there is always still water for swimming, and lots of good things to eat. And there are many other children for him to play with."

"Won't he miss us?"

"I am sure he will," she said, smiling at the boy's innocence. "And we will miss him, too. But we must be happy for him. He gets to live with all the gods, and he will never have any worries again."

Amunmose pulled back from her shoulder. His face was serious, as it had been all these seventy long days. She missed his laughter, his little jests. *His smile will come back with time.* He said, "I don't want to go live with Waser, even if it is nice. I like it here."

Ahmose's ka felt sick. She glanced up at the rock bluff where the vulture had perched. "I don't want you to go live with Waser, either. Not until you are a very old man."

Thutmose came to her that night. They made a desperate, mournful kind of love in the dimly striped light of her bed chamber. They were a soft confusion of flesh and seed, hot living breath and hot living skin, a double proclamation of vitality against the cold, open mouth of the tomb. When it was over, Ahmose lay still and listened to Tut's breathing. He was awake but silent. She remained silent, too, content to let the warmth of their passion burn off her cold fog of sorrow.

Finally Tut spoke. "Why did the gods take him?" His voice was curious, not wounded. He had more than two months to heal that wound, as much as it could ever be healed.

Ahmose said nothing. She did not want to speak.

He rolled over and propped himself up on an elbow, peering into her face to see if she slept.

Finally she said, "I don't know."

Tut was quiet again for a long time. Out in Ahmose's private garden an owl fluted its hollow, repetitive call. The sound caught his attention. He turned toward the pillared wall, and starlight limned the planes of his face, the hard edges, the soft curve of his scalp above his temples, the lines in his forehead, the sharp arc of his nose. She loved him. She would give anything to spare him, if she only could.

"You do know," he said quietly. "Please tell me."

"Tut, don't make me do this."

"Was it something I did?"

"How could it be?" she asked dully.

He lay back again, his fingers laced together over his chest. She loved his thick, strong hands, the strength of his body. She did not know whether his ka inside was as strong as the outside of him. She did not want to see him shake.

"Is it Hatshepsut?" He whispered the question.

Ahmose sat up, rubbed her eyes. She glanced at the jar of water beside the bed, thought of taking a drink to stall answering. Then he touched her arm, insistent.

"Yes," she said.

There was silence again, an uncomfortable, attenuated thing that clung between them like a spider's thread. This time Ahmose broke it.

"The gods are not pleased that you haven't named their heir, Tut."

He laughed softly, a self-deprecating huff. "You are always on me about naming an heir. You always have been."

"It is important."

"I know it is. I know."

The spider's thread stretched and quivered.

"I fear for the other boys," she said. "Of all the ways a three-year-old child can die – a vulture's bite? If ever I saw an omen, Tut..."

"What if I had named Wadjmose heir years ago, when you pestered me about him? What would the gods have done?"

"I don't know," she said truthfully. "I cannot tell what they'll do now. Maybe Ramose was enough for them. Maybe...." She could not finish the thought.

"It's just that...I cannot...I fear doing this thing, Ahmose." Admitting the fear took something out of him. He sighed, trembled.

She reached out in the darkness and stroked him, brushing his shoulder and arm as if he were a flighty horse. "Do not fear what the gods set before you," she told him, although she feared it, too. She feared all the things the gods had ever set before her: the throne of the chief wife, and the temple, and Aiya, and Mutnofret. Ineni. Thutmose. Hatshepsut.

"If they take me from the throne, what will become of me? I can never go back to being a general. Not now that I have been a king."

It was true. If Tut were pulled from the Horus Throne it would not be a gentle thing. He would be lucky to be banished to another land. More likely, he would end up dead. And Ahmose...she would die, too. She was not the God's Wife anymore, with power over the priests. She had no power — no power, except as the mother of a secret half-god. Precious little to stop an uprising.

"I love Hatshepsut dearly, but she cannot be my heir."

Ahmose's hand froze on Tut's shoulder. "You taunt the gods by doing this," she said, afraid. "You put us all in danger."

"Maybe. But perhaps you have read the signs wrong, my love." He rolled over and put a hand on her belly. "Perhaps tonight — or some night yet to come — a son."

"No, Tut. I will never bear a son." Her voice was half whisper, half wail. If she could give birth to a child with a body that reflected his ka, she would. A thousand times over, she wished that she could. Not just for Tut, and not for herself. For Hatshepsut. Was it Ahmose's fault, that the King's Daughter was such a jumble inside? Had she done something wrong during the pregnancy? Had she not said the right prayers, not made the correct offerings, or not made enough? Or was this warrior-girl who housed eight male kas and one female soul a punishment for Ahmose's sins?

313

No. Never – Hatshepsut was never a punishment. She was a blessing and a gift, a delight, though her very presence caused turmoil in the royal family. Ahmose wanted no other child, could imagine herself as mother of no other child. Her life had begun when her daughter was born. Her daughter *was* her life now.

"I am sorry Hatshepsut is female," she said, "on the outside. If her body was like her kas, we would not argue so much."

"It's not your fault, nor hers," he said, taking Ahmose in his arms.

She laid her head on his chest. She listened to his heart beating, gratefully. At length Ahmose said, "What will you do?"

He stroked the smoothness of her scalp. "For now, nothing. I still need time to think. I don't know what to do yet. So I will do what I have been doing: listen to petitions, send soldiers off to dredge canals and build fortresses. And I will pray. I hope the gods will take pity on me and send me a clear answer to my questions."

Hope for anything but that, she wanted to say. But she allowed him to go on stroking her head, and she kept her ear to his heart. How she loved him. How she would hate to see him shake.

CHAPTER FORTY-ONE

FOR MONTHS AFTER RAMOSE'S FUNERAL, Ahmose prayed daily, burning offerings in her bronze bowl before the statue-filled niches in her bedchamber wall. She was tense all the time, especially around her daughter and husband, expecting some terrible, divine blow to fall on her family. Yet none ever did. As the seasons went on in their accustomed march and Mutnofret's two boys grew taller, stronger, more confident, the prayers and offerings did not come so frequently. She allowed herself to hope the boys would be spared. And when Hatshepsut marked her fourth birthday, Ahmose felt sure the gods had been appeased.

Hatshepsut was not like the other four-year-old girls. She shunned dolls, unless it was to rip them apart. When she was made to wear a pretty dress, she rolled it over and over at the waist and tied it with a sash so the skirt hung short like a boy's kilt. When Ahmose encouraged her to let her hair grow, she screamed and kicked until Sitre-In gave in and shaved her scalp bare, just like a boy's. She was not growing long and lean like the daughters of the harem women, either. She was broad, strong, and tanned from playing in the sun at Wadjmose's war games. The only hint of her femininity was a soft half-ruggedness about her face, and matted black lashes so thick she always looked like she was wearing kohl.

Sitre-In worked constantly to teach the wild girl proper behavior. The whole family sat now at a long table for supper, and the young nurse slapped at Hatshepsut's wrists, for she

315

had reached for the bread before the king.

Hatshepsut hissed like a cat. Lately it amused the girl to make animal noises. Sitre-In shoved the platter of bread out of Hatshepsut's reach, and Hatshepsut scowled at the nurse, rocking her bottom side-to-side in the bowl seat of her stool.

"All right now," Tut said. "We must recall our manners, Hatet."

"You recall *your* manners," she shouted. "I'm hungry!"

Tut's eyes crinkled. Ahmose shot him a heavy look. *Don't laugh. It will only encourage her.* The Pharaoh straightened in his chair, frowned at his daughter. Hatshepsut squeaked, and sat very still, her hands resting in her lap, eyes very wide and staring straight ahead – pretending to be a temple statue, Ahmose assumed.

"That's better," Tut said. "Now, Wadjmose, since it is your special day, you shall have the first serving of every dish."

Ahmose beamed at her nephew. The boy eagerly picked up the platter, selected the best piece of bread for himself, and passed it to his mother. It was indeed a special day for him. Wadjmose had completed his first day of real military training. Not just horse care and running with the other boys, but true soldier's work. He had entered training almost three years earlier than most boys. The fact that Wadjmose was First Son of Egypt surely had something to do with it, but all the credit could not go to his blood and birth. Wadjmose was exceptionally bright and serious in his studies. He applied himself wholly to everything he did. The Instructor of Boys had recommended Wadjmose for advanced training without any prompting from Tut's stewards. The boy had his father's ability with bow and horses. He, too, would be a strong arm for Egypt.

"How was your first day? Tell me all about it!" Ahmose leaned her elbows on the table and watched Wadjmose eat. He dipped his bread in honey and stuffed it into his mouth, chewing quickly. They must have worked him hard. She had never seen the boy with such an appetite before.

"It was wonderful," he said, his mouth still full.

"Recall your manners," Hatshepsut yelled.

"Quiet, Hatet. It is your brother's turn to speak."

Hatshepsut knew better than to try scowling at Ahmose. The girl went back into her wide-eyed temple-statue pose. Ahmose held the platter of bread out, but Hatshepsut did not move, staring ahead with her huge, unblinking eyes. Ahmose dropped a piece of bread into the princess's bowl, then passed the platter along to Sitre-In.

"I got to drive a chariot," Wadjmose said. "*Two* horses! And then we ran laps, and then I had to carry a shield."

"It sounds like fun."

"It's hard work. The shield was heavy. I am very sore, and hungry." He took another huge bite of his bread.

"The Instructor of Boys tells me you were especially good with the chariot," Tut said from the head of the table. "I am proud of you."

Wadjmose blushed.

Hatshepsut shifted on her seat. She looked for a long time at Tut, then at Wadjmose. "When do I start soldier school?"

Mutnofret, seated across the table from Ahmose, raised her eyebrows, then turned to smack Amunmose's wrist; the boy had let out a donkey-bray laugh.

"What?" Hatshepsut stared hard at Amunmose.

"You're a *girl*, stupid," he said. "You can't be a soldier."

"I am not!"

"Yes you are! I've never seen you piss standing up!"

"All right," Tut shouted. "Enough! Amunmose, you are old enough to know better."

"So is she," Amunmose muttered. "When is she going to learn she's a girl?"

"She knows she's a girl," Tut said.

Hatshepsut sucked in a breath, ready to shout a denial at her father, but Ahmose and Sitre-In each seized one of her arms.

"Enough out of you," Sitre-In said. "Sit and eat quietly or go to bed hungry."

Desperate to change the subject, Ahmose turned to

her other nephew. "And what are you learning in school, Amunmose?"

"Numbers," the boy said, sulking. "I hate numbers."

"Numbers are important. You will be a great man some day, and you must know how to keep track of numbers."

"Amunmose is excellent with numbers," Mutnofret said, giving him a pat on the shoulder. "He is very clever."

"I'm clever," Hatshepsut said.

Amunmose rolled his eyes.

"I am," she insisted. "I'm cleverer than you!"

"What did I tell you, Hatshepsut?" Sitre-In stood and took the girl's hand. "No supper for you!"

"No!" Hatshepsut screeched, grabbing her bread and stuffing it in her mouth. Sitre-In, with the patience of a goddess, pulled the bread out again. The nurse dragged Hatshepsut out of the great hall.

Ahmose took her time finishing supper. She was in no hurry to rush to Hatshepsut's room to comfort the girl. The King's Daughter had been a trial lately; it seemed every day she craved more and more of her father's approval. Any favor Tut showed to either of the boys was met by Hatshepsut with sulking at best, and outright disruption at worst. Hatshepsut was cultivating a jealous streak as wide as the river. Ahmose was not sure how to curb it.

After supper, she found Sitre-In sewing in the far end of Ahmose's private garden. She asked whether she might sit, too. The evening air was refreshingly brisk, and the garden was especially peaceful tonight.

"Of course you may sit, Great Lady," Sitre-In said, shifting her neat pile of linen on the bench to make room.

"Did you get anything to eat, Sitre-In?"

"Ah, Great Lady. I had a friend from the kitchens bring me my supper."

"And Hatshepsut?"

"None for her, just as I promised."

Ahmose sighed, pinching the bridge of her nose. "I suppose that's for the best."

Sitre-In gave Ahmose a level, matronly look. Were nurses born with that look, Ahmose wondered, or did they have to practice it? "Hatshepsut needs rules, and consequences for breaking the rules. I know she is a King's Daughter, but if she is to grow into a gracious and fair ruler, like you, Great Lady, then she must understand why we have rules."

King, Ahmose did not say. *She is to be king.* Even the girl's nurse would not understand. "She wants to become a soldier."

"No doubt. And she'd be a good one, I would wager," Sitre-In said, laughing.

"I wonder."

The nurse laid her sewing in her lap and looked at Ahmose, not with the nurse's stare this time, but with genuine surprise. "Great Lady? Forgive me, but you cannot be serious."

"I don't know. Would you believe me if I told you..." She trailed off, uncertain. Sitre-In would think her a fool. But the nurse was waiting with her brows still arced over her green eyes. Ahmose took a deep breath. "Would you believe me if I told you Hatshepsut has a male ka?" *Or eight of them?*

Sitre-In did not seem at all surprised. "Yes, I would believe you," she said, and picked up her needle again.

"You aren't startled at all."

"I cannot think why I should be. Just look at how she behaves, Great Lady. Have you ever known a *girl* to be so fierce?"

And suddenly it seemed so easy and natural to share all her thoughts and fears with this sensible woman. She told Sitre-In everything. Ahmose's knowing, from a young age, as if by divine prophecy that she would never have a son; Tut's dream; the vision on the night Hatshepsut was conceived. The rest, too: how the king would not name Hatshepsut heir because of her sex; how Nekhbet took Ramose away as punishment. By the end of it, Sitre-In had laid her sewing down again, and was watching Ahmose's face with rapt attention.

"What do you think, then?" Ahmose said. "What should we do with the girl?"

Sitre-In considered the question for a long time. At last she said, "I do not think the people would understand, Great Lady. You and I know Hatet, but we are her mawats, her mother and her nurse. The court and the commoners and the priests – they will never see her ka. All they can see is her body. And it is a girl's body."

Ahmose nodded. "You are right, of course. It's been a year since...since Ramose. A year, and the Pharaoh still has not said a thing about an heir. Nothing else has happened, thanks be to all the gods. We have lost no one else. Maybe he is right, after all. Maybe I am to have a son one day – an *actual* son, in body and in ka. I have thought for years I would never have a boy, but..."

Sitre-In's needle sparkled in the moonlight. She drew her thread in, out, in, before she answered. "Even a very great priestess might be wrong now and again, Great Lady. You could still bear the king a son."

"Yes. I suppose you are right." But Ramose. Why was that price paid? Why punish the royal family in such a cruel way, if the son who would be heir had not even been conceived? It made no sense. But Ahmose didn't have the energy to fight it anymore. "We should start educating her. She needs to learn to be a proper girl, and some day, a proper woman."

"No soldier-school for her, then?" Sitre-In sounded amused, and a bit disappointed. Ahmose understood. It was a hard thing to deny Hatshepsut, even for a sensible disciplinarian like Sitre-In. There was a power in the girl's eyes when she got what she wanted, when she was pleased. She had a way of making others want to please her.

"I suppose not. We should see about finding her a music teacher. And she should take dance lessons with the girls in the harem. It is time for the Royal Son to become a King's Daughter."

Ahmose nodded, but in her heart she was uneasy. The

words of Mut that terrible night in the temple – the finger touching the water, the ripples spreading. Still, a year later, these things unnerved her.

There was a rustle among the flower beds. Ahmose looked up, startled. Hatshepsut, dressed now in her boy's kilt, stomped over the black shoulder of earth carrying a little white jar in her hands. It was a chamber pot. She set it on the path in front of the bench and stood over it.

"Watch," she said. "I can, too."

And, lifting her kilt slightly, she urinated into the jar, standing upright. Hardly a drop splashed.

CHAPTER FORTY-TWO

A LL IN ALL, HATSHEPSUT ADJUSTED well to life as a
girl. Once she realized the Pharaoh was pleased when she
wore dresses, practiced temple dances with the other harem
children, and plunked clumsily at her harp, she applied
herself to her lessons with a focus Ahmose had never seen
in any four-year-old. The girl even allowed her hair to grow
out. Sitre-In wetted it daily, combing it toward Hatshepsut's
sidelock so it would lay in place until it grew long enough
to work into the braid. In just a few weeks' time she had
learned some basic melodies on her harp, though she often
threw it across the room in frustration. It was hard for her
to sit still and be ladylike, Ahmose knew, especially when
Amunmose and his friends ran about the gardens in their
kilts, making war.

Hatshepsut played her harp now for Mutnofret. The
second wife had come to Ahmose's garden for wine and
fruit on a warm, bright afternoon. The sisters sat beneath a
shade tree while the King's Daughter knelt on a cushion, her
brow furrowed with the intensity of her concentration. Her
deft brown fingers plucked out the notes one by one, and
whenever she dropped rhythm or struck the wrong string,
Hatshepsut frowned and bit her lip. Even Mutnofret had to
smile at the girl's diligence.

When the song was over, Ahmose and Mutnofret applauded.

"Well done," Ahmose said. "You played beautifully."

"A very nice song, Hatshepsut," Mutnofret said, resting her

hands again on the roundness of her belly. Another child was growing there – to replace the one that was lost, Ahmose suspected, although she would never voice such a thought to her sister. No one ever spoke of Ramose.

"Put your harp away, and then you can see if Sitre-In will take you to the House of Women to play with the other girls."

Hatshepsut tilted her head, as if considering Ahmose's offer. *I want to play with the boys.* Ahmose could all but hear the words. But the King's Daughter had learned how to please. "Yes, Mawat," she said, and skipped away with her harp.

"I must say, you have done wonders with her, Ahmose, you and that nurse. I never would have thought she could be turned into a little lady."

"We still have a long way to go. She acts up every day. She kicked Baketamun's youngest girl a few days ago...bruised her leg quite badly."

Mutnofret gave a snort of laughter. "I don't think you will ever train all the ferocity out of that one."

"And what about this one?" Ahmose put her hand, too, on the baby in Mutnofret's womb. "Another boy, do you think?"

"It seems I have a habit of making boys."

Ahmose shrugged away the words. Mutnofret did not mean them to sting, she was sure. Those days were gone for the second wife. "I can't believe it has been seven moons. You do not look so pregnant."

"I suppose I am carrying him high," Mutnofret said. "That, or it's a small child."

"Mawat." Hatshepsut stood near the garden door, waving urgently.

"What's the matter, dear one?"

"Sitre-In says to come here right now!"

Ahmose and Mutnofret shared a glance. A nurse said for the Great Royal Wife to *come right now?* Either Hatshepsut had gotten the message wrong, or something was terribly amiss. "Wait here," Ahmose said, and hurried toward her bed chamber.

She knew the moment she saw Sitre-In that Hatshepsut

had the message right. The nurse was pacing, wringing her hands, and when her face turned to Ahmose it was swollen with tears.

"Sitre-In! What's the matter?"

"Oh, Great Lady," Sitre-In cried, running to her, throwing her arms around her. Ahmose was so startled she hugged the woman back, hard. After a few sobs, Sitre-In pulled away, covered her face with her hands. "It's the Royal Son, Great Lady."

"What? Which one?"

"Am...Amunmose." She choked out the name, her hands still pressed to her face.

No. No, no, dear Hathor, no! Swiftly, Ahmose looked at Hatshepsut. The girl stood silent in her dress, tugging on her sidelock, watching her nurse cry. *All because of this child*, Ahmose thought. *All this sorrow, for her.*

"What happened?"

"A snake, Great Lady. He was playing in the tall grass with some boys from the harem. An asp bit him on the foot."

"An asp bit who on the foot?" Mutnofret had come in from the garden. Her face was pale. Ahmose looked at her sister, at her dark eyes, her wide mouth, the roundness of her belly, and could find no words. Mutnofret stared back. She held Ahmose's eyes for a long, long time. Then her hands clutched at the child inside her. "Who? Tell me who!" Her voice rose to a scream.

Ahmose went to her, took her hand. "Amunmose. I'm so sorry, sister."

Mutnofret's entire body shook hard, like a leaf in a gale. Then she turned her face to Hatshepsut, whose back was against a wall, whose eyes were solemn and knowing. "Another of my children? I must lose *another* of my children?"

Hatshepsut opened her mouth, as if she was expected to answer, but could think of nothing to say.

"Sitre-In, take Hatshepsut out of here," Ahmose said quietly. She pulled at Mutnofret's hand. "Come. Let's go to your rooms. We will learn more from your women."

"No. Ramose died in my rooms." The name was like a slap, it had gone so long in the palace unspoken. Ahmose felt it, and Hatshepsut, too. The girl's shriek carried from the antechamber, and Sitre-In hushed her.

"Then we will go to Tut's rooms. Come."

And they were outside the Pharaoh's apartments, abruptly, in a terrible nightmare jump. They must have walked, though Ahmose could remember not a single step of the way between her hall and Tut's. All she knew was that she held Mutnofret's hand, and that Mutnofret shook and shook. Ahmose pushed open Thutmose's door. The Pharaoh sat on his couch, surrounded by dropped scrolls. Two stewards bent over him, speaking quickly, quietly. And the look on the king's face was terrible.

"Why do you rebel against the gods?" Tears burned Ahmose's eyes. Her face was sticky and hot. "Do you think you know better than they?"

Tut's fists rested still on the arms of his throne. He stared straight ahead, saying nothing. She had searched for him all night, and finally found him here in the great hall, sitting on his gilded chair, the double crown lying on the floor at his feet.

"A vulture took Ramose, and now an asp takes Amunmose. Nekhbet and Apep. Two of your sons dead! How can you doubt?"

Still he said nothing, his eyes hard.

"Tell the people that Hatshepsut is your heir, Tut. Do it before you lose your eldest son."

Finally he turned to her. "No."

The quiet ferocity of the word staggered her. She stepped back, catching her breath. He had never spoken to her before with such anger, with such hatred. She had never seen this mask he wore now. It was not the face of the sweet, boyish man with whom she rode chariots and shared supper. This was the face of Thutmose the general, Thutmose the conqueror, Thutmose who hung his enemy's body from the prow of his ship.

Tears stung her eyes afresh. "Then Wadjmose will die, too."

"He will not."

"Tut, please. Do not challenge the gods this way." She would have fallen on her knees to beg him, if she'd thought it could make a difference.

He was on his feet now, moving toward her with the speed of a stooping falcon. She gasped and skittered backward, trying to stay clear of his fury. Her back hit a pillar, and he was upon her; his hand closed around her arm. He shook her roughly. "Bear me a *son*, and Wadjmose will be safe." His other hand was at her breast. He squeezed it hard, so hard she screamed. He let go, and for one heartbeat relief flooded her. Then horror as he grabbed at her thigh. Not her thigh – the fabric of her gown. And his hand clutched hard, jerked it up, so her legs were exposed. He forced his knee between her own, pushed her legs apart. Shrieking, Ahmose twisted, kicked out at him, but he stepped quickly and her foot connected with nothing. Her dress fell back into place.

Now his teeth were against her neck. He bit, and she cried out again. Why were no guards coming to aid her? "You talk of rebelling against the gods? You? God's Wife? You were supposed to give me a son, Ahmose. That was the duty the gods gave you. A son!"

He pushed away from her, shoving himself back, reeling like a drunkard back up the steps of the dais. He leaned against one arm of his throne, trembling, coughing, and Ahmose leaned against the cool pillar, her breast and neck throbbing, grateful for the space that separated them.

He is mad with grief, she told herself. It was small comfort.

"Gods forgive me," Tut said, softly; and now tears ran down his face. "What have I done to you?"

"I know...I know you are grieving," she said in a small, broken voice. "I will forgive you."

He shook his head.

"I will," she insisted.

"I don't know what to do, Ahmoset."

"The gods want their son. They will have her, whether you give her willingly or not."

He looked up, his eyes so hurt, so angry, so sad. "My dream. You must give me a son."

Two of her nephews were dead. Her sister was shattered. Ahmose wanted to scream her words at him, but she could only summon up a pale whisper. "I already have," she said, and crept out of the great hall.

CHAPTER FORTY-THREE

THE TOMB WAS UNCHANGED. DENSER growth on the bluff above the opening, perhaps, but otherwise it was still cool, still green, still pleasant. Ahmose held Mutnofret's hand through the ceremony, and when Tut came forward with the other men to carry Amunmose into the cold black ground, both sisters turned away.

Mutnofret was silent almost all the time now. She always held her hands upon her belly, and when she did speak it was usually to the growing child. Seeing her this way, withdrawn, gentle, Ahmose had to struggle to recall a time when Mutnofret was ever anything else. When had the second wife been a scheming viper? When had she been full of hate? That was a thousand-thousand years ago, before the world was formed. The world was loss, grief, a pillar against Ahmose's back, Hatshepsut throwing her harp, Mutnofret whispering to the baby she carried. No other world had ever existed for the daughters of Amunhotep. A sapling in Ahmose's hand...no. That other world had never been. That was a story the nurses told their children.

When pleading for Hatshepsut's heirship failed, Ahmose begged Tut to choose Wadjmose instead. She thought perhaps any heir would suffice now, that so long as the succession was secure, even Amun would overlook his own daughter being set aside. Sometimes she even convinced herself that if Wadjmose were proclaimed heir, he would be safeguarded, as though the gods could not touch a Pharaoh's proclaimed

329

successor.

But it was useless. Tut still clung to his long-past dream, the baby in Ahmose's arms, a son to rule after he was gone. She begged for him to be sensible, and he pleaded to come to her bed. But ever since that miserable night when he had shaken her and bitten her, Ahmose had shunned him. As soon let a leopard into her bed. He was no longer the Thutmose she had loved. He was a beast that could not be trusted, terrifying and powerful in his rage and grief.

She walked with silent Mutnofret at the head of the procession, all the way out of the green valley and to their litter. She and Mutnofret rode together, hands clasped, heads leaning. Now and again the baby kicked. Ahmose watched it glide beneath Mutnofret's robe. Would this one, too, be taken?

And Wadjmose...when would the gods come for him? For she had no doubt now they would. The precious boy still studied and trained, all the seventy days while Amunmose's body was prepared for burial. Wadjmose was committed to becoming a general like his father, focused on his target like an arrow fired from a bow. Ahmose was glad. She did not want her nephew to worry over his death.

They were carried all the miles back to the Waset palace. The mourners marching behind their litter keened and cried, and Mutnofret, her head tucked against Ahmose's shoulder, keened with them, a high, piercing, sustained call, grief and loss given form. It flew up into the white sky, up and up, never stopping, a flock of black birds over Egypt.

Mutnofret's cry stayed with Ahmose for days. In her bath, in her garden, in the awkward notes of Hatshepsut's harp, she heard her sister's voice. It was there in her sleep, falling out of the dreaming sky in the form of singed white feathers. Many nights Ahmose would wake crying, too, and would bury her face in her linens, giving full voice to her own grief until her throat was raw. Not only for the boys, nor for Mutnofret. Not even for Tut, for the loss of his gentle hands, his sweet trust. If she had been asked, Ahmose could not have named the exact source of her sorrow. She could not find the dark, cold well from which it rose. She only knew its waters flooded her, and tore cries from her chest in the night. But always Mutnofret's wailing a pallid echo in her ears.

And then, one morning when Ahmose had slept late, exhausted from a dream of choking on black mud and white feathers, Mutnofret's cries were real.

The screaming jolted her out of fitful sleep. For one heartbeat she was hardly more than a girl again, awakened in the harem by the women mourning her father's death. Then she saw her pillared wall, her niches full of the gods' images, Hatshepsut's harp lying in the corner. She sat up on her bed, dizzy. The screaming was high and frantic, and thin as broth, muffled by walls and the distance of the courtyard.

Ahmose ran from her room, never caring that she was naked and unshod. She sprinted across the vined courtyard, into Mutnofret's hall, through her door. Serving women were clustered about the second wife, all of them frantic, all of them weeping. Mutnofret was dressed in a light robe, and its skirts were soaked to the hem. Her feet shone with a slick wetness. She was screaming, crying, the terrible voice of grief come to life again, more shocking and vital than in any of Ahmose's dreams. Mutnofret's fingers reached up to her face, clawed, traced bright red lines down forehead, cheeks, chin.

"Mutnofret!" Ahmose was at her side, shaking her. "What's wrong? Mutnofret!"

If Mutnofret heard, she gave no indication. She scratched her face again, and this time she drew blood.

"Great Lady," one of the serving women cried, "the baby is coming!"

Ahmose looked down at Mutnofret's wet robe. The waters had broken, at least a month too soon. Was this what drove

Mutnofret mad with sorrow?

"And the Royal Son, Great Lady," another woman said, her face distorted with weeping.

"No."

"He was swimming, Great Lady. This morning. Swimming in the river with the other boys. It was a crocodile, Great Lady, took him under the water before anyone even knew it was there."

Ahmose held onto Mutnofret's wrists, trying to keep the sharp nails from her sister's face. But grief weakened her grasp, and she let go, powerless, and pale.

Not even a body to bury. There would be no afterlife for Wadjmose, the serious one, the good boy, the little soldier.

Ahmose watched from a great distance as Mutnofret raked at her face, and screamed. And screamed. And screamed.

Twosre entered Ahmose's bed chamber quietly, taking a long, drawn-out time to close the door so its bump would not disturb the silence. Ahmose watched her serving woman with dull, disbelieving eyes. *I have news, Great Lady.* Were the words coming from Twosre's throat, or from Ahmose's heart, or from Mut's eyes? News, news. News of more grief, news of more loss. Ahmose hadn't the strength to brace herself. She sat, barely holding herself upright, passively waiting the fresh sorrow. *Your sister died in birth, and the baby too. Wahibra cut her open with a copper knife, and she died.*

But no...different words were coming from Twosre's mouth. Ahmose made her repeat them, struggling through the river-fog to understand.

"A healthy boy. Small, as you might expect from an early birth, though he seems strong enough. The midwives are cautious, but they expect him to live."

"Oh." Should Ahmose be pleased or afraid? Another boy for the gods to take. "And Mutnofret?"

"She seems...numb. She has named the baby Thutmose. She said the name will protect him."

Nothing will protect him. Nothing but his father. Ahmose nodded.

"Great Lady, the Pharaoh is outside. He waits to speak to you. He said I am only to let him in if you will have him. He said to..." Twosre flushed, and her hands fluttered at the collar of her dress. "He said to *beg* you, Great Lady. To beg your audience on his behalf."

Ahmose shook her head. She did not understand. Did the Pharaoh want to come to her bed? What business could he have here? "Send him in," her voice said from across the river, from miles and miles away.

When Thutmose came, Hatshepsut came with him. Sitre-In tried to follow, but the Pharaoh stilled her with a gentle hand on her shoulder; the nurse withdrew.

Carefully, Tut picked up their daughter and carried her to Ahmose's bed. He sat with the girl on his knee. "You were right, Ahmose. Right the whole time."

Ahmose said nothing. There was nothing to say. Hatshepsut toyed with something in her lap – a doll made of blue cloth, and for once it was whole, not ripped. The girl held it up to her face, rubbed it against her cheek. Ahmose saw the golden linen plumes rising from the doll's head. Amun. She wondered who had given the toy to Hatshepsut.

"The gods forgive me," Tut was saying, distantly. "The gods forgive this stupid man everything. I did not listen to them. I did not listen to you, and you were given to me so I might do their will. Ahmose, forgive me. Forgive me. Mutnofret, forgive me."

Hatshepsut looked up at her father's face. She used the doll's hand to dab away a tear.

"You must complete the task they have given you, Thutmose, if the gods are ever to grant you peace."

"And yet you know the people may not take it well. I see the gods' power, and I do not doubt them. How could I doubt them now? But my heart still fears. If I lose the throne, Ahmose, it will mean death for all of us."

Inspiration came to her, that true, deep surety that could only come from the gods, that only the god-chosen could know. She spoke Mut's words into her husband's ear. "It may take time for you to grow used to the idea. You are only mortal, after all, and you fear. Proclaim her at the Amun shrine in Annu, Tut, to the priests there. Just a few men need know. For now, it will be enough. And soon word will spread. The people will come to accept it gradually, in the gods' own time. All will be done in the gods' time. And we will be safe."

"Annu." Tut nodded. The ancient capital, a place of great holiness and magic. It was a place where all the gods would see Tut's obeisance. "And I can show her the kingdom on the journey north."

Hatshepsut stirred. "Where are we going?"

At the sound of her sweet voice, Thutmose closed his eyes. He leaned his head against his daughter's. His chin quivered, and his chest. He said nothing.

"Father? Are we going away? Will we see my brothers?"

Tut rose from the bed, so slowly. He handed Hatshepsut to Ahmose, and turned his back on them both, his face in his hands. A choked sound came from the Pharaoh, a painful cry stifled deep inside.

"Father?"

When he could speak again, his voice was soft but even. He returned to sit beside them, and cupped the girl's chin in his strong, rough hand. "You and I are going on a journey, Hatet, together. Just the two of us. Your brothers will not be there."

"I want to see them."

Ahmose tucked the girl's head under her chin, rocked her side to side. "You will see them again someday, precious one. A long time from now."

"Where are we going?"

You are going to fulfill the gods' promise. You are going to claim your birthright, the right of a god, the kingdom of Egypt. "North, up the river," Ahmose said. "You will see the whole of the land, Hatshepsut, my prince. You will see your kingdom."

EPILOGUE

THEY STOOD ON THE QUAY, watching the sun rise.
Hatshepsut was wrapped in a new white cloak, a timid smile on her round face. Even for the bravest of children, a boat voyage without mother or nurse was daunting. But she would be with her father, and Ahmose knew how that thrilled her. The King's Daughter watched Thutmose with an air of worship, a brilliant innocent gaze that knew nothing of his wrongs. He was no stalking leopard to Hatet. To her, no choice he made had condemned her brothers. He was just her father, brave and strong and unfailingly good. Tut looked back at the girl just as timidly, a smile wavering around his eyes. Ahmose had not seen him smile for so long. It was good. This journey: it was maat. Maat for all of them, even Mutnofret's new son, Thutmose. He would be safe now, with Hatshepsut sailing upriver. Mutnofret brought little Thutmose forth in sorrow, but he had restored a tenuous, fragile joy to her heart. The second wife refused to turn him over to a nurse, clinging to him, keeping him at her side every hour of every day, nursing him herself when he was hungry, cleaning him herself when he was soiled. The baby was Mutnofret's ka now, the essence of her life. No one had the heart to separate them.

Ahmose looked at them now, standing apart at the head of the water steps. Mutnofret carried the boy close to her breast, shielding him against the brisk river air. The second wife hardly took her eyes off the baby's face, even when

335

the Pharaoh came to her to kiss her softly in farewell. It was a lingering kiss. Ahmose did not begrudge Mutnofret the affection. The second wife had little enough joy now, with three of her sons gone. Let her find what happiness she could with the king. Ahmose would not be shaken.

She bent to Hatshepsut, pulled her close and kissed both her fat cheeks, then kissed them again. This prince was Ahmose's happiness. This child was the center of the spreading rings on the river's surface. And today, Ahmose would set her adrift on the Iteru to see the world she would rule. The temples, the ancient pyramids against the setting sun, the priests and the people, bent backs in the fields, songs in the sanctuaries – all of these would be hers. And when they reached Annu, far, far to the north, the Royal Son that was not a son would be crowned.

"Be good. Listen to your father," Ahmose said. "It is maat, to listen to your father."

Hatshepsut smiled, nodded, patted Ahmose's hand. *Brave, dear thing.*

Sitre-In cried, blowing her nose into a square of linen. Hatshepsut went to her, too, and allowed herself to be kissed and cooed over. "I will miss you, Mawat," she said, and Sitre-In redoubled her sobs.

Tut came to Ahmose hesitantly, his eyes clouded with regret. She took his face in her hands, and kissed him. "I forgive you," she whispered. "And the gods forgive you."

"Can I forgive myself?"

She stroked his cheek in answer, feeling the planes of his beloved face. He would, someday. She knew it. He was making the right choice now. The sun was rising on a new world. This was a new start for all of them.

"You have found an architect?" he asked, his voice hollowed by grief.

Ahmose nodded, smiling. She had found an architect with clever hands, with a soft voice, with shy, dark eyes. She had sent all the way to Swenet for him, where he had been overseeing the building of some great noble's estate, but he had returned to Waset eagerly when she summoned him. He would build a beautiful temple for the boys' memory, and she would fill his treasury full to bursting in gratitude for all he had done.

She smiled at the Pharaoh, though Ahmose felt little enough of the happiness she put on her face. Wadjmose's body was gone, pulled beneath the waters in Sobek's jaws. No temple, no matter how beautiful, how cleverly designed, no matter how heartfelt its construction, would be enough to see Wadjmose to the Field of Reeds. She knew it, and her heart would bleed every day of her life for the knowing. Yet she could never speak these words to Tut. She would watch over the construction of the Temple of Wadjmose, and every year at the Feast of Wag she would lay out food and drink in her nephew's chapel, though his spirit would never come back to claim her gifts. For Tut and Mutnofret she would do this, though her heart would bleed.

"Take good care of our daughter," Ahmose said, her hands still on his face, unwilling to let him go.

"I will. Most certainly, I will." He glanced at baby Thutmose, suckling at Mutnofret's breast. His eyes flickered away again. "The baby will be safe. We will all be safe."

Hatshepsut took the Pharaoh's hand, pulled him toward the boat that bobbed on the waves below the water steps. "Come, Father," she said, impatient as always.

"All right, all right." Tut held Ahmose's eyes for one last moment, then he was dashing down to the ship with Hatshepsut. The girl's sidelock whipped and bounced in the air as she leaped, two at a time, down the steps. When they reached the plank and scrambled aboard, Tut's jackal-bark laugh came to Ahmose across the morning air.

Her hands were still held up, still caressing his face, though it watched her from the ship's rail now. They waved at her, king and prince, the two halves of her heart – and slowly, she lowered her hands to her sides.

The ship cast off. Musicians onboard rattled their sesheshet, plucked at their strings. The oars came out, shoved away from the mooring. The current caught the great ship and its oars tapped the surface of the water gently, carrying Hatshepsut away, away. Ahmose waved.

When the rising sun set the Iteru afire, she saw how the ship's wake spread from its wooden flanks like a bird's great wings. Ripples flowing outward forever, and at the center, Hatshepsut. All would be well. She *knew*.

Ahmose turned away from the river, and guided Mutnofret with an arm around her shoulders. They walked back to the palace together.

So said Amun, Lord of the Two Lands,
before Ahmose, the King's Wife:
Hatshepsut, Joined with Amun, shall be the name
of this my daughter, whom I have placed in thy
body. Tell the people. She shall exercise
an excellent kingship in this whole land.
My soul is hers, my bounty is hers, my crown is
hers, that she may rule the Two Lands,
that she may lead all the living.

-Inscription from Djeser-Djeseru,
mortuary temple of Hatshepsut,
Fifth King of the Eighteenth Dynasty.

HISTORICAL NOTE

I did my best in writing The Sekhmet Bed to balance clarity and the comfort of the reader against accuracy of historical setting. As a result, many of the names used in this book may be unfamiliar to the casual student of Egyptian history. It was extremely important to me to use the correct names for cities and gods – correct for my Ahmose, Tut, Nofret, and Hatet, who lived a good thousand years before Alexander the Great conquered Egypt, and Greek names and styles began to eclipse old Egyptian culture. Thus most proper nouns and even some "everyday words" have been rendered in ancient Egyptian (or the Anglicized equivalent; the Egyptians did not record most vowel sounds in their written language, so exact pronunciations are anybody's guess.) I have included a glossary to assist the reader, and to explain which words were left in their more familiar Greek or French forms, and why.

Speaking of Tut, this novel deals with the beginning of the Thutmoside dynasty, one of the most powerful, influential, and unusual families in ancient Egyptian history. This is also a family that is not well-known to most readers of historical fiction. Thutmose I was the founder of the line, and he was indeed non-royal by birth and a soldier of some renown. His marriage to Ahmose, daughter or possibly sister of the previous Pharaoh, legitimized his right to the throne. I call him Tut in this book because I liked the way a secret nickname built an age-appropriate closeness between young

341

Ahmose and her new husband; but in The Sekhmet Bed, this king Tut should not be confused with *the* King Tut, whose full name was Thutankhamun, and who ruled Egypt very briefly about 115 years after this book takes place.

Real fans of Egyptian history will be muddled by the names of our Ahmose's mother and grandmother. Historically, the women in Ahmose's family all had the prefix "Ahmose" attached to their names, so her mother was truly called Ahmose-Meritamun and her grandmother Ahmose-Nefertari; and there were more Ahmoses in her family as well, including a king named Ahmose who was a revolutionary and a very important fellow in Egyptian history. For the sake of avoiding headaches, I thought it best to drop as many Ahmoses from the scene as possible, and shortened the old queens' names to Meritamun and Nefertari. I hope the reader appreciates this choice.

As for Mutnofret, she was a real woman, was indeed a lesser wife of Thutmose I (rather than simply a concubine), and was probably related in some way to Ahmose – perhaps a cousin. She was probably not Ahmose's sister, and almost definitely not an elder sister, but I liked the tension such a twist brought to my fictional portrayal of the Thutmosides.

There is considerable debate among Egyptologists as to where Thutmose's sons Wadjmose, Amunmose, and Ramose came from. Some believe they were sons existing from a possible previous marriage to a non-royal wife, in the days before Thutmose was the Pharaoh. They may have been the sons of Mutnofret, and based on how the Thutmosides are depicted on tomb and temple walls, and the fact that a statuette of Mutnofret was found in Wadjmose's funerary chapel, I found this the likeliest scenario.

What is clear is that Thutmose I loved his sons deeply, and that all three of them preceded him in death. He had a mortuary chapel built to Wadjmose's memory, and depicted his son's name in the ring of a cartouche – an extremely rare honor that was typically only granted to kings and queens. The care Thutmose I took to memorialize his lost child speaks volumes as to what kind of a man he was, and what kind of a family he must have led – sensitive, complicated, and tragic.

Notes on the Language Used

This novel is set in historical Egypt, about 1500 years before the common era and roughly 1200 years before Alexander the Great conquered the Nile. With the dawning of the Greek period, a shift in the old Egyptian language began. Proper nouns (and, we can assume, other parts of the language) took on a decidedly Greek bent, which today most historians use when referring to ancient Egyptians and their world.

This presents a bit of a tangle for a historical novelist like myself. Culturally, we are familiar with Greek-influenced names like Thebes, Rameses, and Isis. In fact, even the name Egypt is not Egyptian; it has a long chain of derivations through Greek, Latin, and French. However, the historic people in my novel would have scratched their heads over such foreign words for their various places, people, and gods. And linguistically, the modern English-speaking reader will probably have a difficult time wrapping her head and tongue around such tricky names as Djhtms – an authentic and very common man's name for the time and place where The Sekhmet Bed is set (rather the equivalent of a Mike or Tom or Jim).

On the balance, cultural authenticity is important to me, and so I've reverted to ancient Egyptian versions of various proper nouns and other words in the majority of cases. A glossary of ancient Egyptian words used in this book, and their more familiar Greco-English translations, follows.

In some cases, to avoid headaches and to preserve (I hope)

the flow of the narrative, I have kept modernized versions of certain words in spite of their inauthentic nature. Notably, I use Egypt rather than the authentic Kmet. It is a word that instantly evokes the reader's own romantic perceptions of the land and time, whatever those may be, and its presence in the story can only aid my own attempts at world-building. I have opted for the fairly Greeky, English-friendly name Thutmose in place of Djhtms, which is simply a tongue-twister; and the word Pharaoh, which is French in origin (the French have always been enthusiastic Egyptologists) rather than the Egyptian pra'a, simply because Pharaoh is such a familiar word in the mind of a contemporary reader. Wherever possible, I have used "Pharaoh" sparingly to avoid repetitiveness, and have instead opted for the simple translation of "king." I've also decided, after much flip-flopping, to use the familiar Greek name Horus for the falcon-headed god, rather than the authentic name Horu. The two are close, but in every case reading Horu in my sentences interrupted the flow and tripped me up. Horus flies more smoothly on his falcon wings; ditto for Hathor, who should properly be called Hawet-Hor, but seems to prefer her modernized name.

As always, I hope the reader appreciates these concessions to historical accuracy and to comfort.

GLOSSARY

ankh – the breath of life; the animating spirit that makes humans live

Annu – Heliopolis

Anupu – Anubis

Heqa-Khasewet – Hyksos

Ipet-Isut – "Holy House"; the temple complex at Karnak

Iset – Isis

Iteru – Nile

ka – not quite in line with the Western concept of a "soul" or "spirit," a ka was an individual's vital essence, that which made him or her live.

maat – A concept difficult for modern Westerners to accurately define: something like righteousness, something like divine order, something like justice. It is to a sense of "God is in His Heaven and all is right with the world" as the native Hawai'ian word *aloha* is to an overall feeling of affection, pleasure, well-being, and joyful anticipation. It is also the name of the goddess of the concept – the goddess of "what is right."

mawat – mother; also used to refer to mother-figures such as nurses

rekhet – people of the common class; peasants

sesheshet – sistrum; ceremonial rattle

tjati – vizier; governor of a sepat or district

Waser – Osiris, god of the afterlife, the underworld, and the dead. Also used as a prefix when referring to a deceased king.

Waset – Thebes

Acknowledgments

I am grateful to many people who helped make this book possible.

My family, Cheryl Grant, Georgia Schlegel, and Georgia Grant. Lori Witt, who gave me so much feedback and encouragement early on. My first agent, Natalie Fischer, whose early input shaped this book for the better. Paula Dooley, whose last-minute critique of my first three chapters saved my bacon. Tim Batson, who for some reason appears to be my biggest fan, and everybody at the Cooper's Alehouse writers' group, for all the good times and gooder critiques. Bridget and Dan Lombardo, for being so supportive during some hard times and during the good times, too. Judith Tarr and Stephanie Dray, two wonderful writers who agreed to read advance copies of this book. All my friends, human and otherwise, at the zoological institutions where I worked during the development and writing of this novel: Tracy Aviary, Point Defiance Zoo and Aquarium, and Woodland Park Zoo – your genuine enthusiasm (in the case of the humans) and your calming, beautiful presence (in the case of the animals) kept me focused and charged. Most especially, thanks to Paul Harnden for buying me cupcakes and playing Slug-Bug with me.

So many wonderful people have touched my life and shaped it, and made me the writer and the person I am; I regret that I cannot list all of you here.

Finally, I am indebted to Joyce Tyldesley, an exceptional

historian and a very fine writer. In the creation of this novel I relied heavily on Ms. Tyldesley's large body of work on ancient Egypt in general and on the Thutmosides in particular. All of her books are fascinating, accessible, and entertaining. Any deviation this book makes from known history is a result of my own wild artistic license, and not a reflection on the precision of my primary source of information. I eagerly direct any reader wishing to know the real story of ancient Egypt to Joyce Tyldesley's works.

L. H.
Seattle, WA, 2011

ABOUT THE AUTHOR

Libbie Hawker wrote her first novel, *The Sekhmet Bed*, in 2009 while working as a zookeeper. Although she worked with two different literary agents for two years, the New York publishing world showed no interest in Egyptian historical fiction that didn't feature archaeological celebrities like King Tut or Cleopatra.

When Libbie self-published *The Sekhmet Bed* in 2011, she never expected that readers would embrace the book and her writing so thoroughly. She soon became a leading voice in independent historical fiction, and enjoys contact with readers from all around the world.

When she's not writing, she can be found camping and backpacking, road tripping, rockhounding, and painting. She loves "meeting" readers; find contact information and more on her web site: LibbieHawker.com

Printed in the USA
CPSIA information can be obtained
at www.ICGtesting.com
LVHW040235021023
759869LV00008B/223